BANKED FIRES

BANKED FIRES

ETHEL WINIFRED SAVI

ISBN: 978-93-90058-58-7

Published: 1919

LECTOR HOUSE LLP
E-MAIL: lectorpublishing@gmail.com

BANKED FIRES

BY

E. W. SAVI

AUTHOR OF "THE DAUGHTER-IN-LAW," "SINNERS ALL," ETC.

"Who can find a virtuous woman? for her price is far above ru-bies."

—Proverbs xxxi., 10.

1919

TO
MY SISTER, A. B. B.
IN LOVING APPRECIATION OF HER INTEREST
AND HELP

CONTENTS

CONTENTS vii

BANKED FIRES

CHAPTER I

THE LONELY ENCAMPMENT

An autumn evening in Bengal was rapidly drawing to a close, with a brief afterglow from a vanished sun to soften the rich hues of the tropical foliage, and garb it fittingly for approaching night. The grass beside the Government tents showed grey in the gathering dusk, while a blue haze of smoke, creeping upward, gently veiled the sheltering trees. But for the modulated chatter of servants, the stillness was eerie. The flat, low-lying fields, having yielded their corn to the harvester, were barren and without sign of life, for the cultivators had departed to their homesteads, and the roving cattle were housed.

Far in the misty distance were the huts of the peasantry grouped together, with their granaries, haystacks, and pens; their date-palms, and the inevitable tank illustrating the typical Bengal village—picturesque and insanitary; too far for noxious smells to annoy the senses, or the intermittent beating of the nocturnal "tom-tom" to affect the nerves of the Magistrate and Collector during the writing of his judgments and reports.

The spot for the encampment had been well chosen by the blue-turbaned *chaukidar*—the sturdy watchman of the village—who was experienced in the ways of touring officials; for even such a little matter as a site for pitching the tents of the *hakim*,[1] had its influence for good or ill; and what might not be the effect of a good influence on the temper of a lawgiver?

This one, especially, instilled the fear of God and of the British, into his servants and underlings in spite of his sportsmanship and generosity, for he had a great understanding of native character and, like a wizard, could, in the twinkling of an eye, dissect the mind and betray the soul of a false witness! None could look him in the face and persist in falsehood. He was a just man, and courageous; and when roused to wrath, both fierce and fluent. But the diplomatic domestic and cautious coolie, alike, respect justice and fearlessness, determination, and a high hand.

Servants, engaged in culinary duties before open fire-places, gossiped in lowered tones of standing grievances: It was like the exactness of the Great to require a five-course dinner, served with due attention to refinement and etiquette in untoward circumstances, such as an improvised cooking-range of clay and bricks, a hurried collection of twigs, some charcoal, and every convenience conspicuous by its absence! And what a village to rely upon!—no shops; only a weekly market

[1] Magistrate.

with nothing suitable to the wants of white men fastidious and difficult to please.

Yet, the day that sahibs condescend to study the convenience of their Indian domestics, the prestige of the British Raj will be at an end.

"Ho! *Khansaman-jee!*" cried an agitated voice in Hindustani. "With a little clemency, look quickly in the rubbish heap for the pepper pot. The *masalchi*,[2] out of the perversity of his youthfulness, has lost that and every other ingredient for the flavouring of the soup; and now, what can I do? Of a truth, this night will the Sahib give me much abuse for that which is no fault of mine. I shall twist the idle one's ear the moment he returns with firewood from the jungle, just to stimulate his mind and teach him carefulness."

The *khansaman*[3] uncoiled his legs and rose from the ground where he had been peeling potatoes at his leisure with a table knife, and proceeded to do as he was bid. He was of an obliging nature and could be relied upon to perform odd jobs not strictly his duty, so long as they did not establish a precedent.

After some diligent searching among loose charcoal, dried twigs, kitchen rags, utensils, and vegetable parings, a rusty tin box was discovered and handed to the cook. Old Abdul grunted approval of his own intelligence, and after liberally sprinkling the soup with pepper from between a dirty finger and thumb, he wiped both, casually, in the folds of his loin-cloth.

Altogether, the task of preparing dinner in camp was no mean effort. The business of the moment was to produce a clear soup with its artistic garniture of sliced carrots and turnips; to be followed by tank fish captured that afternoon from the property of a local Hindu landowner and, in the serving, robbed of its earthly flavour by a miracle of savoury dressing. Considering the lapses of the mate-boy's memory, this was a marvel of achievement. Next, the *entrée* of devilled goat (called by courtesy, mutton) was also a difficulty; nevertheless with a lavish addition of mango chutney, it was on its way to completion. The "chicken roast" was a tolerable certainty in a deep vessel where it baked in its own juices, stuffed with onions, cloves, and rice. But the pudding—alas! black despair, invisible owing to natural pigment, was in possession of Abdul's soul. What to do, he grumbled, but to serve, in fear and trembling, that abomination of sahibs, a "custul-bile" (boiled custard), since every possible ingredient for a respectable pudding had been left behind at the last Rest Bungalow! What the master would say, might well be imagined, for these were not the easy-going days of his bachelorhood, when such makeshifts, varied with "custul-bake," could be imposed upon him with the regularity of the calendar; for, after a successful day's *shikar*, with a tiger spread at full length on the grass before the tent for the benefit of an admiring semicircle of enthusiastic villagers, the quality of a meal used to be a secondary consideration.

Well—what use to repine? Even a cook must sometimes be excused, since he was not God to create something out of nothing. Peradventure, the timely indisposition of the babe within the tent would offer distraction. In the interludes of stirring the pots and declaiming against fate and the misdemeanours of the *masalchi*,

[2] Scullion.
[3] Butler.

the cook soothed his ruffled spirits with a pull at his beloved *hukha*.

Yes, the Sahib was married, worse luck! and lived, above all, to please his Memsahib who, to him, was the sun, moon, and stars; the light of the world. And she?—of a sort wholly unsuited to the conditions of his life; a flower plucked to wither in a furnace-blast. The rough soil of the country was no place for a delicate plant; and such was also apparent in the case of her infant. Since its arrival from the hills where it was born, it daily faded as though a blight had descended upon its vitality; and now it was stricken with a fever.

Devil take sahibs for their folly! This one had been content enough as a bachelor, hunting and shooting in his spare time, and consorting with his kind where games were played to pass the time away; what-for did he allow himself to be shackled thus during his visit to *Belait*? It passed understanding; for there were many *Miss Babas* in the country, already acclimatised, from among whom he might have selected a suitable wife; one who could at least have made herself intelligible to his servants in their own language, instead of this one who created endless confusion by non-comprehension. But no! he had been unable to stand the allurements of her person. The rounded outlines of her slender form and the bloom on her flawless cheek had enslaved him, depriving him of the power to resist. Truly she was good to look upon, as every masculine eye betrayed by its open homage.

In all the annals of the District, never had there been a more picturesque creature than this girl-wife, with her hair like ripe corn and eyes like full-blown flowers of heavenly blue. Even the servants in gazing on their wonder forgot to heed the orders she delivered through the ayah, whose linguistic powers commanded the respect of the entire establishment.

The subject of the little lady from *Belait* was a favourite theme of conversation when domestics congregated in the region of the kitchen to gossip and smoke, and criticism was condescending and tolerant because of her good looks, which made their inevitable appeal. But opinion was agreed that no longer was Meredith Sahib the same man. Henceforth, if they would keep their situations, they must satisfy his lady. Her little hand would point the way he must in future tread.

And he, the respected Magistrate and Collector, representative of the Government in the District—a sahib whose word had authority over thousands on the land, and before whom all delinquents trembled!

Such was the influence of beauty!

According to the words of a local poet who sang his verses in the Muktiarbad bazaar to an accompaniment of tom-tomming:

> *A beautiful wife is as wine in the head to her husband; as wax is in the*
> *palm of her hand.*
> *His wisdom cometh to naught in his dwelling; his will is bartered for*
> *the things in her gift.*
> *Beguiled is he by the words of her mouth, and he taketh only the way*
> *that will please her.*
> *Bereft is he of his power to govern, yet happy is he in the bonds of*

enslavement.

And these did he compose out of the rumours current in the market-place respecting Meredith Sahib and the Memsahib he had taken to wife. *Yah, Khodah!* the white race were amazingly simple!

The sound of an infant's distressed wail broke the calm of the descending gloom. Voices within the tent conferred together in agitated whispers. There was a call for hot water, and in a moment the Madrassi ayah rushed forth for the steaming kettle which was boiling for scullery needs, and carried it off without a question. The waterman, clad only in a loin-cloth, hurried round to the bath tent, and a diminutive, tin bath-tub was extracted. Apparently the child was to be immersed.

"What has happened?" called the Sahib's body servant, the *bearer*, who was the major-domo of the camp. But the waterman, fully appreciative of his temporary importance, refused to reply as he disappeared from view.

"Ice—ice!" the lady cried dashing through the bamboo chick and almost tearing it from its fastenings. "Give me ice quickly." She looked haggard and distracted. Dark circles ringed her eyes; her sleeves rolled above the elbows revealed rounded arms from which water dripped; her skirt was splashed; her blouse and hair were in disarray.

"There is none, *huzur*," said the *bearer* in Hindustani. "Hourly is it expected from Muktiarbad, but as yet it is not in sight."

"What is he saying?" she cried vaguely in her distress, refusing to believe that there was none, which the corroborating action of a hand had implied.

"No ice got it, Memsahib," volunteered the *khansaman* in his best English, learned from a teacher in the Station bazaar. "All finish—melting fast—making saw-dust one porridge."

"No ice?—my God! My child will die if I cannot have ice." She disappeared within the tent, wringing her hands, leaving the servants to hold council together on what was the best course to pursue.

"Without doubt the little one is in a fit," ventured the cook. "Such is sometimes the case when the teeth press their way through the gums."

"What folly," sneered the *khansaman*, "when the infant is barely three months old!"

"Without doubt it is a fit," the cook repeated, "else why the hot bath? Such is the treatment the doctor-*babu* ordered for the son of Amir Khan, my relative in Benares when, from fever, his eyes fixed and his limbs grew rigid."

"Thou speakest true words," said the waterman approaching the group in visible excitement. "To see the limbs twisting and the eyes strained upward turns my stomach. Assuredly it will die—and the master away!—*ai ma!*—what a calamity!"

"It will die, and we shall all be blamed because there was no ice," sighed the *bearer* feeling the weight of his responsibility.

"God send that he be even now returning," prayed the *khansaman* devoutly.

"The sun has long set, and any moment he may be here, for who can shoot a leopard in the dark?"

"Tell Hosain to drive the *hawa-ghari*[4] quickly to the Station for the doctor and the ice. If he meet not the ice cart on the road, let him borrow all they will lend him at the houses of the sahibs," said the cook. "*Jhut!*—lose no time. In these illnesses the life of a child is as the flicker of a candle. A breath, and it is out; and once dead, who can restore it to life again?"

Servants ran to do his bidding while he returned to his pots and pans, anxious lest the roast should burn at the bottom of the pan, and the soup boil over.

"For what dost thou concern thyself?" jeered an old watchman who stood a spectator of the scene. "All that thou cookest will be given to the sweeper's family. Who will eat of thy cooking tonight when the child is like to die?"

"Not the sweeper and his family, *bhai*,[5] but we of the kitchen shall have a feast, have no fears." "It's an ill wind that blows nobody good," was the essence of the cook's philosophy, and since there was no swine-flesh in the menu, there was no reason why Mohammedans should not enjoy the repast he was cooking for the Sahib's table. It was a dispensation of Providence that had not made him at birth a Hindu like the watchman, who took pride in the exclusiveness of his caste, yet feasted on the sly, on things forbidden.

Inside the tent the lady and the ayah together ministered to the small sufferer lying in the warm bath. The sympathetic servant supported the light body which had relaxed its rigidity, while the mother bathed the brows and head with cold water.

"He is better, ayah, don't you think?" asked Mrs. Meredith, dependent on the woman's superior knowledge.

"Plenty better, Ma'am. Heaven is merciful."

"Or do you think he is dying? Don't lie to me."

"He not dying, oh, no! See that black round his mouth?—now fast going. This is what they call *bahose*."

"Thank God if it's only that. Children recover from fainting fits, don't they? Oh, ayah, I could not bear to lose my baby!" she cried in choked accents.

"Say not like that. Got is goot and the baba will live. Now take out of the water, dry, and keep head cool," said the woman whose experience in the management of infants had gained her her present post at some considerable advantage to herself.

They placed the limp form, when dried, on the cool sheets in its crib and hung upon its every breath.

"Barnes-*mem* saying, when bad with fever, lap plenty hot place, bed goot," the ayah remarked; "Barnes-*mem*," a former mistress, being a standard reference in nursery difficulties.

---

[4] Motor-car.
[5] Brother.

"Had she many children?"

"Children? My lort! Every year a child. She was plenty blest. One child for every finger, and a grand-child older than her last. Master, he shake his head and say, 'Damn-damn,' but Barnes-*mem*, she say, 'Let come; the Lort will provide.'"

"Were they all brought up in India?"

"In Calcutta they were born and grew up; no Darjeeling *pahar*;[6] no Munsuri *pahar*! All living; all plenty strong."

"Yet most children cannot thrive out here—English, I mean."

"English Memsahib making much fuss, like there is no Got Almighty. Everywhere there is sickness, also in *pahar*."

Mrs. Meredith shivered at the cold consolation. After a short interval spent in anxious suspense, a clatter of hoofs announced the return of the Sahib. Raymond Meredith galloped into the camp and flinging his reins to a *saice*, leaped to the ground. A messenger had met him on the road with the disturbing news of his infant's bad turn. In another moment he was beside his wife, eagerly sympathetic and anxious to comfort her.

At any other time she would have received him affectionately upon his return from a long day's outing, and he marked the change, excusing it on the plea of anxiety and distraction.

"This is very sudden, darling," he said in lowered tones, placing his arms tenderly about her. "How did it happen?"

His wife explained emotionally. "Baby was feverish when you left. You remember, perhaps, that I was worried and did not like being left alone?" she concluded resentfully, her eyes refusing to meet his.

"He seemed a bit out of sorts, but nothing to alarm one," her husband allowed in self-defence. "You know, sweetheart, you are often needlessly anxious." He would have kissed her to soften the reproach, but she turned her face aside. "Anyhow, I had to go, you know that? The leopard had done enough damage in the village and was a danger to human life. An infant had been carried off from the doorway of its dwelling the moment its mother's back was turned. I simply had to hunt and shoot the beast, or let the people think I funked it. I managed to bag it in the end, but the fellow gave us a devil of a time," he continued, warming to his subject. "Had it not been for the pluck of the *chaukidar*, I might never have returned at all—" He waited for some evidence of concern. "He's a fine sportsman," he went on, though disappointed at her lack of interest. "With only a stout stick in his hand, he—" his voice trailed away as he became convinced that he was talking to an inattentive mind. "Don't worry, I'll send post-haste for Dalton. He'll be here before morning."

"Anything might happen before morning," she cried brokenly.

"You mustn't be so pessimistic."

---

[6] Mountains.

"The car was sent for the doctor when Baby was in convulsions," she said coldly. "It was terrible not having you here to advise. I have been desperate, and you—" a sob—"you were enjoying yourself in the jungles." She had not an atom of sympathy for the sport.

"Surely you are not blaming me?" he cried deprecatingly, afraid that he had injured himself for ever in her sight.

"It is not a question of blame; you have failed me, that is all."

"That's a cruel thing to say, dearest!" he cried kissing her unresponsive lips at last, in the hopes of melting her hardness. "It is only that you are in a mood to be unjust, that you say so. You know I am happiest with you."

"This is a cruel country which I shall hate to the end of my days," she returned miserably. "It is trying at every turn to rob me of my little baby."

Meredith winced almost as though he had been struck. It was not the first time that she had expressed disgust for her life in India, which gave them their living, and every time her words gained in feeling. Early in the summer he had sent her to the hills because of an episode with a snake that had unnerved her and imperilled her condition as an expectant mother. He had not forgotten that her first arrival at the Station had synchronised with an outbreak of cholera, so virulent, that half the community of Europeans among whom she was to live were demoralised. It was a crying shame that Life should be so perverse. He yearned for her to settle down and take kindly to Station ways and doings, but fate eternally intervened. Muktiarbad was a merry little station, full of friendly souls eager to accept the youthful bride as a social leader for her husband's sake, he being the most popular of men.

Meredith was aware of his own popularity and enjoyed it as a healthy-minded individual usually does when success has crowned his efforts to govern a large District with sympathy and tact. But already the young wife and mother was pining for "home," and was declaring that the India he loved was a "cruel country," which she would hate to the end of her days. How should he be able to pin her down to his side in a land she detested and feared? She was too young and uninformed to appreciate his position in the Government and her possibilities as a *Bara Memsahib*; and too delicately nurtured to endure the rough and tumble of life far from towns and cities, where money could not buy immunity from inconvenience and climatic ills.

He had expected, as many another husband of a very young wife, to mould her ideas to fit his own; instead, his peace of mind was being steadily whittled away.

"There is not even any ice to be had in this God-forsaken spot!" his wife's voice was saying helplessly.

"Damnation!" he swore under his breath, enraged that the servants should have supplied him at the cost of the child; for he recalled the very acceptable iced beer he had drunk in the jungles after a dangerous exploit that had exhausted his energies and reduced him to a perspiring rag of humanity, even though it was autumn.

The urgent need to find a scapegoat to suffer for this miserable muddle sent him outside with a stride and malignant intentions at heart. Never again while he toured with his family would he drink iced stimulants, however damnably hot it was in the sun.

"What can I say?" whined the *bearer* in indignant sympathy, cleverly averting the storm he saw ready to descend on the head of the guilty. "Such unusual heat for this time of the year, and that swine, the carter, who is now many miles distant, left the ice-box on the sunny side of the tent! Without sense is he, and possessed of a mind equal only to that of a sheep. So much shade to be had, yet of a perversity must he commit this brainless act! What can I do? Had this pair of hands not been incessantly occupied in performing urgent tasks for the comfort of the Memsahib, I might have cast eyes on the packing-case earlier, and myself have removed it to safety. But alas! how much can one poor servant do among so many who are idle and indifferent? So there it lay out of sight and the water running freely through the joins till there was one tank, and my bedding beside it, floating! Tonight I am without bedding, but what of that? With the child ill, will any one care to sleep?" He cast a triumphant eye around on a semicircle of admiring fellow-servants who were envying him his resourcefulness and powers of invention.

"Who sent ice with me into the jungles?" Meredith asked fiercely.

"Who, indeed, Image-of-God? Such an act of folly while the tender babe lay sick is not to be forgiven. Peradventure, it was the mate-boy of the cook who is of an imbecility past understanding, owing to his extreme youth. Not even the intellect of a cow has he. *Urre bap!* Did he not leave at the Rest Bungalow——"

"Be silent, you talk too much," said Meredith. "Go and chastise him for his interference. If I strike him I shall break every bone in his body. Never again let ice be sent anywhere with me if it is likely to run short at the camp, remember that," he said, impressing the fact on the *bearer*, as he knew full well that, in the native mind, very little importance is attached to a woman's needs in comparison with her lord's,—the superiority of the masculine sex being unchallenged. When ice travelled by rail some hundreds of miles three times a week to Muktiarbad, it invariably fell short when the servants were careless or assisted to make it vanish. Every silent witness of the colloquy knew that the Sahib's *bearer* considered an iced whisky-and-soda his perquisite at the close of a strenuous day, and would continue to have it as long as ice came from Calcutta for the alleviation of sufferers from the climate.

"Buck up, darling," said Meredith comfortingly, "you'll have the doctor here in no time. Dalton is a clever fellow and prompt. They say he will make a name for himself some day, he's such an able physician and surgeon. What he doesn't understand concerning the ills that flesh is heir to is not worth knowing, so we are jolly lucky to have him in such a potty little station as ours. What got him sent here is a mystery; usually we get fossils of the Uncovenanted service at Muktiarbad, whereas Dalton is—" "Sorry," interrupting himself as his wife put her hands to her head. "You've a headache, sweetheart, and it's not to be wondered at."

"Is there nothing you can suggest for Baby in the meantime?" she questioned.

"I shouldn't like to experiment, knowing nothing of kids—infants, I mean," he replied with irritating cheerfulness. "Had it been a horse or a dog"—he discreetly ceased and made tender love to her instead, for his darling girl was sobbing piteously. "Don't worry," he advised with masculine lack of understanding of maternal feelings, "babies are marvellous creatures; like sponges, my dear. Squeeze them dry and they swell out again. See how the youngsters swarm in the bazaars and villages. Nothing seems to kill them," he asserted ignorantly. "They get over almost any illness without a hundredth part of the care you lavish on our little scallywag. Keep his head cool and you'll see, he'll be as right as rain in the morning."

"Cool without ice!" she said witheringly.

"Cold water on the head with a dash of vinegar in it will do to carry along with till the ice comes."

Somehow he was less concerned with the child's case than his wife's. Her distress, the added reason for her abhorrence of India, cut him to the heart and made him a coward of consequences. It was the child, that insignificant atom of indefinite humanity, that had intruded itself between them and was daily usurping his place in his wife's thoughts. At first he had been fool enough to imagine that it was going to be the link that would bind them closer together, instead of which it was the wedge that was surely driving them asunder. For its sake she was ready to put the seas and continents between them, and treat him as if he were of secondary importance in her life—the being who had to provide the wherewithal on which the human idol might be suitably reared. His own personal need of her was viewed as masculine self-indulgence and lack of spirituality.

"I don't think you half realise what a wonderful thing has happened," she had once said in the midst of her baby-worship. "Here is a miracle straight from God. A man-child who, if properly cared for, will become a useful citizen of the Empire; and he is my VERY OWN—yours, too," she condescended to add with her exquisite smile.

"But where do I come in? I, who am already a useful citizen of the Empire?" he had delicately insinuated. "With due regard to nature and the multiplication table——"

She had considered him coarse and had refused to smile. The matter of a family was entirely in God's hands and not to be treated with levity. He could have added a rider to that, but refrained; she was only a little girl of nineteen lacking the logical sense in the usual, adorable, feminine way. He was not hankering considerably after a family in the plural sense when in imagination he could see an intensification of the present situation which was forcing him into the background of domestic life. The baby, waking and sleeping, and all its multifarious concerns occupied its mother's time to the exclusion of all else, and it was no wonder that the father was feeling injured and a trifle lonely.

Yet, in her childish way, she was fond of him, while unconsciously learning from him that, after all, men were truly long-suffering and unselfish creatures, patient, and forgiving.

So he possessed his soul in patience, never tired of recalling the supreme episode of their married life, when, after the birth of their son, she had embraced him with a new affection, spontaneous and sincere. She had been so utterly ill that for a day and a night her life had hung in the balance, while he, like a maniac, had paced the footpath in mist and rain, praying as he had never prayed before for her restoration. It was in Darjeeling where he had gone hurriedly on receipt of a telegram, and never should he forget the anxieties of that journey. He had been ready to register any vow under the sun that he might ensure her recovery; and when he had crept with broken nerve and sobbing breath to her bedside, she had clung to his neck with blessed demonstrativeness kissing him of her own accord on the lips. Generally, he had kissed her.

"You love me still, my precious?" he had asked fearfully. Mark the "still," for by her agony he was ready to believe he had forfeited the right to her love.

"Aren't you my baby's Daddy?" she had replied happily with shining eyes and quivering mouth. "Of course I shall love you better now than ever."

She loved him only through the child! However, Meredith did not quarrel with the process, so long as the fact was full of promise. It had always been a calm and unemotional affection, not in the least of the quality he craved, but his love and patience were equal to the demand made upon them, his mind having realised the unawakened condition of hers. "All things come to those who know how to wait," and he was learning patience, for his life was wrapped up in the person of his girl-wife. She was so infinitely lovable even when least comprehending his man's nature and holding herself aloof. Again, her charm was indescribable when, with adorable grace, she offered compensation, sorry for her uncomprehending selfishness; and he eternally rejoiced that, by the law of marriage, she was irrevocably his till death should them part, a bondage which he endeavoured to make her Eden, as it was his.

CHAPTER II
MAINLY RETROSPECTIVE

Dinner that evening was neglected as neither could eat.

Tired and hungry though Meredith had been, his appetite for food vanished under the lash of his wife's resentment. She once said: "If my baby is taken from me, I shall cut this country forever. I shall hate it with an undying hatred. Nothing will induce me to live in it again and risk a repetition of tonight. It is not fit for Europeans—and yet, the tragedy of it is, we can only know it by experience!"

"That is to say, if you had foreseen this, you would never have married me?" he put in sulkily.

Silence gave consent.

"Why shouldn't you give up, and find something to do at home?" she asked unreasonably.

"You don't know what you are talking about," he returned shortly. Give up the "Indian Civil" and his splendid prospects, liberal future pension, and the life of sport men loved? For what? A desk in a city office; most likely a mercantile job on a third of the pay, and a life to which he was as much suited as a square peg to a round hole. All this, that the babe might be spared the illnesses that mortal flesh, in infancy, is prone to, particularly in the East. It was utter nonsense! For the first five years there would be need for special care and intervals spent in a hill climate. In due time would come the change to England and English environment necessary for the proper physical and mental training of his child. This was the course usually followed by English families in India of any social standing, and one which involved submission on the part of the husband to short periods of separation from the wife in the interests of the absent children. Thousands of married couples faced these conditions; why not they?

He felt rebellious.

What was the matter with his luck that it threatened not to work? He had no fortune on which to retire, only a modest return from savings judiciously invested, while his wife would have nothing more than a trifle till the death of her parents; and they were still young. To give up the Service would, under the circumstances, be madness and folly.

Moreover, he loved the East. The climate had no grudge against his English constitution, and had been kind to him. He enjoyed the freedom of the life, India's great spaces; and the lurking risks made existence a great and continued adventure. In England it would be monotonous and flat. Though he loved the Motherland and was proud of her traditions, he was of the stuff that made empires, and his tact and understanding of the natives under his rule, made him an officer of exceptional ability and service to the Executive Government. Then there was big game shooting which he enjoyed, and all the happy freedom from narrow conventions. Give up, indeed!

Time enough to think of retiring when past middle age with shaken nerves and a growing appreciation of golf. Not while he could ride a buck-jumper, handle a hog spear or a polo stick, and shoot straight. The thrill of tracking a wild beast to its lair was something to live for, and the hazards of his life made up its charm.

The greatest of all hazards, had he realised it, had been his marriage with Joyce Wynthrop of Eagleton, Surrey.

She had put up her hair to attend the hunt ball the year he was home on furlough and staying with his widowed sister, Lady Chayne, a neighbour of the Wynthrops, and it was love at first sight, with him. He had been forced to attend the ball against his will, only to meet his fate, it would seem.

Thereafter, he had been obsessed with one ambition, and that was to win Joyce for his wife, in spite of the fact that he was fifteen years her senior and held an appointment in the East.

Touched by his devotion and influenced by the opinion of others, she had yielded, feeling that Destiny was calling to her to fulfill her obligations to Life. Marriage with a good man of irreproachable antecedents, and children to rear in godliness and wisdom, was the religion of her upbringing. It had been impressed upon her as the natural vocation of woman so that the race might continue. She had played with dolls as the proper playthings of her childhood, and was prepared to exchange them for the children God should send her in some mysterious way to which marriage was the true gateway. Raymond Meredith, good-looking, kind, eligible, and full of love for herself was obviously the "Mr. Right" of schoolgirl tradition; the man to whom it would be correct to give herself in the bonds of holy matrimony, even as her mother had long ago given herself to her father—an example of unemotional attachment and tranquil orthodoxy.

At first it had been wofully embarrassing to be made love to; and she wondered if her mother had been kissed so often and called all those silly love-names by her father before they were married?

She also resisted the strange effect on herself of those ardent kisses, and was afraid to encourage feelings she had never before experienced, believing them immodest to indulge, and something she had to subdue with a determined effort. She would die sooner than confess to them. Passion might be all right for men with whom every initiative of life lay, but unbecoming for women to acknowledge, even to themselves. In fact, Joyce Wynthrop was a product of Early Victorian views on the subject of a girl's training, and an anachronism in modern times. She had been reared in rigid ignorance of life, her reading having been heavily restricted, her associates selected, so that when the time came to hand her over to a husband, he should find her beautifully unconscious and unique.

To Meredith, her shy submission to his caresses, and her passionless response were the surest guarantee of her virginal past, and he was in no hurry to awaken the sleeping beauty to a deeper knowledge of herself.

Joyce eventually decided for her peace of mind, that love-making belonged mainly to the period of Engagement, when everything was so new. Once having attained the object of his desire—that is, the possession of a wife—her lover would settle down to normal life, and no longer regard her eyelashes with wondering admiration, or exact kisses because her mouth was shaped like Cupid's bow. Men were so disturbing, if they were all like Ray Meredith!—delightfully disturbing,— only they must not know it, or peace and tranquillity would be impossible! After marriage there would be other things to think about, such as having a home, and, if the Lord willed it, a baby all their own, presented to them in some extraordinary and mysterious fashion.

She had always adored babies and could rarely pass one in a perambulator without wanting to kiss it and know all its little history. To have a baby of her very own was a prospect so full of allurement, that she offered no coy objections when Meredith wanted the marriage fixed at the earliest possible date. Indeed, her calm was the despair of her girl friends who envied her openly. Wasn't she "terribly" in love with him? Wasn't she just "thrilled to death" with excitement at the prospect of having a husband and going all the way out to India?

Joyce did not believe there was such a thing as being "terribly in love," which was a phrase invented by cheap novelists, whose literature she had never been allowed to read. She admitted she was growing very fond of her Mr. Meredith, and preferred him to any other man. Not that her experience of men was great— nevertheless, he was a "perfect dear."

Her sister Kitty of the schoolroom, a young woman of rather decided opinions, reproached her severely for lack of enthusiasm over her very presentable lover. In her eyes, Ray Meredith was the ideal of a Cinema hero, with his clean-shaven, ascetic face, his muscular build, and adorable smile. "You should be flattered, my dear, that he condescended to choose you out of the millions of girls in the world," she remarked sagely. "You may be pretty, but hosts of girls are that. One has to be clever, and ... are *you*?... Why, you spelt vaccination with one 'c,' and vicinity with two only yesterday, and but for me, reading over your shoulder, you would have been disgraced for ever. I am not sure that he would not have broken it off! Then you know nothing whatever of politics—or football. Men are crazy about both, so you really are rather stupid, darling, or cold-hearted. Surely you must feel all squiggly down your back whenever Ray hugs and kisses you?"

"What do you know about it?"

"I'd be thrilled to my boots. Why, I feel like that every time they kiss in the film—really I feel an intruder, and as if I shouldn't look."

"Silly penny stories untrue to life!" Joyce said as an echo of her father's scorn, but blushing, nevertheless.

"Well, if you don't appreciate your lover, tell him to wait for me. I'll put up my hair year after next and take him like a shot."

"Of course I appreciate him, or I should not be going to marry him," said Joyce with the dignity of eighteen. "But it's folly to make so much fuss about marriage, seeing that it's the most ordinary thing in life, like being born, or dying."

"The most incomprehensible thing in life, I should imagine," retorted Kitty, wide-eyed with curiosity. "Especially when you come to think of going away for good—or bad, maybe!—with a strange man you know next to nothing of; and all at a blow, having to share the same apartments with him. Merciful Providence! I am sure the Queen never did!"

"It's supposed to be the correct thing," said Joyce rather scared. "Mother says, 'husbands and wives are one,' and 'to the pure, all things are pure'—whatever that has to do with it—so it would be illogical in the face of that to object to such a trifle as sharing a room. 'One has to tune one's mind to accept whatever comes, and to follow in the footsteps of one's parents,'" she quoted.

"How I wish you were not going right away with him, immediately," sighed Kitty enviously. "You might so easily have told me all about it. Nobody tells one anything worth knowing, just as though there was anything to be ashamed about!"

Joyce made no response for the good reason that her mind was wrestling with disquietude. However, in spite of so much that was mysterious, even alarming, she decided, as a prospective bride, to assume the dignity and reserve she had noticed in others and smile patronisingly on inquisitive sixteen.

Shortly afterwards she was married, and she accompanied her "strange man" on their journey to the Unknown, much as a confiding child trusts itself to the guardianship of a loving nurse; prepared to accept as a duty whatever path he might require her to tread.

In matters pertaining to sex, Meredith found her little more than a child; the result of her narrow upbringing by which she had been reared in ignorance of the primal facts of life and all that was common knowledge to the flapper of the day. But to his fastidious nature her unsophisticated innocence was the most captivating of any of the qualities he had met with in girls, and it became his most earnest desire to preserve it undefiled. The sweet simplicity of her mind he regarded as even more precious than her beauty. Having spent a decade in acquiring a disgust for a certain type of woman, he was inclined to over-estimate his surprising good fortune, and was content in the hope that time was on his side. Like a flower unfolding to the sun, the treasures of her womanhood would be all his one day, drawn forth by the warmth of his steady devotion.

The obstacles in his way, however, seemed to increase as circumstances combined to fret and tantalise his hopes.

The night wore on—the Eastern night of cloudless moonlight with the scents of the earth rising from harvested fields to mingle with the pungency of smouldering fires. Somewhere an owl persistently hooted.

Joyce recalled the superstition that the owl was a bird of ill omen and should not be allowed to perch in the neighbourhood of a sick room. Immediately she was seized with foreboding and her husband was dispatched to scare away the prophet of evil. On his return she was trembling and hysterical.

"You must let me give you something, darling," he pleaded. "You'll collapse for want of food, and how then can you look after Baby?" It was inspiration which suggested the child's need of her, for she patiently submitted and drank a glass of milk. She changed her gown for a silken kimono, and sought rest among the pillows of her bed which adjoined the crib. Then, in subdued tones, she reproached her husband for never having studied the simple diseases of childhood,—so necessary in their case, when for months together they were expected to live in camp, far from the Station, and the reach of medical aid.

"It is criminal," she cried. "If it had been a dog you would have known what to do. But your own child!" words failed her.

"The next time we come out we shall bring 'Good-eve.' I believe it gives everything you want to know and a lot besides."

"There'll never be a 'next time,'" she moaned. "Please God, when my pet is better he shall never again be taken so far from the doctor. This is the end of all camping for him."

"So I am to be deserted?"

"You are a man and able to look after yourself. Baby needs me far more than you do."

Meredith refrained from any argument, feeling the futility of words in her distraught condition. In the darkened tent he brooded over his difficulties while his eyes strayed with jealous yearning to the slim form in the gaudy kimono. Instead of isolation in a canvas chair, he might so easily have shared her pillows while comforting her lovingly in his arms! but for the time being he was out of favour and unloved!

Shortly before sunrise, Captain Dalton motored in.

CHAPTER III
THE CIVIL SURGEON

From the moment of the doctor's arrival the tension of watching was eased; the very sight of his wide shoulders in the doorway of the tent brought instantaneous relief to Joyce whose faith, as far as her child was concerned, was material rather than spiritual. Though she had felt an instinctive shrinking from the man's society on the few occasions on which they had met, her whole heart went out to welcome him with earnest supplication. He possessed the knowledge, under God, to save her child; therefore, surely, was he Superman—a being apart, to be reverenced above his fellows.

Captain Dalton of the Indian Medical Service, and Civil Surgeon of Muktiarbad, was an unfriendly being of peculiar personality, whom no one could comprehend. Ordinarily, he was repellent to intimacies; a reserved autocrat, and content to be unpopular. Though elected a member of the Club, he had little use for its privileges. Having fulfilled his duty to his neighbours by calling on them shortly after his arrival in the Station that summer, he had retired into professional and private life, and was as difficult to cultivate as the Pope of Rome. He rarely accepted invitations, and issued none. Men who called upon him received a rigid hospitality, nothing more, so that they soon ceased to visit him at all, at which he was relieved.

That he was a gifted musician became generally known when classical strains from a grand piano were wafted through the Duranta hedge which encompassed his grounds, riveting passers-by to the roadway at some sacrifice to personal dignity, that they might listen and admire. Sometimes he was heard to sing to his own accompaniment in a voice of extraordinary richness and sympathy. The evening breeze would carry the tones of his fine baritone voice farther than the Duranta hedge; and though bungalows were widely separated by private grounds of many acres, with paddocks and lanes between, his neighbours would hang out of their windows to catch every note, and afterwards at the common meeting ground of the Club, discourse on the advantage of their proximity to the singer.

All persuasions to repeat his performances in public met with obstinate discouragement, till, reluctantly, the Station left him alone. Injured feelings were nourished, and opinions concerning his conduct and manners grew harsh and unrelenting the instant his back was turned. To his face there was no failure of cordiality, for it is not politic in a small station to quarrel with one's doctor.

It was on the polo-ground, on the occasion of a slight accident which might have been more serious, that Joyce first met Captain Dalton, — a bare fortnight ago. His appointment had taken place while she had been at the hills, and at the introduction she had resented the impudent scrutiny of his eyes, not realising the fact that she had been an arresting picture with the hue of mountain roses in her cheeks, and eyes like English forget-me-nots; in beauty and colouring a rarity in that rural district of Bengal.

Perhaps the doctor wondered at the unusual combination of prettiness and simplicity, for, in his experience, good looks without vanity were something unique. Possibly he was sceptical, for a smile of satire lurked at the back of his inscrutable eyes. At any rate, he had found her an interesting study, and the jade-green orbs, reckoned his finest feature, seemed to assess her from top to toe, critically and coolly. Though he made no effort to engage her in conversation, he had lingered in her vicinity, listening to her childish prattle; and, contrary to expectations, long after the need of his services was past, he had loitered on the polo-ground till the Merediths had driven away in their car.

On looking back, Joyce had felt a sense of resentment at his quiet contempt of the ladies present. His cynical study of herself without any attempt to cultivate her society annoyed her self-esteem.

"He's positively rude!" was her indignant verdict, later. "I wonder people put up with him. And he has perfectly hateful eyes."

"The ladies think them very handsome eyes," Meredith had insinuated.

"They are very uncomfortable; like a thought-reader's. Anyhow, I shall not allow him to stare at me another time."

"There's a saying that 'a cat may look at the queen,'" he had remarked mischievously.

"It's a blessing, however, that one may choose one's friends!" she had finally stated; and her husband allowed the subject to drop, not displeased at her repugnance to the doctor whom he marked dangerous to feminine susceptibility and an unknown quantity.

Captain Dalton had called the following Sunday at noon, and was received by both husband and wife for the conventional few minutes. Being the official holiday, it was recognised as the correct day for men to pay formal visits, and by an unwritten law, at the warmest hour in the twenty-four.

Another time they had driven past each other in a lane, when Dalton gravely raised his hat in acknowledgment of her bow. Lastly, he had sat beside her at a Hindu dramatic performance held in the grounds of a local landowner, in celebration of a religious festival, and he had barely noticed her existence, being engaged with his host on the other side.

On the whole, he had not made a favourable impression on Joyce Meredith. But what did it matter, now? He had come out to their camp, many miles away from the Station, post-haste to save her child, and for that she was thankful. All memory of the doctor's bad manners was forgotten when she saw him enter the tent with her husband, a strong virile being, from his keen eyes and locked lips to his brisk tread;—God's own agent to cure her babe; a blessed healer of the sick, to whom the mysteries of the human frame were revealed; who could fight even death!

"Oh, Doctor," she cried piteously, the tears like great dewdrops on her lashes: "Baby has been so bad—I thought, once, I had lost him!"

Without formal greetings, Dalton passed to the cot, and stooping over it, began his examination of the case.

Appreciating the reproof conveyed by his silence, the little mother sat still while the examination proceeded, answering in tremulous tones the crisp, short questions hurled at her from time to time.

By and by, when a certain drug had been administered and there was nothing to be done but wait for its effects to be apparent, he abruptly turned his attention to herself. Had she eaten anything? What had she fed on for the past twenty-four hours? He covered her wrist with his hand, studied her highly nervous face for a full minute, and then ordered her away to bed.

"Take her out of this, Meredith, if you wish to avoid having two invalids on your hands. Is there another bed anywhere?"

Meredith's own occupied the dressing-tent, since he was obliged to give up sharing his wife's on account of the baby's claim to the services of an ayah.

"But, Doctor, I am not ill!" Joyce protested feebly, realising however now, that it was mentioned, that a collapse was imminent.

"You'll do as we think best," he said shortly, "or I had better get out."

"Who is to look after Baby?" she asked faintly.

"I am here for that," he said more gently.

After some futile objections, Joyce departed feeling unable to hold out a minute longer.

"How are you feeling?" her husband's anxious voice was asking. "You are as white as a lily, darling."

"I'll be all right when Baby is," she answered wearily.

In a little while Joyce was put to bed with a sleeping draught and tucked in comfortably, her husband as skilful in his ministrations as any nurse. "Won't you kiss me before I go? Love me a little bit," he pleaded wistfully.

"Go away Ray," she cried irritably. "Don't worry."

"You've made me so miserable!"

"It's nothing to what you made me!"

"I made you!"

"You—you were absent all day when Baby was so ill. It has nearly killed me."

"Dearest, don't blame me unjustly."

"Then let it drop. I am not wishing to discuss it; I am too tired."

So was he, but he had no thought of himself while yearning over her, his love-ly girl, more beloved in her stubborn antagonism than ever.

Remembering the doctor's injunctions that she must sleep, he reluctantly re-tired to pace the grass in the dawn, a dishevelled figure in his shirt-sleeves with hands plunged into the pockets of his trousers. The cool air soothed his nerves and brought him a sense of drowsiness which he indulged in a long cane chair under the eaves of the dressing-tent. The camp was very still after the disturbances of the night, and the sun rose above the flat horizon like a ball of living gold, its searching rays awakening the sleeping servants in their *shuldaris* by their glare and warmth.

But Ray Meredith was worn out and slept heavily, oblivious, for the moment, of his anxieties and his surroundings, for, after all, he cultivated a broad perspec-tive and a wide tolerance for his little girl's humours, since she was only "a kid in years and ideas."

With the sun mounting rapidly into the heavens came sounds of life from the distant village. Far away, cow-bells tinkled musically as the cattle moved lazily to pasture lands; dogs barked and children's voices, shrill and joyous, echoed over the fields.

Domestic servants at the camp were to be seen rolling up their bedding of sacking, preparatory to beginning the common round, the daily task. Not far from the temporary kitchen, the mate-boy squabbled with the village milkman over the supply of milk with its sediment of chalk, which he declared had all but killed the master's child. Let him remember that there was a doctor sahib on the spot, and what availed his protestations?

"A raw infant, too, with a new stomach. Assuredly will the police drag thee into court."

"Who said there was chalk!" almost wept the indignant *guala* gesticulating wildly in self-defence. "As God is my witness not a grain was in the milk. Have I no fear? Straight from the udder was it milked into the brass *lota* and brought to the camp. Ask of all the village if I am not an honest man paying just tribute where it is asked, and giving full measure and pure, to one and all. Would I jeopardise my freedom for malpractices? What evil accusation art thou, *badmash*, hurling at me?"

"We'll see who's a *badmash*!" the youth returned loftily. "Wait till the doctor Sahib gives evidence. Presently the Judge Sahib will say, 'O Amir, faithful one, speak concerning the sediment in the milk which thou didst show to the doctor Sahib, that the pestilential *guala* may receive just punishment for his wrong-do-ing.' But I have a tender heart for the repentant and may consent to destroy the evidence, even refrain from showing it to the Sahib, if it is made worth my while. Allot for my own portion one seer of milk, and two for the servants, free of charge, and, peradventure, my memory concerning the chalk will fail when the moment of inquiry arrives."

"Why didst not thou tell that it was perquisite thou wast wanting, for I would have given to thee without argument," sighed the *guala*, in visible relief. "I am a poor man, and honest, though the ways of my country-men are crooked, and I give in to thy demand that I might be spared false accusation and much humiliation. Take, brother, thy illegal *dusturi*;[7] how can such as I hope to escape *loot*, when from the *chaukidar* to the sweeper all are robbing those who provide the *hakim's* needs? Only from the *hakim* himself is there straight dealing!—*ai Khodar!*"

Within the large tent the silence that reigned boded well for the child who was sleeping peacefully.

Its improved condition was the latest bulletin issued by the ayah who had snatched a moment to enjoy a cheap cigarette in the open.

"What a night!" she said in Hindustani, which she spoke almost as fluently as Tamil. "With both Sahib and Memsahib awake and watching, who could sleep? I had not the conscience to close my eyes. Nor has a morsel passed these lips, for, with the precious one at death's door, food turns to ashes in the mouth."

"Thou art indeed a faithful one, Ayah-jee," said the *peon*.

"It is my religion, for I am a Christian and have no caste to hold me back from any service that is required of me, *Baba-jee*. The child is my first thought, and to guard its life, my first care."

"For which thou art paid handsomely, is it not so?"

"That, of course! and money is a great convenience, *Baba-jee*."

Joyce was still sleeping from the effects of the draught, when Meredith and the doctor breakfasted together. On no account was she to be disturbed. It seemed the doctor took a malicious delight in depriving the husband of the pleasure of carrying his wife the good news concerning the child; and he saw him depart to preside at his court under the trees, without a shade of sympathy for his visible distress.

"Your wife will be all right," he said confidently, "so don't worry, but go ahead with your work. I am capable of looking after both mother and child."

"I have no doubt of it," Meredith grumbled, "but you'll send for me, won't you, if anything's wrong?"

"Most assuredly," was the reply. And the Magistrate took his seat at the camp table under a leafy mango tree, and was soon immersed in his duties to the State. Natives of all castes and creeds thronged the grass beyond the precincts of the court, and a hoarse murmur of voices soon filled the air, above which was constantly heard that of the crier naming a witness, or calling up a case.

When the ayah brought Captain Dalton the news that her mistress was showing signs of waking, he poured out and took her a cup of tea, himself, and asked how she felt. "Not very bright, I can see," he remarked, placing his fingers on her pulse.

"Have I slept long?" she asked drowsily.

"Five hours."

"But Baby?" she cried out in alarm, sitting up in bed, giddy and confused.

[7] Commission.

"Baby's all right. Temperature normal, and sleeping like a cherub," he returned pressing her back on her pillows.

"Oh, Doctor, is that true?"

"You may think me a liar, if you like, but it isn't polite to call me one to my face," he said with a crooked, grudging smile.

"Oh, how am I to thank you!" tears suffused her eyes as she seized his hand and carried it impulsively to her lips. "You have no idea of the relief you have brought me!"

Dalton had; and by the answering gleam in his eye, showed he was rewarded for the whim which had prompted him to be the bearer of the good tidings. It amused him to play with this pretty child-wife, and sound the depths of her nature—if there were any!

"What is your age?" he asked abruptly, with a doctor's licence to question a patient as he chose.

"I was nineteen in summer."

"You have no business with a baby when you are one yourself! Now for your tea," and he held the cup while she leant on her elbow to drink its contents, a shower of honey-gold hair falling about her face.

"Is your head very bad?" he asked when she had finished.

"How did you know that it ached?" she questioned.

"I have ways of finding out. Your pulse and your flush, for example."

"Then I am ill?" she asked in alarm. If she were to be ill, who would take care of the child?

"A little ill."

"Fever?"

"Feverish."

"But I may get up, in spite of it?"

"Certainly not. Nor would you be of any use if you did."

"But I must take care of Baby!"

"I am doing that, already."

"You are going to take care of me, too?"

"Yes, if you are good and do all I tell you."

"I'll be so good, for I want to get well. How long will it last?"

"The fever? Who can say? However, I dare say it will be only a trifling thing."

"Where is my husband?" she asked, wondering if Ray knew, and why he had not rushed to see her. She was so accustomed to being fussed over, that she missed the excitement. No doubt he was nursing injured feelings since her ill-treatment of him last night....

"Listen, and you will hear the voices of the multitude before the Court. Mr. Meredith is trying cases and sentencing malefactors to various degrees of punishment," said the doctor.

"Won't you call him?"

"Are you sure he won't charge me with Contempt of Court?" he teased.

"If I am going to be ill, I must have him come at once. But first promise me something," she cried, clinging to his hand with feverish excitement; "I cannot bear to stay in camp after yesterday's experience. Tell him that I must go back to Muktiarbad so as to have Baby near you. He might be ill again, and what should I do then!"

"He might, certainly. Yes, I'll tell your husband, but not today. Today you will want to be taken care of, and we mustn't pile on the agony."

"On whom? It would be such a relief to me!"

"Not to your husband. I wouldn't mind betting he'd have a fit of the blues and be ill himself as a result."

"Oh, no! Ray never gets ill. He is so strong. That is why he can't understand us. Oh, Doctor, I cannot live in India!" she wailed.

"Are you very homesick?" he asked with the same grudging smile.

"I hate India! It will kill Baby—won't you explain that to my husband?"

"There is no reason why it should kill Baby."

"How can you tell?—everything is against him here!"

Dalton decided to humour her because of the deepening flush and starry eyes. The nervous fingers twined about his were hot with fever. "That's all right. Be happy, you'll go home in the spring if it depends on me."

"Oh, thank you, you are such a dear!"

Captain Dalton smiled less grudgingly. She was so perfectly ingenuous. In his critical eyes was a look of dalliance with a new problem. They were eyes that must often have studied human problems and not always to good purpose.

"I suppose the kid is your first consideration?" he asked, amused.

"He's so helpless!"

"I see," he remarked oracularly. Before he left the tent he gave her a tablet from a phial which he carried in his vest-pocket.

"Do you know," she ventured in the hurried accents of feverishness, "I did not like you a bit when I first met you."

"And now?"

"You are so different from what I had imagined."

"What was that?"

"You seemed an animated iceberg—forbidding and—yes, almost disagreeable. You make most people afraid of you."

"It matters very little to me what people think of me," he returned indifferently.

"Don't you ever care for friends?"

"I have no use for friends—besides, who are one's friends? I have ceased to believe in friendship," he sneered.

She studied his face gravely. "I don't like to hear you speak like that. We would be your friends if you would let us."

Dalton checked a laugh of genuine amusement, the first sound of mirth she had heard from his lips, and it was not pleasant hearing.

"You are very good," he said tolerantly, "but it wouldn't work. I wouldn't suggest the experiment, if I may advise you."

"I certainly shall not, if you are nasty," she pouted.

Dalton laughed again disagreeably and went out.

He was truly a conundrum, she decided, and difficult to know. Yet how kind he had been to her and careful of her child! for that she would always be grateful. But for him, anything might have happened! Strange fellow!—why was he so antagonistic to people when his profession made him a ministering angel to humanity? Joyce felt her head aching so violently at this stage that she abandoned the puzzle of Captain Dalton's nature and indulged in ecstasies over the thought of her baby's recovery. It made her so happy that, when her husband entered with the doctor, she flung her arms about his neck and apologised for her exhibition of bad temper. "I was horrible to you, Ray. Do forgive me," sounded very sweet in her husband's ears. What the doctor thought was of no importance to her.

Meredith mumbled transports of joy on her lips and was beside himself with anxiety that she should be feverish. He plied her with questions in his solicitude, and stood by in sulky jealousy while the doctor made his professional examination of her lungs and heart.

Joyce said "ninety-nine" many times obediently, and was like a child in her unconsciousness of self. One all-absorbing thought occupied her mind, and that was her baby's well-being.

"Isn't Captain Dalton an angel?" she cried when the examination was over and her lungs pronounced in perfect order. "I shall love him for ever after his kindness to us; only, he won't let me. He has no use, he says, for friends!"

Dalton smiled grimly as he put away his stethoscope. "Have you ever heard of the qualities that go to make a good doctor?" he asked coolly.

"Tell me," she demanded.

"An unerring judgment, nerves of steel, and a heart of stone."

"And have you managed to acquire all three?" she asked playfully.

"The petrifaction of the last-named is quite an old story," he remarked, as he passed out of the tent.

"You must not talk so much, sweetheart, with a rising temperature," Meredith cautioned, fussing over her, while, outside, the trial of a notorious criminal was suspended till the Magistrate should think fit to return. "How did Dalton find out that you had fever?" he questioned suspiciously. "Did you send for him?"

"Oh, no. He brought me news of Baby and gave me my tea. Isn't he queer? Not half so bad as people make him out to be. Oh!—and I was so overjoyed and excited that I kissed his hand. I wonder what he thought of my foolishness?" and she laughed at the joke; but her husband seemed to have lost his sense of humour, for he retired from the bedside to pace the drugget in distinct annoyance.

"Damned officious of him," he grumbled. "You were not his patient."

"I am *now*, so it's all right."

"You shouldn't have forgotten your dignity."

"I know it, but that's the way with me. I never remember that I have any!"

"You are a married woman and no longer a child," he continued reproachfully.

"I shall always be a silly fool, I'm afraid," she sighed. "However, he's only the doctor, and a doctor is something between an angel and an automaton."

"The devil he is!" Meredith growled, kicking a hassock to the other end of the tent.

"Come here, you big goose," she said wearily, stretching her limbs; "kiss me this instant, and go back to the malefactors. I want to sleep off this attack and get well quickly."

Meredith could not bear to see her looking ill and wanted no second bidding to demonstrate his love for her. After kissing her most tenderly, he tucked her in comfortably, and, much against his inclination, left her to the doctor's ministrations.

CHAPTER IV
A POINT OF VIEW

Dalton filled the ice-bag he had brought with him and settled down to nursing with the skill of a woman; and no hands could have been gentler. Occasionally the worried husband would pay the tent a flying visit and return to listen to a pleader's lengthy oration with all the attention he could muster under the troublous circumstances. Visions of his wife's flushed face lying still on the pillow with closed eyes would haunt him with agonising fidelity to detail—especially in relation to the attentive doctor hovering near, adjusting the bag or removing it to be refilled, and administering the necessary doses of medicine. He took special notice of Dalton in his new character of nurse, and had no fault to find with his manner. He was as silent as the Sphinx and as professional as a nursing sister, and though Meredith thought it objectionable that his wife should always have to be treated in illness by a male physician—there being no lady doctor within hundreds of miles—he was obliged to take comfort in the fact that his beloved could not be in better hands.

Elsewhere, the ayah crooned lullabies to the baby who no longer needed strict watching. She fed it from the bottle and wondered, philosophically, who would be the next to be taken ill; for experience told her that it was a mild form of epidemic chill, familiar to all at the changing of the seasons.

Meals went forward with clock-like regularity, whether the sahibs were inclined for sustenance or not. The camp table in the dining-tent was laid with silver and crockery; a tight bunch of green leaves adorned a centre vase, and a gong rang at the appointed hour, while the dishes remained warm in the portable "hot case" where an open charcoal fire burned redly.

"Isn't the fever rather persistent?" Meredith asked at dinner while toying with his food.

"It's early to judge," said the doctor.

"What do you think of it?"

"Unquestionably a touch of the 'flu.'"

"It isn't enteric?" the anxious husband asked fearfully. "I have a holy horror of enteric."

"You make your mind easy, it is not going to be anything of the sort. I am afraid, however, you will have to give up all idea of Mrs. Meredith's camping for the present," he added definitely. "She and the child don't take kindly to canvas, and at this time of year we must avoid exposure to malarial conditions."

"The District is particularly free from malaria," said Meredith.

"Bengal is full of it; the many bogs and pools of stagnant water around are responsible for the anopheles mosquito."

"It's dashed inconvenient when I must put in a deuced lot of camping in the cold weather."

"Do most of it after Christmas," Dalton suggested.

"It will be just the same—they won't be able to stand it."

"Frankly, I don't think they will. Perhaps, both might be more acclimatised later on," was the diplomatic reply.

Meredith passed another night on the cane chair which he placed alongside of his wife's bed, and was conscious during periods of rest that the doctor never slept at all. He was in and out of the tent at all hours of the night looking after his patient with untiring zeal. An easy chair in the dining-tent had served as his couch, and the English newspapers entertained him during the long hours of the night.

Yet at the end of the vigil, Meredith knew Captain Dalton no better than before. He was still the silent, repellent being, with eyes of a thought-reader and a baffling smile which might have meant contempt or tolerance; he was altogether incomprehensible.

By morning, Joyce was free of fever with a temporarily lowered vitality, and showing no ill effects. All day she convalesced happily, enjoying the petting she received from the men; Captain Dalton's methods being unobtrusive, but effective; Meredith's, on the other hand, being tactlessly affectionate and blundering.

"You are a darling, Ray," she laughed, after a specially clumsy service, "but you were never born with a faculty for nursing, like Captain Dalton's. He is so capable; he never spills my mixture down my neck before I can drink it; nor does he pour out over-doses, and empty the surplus on the drugget!"

"'Comparisons are odorous,'" he returned, looking hurt.

"The tent is, if you like. It smells like a chemist's shop! Your proper place and function are in the court, and sentencing criminals to punishment."

"You want to get rid of me so that you may have the doctor all to yourself! I wonder what you find in him at all. He fairly chokes one off."

"I told you he was either an automaton or an angel; I find he is both, only he would like us to think him a bad angel."

"A man knows himself best. So you want to desert me tomorrow?" he cried reproachfully.

"Dear old thing!—you wouldn't have me stay if you knew that I should be miserable?" she coaxed, drawing down his face to be kissed.

"Miserable with the husband who adores you?"

"If you love me so much, you should be unselfish and think more of Baby."

"Must Baby always count above his Daddy?"

"Naturally he must be considered more, while he is so young and delicate."

"Where then do I come in?"

"You mustn't be jealous of your own child!" she cried reproachfully. "Think of his helplessness, his need of me!—Of course you need me, too," she said putting her palm over his mouth to stifle his eloquence on the subject of a husband's rights, "but then, there's a difference. You can manage without me, while he must not. A babe is a sacred trust to its mother."

"And when he grows older and is impressionable, there will be a mother's *moral duty towards his soul* to separate us. You and he at home, and I out here, alone! I know the jargon, having watched such comedies for years. Now it has come home to me. One hears that a child is a blessing from God.... I believe it is a blessing very much in disguise, for I see only the disguise at present."

"Why look so far ahead?" laughed Joyce, determined to mend his humour. "By the time he is old enough to become a 'moral' responsibility, you will probably be only too glad to get rid of me. I am such a worry as a wife."

"I wonder!" he ejaculated ruefully.

Joyce reminded him of the many week-ends he could spend at the bungalow, when they would contrive to have very happy times. "I shan't be so anxious with a doctor on the spot, so to speak; and shall be ever so much more of a wife," she promised, looking adorable in the ribbons and laces of her snowy night-dress, backed with befrilled pillows.

The prospect had compensations, he felt, but he found it hard to explain without incurring the imputation of selfishness, that, parted day after day from the light of her presence, deprived of the sight of her loveliness and the natural expression of his passion for her, he would assuredly ache unceasingly and pine himself sick. She would not understand, since she had little comprehension of the ways of mankind, so he could only sigh and capitulate.

"At least there will be many honeymoons!" he allowed, trying to hide his disappointment in satire.

"What a man you are!" she laughed. "Won't you ever get used to being married?"

Meredith returned to his files and the clamouring multitude under the trees, for the remainder of the afternoon, with the noxious odours of bare-bodied humanity, besmeared with mustard oil, assaulting his nostrils. Meanwhile Joyce cultivated the doctor with innocent feelers of friendship while he administered afternoon tea.

"I do think you are such a clever nurse," she said flatteringly, while he fed her on bread and butter. "You are like two persons in one—both doctor and nurse!"

"Necessity is a good teacher," he returned shortly. "I have never nursed any one myself; others have generally taken my orders."

"I should have imagined that you had done this all your life."

Viewed in broad daylight at close quarters, when her brain was cleared of feverish delusions, he was not at all a handsome man. Too blunt-featured and heavy in the jaws; too square in the frame and thick of neck; but his eyes, with their power of reserve, were always a splendid mystery; deep-set and provoking, yet suggestive of nothing so much as banked fires, glowing and suppressed. Frequently they dwelt on her with the same satirical amusement of the polo-field, and she would waste much of her thoughts in wondering why. It was the look of a sceptic who had no intention of expressing his unbelief, and Joyce was irritated and annoyed. But she had no fault to find with his attentions, and was invariably won to gratitude for services rendered.

She was very pretty—exceptionally so—and very simple; but, as pretty women were never simple, Dalton found entertainment in the study of her particular pose, as it seemed to him. If it were not a pose, then her husband was a short-sighted fool and he had no patience with him. The time was past for childish innocence and folly. Coquetry was very captivating, but to play with fire was dangerous, and if he mistook not, she would some day arrive at an understanding of human nature when it was too late to save her self-respect. Her beauty appealed to his artistic sense, but he had no admiration for shallow natures; hence his amused contempt.

"You remind me of nothing so much as an oyster," she laughed, picking up a dainty piece of bread and butter and putting it in her mouth.

"Why so?"

"You are living so much in your shell. Why do you do it?"

"Why not, if it pleases me?" he asked pouring out two cups of tea.

"Think of all you lose!"

"I generally manage to take what I want," he replied with an insolent smile. "I rarely suffer from loss."

"You lose love," said she wisely.

"What do you know about it?" he questioned, fixing her with his penetrating eyes.

"I love my husband——"

"—And your baby, even more. Of course your experience is immense!"

"You are sarcastic," she said reproachfully. "I love my husband and my baby in quite different ways. You have no wife or baby, so you cannot understand. Men like you go through life without knowing any of its real joys."

"That is according to your point of view," he retorted. "In any case, marriage is a great gamble and it's best to avoid risks."

"There's a girl you and I know..." Joyce put in reminiscently, seeing in mind a pleasing vision, "and the man who gets her will be the luckiest fellow in the world."

"He certainly will."

"How do you know whom I mean?"

"You mean Miss Bright of Muktiarbad."

Joyce opened wide her blue eyes which were the colour of forget-me-nots, and stared. "Are you a thought-reader?"

"It was easy reading, for there is only one girl we mutually know who fits your description entirely, and she is Miss Honor Bright. She has been reared to live up to her name."

"And you found that out though you hardly ever speak to her?"

"It is rather wonderful, isn't it?" he asked with his crooked smile.

"Then—why—?" There were limits to curiosity, but her expressive eyes spoke the rest of her question direct to his.

"Why don't I cultivate Miss Bright? The answer is simple. I am not seeking a wife, and I have no interest in friendships."

"How rude!" she cried reproachfully.

Dalton laughed disagreeably and offered her more tea which she accepted, not knowing whether he was not after all the most churlish being she had ever met.

"I wish I could understand you, Doctor, but I never shall," she sighed hopelessly, as she endeavoured to make herself comfortable among the tumbled bed-clothes. "I give you up as a difficult riddle."

"You want your bed re-made," he returned changing the subject. "Shall I do it for you?"

"You?—I can't fancy your bed-making!"

"I'll show you that I can do that as well as most other things. But you'll have to move out."

The cane lounge had been put out of the way and was not within easy walking distance for a shaky invalid; nevertheless Joyce was determined to try. While he transferred the cushions, she rolled herself in a shawl and made a brave effort to walk across, only to be overcome by giddiness.

Dalton was in time to save her from falling and she was carried clinging in her panic to the column of his neck. "You shouldn't have attempted it," he scolded.

"But I liked the way you swung me off my feet!" she said contentedly.

"It is not one of my duties to wait hand and foot on my patients, I would have you understand," he said grimly with a lurking twinkle in his eye, wondering, the while, whether the giddiness was another pose. "It seems you like being fussed over," he remarked before laying her down among the cushions.

"I love it!" she cooed ingenuously. "It's the only reason I don't mind being sick, to have Ray fuss and carry me about."

He put her down immediately with the familiar expression of indulgent satire in his eyes. "You'll probably get plenty of fussing from everyone; but, in the case of the boys, remember to be merciful."

"What on earth do you mean?"

"There are some young fools who might, if encouraged, lose their heads, you know."

"But there'd be no excuse, for I never flirt."

"Pardon me, you flirt like an artist."

Joyce thought it was horrid of him to say so, and wondered if she should snub him for his impertinence; only she did not quite know how. He had been so kind—perhaps he was only teasing? However she was reduced to offended silence while he made her bed with skill and expedition. He was not anxious that her husband arrive and find him so employed, and was glad to restore Mrs. Meredith to her nest of pillows without interruptions from without. Her utter lack of concern, either way, was illuminating, so that he had to revise his estimate of her once again, while his smile lost its satire.

"Sure you are comfy?" he asked before leaving her.

"Yes, thank you," she answered stiffly.

"Haughtiness does not become you, dear lady. What have I done?" he asked coolly.

"You said I was a flirt!" she pouted.

"I'll take it back," he returned smiling broadly, thinking that she certainly flirted delightfully. But shallow natures always flirted just so.

"I have never been accused of that—in my life."

"It would be such a libel!" he conceded.

"Thank you," she said graciously as she shot him a forgiving glance both radiant and alluring. "Do you know, I like you tremendously, though I began by thinking you hateful."

"First impressions are often correct," he returned grimly, and retired.

By and by, when she was alone with her husband and childishly about to recount the events of the afternoon with fidelity as to detail, she was diverted by his grave distress at the coming parting. It was cruel to inflict grief, and she wished he would be more reasonable.

"Old thing!" she said affectionately, rubbing her soft cheek against his rough one; "think how much I, too, shall miss you! It won't be only on your side!"

"Will you really miss me?" he asked infatuatedly.

"All the time. I love having you about, and if I am lonely at nights, I have only to creep into your bed in the next room to be comforted. What ever shall I do when that bed lies empty?"

It was heavenly to Meredith to hear this intimate revelation from her lips, always so shy of expressing her need of him. It was a great advance in the right direction, and his skies cleared as by magic. If absence truly made the heart grow fonder, he would have no cause of complaint against this short parting. It was the greater one in the spring, the shadow of which was already darkening his horizon, that he dared not contemplate.

However, there was plenty of time yet, and no earthly good was to be gained by crossing bridges in anticipation.

The following day saw an exodus from the camp. Meredith took his wife and child to Muktiarbad station, and saw them comfortably established in the Collector's bungalow, known as the Bara Koti,[8] then returned to his duties in the rural parts of his District, resolved to support his deprivations with cheerful resignation.

---

[8] Big House.

CHAPTER V

WHAT CAN'T BE CURED

Ray Meredith tried for the first few days to submit to his loss with fortitude, but the loneliness of the camp, after the experience of a sweet wife's companionship, was insupportable. There were no Europeans for miles around and there remained only the diversions of an occasional *shikar*. The tour of the previous autumn and winter months on which he had been accompanied by his girlish bride, had spoilt him for bachelor life; for though Joyce had disliked the inconveniences of camping, she had suffered them meekly, seeing that to have objected would have been both selfish and unkind. But the coming of the child had roused in her active opposition to all that might be harmful to its most precious health, and her husband was gradually discovering that he would inevitably have to accept the back seat.

For the first time in his official career, the routine of his work wearied him with its monotony and staleness. Having his meals in solitary state affected his appetite and digestion, for he took to bolting his food just to get rid of the automaton behind his chair who, no doubt, mentally criticised his every act, and treasured up the memory of his idiosyncrasies to comment upon them, later, in the kitchen.

During the day the business of hearing petitions, trying cases, and delivering judgments, occupied his mind and brought distraction, but in the evenings he could settle to nothing. Even his beloved pipe failed to bring him consolation.

When darkness closed in with dense shadows where the moonlight failed to penetrate, and the peace of a world at rest was upon the countryside, when even the birds had ceased to chirp and flutter in their nests, the air would feel charged with expectancy. A footfall without would cause Meredith to lift his head from his papers or book, wondering if there was a message for him—Joyce taken ill—or the baby? The silence bred nerves, till a chorus of jackals howling in an adjacent paddy field would break the spell and come as a welcome relief.

Often, the words of a book he tried to read conveyed no meaning to his mind till he had re-read a paragraph several times. Or the official report he had set himself to write was disturbed by mental visions of Station doings in which his young wife was perhaps taking part without his support and protection.

She was so young and unsophisticated! It was perhaps his own fault that she was so, but he loved her all the more on account of it, and would not have had her otherwise.

An instinctive distrust of Captain Dalton would not be stifled, and he disliked the thought of his innocent young wife being exposed to the subtle flattery of such unusual attentions as he had paid her in camp,—strictly professional, no doubt, but disagreeably intimate from a husband's point of view. Confound him!

A young man of arresting appearance and strange personality, whose private life was unknown and whose conduct towards his neighbours was aloof and repellent, was best kept at a distance and treated with the formality which accorded with his profession, otherwise he would become a disturbing element. Already Joyce seemed to consider herself under obligations to him, and in her enthusiastic gratitude was prone to overstep the limits of dignified propriety which he wished her to observe. Would to heaven that the Government had sent them a married man as Civil Surgeon of Muktiarbad! Bachelors of mysterious habits and manners were totally out of place in a station so well supplied with womenkind.

Meredith was thankful that there were so many women in the Station and all likely to be lavish with their attentions to his wife. She would seldom be left to her own devices or the society of the doctor, in whose care she was unreservedly placed. And Joyce was popular with the ladies despite the fact that she was too young to play her dignified rôle of leading lady with success. She played it with a charm all her own, and drew towards her the members of her own sex as well as those of the masculine. She was unique, he assured himself. He could trust her blindfold, even among wolves in sheep's clothing; for essentially she was a mother, and had every incentive to keep pure. Love of children and a respect for religion were sure safeguards against the wiles of the tempter; he could therefore make his mind easy, feeling that his wife possessed both.

But jealousy is a weed of hardy growth, and once having taken root is difficult to destroy. There were memories to haunt him and give him many a sleepless night: Joyce seizing and kissing Dalton's hand in her frenzy of relief when he told her the good news concerning the child; her milk-white shoulder and bosom exposed for the stethoscope.... She might look upon Dalton as an "angel" or an "automaton," but no man, unless superhuman, is a stoic where a lovely woman is concerned.

On the whole, it was a miserable week for Meredith in his solitude, despite the distractions of his office and constant journeys over the plain.

His next encampment was a large Mohammedan village on the outskirts of a silk factory,—an important industry owned and worked by a prosperous Anglo-Indian.

In duty bound, the Magistrate and Collector called on the ladies of the house, sending in the usual piece of pasteboard with his name printed thereon, and caught a fleeting glimpse of the wife in a dressing-gown and slippers scuttling to cover from the out-offices in the rear.

After keeping him waiting for sometime in a musty drawing-room where cobwebs lurked in corners and everything looked the worse for time, she appeared in fearful and wonderful array,—layers of powder concealing the dusky tint of her complexion, innumerable jewels tinkling on her person, and hands badly manicured, but richly be-ringed.

During his brief visit she talked volubly in "chee-chee," vigorously assisted by gesticulations, and her laughter was ear-splitting and vulgar in its enforced hilarity; so that Meredith, whose nerves felt badly jangled, rose to beat a hasty retreat, courteously resisting all the hospitable efforts of the hostess to keep him as a guest.

At the Subdivision of Panchpokhur, he was introduced to the Deputy Magistrate's wife and twin baby boys who were splendid specimens of infantile vigour; and his praise and admiration were the passport to their mother's instant regard. She was a devoted wife and mother, placid and easy-going, and carried the air of one equal to any emergency.

"I am amazed that they should look so strong," Meredith said as he watched the children racing over the grass in pursuit of straying poultry.

"They seldom ail," said their mother, who, though country born, was perfectly English in her speech and manners. "I nursed them both, unaided," she said proudly, feeling disposed to venture this confidence to a man who was married and a father.

"That, I suppose, makes a heap of difference," he remarked diffidently. "My wife was too ill after the birth of the kid, so it was put on the bottle from the start."

"What a pity!" and the lady forthwith entered upon an instructive dissertation on the particular artificial foods that could be recommended.

"Will this always make him delicate, do you think?" Meredith asked anxiously, not so much for the sake of the babe, as from the fear of all it would mean to himself in regard to his wife.

"Perhaps not, but it is a bad handicap."

Meredith sighed as he explained the reason of his touring alone. "Captain Dalton thinks the child should be within reach of medical aid after its go of fever. My wife, too, was a bit knocked over and cannot rough it this winter, I'm afraid."

"The new Civil Surgeon?"

"Yes. Came direct from Calcutta after the rains set in."

"He is said to be very clever, but the natives don't seem to like him at all, as he is supposed to be rather fond of the knife."

"A good surgeon, I am told. The natives are great cowards of surgery, and risk gangrene before they will consent to an operation."

"That is so. He has his hands full, I should think," said the lady. "Elsie Meek, the daughter of a dear friend of mine, is dangerously ill at the Mission not far from Muktiarbad. I suppose you know that?"

Meredith had heard a rumour to that effect, and wondered how Captain Dalton had managed to spare so much of his valuable time to the camp.

"Mr. Meek is a Methodist who came out some years ago and married a school friend of my mother's. Their daughter was educated in England and joined them a few months ago. I am told she is a talented girl and totally unsuited to her life here," said his hostess. "Have you seen much of her?"

"Very little, indeed, for her people don't belong to the Club and Miss Elsie has only been to see the Brights who are rather friendly with her parents. She came out in the summer."

"Poor thing! Enteric is such a terrible disease, and she is very bad I hear."

"She could not be in more skilful hands," said Meredith.

Before he left the Subdivision, he had many illuminating talks with the wife of the Deputy on the subject of infants and how to rear them in Bengal.

"I suppose," said he, "when my kid begins to teeth, the doctors will advise sending him and the mother home?" It was the probability he most dreaded.

"I see no necessity for that," was the assured reply. "Doctors take too much responsibility upon themselves, when they so readily part husbands and wives. It has often been the cause of greater trouble than is to be feared from the climate. It should be remembered that teething is not a disease, but a natural process, which might be influenced by the digestion in any part of the globe. Poor India gets all the blame!—even when an ayah is careless with the feeding bottles. Why! those iniquitous ones with a long rubber tube, used in my mother's day, were called 'Herods' for the number of children they killed. With proper attention, and the hills for a change when necessary, there is no reason why babies out here should not do perfectly well till they are seven. It is the growing and impressionable stage, and I'll allow that the moral example of human nature in the East is not of the best. I say it, who have been brought up entirely out here."

"You are a tremendous credit to your upbringing," put in Meredith.

"My people were very particular and I was never allowed an ayah to teach me self-indulgence, nor to associate with the servants' children on the estate; for what native children do not know of evil isn't worth knowing."

The Subdivisional Officer's bungalow was a type usually to be found in rural Districts, built of bricks and mortar, whitewashed, and roofed with the thatching grass that grows on low-lying lands by the Ganges. Earlier in Raymond Meredith's career, Panchpokhur had been one of his own appointments, and every corner of the dwelling and its grounds was familiar to him: the tall goldmohur trees beside the gate, the range of out-offices and stabling, the high, flowering hedge of hibiscus, the primitive well by the palm tree, with its screeching pulley. Gazing from the verandah he could almost imagine himself a bachelor again in the first flush of an opening career, keen and interested. The low verandah was the same on which he was wont to sleep on hot summer nights, and breakfast upon, at sunrise, in his pyjamas. The deep, thatched roof was as cool and as picturesque as of yore, having been renewed many times in the seven or eight years that were gone. The difference in his surroundings lay in the greater cleanliness—which usually distinguished the abode of a married man from that of a careless bachelor—and also in the supplementary furniture which threw his old camp articles into the shade. He was able to recognise the more durable of his past possessions in various parts of the house where they appealed to him as old friends. In those days how little had sufficed him!

All was now changed, for his life was dominated with the one idea of making his home attractive and suitable for the treasure it held.

After Panchpokhur, he moved on with his tents and the paraphernalia of camp life to parts thickly populated by Indians of all castes and creeds, and was received with pomp and ceremony befitting the representative of the Ruling Power. Addresses were read to him before a vast concourse of humanity; and members of the Local Municipal Board vied with one another in paying him the respect due to his official position.

In the intervals of duty, he tramped jungle places for game, alone or in company with gentlemen from the neighbourhood; and, at the week-end, prepared to spend Sunday with his wife at Muktiarbad.

CHAPTER VI

THE LEADING LADY

Meanwhile, Joyce at the Bara Koti, partially regained her confidence in life, and tried to make the best of her surroundings.

The house stood imposingly in extensive grounds which had been artistically laid out by successive officials, in lawns, flower-bed, ornamental shrubberies, and a kitchen garden, all of which were maintained by four *malis* and a regiment of coolies. A dense hedge of cactus separated the grounds from the roadway, with graceful bamboo clumps at intervals for shade; and a rustic gate led to the carriage drive, an avenue bordered by goldmohur trees.

The building, which was one-storeyed, was of solid masonry, the floor being well raised upon arches. Wide pillared verandahs ran on every side, and the roof was of concrete supported by iron joists. The rooms were lofty and spacious, with high doors and many windows, furnished with glass shutters and Venetian blinds; and were designed to fulfil the requirements of married officials of important position in the Government, who were expected to maintain a dignified state and entertain in a style to correspond. In a word, it was Government House on a minor scale, with a lordly status to keep up in the Station and District.

For his wife's sake, Meredith had endeavoured to make his home as attractive as possible so as to save inevitable comparisons between her present and past circumstances.

However, there were drawbacks which even he could not avoid: the lack of the most ordinary conveniences of daily life, such as electric lights and fans, water pipes, telephones, and English shops; and of them all, it was to be feared that the last might yet prove the most to be deplored.

The bathrooms, which were numerous, had no hot and cold water laid on; nor were there any but kerosene lamps to give light; and in lieu of electric fans, *punkhas* with gathered frills were worked by means of a rope through a hole in the wall. Kurta, Moja, Juti, and Paji, were the four Hindu coolies employed in summer to keep the frill perpetually waving in whichever room it pleased the sahibs to sit; and the patient creatures sat cross-legged on the verandah floor, nodding over the rope till galvanised into activity by a shout from within.

For baths, kettles of boiling water were fetched from the kitchen, fifty yards or so distant, and cans of cold water from a tank beyond the vegetable garden, by a semi-nude servant whose duty it was to do this and nothing else. It took

Joyce many months to realise which of the numerous servants in her pay could be required to perform a particular task, so complicated were the differentiations created by caste.

Muktiarbad was very much behind the times as to modern comforts and conveniences, but was entirely up-to-date in the fashions which the weekly journals depicted for the advantage of the gentler sex, and which the latest arrivals from "home" expressed. Moreover, Calcutta was only a few hundred miles away—a trifle in India—and contained first-rate shops and dressmakers. A week-end visit to the Metropolis for a round of shopping was a common habit of the ladies of Muktiarbad, with its handy train service; and if it added considerably to the cost of living, what would you, when the bazaar sold only Manchester goods in bales, and *saris* for feminine apparel?

Old Khodar Bux, who was available for eight annas per day, was a treasure to bachelor servants, as the only tailor to be had in the District.

In all other matters, the Station was content, for officials were birds of passage, and what had sufficed the residents for years, was good enough for today. Private enterprise was sluggish, and the cost of transporting plant and material for the installation of electricity, prohibitive; so the sahibs continued to use kerosene oil; were fanned by coolies, and were dependent on wells and tanks for their water supply, leaving it to the larger towns and great centres to revel in all the luxuries of modern times.

The possession of a large Daimler by the Collector, and of a two-seater Rolls-Royce by the doctor, filled the other English residents with envy; but they were anathema to the natives of the bazaars and villages. Rich Indians followed suit with cars of various sorts, but, generally, the machines were looked upon by the ignorant as ruthless inventions of the devil, and to be feared accordingly.

Joyce lived an idle life at Muktiarbad, served hand and foot by a host of servants, and treated as a little queen by her neighbours. She did not even try to "keep house" after the approved method in the East, a bunch of keys jingling in her pocket, and everything that was of value locked safely away; a cook to stand behind her chair, once a day, to render the bazaar accounts; visits of inspection to the kitchen, an eagle eye kept on the dusting and sweeping, and the laundry-man's weekly wash duly checked; for Meredith's head *bearer*, who had assumed responsibilities in his master's bachelor days and was too valuable to be deprived of his office, continued to keep accounts and run the establishment on oiled wheels. Joyce held him in secret awe and respect.

Her ayah instructed her in Indian ways and customs, and caste susceptibilities; and it was no little tax to remember how not to offend. The *bearer* was not to be asked to carry trays of food, or the *khansaman* to trim the lamps; the *masalchi* had no responsibility with regard to the boots, or the sweeper with scullery concerns; and so on, and so forth. It was all very bewildering and made her nervous. She cared too little for India to take much trouble to improve her knowledge of the country or of the people, and was content to remain as an honoured guest in her own house, with her precious babe to worship and cherish with jealous devotion.

On her return from camp, visitors dropped in to see her, foremost among them, Mrs. Barrington Fox, the wife of a railway official of some importance in the District; a lady young enough to have retained a belief in her power to charm. She had been very handsome at her *début*, ten years ago, but the ravages of the climate had not spared her complexion which was delicately assisted by art to retain its bloom. She had the air of being languidly bored with the monotony of her life, and seemed disposed to patronise the "leading lady" who never led, save when the laws of precedence obliged her to occupy the seat of honour at dinner parties in the Station. It was a temptation to Mrs. Fox to advise her in the way she should go, and she tactfully managed to hint at it. "India is naturally strange to you, yet you do wonderfully!—I am sure you are very clever," she would begin, and then make some suggestion which Joyce was very glad to follow. For instance—"I hear the Padre from headquarters wishes to hold service here next Sunday. He ought really to put up with you, but the Brights have had him lately and unless you write and invite him he is likely to go straight to them. What do you think?" she asked lighting a cigarette.

Joyce had been in the hills on the few occasions when the Reverend John Pugh had visited Muktiarbad from Hazrigunge and conducted Divine service in the reading-room of the Club.

"Do you think I should?" she asked, anxious to do the correct thing.

"I was thinking that the Brights take too much upon themselves. Mrs. Bright is only the wife of the Superintendent of Police after all, and your husband is the Collector."

"But Mrs. Bright is a perfect dear."

"Still she should not encroach on your rights. The District Chaplain usually stays with the Collector unless he has special friends in the Station with whom he divides his time. But do just as you like. I thought perhaps he would think you did not want him."

"I should like to have him very much," Joyce said eagerly. "My husband will be here and it will be quite a pleasure to us both." So Joyce promised to write her letter of invitation.

On the whole, she was never at her ease with Mrs. Fox, who had rarely a good word for her neighbours and voiced strangely radical sentiments concerning Life and its obligations. They were often startling, particularly as she made no secret of the fact that she and her husband never "got on." Between puffs of cigarette smoke she would scoff at the laws of marriage and speak with much leniency of divorce. Her sympathies were invariably with offenders, and Joyce thought her rather too fond of the society of men. Meredith feared and disliked her. The fear was on his wife's account, lest she should be contaminated. "I have no use for a woman of her type," he would say. "She has made a mess of her own life and is a poisonous influence to young women."

"But it seems she has a perfect brute of a husband, who leaves her to herself while he runs up and down the line amusing himself with other women."

"It's a lie," said Meredith sternly. "Fox is not a bad sort. Men rather like him, and he is a jolly good Traffic Superintendent. The Railway staff think a lot of him. I should not be surprised if he is fed up with her selfishness and the way she carries on with his assistants. No decent man tolerates that sort of thing."

"If you talked to her for an hour, you'd think she was the injured party," said Joyce.

"Then I'd rather you never talked to her."

But that was ridiculous in a small station where everyone met everyone else every day, Joyce explained.

So when Mrs. Barrington Fox called, full of gossip and friendliness, she was received politely. After the matter of the Padre was settled, she demanded to see the child and a quarter of an hour was spent in baby-worship.

"He's certainly not looking so well as when you brought him from Darjeeling. Weaker, I should say, poor little chappie! I don't believe the place agrees with him—or with you, for that matter. You look a good deal paler. How do you feel?"

"I am quite all right now, only a bit shaken," Joyce said doubtfully. Possibly she was not conscious how bad she actually was? Mrs. Fox was not comforting.

"You mustn't run down, you know. The surest safeguard against epidemics and illnesses peculiar to this miserable climate is never to allow yourself to run below par."

"But what is one to do? One doesn't deliberately do it."

"No, but you should eat heaps of nourishing things. Drink plenty of milk, for instance. But never fail to boil it, and never leave it exposed to the air. Milk is the most dangerous thing you can take, on account of its susceptibility to germs of every kind; especially enteric and cholera. It simply asks for germs!"

"And if you keep it covered, it goes bad!" cried Joyce alarmed since it formed the sole diet of her beloved infant.

"It wouldn't be a bad plan to keep it in the refrigerator in bottles. I did that all the winter, last year, when I was on milk diet."

"It will turn me grey to keep in mind the many things I must not do out here!" sighed Joyce.

Mrs. Fox condoled with her out of fellow-feeling and congratulated her for having given up camping. "If it doesn't suit you or the kid, I don't see why you should be obliged to do it. Men have to learn not to be selfish."

Joyce fired up. "Ray is anything but selfish. Sometimes I think it is I who am selfish; but if it were only myself, I would never say a word. We have to do our duty by the child."

"Exactly so. I quite see the point of view. Here you have the doctor at hand. I am told he nursed you like a mother."

Joyce wondered how Mrs. Fox had come to hear of it as, since her return to the Station, she had seen no callers. "How *ever* did you know?" she asked ingenuously.

"Oh, one hears things!" Mrs. Fox blew smoke through her nostrils and smiled knowingly. "And how do you like him on closer acquaintance?"

Joyce thought he improved on acquaintance. Mrs. Fox annoyed her by that smile.

"He is an enigma to most, but if I know his type, he is not a little dangerous. He can be exceedingly rude. I passed him on my way here and common politeness should have made him pull up for a word or two. But he rushed by in a cloud of dust with two fingers just touching the brim of his hat!—considering I was on foot, you can imagine my feelings. I have never been treated so by a man in my life—unless it is by my own husband; but then, there's no love lost," Mrs. Fox remarked.

"Perhaps Captain Dalton was in a hurry," Joyce suggested.

"Don't excuse him. He can be very nice when he likes. Yesterday there was Honor Bright hanging over her fence to talk to him, and though it was his busiest time, he was there quite a long while,—you know their gardens join. I saw them through Mrs. Bray's field-glasses. The Brays' verandah, as you know, looks on the Brights' grounds from beyond a paddock."

"He thinks a lot of Honor," said Joyce remembering their conversation in camp.

"Any one can see she is making up to him. But Mrs. Bright had better take care. No one knows anything of Captain Dalton's affairs. He might be married for all one knows. Honor Bright may be very popular in the District, but she'll get herself talked about and end all her chances of marrying well. Naturally it is the ambition of her parents to see her well settled, but she's far too unconventional. Did you hear of her escapade while you were in camp?"

Joyce had not heard, but was eager to know all about it. She knew Honor was careless of conventions out of a contempt for small minds and a love of independence. All who knew her allowed that she was as "straight as you make 'em," and admired her open nature and clear eye.

"Didn't she write and tell you?"

"We seldom write to each other."

"I thought you were bosom friends!—well, she was out alone looking for early snipe—someone had seen one in the fields beyond the bazaar—and while out, she was supposed to have been bitten by a snake——"

"—Why do you say 'supposed'?" Joyce interrupted ready to spring to arms for her friend.

"We'll say she was bitten, if you like; only, people bitten by snakes generally die, and she didn't. She tied a ligature and was limping home when she met Captain Dalton in his car on his way to a dispensary somewhere in the District. He took her up and home to his house where she stayed half the day alone with him.

Her mother was week-ending in Calcutta, and Honor was in charge of her father's comforts and the home; but her father happened to have run out to Panipara for a rioting case which he and the police were bothered with; so Miss Honor stayed with the doctor till she thought fit to come home."

"Bitten by a snake!" gasped Joyce in consternation. "Poor Honor!—how terrified she must have been!"

"That's best known to herself and him. Since then, you'll observe that there is a sort of understanding between them."

"How do you mean?"

"They seem to be on far better terms than he is with any one else in the Station, and Honor is falling in love with him. I am anything but blind to the symptoms!" and Mrs. Fox struck a match and lighted another cigarette.

"I suppose they grew friendly over the treatment of her wound," said Joyce beginning to understand how it was that the doctor had learned to appreciate Honor Bright. Yet he was "not seeking to marry her."

"I must get Honor to tell me all about it when I see her. Perhaps she does not know I am back?"

"She knows right enough, for, as I have said, the doctor was with her yesterday, talking across the garden fence."

Mrs. Fox smoked her second and third cigarette, drank tea with Joyce, and, when every topic of interest was exhausted, wended her way homeward, deploring the fact that her husband was too selfish to give her a motor-car. "He doesn't care for one, so I have to do without; and with only one riding-horse and that one lame, I am obliged to tramp the dusty lanes on foot."

"I am also without a conveyance while my husband is in camp," said Joyce, "but it does not matter as I like walking."

"I don't. My frocks are not suited to pedestrian exercise and cost too much—" which suggested the idea to Joyce that Mrs. Fox's expensive clothes accounted for her husband's economy in other directions. She watched her swaying languidly down the drive, a tall and graceful figure, stylishly dressed and pretty in a faded way, in spite of the delicate pink of her oval cheek and the brightness of her thin lips. What a pity it was that she had never a good word for any one, and made herself so ridiculous with the men, thought Joyce; it lowered her in their estimation and laid her open to impudence. Though she was attractive to many, she never succeeded in holding the attention of her admirers very long; which was humiliating to say the least of it. Joyce looked upon her as an example of a true flirt, and feared her accordingly—not on her husband's account, for Ray gave her a wide berth—but as a criminal at large. Women had whispered tales which she found impossible to credit; the world was so censorious! But on the theory that there was never any smoke without fire, she decided that Mrs. Fox was unscrupulous, and deplored the fact that the Station was obliged to put up with her. Apparently, so long as a husband countenanced his wife, no one else had any right to object to whatever she might do! It was a strange world!

The trend of her thoughts reminded her of the doctor's estimate of herself, which he had subsequently withdrawn. But then, he could only have been teasing, for Joyce knew herself, and flirting was very far from her intentions at any time, or under any circumstance. For instance, she was very sure she would never allow any man but her husband to kiss her!—the bare idea was appalling!

After the tennis hour at the Club, Honor Bright cycled up to the steps of the Bara Koti, and ran in to embrace Mrs. Meredith and welcome her home. "I am sorry not to have been able to come earlier, there was so much to do, and a tennis match in the afternoons," she said in her full, deep voice which Joyce thought so musical. Yet she never sang. God had given her a larynx, but the wicked fairies had robbed her of ear, so, though she loved music passionately, she could never produce a tune. "I must be fit only for 'treasons, stratagems, and spoils,'" she was once heard to say, "for it seems I was not born musical."

However, it was pointed out to her that she was not just to herself; she had plenty of "music in her soul" to satisfy even Shakespeare; it was only her inability to use the divine instrument in her throat. "You put me in mind of 'Trilby.' Perhaps you will sing if you are hypnotised!" Joyce had told her.

"Captain Dalton mentioned that you and Baby had both been ill. However I am glad to see *you* so well. How is Squawk?"

"How can you call him such a horrid name!" said Joyce reproachfully.

Honor laughed heartily. "Tommy is responsible; you must scold him."

"I shall, indeed. He's a bad boy!"

"Not at all!—he's a Deare!" at which they both laughed, for Mr. Bright's assistant, like the Assistant Magistrate, had a name of infinite possibilities. A comic fate had thrown him and Jack Darling together in the same Station, and they were provocative of fun in more senses than the coincidence of their names afforded.

The guest was carried off to see the son-and-heir in his crib and admire his indefinite features that were prophetic of beauty, and his limbs that were a miracle of elasticity.

By and by, they settled down to talk and Honor was told of the Padre's approaching visit. "Mrs. Fox thinks we should ask him to put up with us this time, or he might be offended," she explained. "Will your mother mind?"

"Mind? she'll be only too glad, for in private life the old man is a terrible bore! he tells the same joke over and over again, and Mother says she is determined not to laugh the next time. There ought to be some way of choking off stale jokes, don't you think, without offending the poor dear?"

"Tell him one of his own. I am sure it will make such an impression that he'll never forget it."

"He's so polite, that he'll laugh heartily as though he'd never heard it in his life!"

"What a hopeless person! However, I shall be glad to save your mother from nervous prostration," said Joyce.

"Mrs. Fox always gets news in advance of everyone else," said Honor. "I wonder how she does it?"

"She says she hears a lot—Ray says, servants carry news about the District as
fast as telegrams."

"I hate to think that she takes the liberty of dropping in upon you whenever
she likes. She's not a safe person, so I hope you are careful of what you tell her."

"Generally, it is she who does the telling, and I the listening."

"It won't do you any good, what she has to say!"

"It won't do me harm. I heard from her today, that you had been bitten by a
snake while I was in camp. How too terrible!—oh, Honey, how frightened you
must have been!" In emotional moments, Joyce called her friend by her family
pet-name.

"I was dreadfully frightened—afterwards," said Honor, shuddering violently.

"And you never told me!"

"I could not write about it," said the girl with a sudden gravity that ennobled
her face. "I don't like talking about it; it was a bad shock."

"Tell me this once, and we shan't speak of it again," Joyce pleaded.

She thought Honor's a beautiful face, though it had no actual claim to beauty apart from the brown eyes that were so frank and steadfast, and her regular
teeth. The eyes were arresting in their depth of shade and power of expression,
with dark lashes of unusual thickness; but for the rest, her complexion was tanned
by reckless exposure to the sun, her nose had a saucy tendency, and her mouth,
though shapely, was not by any means a rosebud; indeed, she had a wide smile
which was readily excused for the charm of it, and because of her splendid teeth.
Soulless men admired Honor for her eyes, her teeth, and her figure which was
truly classical; others, for her honesty and directness, and the womanly sympathy
which never failed. Tommy Deare was among the latter, and he had known her for
the greater part of his life.

Asked to talk of the episode of the snake, Honor's expression changed and she
was strongly moved.

CHAPTER VII

AN ANXIOUS EXPERIENCE

"Have you ever wondered what it must feel like to have sentence of death passed on you?" said Honor Bright thoughtfully leaning her chin on her hand, her elbow on a low table before her.

"It must be too awful for description," murmured Joyce, large-eyed and sympathetic.

"I shall always understand and feel for any one under sentence of death either by the Courts of Justice or from disease. When I felt the sharp prick on my ankle and looking down saw the snake glide into the undergrowth I believed it was all up with me. I had seen two or three natives who came up to the house for treatment die before my eyes. A *saice* bitten in the stables by a cobra died in twenty minutes. A *mali* cutting grass was struck on the hand and died in three quarters of an hour. A *punkha* coolie on the verandah lost his life within an hour after being bitten by a karait.

"I could not tell the character of the snake that had bitten me, but it was large and long, and many cobras are dark and lengthy creatures. My father shot one with No. 8, in the roots of a banyan tree this very year, and it measured over four feet."

"But, Honey, dear, why ever were you walking in jungly places?" Joyce cried, wrought up to the verge of hysteria.

"I was out after snipe. You know how I enjoy shooting, and I generally go alone, for I am not clever enough yet with my gun to be trusted to shoot in company with others. One is so afraid of accidents!

"I had been walking along the 'aisles' of the paddy fields till I came to a swampy bit and found I'd have to walk through it if I had any hope of starting a bird. Just as I was stepping off the 'aisle,' a snake passed over my foot, and biting me on the ankle vanished in the swamp. It must have been some sort of a water-snake, but I did not know. All I knew was that I had been bitten by a snake that might be poisonous. It could easily have been an adder, or a karait—even a cobra—though I had not a minute in which to observe a hood or any distinctive marks. I immediately collected my faculties to think what was the best thing to do. I knew I had no time to lose. Mother was away in town shopping for the cold-weather needs, Dad was out for the day on a riot case. I did not even know if I should find Captain Dalton at home.

"On the instant, I tied a ligature as tight as I could under the knee, and then started to run back to the Station as fast as my breath would allow. As I reached the main road I heard the sound of a motor, and, to my intense relief and thankfulness, it was the doctor on his way somewhere—I never asked where—my case was as desperate as any, and I put up my hand. He saw the 'S.O.S.' message in my face, which he afterwards said was the hue of chalk, and when he found out what was wrong, he just bundled me in and drove home like a streak of lightning. I wonder we did not kill someone or something in the bazaar. I shall remember to my dying day the way the people fell to right and left thinking, no doubt, the doctor was mad.

"When we arrived at his bungalow he sprang out, ordering me to find my way to his consulting room while he went straight to his medicine chest for the remedies he keeps for cases of snake-bite. By that time my leg was feeling as heavy as lead—whether from the ligature or the poison, I do not know—but I could hardly put my foot to the ground. Still, I hobbled in and sat down to wait. It seemed ages, but was in reality only a minute or two, when he came and knelt down before me to deal with the wound. There was very little to be seen, just the punctures and a livid disk round them. Up till then we had scarcely spoken a word, or I have no memory of words having passed between us, but I can see his face, all set and stern, his mouth compressed, his eyes like living coals in his head intent on his work of rescue.

"I hardly felt all he did; I was so deeply excited inwardly. Outwardly I was as calm as a stoic. I felt whatever happened I would have to keep my head to the last. I fully expected to feel desperately ill, and almost imagined the sensation beginning to creep over me, of numbness and chill. I had watched the symptoms in others, and could almost trace them arriving in me. Oh, Joyce, I wouldn't go through that time again if you gave me a fortune!—yet, I don't know—for one thing, I shall always be glad."

"And that?" asked Joyce.

"Oh, nothing—just an idea," she said hastily. "Captain Dalton cut deep into the flesh of my ankle and cauterised the wound; after that he injected something above my heart. I believe he was not satisfied with my pulse, for he brought me a stiff brandy-peg to drink. My hands were stone cold; he chafed them in his. In the meantime my leg swelled and looked all colours. It was most alarming yet he would not let me think of it. He, who is usually so silent, talked all the time of a thousand things that had nothing to do with snakes and their deadliness. He even made a joke or two. Once he wanted to know if I wanted any one—a lady to sit by me and cheer me up. But when I couldn't have Mother, and you were away, I wanted no one else, and told him so. I think he was rather surprised that I wasn't hysterical or troublesome; that I bore all that cutting about without uttering a sound. Every now and then he felt my pulse, and as time passed his face took on a wonderful look. You would hardly have believed he was the same man. The hardness was all melted and broken up, his eyes were so kind—he talked so pleasantly.

"After some time I asked if he thought I was well enough to go home, but he preferred to keep me longer. He thought I would have to be watched for a bit and looked after. Later he explained that he was afraid of shock. I had been through such an anxious time. He carried me to his drawing-room, and while I rested on the sofa he diverted me with music. He played the most exquisite music, and sang me ever so many songs. Really, Joyce, nobody knows Captain Dalton. He has most extraordinary depths in his nature of which I have had only a fleeting glimpse."

"Why is he so antagonistic to people as a rule?" Joyce wondered aloud.

"He has had some great disappointment in his life. Someone has smashed up all his ideals and beliefs, or he would never be so suspicious and unfriendly. He is that; for who knows him a bit better today than five months ago when he first came among us?"

"*You* do, certainly, Honey!"

"Not even I. I have been favoured with only a glimpse of his inner self. There are stores of wonderful goodness all hidden away underneath the nastiness and ill-humour he shows to the world!"

"Do go on and tell me the rest," urged Joyce, excitedly. "What a fearful experience!"

"It was. I thought of Mother and her grief were I to die,—of my father's desolation. They are both so wrapped up in me, having no other child, you know. I pictured myself lying dead and covered with flowers—you have no idea how involuntary was all this thinking!"

"And you never cried or lost your head?"

"I had not the slightest leaning that way. All I wanted was to die 'decently and in order,'" Honor returned, smiling reminiscently. "I did not want to make a scene and upset Captain Dalton's nerves. Once, while feeling faint and sick, I gave him messages. I wanted him to tell Mother that I did not mind dying, a bit. That was not strictly true, for I love life as much as any one else, but I thought it would comfort her. I sent her my love and said that if I had to die, I was sure it was best for me, because everything happens for the best. 'Do you really believe that?' he asked. 'I am not quite sure I do,' said I, 'but I must think of everything that will cheer Mother and help her to be reconciled if I have to go.'"

"How long were you obliged to be in suspense?"

"Time passed so fast that I had been there four hours before he judged it was safe to bring me home. He drove me in his car and carried me to my bed where the ayah took over charge. He then went about his other duties. He was so kind and wonderful to me...." The colour rushed into Honor's face at a memory that would not be suppressed. "Just before he left, he came and stood beside me, looking so queer...."

"How?" Joyce asked curiously. The only expression familiar to her on the doctor's face was quizzical amusement.

"He has rather wonderful eyes," Honor said reminiscently, "and they seemed suddenly soft and misty. 'You are quite a heroine, Miss Honor,' he said. 'I shall think of you often when I am alone in my diggings, as the bravest girl I know;' and without any warning he took my hand and kissed it, ever so reverently, almost as though it were the hand of a queen, and was gone."

"Didn't he come again?"

"Many times to see how the wound was doing. The swelling had to be fomented—he had shown me how—the ayah was quite a brick about learning the way. Father was there too, and Mother had returned. Poor Mother wept enough for two, and Father drank a stiff whisky-and-soda to steady his nerves. Altogether it was a ghastly experience. I wonder what particular kind of snake it was!"

"It was evidently poisonous, and the bite would have killed you if the doctor had not found you in time," said Joyce.

"I have no doubt of it." Honor became suddenly aware of the lateness of the hour and rose to go. "I shall have to dress for dinner, and there's only a quarter of an hour to do it in!—Dear me, how I have talked!"

"One minute—this happened only the other day, and yet you had associated with the doctor for five months before you were properly on speaking terms?" said Joyce, detaining her.

"We used to see each other in the distance occasionally. He never came to the Club and showed no inclination for feminine society, so we never spoke more than to say 'Good-evening' once in the way!"

"Yet he said quite a nice thing about you to me in camp."

"Did he?—What did he say?" Honor asked, flushing.

Joyce related the conversation faithfully, even to the doctor's concluding remark—"I am not seeking a wife, and have no interest in friendships."

Honor winced as under a lash, and straightened herself.

"You should not have pressed the point, Joyce. However, what does it matter? I am glad he thinks well of me, and that's all there is to it. He and I are of the same mind. I, too, am not seeking a husband, for I am very happy as I am. Good-bye, dear, I was commissioned with a message for you, but I have talked so much that it has been nearly forgotten. Mother wants you to dine tomorrow; just a few friends and Captain Dalton; and he has actually accepted the invitation."

"It is never safe to ask me to dinner," said Joyce doubtfully. "I hate leaving Baby all alone at night."

"He has a good ayah."

"Oh, yes. She is absolutely trustworthy; but should he ail ever so slightly I shall stay at home. I could not go out and leave him the least bit out of sorts."

"We shouldn't wish it. However, he might be quite all right, and then you'll come—bye-bye!" she waved her hand from the steps, mounted her bicycle, and was gone.

So the dinner-party at the Brights' was a settled engagement and Joyce prepared to keep it. She had never been anywhere without her husband, and felt nervous and shy for the lack of his support. Moreover, her mind was haunted by nameless fears for the child who was to be left behind to the tender mercies of native servants. A thousand possibilities of evil presented themselves to her mind and robbed the outing of prospective enjoyment; consequently the next night when it came to the point of starting, she was full of regrets for her weakness in having consented to go. "Ayah," she said in a fit of childish confidence, "I care for nothing on earth so much as my darling baby, how can I leave him for an hour or two not knowing what is happening to him in the meantime?"

"My Lort! what-for be frightened? Baba plenty well, sleeping sound. What can be?" the woman cried irritably. Could she not be trusted?

Nothing could possibly happen in so short a time. How did other mothers fulfil their social engagements? Surely they did not all worry themselves and others to death over nothing? Joyce therefore resolved to become more normal in her habits, and proceeded to dress.

Hardly, however, had she put foot in the hired victoria, when the ayah appeared, suggesting another look at the child. He had been coughing in his sleep, and considering the mother's anxieties she feared the responsibility of keeping the fact to herself.

Joyce immediately sprang from the carriage and hurried to the bedroom where the child lay sleeping in its cot. "You are sure he coughed?" she asked listening in vain for a repetition of the sound.

"Would I say it for nothing?" the Madrasi asked testily.

"What would it mean?"

"A little cold he has caught, or indigestion."

"Then I cannot go out with any peace of mind," Joyce cried definitely. "What if he should have croup?"

"Why say such words? Give little honey, and cough go."

But Joyce was not satisfied. What was a dinner-party to her if her precious one was sickening for croup or any other fatal malady? Most infant maladies were fatal unless taken in time, and if she were away and he be taken ill, how would he fare? She decided that the Brights would have to do without her, and forgive the disappointment.

Forthwith she unwrapped, and settled down to spend a quiet evening alone, with an ear strained to hear any return of the cough, and quite determined to send for the doctor should it recur.

However, having upset his mother's nerves and thrown a dinner-party out of order, the infant slept soundly till morning.

CHAPTER VIII
THE DINNER-PARTY

At Muktiarbad, the usual form of evening entertainment was a dinner-party with music and bridge to follow; and Mrs. Bright, wife of the Superintendent of Police, was specially noted for her hospitality in this respect. The brief intervals spent at home by her husband between his rounds of inspection or inquiry in his District were always celebrated by herself and her daughter as festal occasions; and their friends were gathered together at short notice to eat, not the "fatted calf," as that would have offended the religious susceptibilities of the Hindus who held the animal sacred, but one of the fattened geese kept available for such occasions.

The ladies did not always accompany Mr. Bright on his journeys about the District, as they were usually hurried and undertaken with scant preparation. Very little of the flesh-pots of Bengal sufficed to satisfy Muktiarbad's Chief of Police, who had been thoroughly broken in to the rough-and-tumble of official life in the *mafasil*. The presence of his family in camp was a hindrance to Mr. Bright, and he was better pleased to return, after his strenuous duties, to the peace of domesticity at his bungalow in the Station. Moreover, there was little of interest in the monotony of camping in lonely places for a young girl to whom her mother wished to give every opportunity of settling in life, whatever might be her own ideas respecting a vocation. Muktiarbad, though a rural backwater of Bengal, and pronounced by the gay-minded, a penal settlement, had matrimonial possibilities not to be despised by anxious parents with daughters to be happily disposed of.

On the whole, it was a highly social if small community who made the most of their opportunities for enjoyment, accepting the limitations of the place to which it had pleased Providence and the Ruling Power to appoint them, with the usual healthy philosophy which has made India so rich in memories.

It mattered little if they had to endure the discomforts of the climate and various inconveniences besides; others were in a worse case. Nor did it matter if they never reached the goal for which they strove—it was Kismet!

Fatalism is a habit of mind peculiar to the people of the East, where the unexpected might happen at any time without warning; and it is not unusual for Europeans to slip half-consciously into the same mental attitude.

It is consequently not surprising that, in spite of many lurking dangers, life in the rural districts is careless and free. Risks of cholera, sunstroke, and snake-bite, are taken boldly without a thought of possibilities. India has need of resourceful minds and nerves of steel; and no use for the faltering and irresolute.

Even Mrs. Bright took chances for her family and friends when her cook at the eleventh hour sent to Robinath Mukerjea's store in the bazaar for tins of salmon (the fish procured from a local tank being deemed inevitably earthy in flavour); for Mukerjea bought his provisions at sales of old stock from the Army and Navy Stores, vowing they were fresh consignments from *Belait*; but no one was deceived when patronising his shop in spite of risks of ptomaine. However, a dinner cooked by Kareem Majid was an achievement more worthy of a Goanese than a Mohammedan, and none who dined at the Brights' was ever the worse.

"My dear," Mrs. Bright had been heard to observe in earlier days, "were it not for Honor and the necessity to cultivate the acquaintance of one's own child, I should never leave India. How I miss that treasure, Kareem! He has been with us since we were married, and there never was a more useful servant. Whether in camp or in my own bungalow, it is just the same; he rises to every emergency and cooks like a French *chef*. At a pinch he'll valet my husband. He has even in an emergency fastened the hooks of my blouse at the back; and when Honor was a child, played with her when she had the measles and kept her from crying herself into a fit. When other servants ran away from the cholera, he stayed and did everything but sweep the floors! And when any one is sick, I have never known the equal of his 'chicken jugs'! He is so self-reliant, too. I have only to say, 'Kareem, six guests for dinner tonight. Don't ask for orders—do just as you please, only don't mention the subject of food as you value your life!' And he will *salaam* and say, '*Jo hukum*,' after which I have no responsibility whatever; dinner up to time, everything cooked to perfection, and when you think of what an Indian cook-house is, really, you are overcome with admiration. Can you fancy an English cook consenting to turn out dinners under like conditions? You get notice in a day! And who thinks of sparing Indian servants? As many courses as you like, with a wash-up like a small mountain, which the *masalchi* disposes of behind the pantry door on a yard or two of bamboo matting, with an earthen *gumla*, a kettle of boiling water, and an unthinkable swab! An English maid would have hysterics."

To make existence possible to the residents of Muktiarbad, there was the great, straggling bazaar on the outskirts of the Station ready to supply the necessaries of life. An enlightened confidence in the rule of the sahibs and in their honour and justice was a tradition with the local population whose trust in the *Sarcar* was unbounded; for sedition had not yet poisoned the minds of the peace-loving, contented agriculturists and shopkeepers who were as conservative as they were simple. It was only in outlying villages that occasional trouble brewed when ignorant and superstitious minds were played upon by malcontents.

Ten minutes' grace was allowed to Mrs. Meredith—no more—and Mr. Bright offered his arm to Mrs. Barrington Fox and led the way to the dining-room. Mr. Barrington Fox was seldom to be persuaded into accepting Station hospitalities; and usually made the time-worn excuse, as on the present occasion, of inspection duty on the line. The Station, however, understood it to mean that he had ceased to find pleasure in his wife's company and was determined not to be victimised.

The dining-room at the Brights' was a large apartment, whitewashed like a hospital ward, but redeemed by hunting pictures on the walls, graceful drapery, and good furniture. A *punkha* with a mat frill hung motionless overhead, as weather conditions were sufficiently altered to dispense with an artificial breeze; and the dining table beneath it presented an inviting aspect with its glittering mass of silver, glass, and flowers. A draught-screen concealed the door of ingress from the pantry where the business of serving was carried on by the *khansaman* assisted by a group of white-robed domestics. Agitated whispers from behind the screen were infallible indications of mistakes retrieved in the nick of time; otherwise, the occasional blow of the ice hammer, or the rolling of the ice machine on the outer door-mat were the only sounds audible from the dining-room.

Mrs. Bright, full of confidence in her staff and indifferent to mistakes which were not inexcusable, showed a complete detachment from the details of serving while she entertained her guests.

A little reshuffling of the order of precedence, when Mrs. Meredith's non-appearance was assured, had disposed of Tommy Deare to his entire satisfaction. Left to shift for himself he moved to the other side of Honor Bright whom Jack Darling had piloted in. He was a plain, freckle-faced boy of twenty-two with plenty to say for himself, and a most engaging smile. In height he was on a level with Honor who was considered tall; yet, to his disgust, he was referred to as a "little man." But since it was recognised that "valuable goods are packed in small parcels," he assured his friends of his inestimable worth, and was comforted.

"Mrs. Meredith is too absurd about that kid of hers," Mrs. Fox was heard to remark in the first hush that fell with the arrival of the soup. "Isn't it the baby who is ill tonight?" to Captain Dalton.

"If I had known, I should have mentioned it," said the doctor above his soup plate. The rudeness of the reply was characteristic of him.

"I understood from Mrs. Meredith that she and her offspring are in your charge. How neglectful of you to know nothing!"

"I am ready to attend to them when called in," he replied.

"Then you have not been wanted!" she laughed spitefully. "It must be very mortifying never to be wanted except when you are of use!"

"A doctor is the one man whom you are only too glad to see the last of," said Dalton coldly.

"All the same, I shouldn't be a bit surprised if it's the baby who is ill, and you are sent for before dinner is over. Mrs. Meredith said it would be the only reason that would stop her coming," put in Mrs. Bright, anxious to soothe.

"I hope not, indeed!" cried Mrs. Fox. "For now we've got you we mean to make you sing. Don't imagine we'll let you off."

The doctor bowed a stiff acknowledgment, which meant nothing, and entered into conversation with the Executive Engineer on the subject of a morass which he had condemned in his Sanitary Report, and recommended to be drained.

"The villagers won't stand it," said Mr. Ironsides. "They draw their drinking water from that *jhil*, and providing them with wells instead will not console them for its loss. Incidentally, they use it also for laundry purposes and bathing," he laughed.

"Exactly. So the sooner it is done away with the better for their health and the health of the District. Malaria and cholera have their source at Panipara."

"I hope you are not trying to deprive us of our duck-shooting, Doctor," said Mr. Bright in alarm. "We depend upon Panipara Jhil for game in the winters, and there is little sport besides, in this God-forsaken place."

"It will have to go if you want immunity from sickness," said Dalton.

"If *they* don't mind it, I don't know why *we* should. It rages chiefly in Panipara village itself, and is nothing to us."

"It comes on here afterwards with the flies," said Tommy.

"A few natives, more or less, wiped off the face of the earth hereabouts would be a benefit to Muktiarbad," drawled young Smart of the Railway from his seat on Mrs. Fox's right, which, by an unwritten law was always accorded to him at Station dinners.

"How very unfeeling!" cried two or three ladies in unison.

A vigorous argument arose to which Honor listened, deeply interested. Panipara Jhil lay a few miles outside the Station, with the village of the same name lying on its banks. It occupied an area of a square mile or two of marsh land, was overrun with water-weeds and lotus plants, and dotted about with islands full of jungle growth and date-palms—a picturesque but unhealthy spot, dear to lovers of sport.

"The natives haven't the foggiest idea of hygiene," said the doctor finally. "But they cannot be argued with. They will continue their filthy habits though twenty to thirty per cent. of them get wiped out by cholera annually. Drain the *jhil* and give them wells, and there'll be little or no sickness afterwards. Incidentally, several hundred *bighas* of ground will be reclaimed for agricultural purposes, which will be a benefit to the owner."

"The Government will take its own time to consider the proposition, and a few years hence, when it has exhausted all the red tape available, it will be put through," said Honor. "In the meantime, the cholera, like the poor, will be 'with us always!'"

"I shouldn't be at all surprised," said the doctor meeting her eyes in swift appreciation of her verdict.

He said no more to her, for others intervened and the conversation changed.

Captain Dalton looked a trifle more cynical and dissatisfied than usual, Honor thought. His strong jaw and irregular features hid his thoughts, but not their reflection which showed a mental unrest. He was clearly not a happy man, and was plainly a discordant element in light-hearted company. "A real wet blanket," Tommy whispered in her ear. "If one makes a joke he either doesn't hear it, or thinks it not worth laughing at. Something has turned him sour, so he hates to see people happy."

But Honor was not in agreement with him. "I grant he is an embittered man—he looks it; but he is quite willing that you should enjoy yourself so long as you don't force your high spirits on him. If one's mind is not in accord with blithesomeness, one surely might be excused from taking part in it."

"I do believe you like the blighter?" Tommy cried reproachfully.

"I have every reason to," she answered stoutly.

"Because he cured you of snake-bite? Doctors get a pull over us poor laymen when it comes to matters of life and death. They do their duty, and you are grateful for all time," at which Honor laughed heartily, for Tommy was looking personally injured.

"There's Mrs. Meredith!" he continued. "She talks of him with tears in her eyes as though he were a saint—Old Nick, more likely!—He has been endowed with every virtue when he has none, simply because he put the Squawk to rights." Tommy had seen Joyce that afternoon and went on to describe his visit. "She was looking topping, so was the kid; which makes it all the more mysterious, her not turning up. But, my word, she is pretty! One might be excused for any indiscretion when she makes eyes at one!"

However, to his disappointment, Honor showed no symptoms of jealousy. "I'll wager she neglected you for her baby!" She said. "Mrs. Meredith has no interest in young men."

"She had plenty in me. We grew quite intimate—talked of the weather and *anopheles* mosquitoes, and improved the occasion by rubbing *eau de Cologne* on the bites."

"How very thrilling! and she forgot all about you the moment you had left!"

"Everyone forgets all about Tommy the moment he has left," put in Jack, thinking it about time to remind them of his presence.

He was a handsome young athlete of twenty-five, with the reputation of having played in the Rugby International. He owned a complexion inconveniently given to blushing. He and Tommy chummed together in a three-roomed bungalow near the Police Court and were generally known as inseparables. Both played polo and tennis with skill and kept the Station entertained by their high spirits and resourcefulness.

Honor's attention was diverted by an animated discussion among her elders respecting the duties of a wife and mother in the East.

"A mother is perfectly justified in taking her child home if it cannot stand the climate," Mrs. Fox was saying.

"I suppose the question to be decided is, whom a woman cares most for, child or husband—whether she will live away from her husband for the sake of the child, or from the child for the sake of the husband, presuming that the climate is not suitable to children," said a guest.

A strident voice was heard to remark that women had no business to marry men whose careers were in the East, if they meant to live away from them most of the time. "It's a tragedy for which doctors are mainly responsible," with a sniff and a challenging glance at Captain Dalton.

"Oh, you doctors!" laughed Mrs. Bright, shaking her finger at him. "See what mischief you are accountable for!—ruined lives, broken homes!"

"In many cases, it is a charity to part husbands and wives," said the doctor grimly.

"Hear, hear!" from Mrs. Fox, at which Mrs. Ironsides was shocked.

"I hope Mrs. Meredith will not go home so soon," she said. "It will be a pity, when she and her husband have been so lately married. Somebody should influence her to remain and give the hills a trial. They seem to suit children very well."

"If she goes home it will be nothing short of a calamity," said Honor quietly, thinking of Ray Meredith's devotion and his wife's unsophisticated and undeveloped mind. "It would never do unless she means to return immediately."

"A child of tender years needs its mother," said a lady whose heart yearned for her little one in England. "No stranger will give it the same sympathy or care."

"It is a difficult problem to which there is no solution," said Mrs. Bright.

"I always feel, when I see a wife living for years at home while her husband remains out here, that there is no love lost between them. The children serve as an excellent excuse for the separation," said Honor, colouring at her own audacity in voicing an opinion so pronounced. "No reason on earth should be strong enough to part those who care deeply for each other."

"Hear, hear!" murmured Tommy under his breath, while Mrs. Fox laughed disagreeably. "An excellent sentiment coming from you, Miss Bright, who have no experience. Long may you subscribe to it."

Honor blushed still deeper. "I have my ideals," she returned.

"I trust they will never be shattered!" the lady sneered.

Again Dalton's eyes met Honor's with strange intentness. Feeling out of her depth she had looked involuntarily to him for the subtle sympathy, instinct told her was in his attitude to her, and she had received it abundantly in the slow smile which softened his expression to one of absolute kindness. It created a glow at her heart, to linger with her for the rest of the evening.

"Whenever I used to run home on short 'leave of absence' to see if Honor had not altogether forgotten me," said Mrs. Bright, smiling reminiscently, "and dared to hint at an extension, my husband would squander all his T.A. in cablegrams threatening to divorce me on the spot in favour of some mythical person if I did not return by the next mail. Wasn't that so, dear?"

"Gross exaggeration, my love. I could never get you to take a respectable holiday, for just as I was beginning to enjoy my liberty as a grass-widower, you would bob up serenely with 'No, you don't' on every line of your rosy face. It was worth anything, however, to see those English roses back again."

("The reason why Honor is such a nice girl," a lady once told Captain Dalton, "is because she has such a charming example of love in her home. Love is in her bones; her parents are so perfectly united that it is impossible for Honor to be anything but a good wife. Parents are immensely responsible for their children's psychology.")

"I have never ceased to thank Providence that I have no children!" said the wife of a railway official, with a sigh of contentment, "so the tragedy of separation has never affected me. I can honestly say that I have never left my husband for more than a day since we married, fifteen years ago!" and she reared her thin neck out of her evening gown and looked about her for congratulations.

"Lord, how sick of her he must be!" whispered Tommy under his breath, to the delight of Jack and Honor. "Life would be stale and unprofitable if I could not repeat the honeymoon every autumn when my wife returned from the hills. So thrilling to fall in love with one's own wife every year!"

"Which proves that you will make a very bad husband," said Honor severely. "Out of sight out of mind."

"He won't talk so glibly of sending his wife to the hills when he has discovered that she has been carrying on with Snooks of the Convalescent Depôt while he has been stewing in the plains," said Jack with a *blasé* air.

"Since when have you turned cynic, Mr. Darling?" Honor asked, astonished. "It doesn't become you in the least!"

"Jack had an enlightening holiday in Darjeeling last month when he had ten days during the *Pujas*," Tommy explained with reprisals in his eye. "It accounts for his attitude of mind. Having strict principles and a faint heart, no one had any use for him up there but Mrs. Meredith and the Y. M. C. A. ——"

"Don't listen to him, Miss Bright," Jack interrupted.

"—So in sheer desperation he turned nurse to Squawk and ran errands for its mother, wondering the while how it was that some men had all the luck!"

"Draw it mild, I say!"

"And now he sits up half the night composing odes to her eyebrows and boring me stiff with his sighs."

"Liar!" laughed Jack. "I couldn't write poetry to save my life."

"It doesn't prevent him from trying. Then there's her photograph——"

"It isn't hers, I told you!" Jack protested. "Tommy, you're a villain."

"It's jolly like her, what I saw of it when it fell out from under your pillow."

By this time Jack was crimson. He relapsed into sulky silence and devoted himself to his plate with appetite. Honor Bright wanted no better evidence of the fact that he was heart-whole, though she continued to wonder whose was the photograph he was treasuring so sentimentally.

Dinner progressed through its many courses towards dessert, when toasts were drunk to "Absent Ones," and "Sweethearts and Wives," —the usual conclusion to dinners at the Brights'; then, with a loud scraping of chairs, the ladies rose and filed out of the room.

Later, when the gentlemen appeared having finished their smokes, it was discovered that Captain Dalton had retired. He had excused himself to his host on the plea of a late visit to his patient at Sombari, three miles out, and was gone.

"Dear, dear!" sighed Mrs. Bright. "How very disappointing! Evidently he had no intention of singing tonight, and I hear he has such a divine voice!"

"But we don't begrudge that poor girl his attention when she is so ill," put in Mrs. Ironsides.

"Indeed, no. I wonder how she is."

"Pretty bad, from all accounts," said Mr. Bright.

"Her poor mother must be distracted. The only real happiness she has in life is the companionship of this only child. Mr. Meek is so narrow-minded and autocratic in domestic life. He must be sorry now that he deprived the child of so many opportunities of innocent amusement."

"Not at all," said a guest. "He will congratulate himself that he kept her unspotted from the world. Muktiarbad is his idea of unadulterated godlessness. We are such a bad example to his converts, you know, with our tennis on Sundays!"

"Poor little Elsie! I hope she will recover," said Mrs. Bright.

Honor felt a distinct sense of depression when she heard that Captain Dalton had gone quietly away without even a hint to herself that he had had no intention of staying. It was clear that he had no interest in remaining; his excuse she disregarded, for he could have visited Sombari earlier in the evening when he knew that he was engaged to dine out. She believed he liked her ... but he was "not seeking to marry her," as he had said to Joyce in camp, so it was her duty to rise above the folly of thinking too much of a man who would never be anything more to her than a mere acquaintance. With a determined effort to stifle feelings of wounded pride and disappointment, she ordered Tommy to the piano to beguile the company with ragtime ditties at which he was past-master, and while he played and others sang, notably Bobby Smart, who was not to be chained to the side of Mrs. Fox, the latter was left to cultivate the acquaintance of the shy Apollo, Jack Darling, whom the Brights and Tommy had hitherto absorbed.

Jack met her ravishing smile with a blush of self-consciousness, fearing all eyes upon himself as he accepted the seat beside her on a chesterfield. He was so obviously new to the art of intrigue, so conspicuously ingenuous, that he had the charm of novelty for her. She believed that Mrs. Bright was manoeuvring to get him for a son-in-law and was chafing at Honor's lack of worldly wisdom in dividing her favours equally between him and Tommy whose prospects in life were less brilliant. The situation was one entirely after her own heart, to make or mar with impish deliberation. In spite of his comparatively inferior social standing and unattractive appearance, Tommy was popular with the girls for his ready wit. He dared to be unconscious of his disadvantages and stormed his way into the front rank of drawing-room favourites; but he was too unimpressionable and discerning to suit Mrs. Fox's taste, so she left him alone to see what she could make of Jack whose guilelessness was a strong appeal to women of her type. His development under her guidance seemed the only excitement life had to offer her in this rural backwater, and she was not one to miss her opportunities.

"I'd dearly love to act sponsor to a boy like you in the beginning of his career, Jack," she cried with a tender inflection of the voice. "By the way, I'm going to call you 'Jack'—may I?"

"Certainly, if you care to," he returned awkwardly.

"Oh, you are priceless! What an opportunity you missed for a pretty speech!" and she laid her hand caressingly on his for a moment to emphasise her delight in him.

"Why? what should I have said?" he asked, laughing boyishly, and wincing under her touch. The suggestion of intimacy in her manner somewhat embarrassed him.

"I should like to see you a few years hence when your education is complete," she returned, evading his question teasingly. "But you mustn't marry, or you will be utterly spoilt."

"There is no immediate prospect of that!" he said laughing and giving away the fact that he was heart-whole. "But won't you take up the job tonight and begin instructing me?"

"I am sorely tempted to," she replied, smiling affectionately on him. "You must really learn your possibilities. They are limitless. After that, everything will come naturally,—assurance, the wit to grasp opportunities, and a bold initiative, without which a man is no good."

"No good?—for what?" he pressed ingenuously.

"To pass the time with, of course, O most adorable infant!" she laughed silently, returning his look with an expression of half-veiled admiration.

In stations where officials came and went with meteoric suddenness owing to the reshuffling of the governmental pack of human cards, friendships were as sudden as they were transient. Jack Darling having arrived at Muktiarbad while Mrs. Fox was at a hill station, their acquaintance was only in its initial stage.

"Look at Mrs. Fox," whispered Mrs. Ironsides to Mrs. Bright. "She is doing her best to spoil that nice boy with her flattery! You can tell that she is pouring conceit into him by the bucketful. Shameless creature! I wonder her husband doesn't send her home."

"She prefers India," Mrs. Bright showed a restless eye.

"Mr. Smart will be only too glad if Mr. Darling relieves him of his attendance on Mrs. Fox. Did you notice how he yawned at table while she was talking to him?"

"He lives in her pocket, all the same, and is always at her beck and call."

"Was my dear. I have noticed a great change latterly, and I hear he is going to be transferred. Mr. Fox knows his people at home and is arranging it."

"And he knows his wife better," said Mrs. Bright with satire. It seemed at Muktiarbad everybody knew everybody else's affairs.

She allowed a brief interval to pass and then, using her privilege as hostess, captured Jack on the pretext of sending him to the piano, with Honor to select his song from a pile of music in a canterbury. By the time the ballad was finished and a chorus was in full swing, Mrs. Fox had been carried away by Mr. Bright to make a fourth at auction in another room.

Jack watched her go somewhat regretfully, wondering the while, shamefacedly, if he would be able to have another talk with her that night, and consigning all scandalmongers to perdition, who had dared to make free with her name. He refused to believe ill of so charming a lady, and was not surprised that Bobby Smart had found her company attractive—why not? When a brute of a husband spent all his time down the line instead of trying to make life pleasant for his wife, it was no wonder she was obliged to find entertainment for herself in the society of other men! Hers was a poor sort of life, anyway.

When the party broke up, Mrs. Fox elected to walk home as a tribute to the glorious moonlight, and Jack was commandeered to act as her escort. It was a good opportunity for the lady to show that renegade, Master Bobby Smart, that he was not indispensable. His yawn at dinner deserved a reprisal.

Bobby Smart, however, was not slow to profit by his release from escort duty, and wasted no time in pleasing himself. "I'll drop you home, Deare," he said cheerfully, "and we'll have a whisky-and-soda at your bungalow before you turn in."

"I should wait till I'm asked," said Tommy lighting a cigarette and dropping the match in a flower-pot on the verandah.

"I knew you were pining to have me round for a *buk*."[9]

"You can come in if you promise to go home by midnight," Tommy condescended. "I'll not be kept up later."

"On the stroke. That's a jolly good whisky you have. I was going to send to Kellner's for the same brand today, but forgot."

Tommy climbed into Smart's trap and consented to be driven home. His hospitality and Jack's was proverbial at Muktiarbad.

---

[9] Chat.

CHAPTER IX

A MOMENT OF RELAXATION

On leaving the Brights' dinner-party, Captain Dalton made his way to his car and sped out upon the moonlit road. An appreciable hesitation at the gate ended in his taking a course in an opposite direction to that in which lay Sombari and his patient.

A misty peacefulness of smoke and quietude brooded over the Station. Darkened bungalows looked like sightless monsters dead to the world, and the silent lanes were alive alone with fireflies scintillating like myriad stars in a firmament of leaves. At Muktiarbad, there was little else for the English residents to do after the Club had closed its door at nine, but eat, drink, and sleep. Theatres never patronised *mafasil* stations, and cinemas had not yet found their way so far into rural Bengal. In the bazaar also, which was strictly the native quarter of the town, the night was silent save for intermittent tom-tomming on the favourite *dholuk*,[10] or, here and there, the murmur of gossiping in doorways. Behind mat walls men gambled or slept, and by the pale light of the moon could be seen the smoke of burning cow-dung—kindled for the destruction of mosquitoes—curling upward from the clusters of thatched huts, and filling the air with opalescent mist.

But Captain Dalton had no business in the bazaar.

If Honor Bright could have seen him then, she would have been surprised at the look of indecision on his usually determined face. Freed from the restraint of curious eyes watching for revelations of himself, the man's face wore a more human expression; his peculiar half-smile of toleration, or contempt, relaxing the lines of his stern mouth.

For a couple of furlongs he drove fast, then slowed down to a noiseless glide as he ran past the tall cactus fence bordering the Collector's domain. At the end of the fence where it turned at right angles dividing the "compound" from a paddock, the engines were reversed in the narrow lane, till the car came back to the rustic gate beyond the culvert.

It lay hospitably open in the usual way of gates in the Station, and gave access to the grounds. There was only a momentary pause while Dalton seemed to make sure of his intention, and the next instant he was moving slowly up the drive between the handsome goldmohur trees of the avenue. In the dark shadow of one of these, he shut off his engines and stepped to the ground.

---

[10] Indian drum.

All about him, the garden was bathed in silver light, each shrub and arbour steeped in tranquil loveliness, while footpaths gleamed white amidst stretches of dusky lawns; the whole presenting a scene of veritable enchantment under the soft radiance of the moon; a gentle breeze, the while, rustling among the leaves.

In front of him lay the wide, squat bungalow with its flat roof ornamented by a castellated balustrade of masonry, and supported by tall pillars. The verandah was in darkness but for a hurricane hand lantern on the top step.

He was not sure that he had the right to intrude at that late hour even with the pretext of a semi-official inquiry ... but lights in the drawing-room and the tones of the piano, rich and sweet, ended his indecision. The staff of servants being reduced by their master's requirements in camp, there was no one at hand to announce his arrival. Even the peon, supposed to keep watch against the intrusion of toads and snakes, had betaken himself to the servants' quarters behind the bungalow, for his last smoke before shutting up the house for the night.

Joyce was playing Liszt's *Liebestraum* with diligence, but no feeling. Her execution was good, but her soul being yet unawakened, she played without understanding, and Dalton's musical sense suffered tortures as he listened for a few moments; then, abruptly parting the curtains, he ruthlessly interrupted the performance by his entrance, conscious on the instant of the alluring picture she made, — or, rather, would make, to senses that were impressionable. Having outlived that stage, he could only survey at his leisure the curve of her youthful cheek and the small bow of her mouth that seemed to demand kisses; watch the lights dance in the gold of her hair, and amuse himself with the play of her eyelashes. She was dressed in rich simplicity, the only colour about her, apart from the shell-pink of her face and the natural crimson of her lips, was a deep, red rose in her bosom. He inhaled its perfume as she ran to him and seized his hand in impetuous welcome, while he could not but appreciate the exceptional opportunity afforded him of improving their acquaintance.

"How did you know that I was longing to send for you but lacking in courage?" she asked, holding his hand in both hers with extreme cordiality, born of her gratitude for his late services. Her manner was that of a child towards a respected senior, and was not without a certain charm.

"You did not come to dinner," he replied with his grudging smile, "so I had to call and see why. You are such a grave responsibility to me in your husband's absence."

"Does it weigh very heavily on you?" she asked coquettishly.

"As you see, it dragged me here at this late hour!"

"Poor you!" she sympathised; then instantly pulled a long face and explained her alarms deprecatingly while she drew him—still holding his hand—to her bedroom that he might see the child for himself and judge of his condition.

It was her habit to have the baby's crib by her bed, and the ayah close at hand in case of disturbed nights, while Meredith was compelled to retire to a separate suite, adjoining hers. "Such a young infant needs his mother, you selfish old Daddy, and must not be deprived." Arguments respecting the advantages of employing an English nurse and establishing a nursery had been swept aside as arbitrary and unfeeling. As if she could ever consent to a hireling occupying her place with her beloved child! Others might do as they pleased and lose their place in their little ones' affections, but not she! Fathers should consider their offspring before themselves. When Meredith had looked unconvinced and injured, she had tried to soften the blow by cajoleries, in the use of which she was past-mistress. Silly goose! as if the same roof did not cover them both! and didn't she belong to him and no one else in the world?—"Was he going to be a cross boy, then, and make his little girl's life miserable with big, ugly frowns?..."

The doctor gave the child a brief examination as he and Joyce leant over the crib, shoulder to shoulder. She seemed so unconscious of the close contact and of its effect on the average masculine nature that he mentally decided she was either a simpleton or a practised flirt, given to playing with fire.

"I shall sleep so much better tonight now that I know there is nothing seriously wrong with my precious darling!" she said, returning beside him to the drawing-room and tantalising him with brief glances from her shy, sweet eyes.

"You worry quite unnecessarily, take it from me," he returned. "Don't put him in a glass case, and he will do all right. You should go out more."

"I shall, when Ray comes back. He has the car."

"Play tennis every afternoon at the Club."

"I daren't! I play so badly," she pouted.

"Then come driving with me," he said on an impulse which he regretted the moment after, for it would deprive him of the scant leisure he usually devoted to a treatise he was writing. It was not his habit to sacrifice himself to strangers and people in whom he was not greatly interested. However, the study of the little spoiled beauty might prove entertaining since she was not as transparent as he had imagined. The mystery of her undeveloped nature, her childish outlook on life, her ingenuousness and coquetry, were all somewhat unusual and appealing. He could not quite gauge her feeling for her husband who worshipped the ground she trod on. She probably took him for granted as she took the solar system, and was not above practising her arts innocently on others to relieve the monotony of her days. Like most pretty women, he judged her fully aware of her prettiness, and not bound by too rigid a sense of propriety. It might amuse him to test how far she would permit herself to go—or the men who admired her physical beauty; and as he had no friendship for her husband, he was not troubled by too many qualms on Meredith's account. With a big score to settle against Life, he considered himself at liberty to choose the nature of his compensation, and so be even with Fate.

"I should dearly love to drive with you," Joyce said engagingly, thinking of his perfect little car and the triumph it would be to tame this unsociable and reserved person in the eyes of all the Station. What a score for her little self!

Being essentially of a friendly disposition, she saw no reason why he should not become her particular friend. Not as if she were a creature like Mrs. Fox, or other women who flirted—perish the thought! There could therefore be no possible wrong.

"Have you ever driven your car?" he asked indulgently.

"Never."

"Nervous?"

"I don't think so, only no one ever showed me how."

"Shall I teach you?"

"Will you? What a dear you are!" she cried with eyes sparkling and dimples in full play as she seized the lapels of his coat and made him swear not to back out. "It will be great! What a surprise for Ray—you won't mention it? I can fancy myself hopping into the chauffeur's seat, and whoof! gliding away before his eyes. I shall dream of it all night."

"And of me?" he asked looking at his watch and recalling his intention to visit Sombari before midnight.

"Of course. That goes without saying if it is about your car!" twirling lightly on her toe with the grace of a born dancer.

"I find it difficult to believe you are married," he said with a crooked smile. "Your husband should call you 'Joy.'"

"He invents all sorts of pet names far sweeter."

"Anyhow, I shall think of you as 'Joy,'" he amended, taking up his cap from the piano.

"I can't fancy you thinking of any one so frivolous as myself," she laughed. "But you are not going, surely? We haven't even begun to talk!"

The open piano and her frank disappointment drew him to dally with temptation, and he seated himself on the music stool, uninvited, to run his fingers over the keys. "You were playing the *Liebestraum*. Will you let me play it to you?" he coolly suggested, anxious to give her a lesson as to how it should be interpreted; and without waiting for her consent, began to play.

Joyce drew up full of interest and pleasure to listen and watch, instantly aware that he was no self-advertised musician. As she had no conceit in regard to her one and only accomplishment, she was ready and willing to learn from him.

Dalton played with the technique and sympathy of a great artist. Though the opening movement was soft and low, every note fell like drops of liquid sweetness, clear and true—the melody thrilling her with its tender appeal. Insensibly it grew stronger and louder, the pace quickened, till the crash of chords and the rippling rush of sound caused her to hold her breath in an ecstasy lest she should be robbed of a single delight. Now and then, she glanced at his face and she knew that, for the moment, she had ceased to exist for him. His strange, jade-green eyes with their flecked irids had widened as though with inspiration. He saw visions as he played, gazing intently into space; Joyce wondered what he saw, sure that it was beautiful, and passionately sad. Gradually, the passion and dignity of the music having reached its climax, it grew weary and spent. The glorious melody sighed its own requiem and softly died away on a single note.

For a moment neither spoke, till Joyce gave a hysterical sob that broke the spell. "It is too wonderful—the way you play!" she cried breathlessly. "It makes my flesh creep and my heart stand still. I know now why you chose to play the *Liebestraum!*—--"

He smiled back at her like the culprit he was.

"I had dared to attempt its murder!—believe me, I shall never play it again!"

"I wanted to show you how it might be played, but I do not dare to criticise."

"You have done so, scathingly!—Oh! I feel so small."

"Then I am sorry I played it."

"I am infinitely glad. You will have to teach me something more than motoring," she said wistfully, her blue eyes pleading. "You will have to tell me how I should play. I want to hear you all day long!"

He smiled at her enthusiasm. "I shall be delighted to give you all the help I can."

"Honor Bright said yesterday that you once sang to her—I am jealous! Won't you sing to me?"

"Did she tell you of the occasion?"

"Yes, and how good you were to her."

"She is a heroine—*Honor Bright*," he repeated her name with curious tenderness.

"She thinks you are a wonderful person, altogether."

"Does she?" he asked quickly, a shadow falling suddenly over his face at a thought which was evidently disturbing. "How am I wonderful?"

"I don't know. She said something about great depths in your nature. She believes you are tremendously good, inside, but that you will not show it because you have been hit very hard and feel like hitting back."

He was silenced for a moment.

"What made her say that?" he asked while continuing to draw subdued harmonies from the instrument.

"It was to explain your attitude towards people. You are so hard and cold. But what does all that matter? The main thing is, I want you to sing, and you must!" She laid her hands over his on the keys with pretty imperativeness, and put an end to the chords.

"Look at the time," said he, drawing attention to the gilt clock on an occasional table. The phrase "hard and cold" echoed in his ears to mock him.

"It is certainly late!" she gasped, as she realised that the hands pointed to a quarter past eleven. "But I am so lonely and dull. Do sing to me!"

A mischievous smile twisted his lips as he struck the opening bars of *The Dear Homeland*. "It's an old ballad and will probably bore you to tears," he said, before beginning to sing. Joyce had often heard it sung, but never with the feeling Captain Dalton threw into it for her benefit alone. It was a strong and direct appeal to nostalgia, and the quality of his voice, together with the words, dissolved her into tears of positive distress. When he had finished, she was weeping silently into her little hands,—unaffectedly and sincerely.

"I cannot bear it!" she sobbed childishly. "Why did you choose that when you knew how I am longing for home and the home faces!"

"I am a brute, am I not?" he said repentantly, taking down her hands and drying her eyes with his handkerchief. "Was it a nasty fellow, then, to tease?"

"It was," she laughed hysterically with downcast lids and sobbing breath, looking adorable with her saddened wet eyes and crimson flush.

"Come, I'll make up for it and sing you something quite different." And he was as good as his word, singing passionate love-songs that swore eternal devotion to a mythical "Beloved," till a clock, striking twelve, brought him abruptly to his feet.

"Do you always allow your visitors to stay so late?" he asked while saying good-night.

"I never have visitors at night when I am alone," she returned, surprised. "Why do you ask?"

"Because you are too pretty and will have to be careful. Pretty women have enemies of both sexes."

"What do you mean?"

"I mean that men will want to make love to you if you are too kind, and women will tear your reputation to shreds."

He watched the flush deepen in her cheeks: she was uncertain how to take his remark, but decided he had not meant a liberty.

"I think I shall always fear women more than men," she said finally, thinking of the slanderous tongues of her sex.

"Am I forgiven for having made you cry?" he asked.

"Of course. Thank you so much for the songs. You sing like an angel."

"A very bad one I'm afraid," he returned. "With your leave I shall take this rose as a pledge," he said drawing it from the brooch at her bosom and laying it against his lips. "Look, it is fading fast. Will you fix it in my coat?"

Joyce unaffectedly complied. He was welcome to the rose as a reward for his beautiful music. "When you get home, put it in water, and it will fill your room with fragrance," she said patting it into position.

"—And my mind of you?" he suggested tentatively, knowing full well that he would forget all about her and her rose the moment he was out of sight of her dwelling. Already he was wondering why he had allowed himself to waste so much of his valuable time in trifling and whether he would have dared the same liberty with the rose had it been resting on Honor Bright's bosom. With Honor, somehow, a man would have to plead for favours and value them for their rarity when obtained. No man in the Station took liberties with Honor Bright, and every man thoroughly respected her. Dalton shook his mind free of the thought of Honor Bright.

"I shan't mind if the rose recalls me to you, so long as you promise to forget my *Liebestraum!*" said Joyce.

"I shall remember only the tears I caused you to shed, and never be so cruel again." Dalton passed out into the verandah accompanied by his hostess who desired to speed the parting guest. "When does your husband return?" he asked.

"Tomorrow night. I am counting the hours," she replied. "Haven't you heard that 'Absence makes the heart grow fonder'?"

"I don't subscribe to that sentiment," he retorted with a disagreeable laugh as he walked towards the car.

She certainly had the makings of a dangerous flirt, he decided, though, at present, she was only feeling her way. Time would develop her powers and then, God help the young idiots who would lose their heads! Most of all, God help her fool-husband—the besotted idealist! In a few years, Joyce Meredith would be no better than most lovely women in the East—notably such as flourished in the hill stations of India.

Dalton was amused, and laughed aloud at his own weakness and folly. He had not wanted her rose—yet, at the moment, the propinquity of her beauty had magnetised him and given him the desire for a closer intimacy—possibly a kiss!—so he had put his lips to the rose! Feminine witchery had made utter fools of men through the ages! Given further chances of intimacy, a rose might not again suffice!

By the time Dalton had reached the crossroads, indecision had again taken possession of him, and he hesitated at the wheel. He had left the Brights' party fully intending to run out to Sombari, but had been diverted; and now it was too late. They would not be expecting him after midnight. He yawned, thoroughly tired, as he had had a strenuous day, and decided to call at the Mission fairly early in the morning, instead. There was nothing he could do for the sufferer more than was being done by the trained nurse he had procured for the case.

Satisfied in mind that bed was the best place for tired people, Dalton turned his car and drove it to his own bungalow next door to the Brights'.

CHAPTER X

THE MISSION

Life at a small station like Muktiarbad would have been a dull affair for any young girl not constituted like Honor Bright. Being endowed with plenty of common sense and sincerity of purpose, she found a great deal to occupy her in her restricted circle by throwing herself into the business of the moment, heart and soul. If it were an early morning ride, she enjoyed every yard of it, and all there was to see and do. Even the flat countryside with its endless fields of paddy and mustard were good to view because Muktiarbad was "home" to her.

"Define the word 'home,'" she was once asked when very young. "Where Mother is," was her ready reply. "Where Love is," would be her later and more comprehensive amendment.

When she played tennis she played to win, and her enthusiasm infected others, till the game was worth the energy, however great the heat. If house-duties were imposed on her, they were accomplished thoroughly and cheerfully. Honor striding across the back-yard to examine the horses in their stalls, the condition of their bedding, and to see them fed; or to inspect the chicken run; or visiting the kitchen to view pots and pans which were arranged at a particular hour, bottom up, in a row, to prove how perfectly aluminium could be made to shine, was a refreshing sight; and the grace of her gait, the freedom of her movements, and the brightness of her looks, brought sunshine to hearts on the darkest days.

In spite of Mrs. Bright's confidence in her faithful Kareem Majid, she never neglected to supervise those details of housekeeping in India that make all the difference between sickness and health, economy and extravagance. "For, however wonderful the dear servants are, they do want watching," she would explain to inquiring friends. "You simply have to see what they are up to, or run terrible risks of microbes in the kitchen, horses falling ill, and eggs getting beautifully less. They are without the remotest idea of sanitation for man or beast, and revel in dirt if you let them, poor things! And honesty is not their strong point; they have to be checked on all accounts, or they will sell vegetables from your kitchen garden to your neighbours who have none; or sell you your own hens' eggs, and do heaps of other iniquitous things you could hardly dream of!" So Honor was carefully instructed in the ways of housekeeping from the moment of her return to the East, and was an able lieutenant to her mother.

"Besides, it is only right and proper, since, one of these days you will have a house of your own and ought to know how to run it, or I pity the unfortunate man you marry!" Mrs. Bright remarked when introducing her daughter to further mysteries in the art of housekeeping. "Which puts me in mind of Tommy Deare," she continued, eyeing Honor gravely. "What do you mean to do with him?"

"I don't mean to do anything with him," laughed the girl.

"You know he is in love with you—any one can see that."

"I know, because he won't let me forget it," Honor said ruefully.

"Yet you are often about with him, riding and playing tennis—is it fair to fan his hopes?"

"He knows perfectly how I feel towards him. Short of putting him in Coventry I can do nothing less than I am doing."

"But the worst of it is that he keeps others off!" Mrs. Bright exclaimed. "There's Jack Darling who lives with him—such a nice boy and a very excellent suitor from every point of view— —"

"He is not a suitor, by any means," interrupted her daughter.

"He might have been if his friend were not over head and ears in love with you!"

"I should not have encouraged him. Jack does not appeal to me. He is very dear and charming, but not the sort of man I should lose my heart to. He is weak— and I love strength."

"But, dear, surely you are not favouring Tommy?—he will never be anything great in our Service. You have the example of your own father who has come to the end of his prospects on an income that would have been hopelessly inadequate had there been boys to educate and start in life! That's what our Service is worth! While Jack—!" words failed her to express her estimation of the Indian Civil Service of which Jack was a promising member.

"But dear Mother, I am not going to marry a Service!" laughed Honor. "When I fall in love with a Man it won't much matter what job he is in, or what prospects he has. And if he is in love with me, and wants me, why"—she left the obvious conclusion to her mother's imagination. "But rest assured, whoever he may be, he will never be Tommy!" she added by way of consolation.

The morning after the dinner-party was typical of late October in the plains of Bengal, with its dewy freshness of atmosphere and a nip in the north wind that was an earnest of approaching winter—if the season of cold weather might be so termed, when fires were never a necessity, and frost was rare. It was, however, a time of pleasant drought when the state of the weather could be depended upon for weeks ahead, with blue skies, a kinder sun, and dead leaves carpeting the earth without denuding the trees of their wealth of foliage.

Outside the Bara Koti a light haze was visible through the branches of the trees, lying like a thin veil on the distant horizon; and, overhead, light fleecy clouds drifted imperceptibly across the blue sky. It was the hour popularly believed to be the best in the twenty-four, which accounted for Mrs. Meredith's ayah wheeling the baby through the dusty lanes, in a magnificent perambulator, "to eat the air."

"*Hawa khané*," translated Honor Bright critically, as she drew rein and moved her pony aside to make way. She was riding, in company with Tommy Deare, to Sombari that she might learn the latest news of Elsie Meek, a girl of her own age and one for whom she had much sympathy. Elsie had been undergoing the training necessary to fit her for becoming a missionary, irrespective of her talents in other directions; and Honor had often thought of her with sympathy. But Mr. Meek had his own ideas respecting his daughter's career, and Mrs. Meek had long since ceased to voice her own. "*Hawa khané!*—how queerly the natives express themselves!" Her remark had followed the ayah's explanation of her appearance with the child. "Mother says it is a mistake for delicate children to be out before sunrise to 'eat the air.'"

"Eat microbes, I should suggest," corrected Tommy. "A case of 'The Early Babe catches the Germ.'"

"How smart of you!—how do you do it so early in the morning?"

"Inherent wit," said Tommy complacently. "You press a button and out comes an epigram, or something brilliant."

"You've missed your vocation, it seems. I am sure you might have made a fortune as another George Robey!"

While Tommy affected to collapse under the lash of her satire, she leapt from the saddle to imprint a kiss on the rose-leaf skin of the infant's cheek. "What a perfect doll it is—did any one see any thing half so adorable!"

"It seems to me like all other babies," Tommy remarked indifferently. "When it isn't asleep it is bawling; when it isn't bawling it's asleep. I have yet to understand why a girl can never pass a pram without stopping to kiss the baby in it!" Nevertheless, he thought it a pleasing habit with which he was not inclined to quarrel, but for the delay it occasioned in the ride.

"I would like you to tell Mrs. Meredith that the Squawk is like all other babies in the world and hear what she has to say!" Honor said indignantly. "This one is angelic!"

Tommy dismounted with the air of a martyr and peered at the bundle containing a human atom almost smothered in silk and laces. "Hallo! its eyes are actually open! It is the first time I have seen the miracle. Peep-bo!" he squeaked, bobbing his head at the apparition and crooking a finger up and down a few inches from the infant's nose.

"Tommy, you are a silly!" Honor exploded with laughter. "As if it can understand. You might be a tree for all it knows!"

"Then all I can say is, I have no use for kids until they develop some intellect." He assisted her to remount and they continued their way to Sombari. Soon, the last of the bungalows was left behind and they were cantering side by side along the main road which divided paddy fields still containing stagnant rain water and the decaying stalks of the harvested corn. At intervals on the road pipal trees afforded shelter to travellers by the wayside. In the distance, across rough country over-grown with scrub and coarse, thatching grass, could be seen the minarets of an ancient ruin—Muktiarbad's one and only show-place for sightseers—too familiar to the inhabitants to excite even passing notice.

In the meantime Honor soliloquised aloud—"I do so wish we could get Mrs. Meredith more reconciled to India," she sighed. "She has only one point of view at present, and that is a mother's. If she could only be made to see her husband's point of view and realise also her duties as a wife, she would be perfect, for Joyce Meredith is very lovable and good. I never knew any one so pretty and so free from personal vanity. But she is too sure of her husband. Too certain that he will go on worshipping her no matter what she does or how she treats him; and, after all, I suppose even love can die for want of sustenance. It seems to me she gives all she has to give to the baby, and her husband is left to pick up the crumbs that fall from her table!"

"It will end as all such marriages end," said Tommy. "She is only half awake to life, and too pretty for every-day use. Meredith should awaken her by flirting with Mrs. Fox; otherwise someone else will do it by flirting with his wife. I wouldn't put it beyond the doctor."

Honor stiffened visibly. "Why do you say that?" she asked coldly.

"Well, he is given every opportunity. Last night, for instance, on our way home from your place, Smart and I saw his motor in the avenue of the Bara Koti. It was under the trees with a shaft of moonlight full on the steering wheel. If he had wanted to make it invisible, he ought to have reckoned on the hour and the moon. We thought he had gone to Sombari, but he was singing to Mrs. Meredith."

"Is that true?" Honor asked in low tones of pained surprise.

"We both pulled up outside the cactus hedge till the song was finished. He was singing *Temple Bells*!"

So he had not gone to Sombari after all! It had only been an excuse for him to get away from the party. He was evidently not above lying, and—Joyce Meredith was so beautiful!

And Joyce had been alone!

Honor flushed hot and cold with sudden emotion which she could hardly un-derstand because it was so new to her: passionate resentment towards Joyce Mer-edith for the impropriety of receiving a visit from Captain Dalton at that late hour. Her position as a married woman did not cover such indiscretion. How would Ray Meredith feel if he heard that his adored wife was entertaining the doctor at midnight, and alone? It sounded abominable, even if innocent in intention.

It was not right! it was *not* right!...

At the same moment, pride rose in arms to crush her resentment. What busi-ness was it of hers what Joyce Meredith did, or Captain Dalton, either? They were not answerable to her for their conduct—or misconduct....

Captain Dalton might please himself as far as she was concerned. He was hardly a friend. Why should she be so deeply affected by his acts? Yet her heart was wrung with pain at the mere thought that he had spent the rest of the evening entertaining Joyce Meredith who was as beautiful and as foolish as a little child. Any man might be excused for losing his head when treated to her innocent familiarities.

They were innocent. Of that she was sure, for Joyce coquetted with either sex impartially and unconsciously.

All through her silent brooding Tommy talked incessantly. He had passed from the subject of the doctor and Joyce Meredith to Bobby Smart who had obtained a transfer to a distant station on the railway, and was rejoiced that he would soon see the last of Mrs. Fox with whom he was "fed up."

"I don't admire him for talking about her, or you for listening," said Honor, paying scant attention to the subject of Bobby Smart.

"I didn't. I had to shut him up rather rudely; but Bobby is thick-skinned and, like some fellows one meets, a dangerous gossip, and the last man a woman should trust."

"I wonder much why women are so blind. They are fools to care for, or trust men," Honor said gloomily, and looking depressed.

"You must never say things like that to me," Tommy blurted out, offended. "You must discriminate between those who are honest and those who are the other thing. You might trust me with your life—and more——"

"I dare say all you men say that!"

"And all don't mean it as I do. *I* am discriminating; consequently, there is only one girl in the world for me...." He choked unable to proceed, and looked the rest into her clear eyes.

"Don't, Tommy!—this is why I hesitate to come out with you," she said, looking annoyed.

"I can't help caring for you," he answered defiantly. "It's an unalterable fact, and you may as well face it. I have cared ever since school-days. It has been my one hope that you too would care—in the same way."

"And I have tried to show you in a hundred ways that it is of no use," she said kindly. "Can't you be content to be—just pals?"

"No. So long as you remain unmarried I shall keep on hoping."

"And I cannot do more than tell you it is of no earthly use." She avoided looking at him again for the knowledge that his face betrayed the depth of his disappointment. "Perhaps it would be better if we gave up riding and tennis together, and you tried to take up some other interest?" she suggested.

But Tommy laughed unboyishly with a cracked sound in his throat. "I won't say anything more about it, if it annoys you, Honey, but don't for God's sake give me the push. I'm coming to the Club just the same for tennis with you, and shall call to take you out riding when I may—like this. You need not worry about what

I have said. I dare say I'll get along—somehow ... so long as you are not keen on someone else," he added. It seemed he would never be able to stand that!

"I am not keen on—any one else," she said, lifting her head with a resolute air. "But I do want you to know that I am not the marrying sort. I love the idea of being an old maid and having crowds of friends—and perhaps a special pal—that's you, if you like, old boy," she added graciously holding out her hand which he gripped with energy. "So that's all right, eh?"

While he made the expected reply, which was naturally insincere, considering the state of his sore heart, both observed a cloud of dust moving rapidly towards them which quickly resolved itself into a rider galloping at full speed.

When he was nearer his pace slackened from exhaustion, and Honor recognized one of the pastors of the Mission, an Eurasian, his face pale and stricken and dripping with sweat.

A chill of foreboding struck at her heart as she asked for news of the sick girl, Elsie Meek.

"She is dead," came the blunt reply. "I am now on my way to the doctor who should have seen her last night, but he never came." He rode on without waiting to hear Tommy exclaim, "Good God!" and Honor give an inarticulate cry of surprise and sorrow.

"I thought she was going on all right," said Tommy gravely.

"I had no idea she was so bad!" said Honor. Both had pulled up uncertain what to do. "Poor, poor Mrs. Meek!" said Honor, thinking of the lonely woman who struggled to live her life happily in surroundings which had failed to prove congenial, and whose one compensation was the companionship of her daughter,—the one being in the world she loved and lived for. She thought of the unsympathetic husband whose Christianity savoured of narrow prejudices and exacting codes, and she pitied the bereaved mother from the bottom of her heart. "I feel so guilty to think that we had the doctor to dinner last night when he might have spent that time at Sombari!" Honor cried regretfully.

"That was for him to judge. At any rate, he need not have finished the evening at the Bara Koti singing love-songs to Mrs. Meredith."

"Poor little Elsie!" Honor sighed, ignoring the allusion to Joyce. She was guiltless of blame as she did not know. "Tommy, you had better return and tell Mother. I am going straight on. There is now more reason for my calling on Mrs. Meek."

"It will be a painful visit—can't you postpone it?"

"I would rather not. I feel someone should be with her. Mother will go later, I know; but I must go at once."

Very reluctantly, Tommy turned his horse's head homeward, and lifting his *topi* in acknowledgment of her parting gesture, rode swiftly away leaving her to continue her road to the Mission.

The settlement came into view beyond a straggling village which had given the Mission its name, and was composed of bungalows grouped about a wide "compound": chiefly schoolhouses of lath and plaster, with innumerable sheds and outhouses for dormitories and technical instruction. As Honor approached, she was conscious of a great stillness broken only by the sound of intermittent blows of a hammer. When she passed into the grounds through a gate in a neatly kept fence of split bamboos, she saw through the open window of a shed, a carpenter busily engaged on the grim task of preparing a coffin out of a deal packing-case. In India burial follows on the heels of death with almost indecent haste, and the sight of a rude coffin in the making, sent no thrill of horror through the young girl. It was something to be expected in a place where no professional assistance of that sort could be reckoned upon in circumstances as sudden as these. Instead, a great sadness came over her, and tears filled her eyes to overflowing, for it was not so very long ago that Elsie Meek, a young girl like herself had come out to India full of life and laughter, yearning to give her energies scope, and trying for the sake of her gentle mother, to appear contented with the meagre life afforded by her surroundings. Honor suffered a pang of regret that she had not spared more time from her own pleasures to help Elsie to a little happiness. She had so appreciated visits from the Brights, and had been so keenly interested in the doings of the Station people, with whom she was rarely allowed to associate.

What a futile life! Poor little Elsie Meek!

At the Mission bungalow where Honor dismounted, a group of missionaries were sombrely discussing in whispers the necessary details connected with the funeral. Mr. Meek sat apart, bowed with depression, his face lined and haggard with grief. This was the man's world—Sombari Settlement—the child of his creation; yet how hollow were his interests and ambitions today!

Many years ago he had been financed by zealous Methodists and sent out to India to establish a mission in rural Bengal. After careful search he had chosen Sombari on the outskirts of Muktiarbad for the field of his labours. By degrees, his untiring efforts had prospered and Sombari was now a large community of pastors and converts, and he, himself, an Honorary Magistrate of second-class powers, in recognition of his influence among the people. Mr. Meek had a reputation for converting the heathen with a Bible in one hand and a cane in the other, and his methods were justified by the results seen in the confidence he inspired in his followers. He was a strong man, popularly credited with being just, if unmerciful, and was respected by the natives for miles around as hard men are, in the East; and they rarely appealed against his judgments.

The same spirit had ruled Mr. Meek's domestic life and had reduced his wife and daughter to the position of appendages of the Mission. It was nothing to him that they professed no vocation for the life; the discipline was wholesome for unregenerate human nature which is prone to crave for what is worldly and unprofitable. He was responsible for the souls in his care; and he conceived it his duty to protect them according to *his* lights—not *theirs*. Having safeguarded them from the snares and temptations of Station life which represented the World, the Flesh, and the Devil, he was filled with righteous satisfaction concerning their safety hereafter, and ceased to trouble himself with their yearnings in the present.

Mrs. Meek, who had once been a governess in a private family, was of a mild, easy-going nature, incapable of resisting tyranny. Since her marriage, her naturally submissive mind had become an echo of her husband's, although she was not always in agreement with his opinions; yet it was the line of least resistance, and "anything for a peaceful life" was her motto. Her greatest comfort had come with the birth of her daughter, who, later, was reared by her maternal relatives in England. They had means, while the Meeks had barely enough for their own needs, so Elsie had received a good education of which her relatives had borne the cost, and at the finish, came out to her home at Sombari under the protection of missionary friends travelling to India.

Though Mrs. Meek had not seen her daughter for the best years of her childhood, her love for her had become the absorbing passion of her life. For years she had carried about a heart aching with longing for this treasure of her own flesh and blood, so that their reunion altered her whole life. So long as she had her child's companionship and affection, she was blessed among women; even the little world of Sombari was glorified.

But, alas! on that morning of Honor Bright's visit, death had robbed Mrs. Meek of all that life held for her. Honor understood how completely she was bereft, and her own heart overflowed with sympathy. Her one ewe lamb had been taken, and in her grief, the foundations of the mother's faith were shaken.

She turned her face to the wall and cried out against her Maker. "From him that hath not shall be taken away even that which he hath!" was the burden of her sorrowful cry.

"What had I to make life worth the living! My child was all in all to me, and she has been snatched from me! Of what use is religion since even my prayers could not avail? It is comfortless. God is cruel. He tramples on our hearts. He has no pity." Such were the outbursts of the poor, stricken heart.

She was the picture of abandonment in the comfortless room, ascetic in its lack of dainty feminine accessories. The floor was covered with coarse bamboo matting such as the Brights used in their pantry and bathrooms. Cretonne *pardars*[11] hung in the doorways; the furniture was rough and country-made; the bed-linen and coverings were from the mills of Cawnpur. "Lay not up for yourselves treasures upon earth," had been Mr. Meek's justification for confining his expenditure to the barest necessaries of life. But, on the other hand, he indulged himself in his hobby for raising prize cattle for the local *Mélas*[12]. Prize cattle had their use and did not come under the head of extravagance as did furnishing according to taste and fancy; so Mrs. Meek and her daughter had to suffer the lack of the refinements of life to the mortification of their spirits and the discomfort of their bodies, in order that their souls might be purged of the vanities and lusts of the flesh.

"You must not fight against the decrees of the Almighty," said the nurse reproachfully, as Honor knelt beside the bed and embraced the unhappy mother.

---

[11] Curtains.
[12] Fairs.

"Don't talk all that clap-trap to one in torment," said the girl contemptuously. "People are too ready to put all the blame on God when they are bereaved."

If a thunderbolt had fallen in the room it could not have had a more startling effect than this outburst of Honor's. The nurse recoiled in horror thinking she was in the presence of a free-thinker who is first cousin to an atheist, and Mrs. Meek choked back her sobs to stare wide-eyed at her visitor who had dared to voice such heresy under a missionary's roof.

"Isn't it God's will when one is afflicted? That is what we are taught," said the nurse indignantly.

"We are taught a lot of stuff which is not true," said Honor firmly. "It isn't sense to impute to a loving God acts of wanton cruelty, and we dishonour Him by so doing." She kissed Mrs. Meek's cheek and spoke tenderly to her of her sympathy and sorrow.

"But, Miss Bright, are not life and death in God's hands?" the bereaved lady asked astonished.

"Indeed, yes—with our co-operation. God needs our help as we need His. I could never believe that our dear ones are taken from us by God's will. He could not will us unhappiness. We have got to suffer as the result of ignorance and neglect, and a thousand other reasons which are Cause and Effect. Where we fail God, we must suffer."

"How did we fail God? We did all we could!"

"Yes—we always shut the stable door after the steed is stolen. God did not give your child the germ of enteric which constitutionally she was unfitted to cope with. It happened through some misfortune that God had nothing to do with, and, simply, she hadn't enough fight in her. There are times when we cannot understand why some things should be, especially if we feel that by stretching out His arm God can save us; yet He does not do so," continued Honor. "I prefer to believe that God fights for the life of our dear one along with us, and we both fail, we and God, because of some lack on our side that has hindered." Honor was not accustomed to holding forth on the subject of her views and would have said no more, but Mrs. Meek was roused to a new interest and persisted in drawing from her all she felt regarding the matter.

"If you put your foot on a cobra and you are bitten, and no immediate remedies are at hand, you will certainly die. If you prayed your hardest to be saved and did nothing, you would certainly be disappointed. God has given us the means of saving life—science and medicine are His way of helping us through doctors—even then we fail if the patient has no strength to battle with disease. That is how I feel," she added loyally. "We don't blame those we love—so don't blame God unjustly."

"Doctor Dalton said Elsie's heart was weak," moaned Mrs. Meek. "Perhaps had he come last night he would have noticed the change in her and done something to have helped her to live! Oh! Miss Bright, I feel it is owing to the doctor's neglect that I have lost my child. Why didn't he come last night?"

Honor's eyes fell before the anguish in hers. "He was at dinner with us, and left us early intending to come on here. I don't know why he changed his mind," she murmured, feeling again the rush of wild resentment against Joyce Meredith for her beauty and allurement.

"How strangely you talk!" Mrs. Meek went on as Honor relapsed into silence. "I never heard any one speak or think like this."

"I have always felt that nothing harsh or bad can come from God," said Honor gravely. "He does not treat us cruelly just to make us turn to Him. It would have the opposite effect, I should imagine, and He knows that as he knows us. It is presumptuous of me to say anything at all, but it seems to me, we are responsible for much of our own sorrows, or it is the way of life since the Fall. Humanity has foiled the designs of God from the time of Adam, and has had to bear the consequences. But, always, God's goodness and mercy triumph, and we are helped through the heaviest of tribulation till our sorrows are healed. Pity and Love are from God, never agony and bereavement!"

"Yet my husband says that the *cross is from God*, a 'burden imposed for the hardness of our hearts'!"

"So that to punish you, God is supposed to have caused an innocent one all that suffering, and has snatched her from the simple joys of her life! Is that your husband's conception of a loving God? If I believed that, I would become a heathen, preferably."

"It doesn't seem to fit in with such attributes as Mercy and Love!" cried Mrs. Meek, relapsing again into a flood of grief; for, after all, there was poor consolation for her in any theory since nothing could restore to her her beloved child.

"Tell me," said Honor to the nurse who had led her to the adjoining room to take her last look at her dead friend, "wasn't her death rather sudden and unexpected?"

"The doctor should have been here last night," said the nurse looking scared and uncomfortable. "She was so wild and restless and kept exciting herself in her delirium. Her heart was bad and nothing seemed to have effect. He should have been here, and not left her to me for so many hours, since early morning!"

"When did the change set in?—could no one have gone for the doctor?"

"It is a great misfortune that there was no one capable of relieving me," said the nurse looking distressed. "There was only the ayah, and she was supposed to be watching, yet allowed the patient to sit up in bed in her delirium when to lift an arm had been forbidden. All she could do was to cry aloud and remonstrate, which woke me and before I could do anything, the poor girl was—gone! Simply fell back dead. It was terrible! I fear I shall get into trouble, but the Meeks could not afford more than one nurse and Mrs. Meek and I were both worn out. I knew the ayah would blame me, as I blame her; but, humanly speaking, it would have happened in any case—even had her mother been in the room. It was truly most unfortunate. If the doctor had only been here he might have seen the necessity for a sedative or something!"

It was the same cry: "If the doctor had only been here!" From all she could gather, Elsie had passed a restless night and had died of heart failure in the morning. An overtaxed heart had given out by the exertion of suddenly rising in bed.

Honor doubted if Captain Dalton could have done anything by visiting his patient at night, yet his not having done so would always leave a reproach against him. She felt it and, yet, strangely enough, wanted to combat every argument that would have held him to blame.

When she was leaving the bungalow she came face to face with Captain Dalton descending from his car; and so moved was she for the moment, that she would not trust herself to do more than bow stiffly as she passed, her face white in its repression, her eyes cold and distant. At sight of him her agony returned in force; her heart for a moment stood still. Why had he lied to them about visiting Sombari when it was Joyce Meredith he had meant to see? Joyce with her lovely face and winning, childish ways? Everyone must love Joyce because of her ingenuousness and extraordinary beauty. The doctor had nursed her in camp under intimate conditions ... and he had stolen a visit to her when duty had required him in an opposite direction.

How was it possible to feel the same friendliness towards him with that wild resentment raging at her heart? So Honor ran out to her pony, sprang nimbly into the saddle, and rode rapidly away, feeling his searching eyes upon her till she was out of sight.

CHAPTER XI
A SUNDAY OBSERVANCE

Honor Bright rode straight to the Bara Koti to tell Joyce of Elsie Meek's death, not without a grim satisfaction in the thought that the news was certain to fill her friend with self-reproach; on other accounts her feelings defied analysis.

Joyce was writing home-letters for the mail in her morning-room when Honor was announced, and she was arrested, in her expressions of welcome by the look on her visitor's face, which was unusually pale and her great brown eyes, always so friendly and tender, cold and grave.

"What is it?" she asked fearfully, as she searched her memory for any unconscious offence to her friend.

"I have just come from Mrs. Meek who is prostrated with grief. Elsie is dead. She died at sunrise this morning."

"Dead?—Elsie Meek?... I did not know she was so bad!" Joyce looked shocked and distressed.

"I left as Captain Dalton arrived—they are blaming him for not having gone there last night. He was expected, but"—she made a gesture of despair.

"Oh, Honor!—was it because he was here? He came to see if we were ill—I had been nervous about Baby—and when I knew that it was nothing, I kept him for music till—till quite late. Is it my fault?" The lovely face looked stricken and blanched.

"I don't know—perhaps indirectly; but *he* knew. He should not have stayed."

"I persuaded him because I was dull—but I never knew!—I never dreamed she was so bad! Oh, Honey!" and Joyce broke into a passion of tears. "I shall never be happy again. I shall always feel that I was responsible!"

"He should never have stayed with you!—his duty was clear," said Honor sternly. "The responsibility rests entirely with him. But didn't you know that being alone and without your husband, you were inviting criticism by allowing him to stay—at that late hour? People in these *mafasil* stations are so censorious."

"I did not think it mattered," said Joyce without a shadow of resentment at such plain speaking. She stood with hands clasped, looking like a child in trouble, and Honor's heart began to melt. "He's only the doctor, you see, and he was so good to us in camp. Do you think I was wrong, Honey?" flinging her arms about Honor's neck and hiding her face in her bosom. Who could censure so much sweetness? So she was held in a close embrace and tenderly kissed.

"I have no right to speak—forgive me," said Honor.

"But you are privileged, because I love you," said Joyce. "Say what you please. I am so unhappy!—so miserable!"

"We must be miserable only for harm consciously done. You could never do that."

"I could not bear that you should condemn me," Joyce went on, clinging to her for consolation. "It seemed such a simple thing—it *was*."

"Yes, of course," Honor agreed against her judgment. "Only it would be hateful that you should be talked about by the people here—as Mrs. Fox is, for example."

"I should loathe it!—for I am not like her. You don't think that for a moment?"

"Never!—that is why I'll not have you misjudged," said Honor kissing her wet cheek.

"Why are people so horrid? I like Captain Dalton. He is so nice—so different from what people think him—agreeable! He took my rose, and I pinned it in his coat. He showed me how I should play the *Liebestraum*, and——"

"He—took—your rose?"

"Yes. It was in my dress ... and was so sweet—and he said I should be called 'Joy.' He is going to show me how to drive his motor-car so that I may take Ray by surprise one day. I must go out more than I do, and not worry so much about Baby for he is here to look after him. Oh! he is very kind—surely he never meant to neglect Elsie Meek?"

"He knows best about that—but, Joyce," Honor was strangely agitated and hid her telltale eyes in a cloud of Joyce's sunny hair, "you will never do anything that you cannot tell your husband?"

"How do you mean? I always tell Ray everything."

"That is all. He will advise you what it is best not to do. It is no business of mine."

"And I'll always tell you, too," the little wife said affectionately.

But Honor mentally decided it would be better for her not to hear anything more about Captain Dalton's visits. "I don't count—I am a mere outsider."

"You do. You are such a great help to me. I wish I had half your manner and self-confidence."

Their talk reverted to Elsie Meek, and Joyce learned something of the mother's grief. She was anxious to call immediately at the Mission to offer her condolences, and decided to attend the funeral which was to take place that afternoon. It was eventually settled that Mrs. Bright should call for her in the dogcart, and Honor would ride.

Consequently, when Ray Meredith motored in that afternoon, his wife was absent attending Elsie Meek's funeral, a simple ceremony at a tiny cemetery on the Mission property. The coffin, made of packing cases and covered with black calico, was carried by pastors, and the service was conducted by Mr. Meek himself, who scourged himself to perform the pathetic task as a penance to his soul.

It was dusk when Joyce returned, a subdued little person in black with a bursting heart which was relieved by a flood of tears in her husband's arms. He was very pitiful of her in her wrought-up state, and he soothed her with tender caresses.

It was very comforting to Joyce to be petted, and by degrees her weakened self-esteem was restored. Nothing was very far wrong with herself or her world while her husband loved her so, and Honor Bright remained her friend. Meredith would not allow his beloved to blame herself, though it was hardly the thing to entertain a visitor of the opposite sex so late at night when her husband was in camp; but the circumstances were exceptional; his little darling was nervous and lonely, and Dalton was a gentleman. Poof! he wouldn't for a moment allow that the doctor did not know his own business best; and very likely Elsie Meek's case had been hopeless from the start. With a weak heart, anything might happen in typhoid. Anyhow, he was not going to let his little girl worry herself sick and she was to cheer up on the instant and think no more about what did not concern herself. The main thing was, he had returned for the week-end, and wanted all her love and all her smiles to reward him for his long abstinence; and Joyce obediently kissed him and beamed upon him through her tears, wondering in her childish soul why husbands were so exacting in their love—their ardour so inexhaustible. Women were so very different—but men!

"With a wife like you, what can you expect?" Meredith cried, when she had expressed her views with naïveté. Which was all very flattering and calculated to spoil her thoroughly, but Meredith was in a mood to spoil her thoroughly after their enforced separation.

On Sunday morning, Honor followed up the notice which had been pinned on the board at the Club concerning evensong at the Railway Institute, by cycling round to various bungalows and exacting promises of attendance from her friends.

Muktiarbad was behind hand in the matter of a church building, the proposal having been shelved by the authorities with the usual procrastination. The Roman Catholic missionary lived in ascetic simplicity in the Station, and took his meals in native fashion wherever he preached the Faith.

There was no Episcopal clergyman nearer than the headquarters of the Division, eighty miles away; so it was only when his duties permitted it, that the District Chaplain paid a flying visit to Muktiarbad to minister to the spiritual welfare of his flock. Otherwise, it devolved on the Collector to officiate at Divine worship, as a paternal government enjoined this duty on the leading official in the stations not provided with resident clergy.

Thus it was that on most Sunday evenings Mr. Meredith read the Church Service in the general room of the Club to a congregation consisting mostly of ladies, while Jack Darling, usually flushed and breathless after tennis and a lightning change, went through the ordeal of reading the lessons.

To make certain of a couple of unreliable members of the choir, Honor cycled last of all to a picturesque little bungalow near the Police Court, and dismounted at its tumble-down gate. From frequent removals for jumping competitions for raw ponies, it was considerably damaged and swung loosely on its hinges, swayed by every wind that blew.

The bungalow was thatched, the eaves supported by square pillars; and the verandah was screened by bamboo trellis-work up which climbed the beautiful *Gloriosa superba.*

Boars' heads, buffalo horns, and the antlers of deer, ornamented what could be seen of the walls inside, and the tiled flooring was scattered over with long-arm easy chairs and "peg-tables."

A gravelled walk led to the steps, bordered on either side with straggling marigolds and dwarf sunflowers, dear to the hearts of *malis*, but evidently the worse for the depredations of the village goats. Date-palms drooped gracefully above a tank in the background, and a gorgeous hedge of acalypha hid the out-houses and kitchen.

Honor's appearance at the gate was the signal for a wild stampede from the verandah by Jack and Tom, who were enjoying a "Europe morning," to change into suitable garb; an orderly being dispatched meanwhile to crave the lady's indulgence. Rampur hounds and fox-terriers received her effusively on the road, and showed their appreciation of her presence by leaving marks of muddy paws on her drill skirt.

Tommy was the first to appear neatly apparelled, and smoothing his wet hair with both hands. He was followed soon afterwards by Jack, looking like an over-grown schoolboy in flannels. They hung about the gate since she could not be induced to enter, and pulled rueful faces on receiving instructions as to their duty at six-thirty, sharp.

"I believe there has been a riot at Panipara," put in Tommy with inspiration. "It is my duty as a police official to take instant notice of the fact and visit the spot for an inquiry."

"It can wait till Monday morning—or, you can send your Inspector," said Honor.

"I have a poisonous report to write"—began Jack.

"No sulking!" said Honor with determination. "You have to set a good example, both of you."

"I don't mind the service, a bit, and the hymns are fine," said Tommy, "but I distinctly object to sitting still and having illogical arguments when I cannot answer back hurled at my head."

"I shouldn't mind even that, for I needn't listen to them," said Jack; "but I do wish he would cut his sermons short. The last time he was at it for half an hour till I fell asleep and all but swallowed a fly."

"You and Tommy are worse than heathens and want a Mission all to your-selves," said Honor with twitching lips. (When Honor's lips revealed a hidden sense of humour, the boys' spirits effervesced.) "There is hymn-practice at three this afternoon at the Institute," she informed them. "Shall we have *Abide with me*, for a change?"

"'Abide with you,' certainly," said Tommy bubbling, while Jack put in a plea for one of the old favourites. "*Sun of my soul* is hard to beat," he said.

"Jack has a fixed belief that the world has missed a great tenor in him," re-marked Tommy. "He was bawling so loudly in his bath yesterday morning, that I was on the point of fetching my gun thinking there was a jackal around,—fact!"

"Liar! I was singing *O Star of Eve*, and you annoyed me by joining in. Execrable taste."

"Well?—we shall count on both of you for the choir."

"If any one will be so kind as to lend me a prayer-book," said Tommy reluc-tantly. "Jack used mine on a muggy night to keep the window open, and as it rained half the time, my property was reduced to pulp. The least he might do is to give me another."

"You can share mine," said Honor magnanimously. "That's fixed."

"Thanks, awfully. I love sharing a prayer-book with someone who knows the geography of it. The last time I went to church was at Hazrigunge when the Commissioner's Memsahib collared me as I was going to bridge. Miss Elworthy, the parson's sister,—elderly and still hopeful, handed me her book of Common Prayer; but I'm dashed if I could find the Collect! At any ordinary time I would have pounced upon it right enough, but knowing her eyes were upon me, I could do nothing but make a windmill of the pages with only the 'Solemnisation of Mat-rimony' staring up at my distracted vision, till I began to think Fate had designs. Really, it made me quite nervous, I assure you!"

"I shall have to give you Sunday-school lessons," said Honor, laughing heart-ily. "You are a bad boy, Tommy."

"I never attempt to find the places," said Jack. "It's the most difficult thing in the world when you are nervous and the parson is off at great speed, like a fox with the pack at his heels. My Church Service was a present from my old aunt when I was confirmed and is in diamond print, so that when I hold it upside down, no one is a bit the wiser."

"You ought to be ashamed of yourself!" cried Honor.

"Not at all. I always say 'Amen' at the right moment."

"It is always a case of 'Ah, men!' at Muktiarbad, where church is concerned," saying which she sprang on her bicycle and fled with the sound of loud groans in her ears.

Choir practice was well attended, and the "Inseparables" were obediently on hand to swell the singing of the popular hymns and even attempt a few chants. At the finish, Mrs. Fox made room for Jack on the organ stool, and while he worked the pedals, she played a voluntary by Grieg to their own entertainment and the distraction of the company.

"Fair joint production, if Jack would only remember he is not working a sewing-machine," said Tommy. "It puts me out of breath to listen."

"The bellows sound like an asthmatic old man about to suffer spontaneous combustion," said Honor moving away from the vicinity of the American organ, vexed to see the transparent arts practised by Mrs. Fox to lead Jack captive.

Divine service when conducted by the District Chaplain was held at the Railway Institute which was more centrally situated than the Club for the bulk of the European community at Muktiarbad, and the occasion was typical of the generality of such functions in the small, *mafasil* stations lacking a church building. Families of officials,—Government and Railway, non-officials, and subordinates, found seats for themselves in the neighbourhood of their respective acquaintance, and there was only a sprinkling of the masculine element, the majority being husbands whose demeanour, as they followed in the wake of their wives, was suggestive of derelict ships being towed into port.

The choir were accommodated near the American organ at which Mrs. Fox presided with ostentatious skill. Jack's stealthy effort to elude observation in a distant corner was frustrated by Honor on her way in, who whispered her commands that he was to occupy the seat reserved for him as the sole tenor available.

Tommy, on the other hand, put in attendance with laudable docility, claiming a place beside Honor; and all through the sermon occupied himself with the marriage service, till a gloved hand recovered possession of the prayer-book and a pair of brown eyes reproved him gravely.

"You paid no attention whatever to the service," she afterwards remarked scathingly.

"It is just what I did, right through," he returned meekly. "It's the only service that interests me."

"It was irrelevant matter!"

"Which made me miss the benefit I might have derived from the seed falling on prepared soil. Alas! see what you are responsible for!"

"I? I take no responsibility for you. And was the soil really prepared this time?" she teased.

"It was torn by the plough of eagerness and harrowed with anxiety lest I should be late and lose my place beside you," he returned feelingly.

Outside on the gravelled path, Mrs. Bright was informed by Mrs. Ironsides that she had counted sixty women in "Church," and only sixteen men, twelve of whom were married. "Scandalous!—I call it. And this is a country, where, in the midst of life one is in death!"

On their way home, Meredith and Joyce, with the parson in the car, came upon the doctor taking a "constitutional" in the moonlight and insisted on carrying him off to pot-luck.

Tommy attached himself to the Brights and received a similar invitation, while Jack was annexed by Mrs. Fox whose husband was at home and "would be charmed."

The invitation was given openly and Jack had no hesitation in accepting it, curious to know how the elusive Barrington Fox would appear on closer acquaintance.

They walked together across the railway lines and past unkempt hedges of Duranta in full bloom towards the group of residences reserved for officials of the Railway, each within its own garden and bounded by barbed wire as a protection against stray cattle.

The Traffic Superintendent's house was built on a more generous scale than the others, though uniformly of red brick picked out with buff. Shallow arches supported the concrete roof, and the verandah in front was gay with ornamental pot-plants and palms of luxuriant growth. Many doors opened upon it, and through them could be seen a lamplit and graceful interior, veiled by misty lace curtains. The verandah itself was left for the moon to illuminate.

Long residence in India and natural good taste had taught Mrs. Fox the art of furnishing with an eye to the needs of the climate, so that her rooms had the charm of restfulness, ease, and coolness. Most of her drawing-room chairs were of Singapur rush-work; the mat was of green grass, the *punkha* frills of art muslin. The walls were distempered in cool greys and neutral tints; while on all sides were palms, large and small, and china-grass in dainty flower-pots of coloured earthenware. A Japanese draught screen, embroidered in silk upon gauze and arranged carelessly, put a finish to the most picturesque drawing-room Jack had yet seen in Bengal.

Mr. Barrington Fox, however, was not at home. A telegram was found to have arrived, intimating that he had been detained at a wayside station.

"Such a nuisance!" Mrs. Fox exclaimed, laying down the telegram which, as a matter of fact, she had received earlier in the day. "You'll have to put up with only me. Do you mind?"

"It is not for me to mind," he answered awkwardly. "If you think I might stay, I shall be delighted."

"Then you shall. Who cares?—not my husband who has long ceased to mind what I do or how I am left to pass the time," she said bitterly.

"You must often be very lonely?" he ventured sympathetically. He had heard many rumours of Fox's neglect of his wife—of the temptations to which she was exposed and to which a woman placed as she was might be excused for yielding. Plenty of fellows paid court to her, and a good few had grown attached—yet, barring Smart who was a cad and a bounder, he was sure that none could cast a stone.

"I am always desperately lonely," she sighed, as she sank into a chesterfield and motioned him to the seat beside her. "You little know how it preys upon me; how I welcome a sympathetic friend! but—why speak of it?" she passed him her cigarette case, and they began to smoke companionably. "So few understand me," said she in subdued tones. "So many misunderstand! I ask you, what is life worth to a young woman in my position?" her chest heaved, her eyes filled with self-pity. "And who can stifle nature and be happy?—the ache for human sympathy—tenderness—love...." she brushed the moisture from her eyes with a diminutive handkerchief, and smiled a wintry smile. "I refuse to talk only of myself!—let us talk of you, dear Jack. You are a dear and I have so longed to make a friend of you," she interrupted herself to say.

Jack coloured furiously while filled with indignant pity for her. Poor girl!—after all, she was quite young!... He did not care how old she was; she was young enough to be pitied for the rotten time her selfish husband gave her.

They spent a supremely innocent evening looking through albums of photographs and talking football and polo. The dinner was excellent, and Mrs. Fox, clever in the art of entertaining, modelled her conversation to suit his manly tastes, in the end breaking down all his natural shyness and placing him on terms of easy friendship. When Jack eventually rose to go he was flattered by her open reluctance to part with him; her pleasure in his society had been so frank and appealing.

"I have never enjoyed an evening so much in my life, Jack," she said cooingly. "Why are you so different from other men?"

"Am I?" he asked in some confusion as she retained his hand in hers.

"In a thousand ways. I almost wish I had never met you, Jack!"

"Why?" he asked, his breath suddenly short, his heart beating a rapid tattoo in his breast. For the life of him he could not say the easy pretty things that fell so naturally from other men's lips.

"Because—Oh! why, you must know—I shall always be making comparisons which are odious, and remember, I have to put up with only odiousness!"

"I hate to think of it," he said huskily.

"It is sweet to think you mind."

"It makes a fellow—mad to do something. It's damned hard and cruel for you!"

"Never mind, dear boy. Come again, come often, will you?" she pleaded, leaning her head against the pillar behind her and looking languishingly up at him with the moonlight full on her face and throat, bathing her in a pale radiance.

Jack's eyes swept the deserted verandah. He did not know that the servants were well drilled in the etiquette of keeping out of the way when the lady of the house entertained a male visitor. "Good-bye," he said indistinctly, moving a step nearer.

"Good-bye," she returned almost inarticulately, her eyes melting to his own. "I shall weep my heart out when you are gone."

"Why?" he demanded unsteadily.

"For the things that I have missed. I always dream of a man just like you—you are the man of my dreams come to me—too late!—and my heart has been starved so long!"

"Don't," he said sharply. "I am not made of stone."

Their faces were very near together, so near, that Jack had only to stoop to press her lips fiercely with his.

"Oh, Jack!—" she cried emotionally. "You mustn't make me love you—you darling!" yet she returned his kiss with equal fervour. "Oh, go—go quickly," she breathed. "You must not stay——"

Dazed and bewildered, Jack took her at her word and went swiftly down the steps, nor did he halt when her voice called after him to stop and return. "Oh, Jack!—come back—come back, I cannot let you go!"

Nevertheless, he went without a backward look, wondering within himself if all men found it so easy to tread the path of dishonour. Where it might lead him if he allowed his baser instincts headway, he could guess, and with a mighty effort he made up his mind to apply the brake there and then. Poor woman!—he could not blame her—it was he alone who had had no excuse—not a shadow of an excuse for the outrage. She, a disappointed wife was like a being temporising with suicide. Small blame to her if she took the plunge. It was for men of sound brain and clear judgment to save her—not supply the means of self-destruction.

Did she wish him to believe that she already loved him?

Then he must assist her quickly to recover from the delusion, for Jack well knew that there is a difference between love and the feeling that could simulate it to the destruction of honour and self-respect. Passion had swept him off his feet with sudden violence and he was shaken to the depths with fear of himself, for he had let himself go unpardonably and was ashamed.

All the way to his bungalow he walked with bowed head, alternately thrilled with temptation, and abased at his moral collapse; the latter, because he cherished an ideal and was now convicted in his own estimation as unworthy.

The ideal had been established in the *Puja*[13] holidays he had spent in Darjeeling playing with the "Squawk" and listening to its mother's innocent reminiscences of her home and her people in England. He had found a wonderful thing: a beautiful woman without vanity—a child-nature in a woman; an ideal wife; one who respected her husband and obeyed him while idolising their child. Wedded to such purity a husband's life was paradise, and Jack accounted him a lucky man. It was refreshing to bask in her presence and hear her describe her simple past, so transparently virtuous and inexperienced, into which a certain name was always intruding. "Kitty" the little sister was mentioned constantly. Always "Kitty!" She had said this or that, she had done so and so. She was a little wonder, full of charm, and so intensely human that the picture of her had haunted his imagination.

---

[13] Hindu festival.

"Is she like you?" he had asked wondering if Nature could possibly have twice excelled herself.

"We are considered rather alike, but she has twice the courage and initiative that I have, and her eyes are the deepest violet you have seen."

"Haven't you a photo of her?" curiosity had impelled him to ask.

"Oh, yes. A beauty, taken by Raaf's in Regent Street." She had fetched the photograph and Jack had fallen straightway in love with the sparkling face so full of charm and sunshine. The small features were not unlike Mrs. Meredith's, but where they lacked her beauty, they made up a thousandfold in attraction. It was a face to hold the attention, to follow to the ends of the earth. From Mrs. Meredith's description, Kitty was brimful of life and high spirits, affectionate and generous, but quite a "handful" to manage. "She always dared infinitely more than ever I did, and was always the first to get into scrapes! But so loyal and honourable!"

"I should imagine every fellow for miles around must be head and ears in love with her!"

"That, of course, but she is not a bit silly about boys, being practically a boy herself in disposition. Only lately she has begun to do up her hair and is to be presented next season when she will be considered 'out.'"

"And be married straight away!"

"I suppose so," said Joyce proudly. "She is such a darling!"

"I can believe it," said he.

Jack had been so completely captivated by Kitty's photograph that Joyce had generously told him to keep it. She had other copies and thought it as well that he should cultivate an ideal for the elevation of his soul. "It is good for a man to look up to a really good girl with admiration and trust; it should make him determined to become worthy of the possession even of her picture."

"It is something for a fellow to live up to," Jack had blushingly returned, full of delight in the gift. He mentally resolved to go in search of the original the very first time he obtained furlough and to be satisfied with no other. If the Fates would only keep her fancy-free for himself!

He carried the picture home and Tommy was tormented with curiosity concerning the face which was so like Mrs. Meredith's and yet not hers.

The memory of that afternoon at Darjeeling and of the photograph in his dispatch-box came to taunt Jack in the moonlight as he wended his way to the bungalow at the Police Lines, fresh as he was from the experience of a married woman's kisses given in response to his own.

Tommy was at home and awake when he came in, and remarked bluntly concerning his extraordinary pallor.

"How did it go off? Was Barrington Fox Esquire particularly cordial?"

"He wasn't there," came gruffly from Jack.

"Not there?"

"I'll repeat it if you like."

"Don't be ratty. I was only expressing natural surprise. Possibly she knew he wouldn't be there when she asked you."

"You are as uncharitable as everyone else."

"No, I am merely somewhat discerning."

"It does you credit."

"My son, hearken to the words of wisdom and the voice of the sage—'Whoso is partner with a thief, hateth his own soul——'"

"Oh, go to blazes," said Jack pouring himself out a whisky-and-soda.

"'A man that flattereth his neighbour spreadeth a net for his feet.'"

"I've been to Church—Drop it."

"'Iron sharpeneth iron; so a man sharpeneth the countenance of his friend,'" Tommy persisted with a twinkle in his eye.

"Thanks, I'm much obliged but it isn't necessary. Have a cigarette."

It was mentioned that the doctor dined at the Bara Koti that evening.

When the news of an extra mouth to feed was conveyed to the cook in the kitchen, Abdul surveyed three snipe among potato chips with a problem of multiplication vexing his soul.

"With the *padre-sahib* they are three, yet without warning they bring a fourth! Now what to do? *ai khodar!*—how to arrange?"

"Why disturb thyself, brother?" said the *khansaman* sympathetically as he put extra plates on the rack of the hot-case in which an open fire in a cast-iron cooker burned fiercely. "Cut each bird in two and make toast for each portion, in this way there will be some left for thee and me. If the master say aught, ask if it is his almighty will that the *shikari* be sent out at a moment's notice in the moonlight to shoot another bird."

The fine sarcasm of his advice created a general laugh of good-humour among the servants assembled to serve the dinner. "In my last place," continued the Mohammedan butler, "my Sahib who had no wife would, out of sheer provocation, bring six or eight sahibs home to eat with him, and could we protest? *Yah, khodar!* that instant with two kicks would we have been dismissed, and he so ready with his boot! No! Quickly we put water in the soup; with much energy we opened a tin of salmon, cut up onions, fetched a cucumber from the vegetable garden for salad. Then in the fowl-house, what a cackling and screeching as the *masalchi* chased fowls and cut their throats! *Jhut!* they were cleaned and how long does it take to grill meat? In fifteen minutes from the order, the dinner was ready, pudding and all. When a store-room is well-stocked, it is like *jadu*[14] to make a dinner for one capable of feeding six and even eight!"

---

[14] Magic.

All great talkers are unconscious egotists, as the Merediths found the Reverend John Pugh who enjoyed the sound of his own voice even when he was not in the pulpit, and retailed stock jokes and anecdotes to the company in general, forgetful of the fact that the same jokes and anecdotes had been recounted by him at every house on his visiting list. At dessert Joyce was glad to slip away to the drawing-room taking with her the doctor, who was permitted to smoke while he played to her on the piano.

Joyce noticed that he was disinclined for conversation and was out of sorts and dull, as though inwardly disturbed and uninterested even at his music. He took an early opportunity to leave and was accompanied to the doorstep by Joyce, her husband being still pinned to the dining-room by the parson whose anecdotes were inexhaustible.

"When next you see your friend, Miss Bright," said he, apropos of nothing, as he shook hands again, "tell her, will you?—that I know how to take a snub."

"Why?—has Honor snubbed you?" she asked surprised.

He smiled unpleasantly. "It was equal to a knock-down blow."

"But that is so unlike Honor. How do you mean?"

"I am not complaining, for I dare say I deserve it, but I would like her to know that I shall not willingly put myself in the way of the same again."

"Oh—" light had dawned on Joyce. "It must be because she thinks you failed Elsie Meek. She heard that you never went to Sombari on Friday night though you left the party for the purpose of seeing how she was doing. Honor came here straight from the Mission."

"It was on the steps of the Mission bungalow that we met, and I was sentenced without a charge."

"Are you very angry?"

"I don't think I am," he returned proudly. "It is nothing of consequence."

"But would it have made any difference had you gone?" she pressed. "I ask because I feel responsible for having kept you with me." Her voice quavered with emotion and her lovely eyes drooped.

"It would have made no difference." Captain Dalton condescended to explain Elsie Meek's condition and the fatal consequence of the sudden exertion she had taken in her delirium and high fever. "She needed very close watching. Unfortunately that was not given."

"Then it was the nurse's fault?"

"It was an accident. They could not afford a second nurse and Mrs. Meek was physically unfit to do her share."

"I shall tell Honor."

"Please do not do so. I prefer to let the matter stand. It will be quite for the best," and with that he was gone.

However, Joyce took the first opportunity of repeating the conversation to her friend. "So you see, dear," she concluded as they talked together at the Club the following afternoon, "he was not at all to blame."

"Perhaps not, but it makes no difference. I am deeply disappointed in him. It was his duty to have gone, and a man who is capable of neglecting a duty for pleasure falls short of the standard I cherish," returned Honor coldly.

"I did not know you could be so hard!" said Joyce reproachfully.

"I am not hard. It is absolutely nothing to me and Captain Dalton cares very little what I think."

Joyce wondered if that were so, for she remembered his abstraction; his mention of Honor had been a bolt from the blue.

"I do not understand why he said 'it would be quite for the best,'" Joyce speculated.

"It proves how little he cares one way or another!" Honor answered, wounded but proud. "And I have had a lesson never to mistake a goose for a swan again."

"But he was good to you!"

"And for that I immediately dressed him up in every virtue; I was just a fool—like any schoolgirl! Please don't let us talk of Captain Dalton any more. He does not interest me at all."

She knew it was untrue to say that, but it was too late to recall her words as she turned and faced Captain Dalton, himself, who had come up from behind them and must have heard her concluding remarks. He was apparently searching for the Collector who had returned reluctantly to camp and, as Honor passed on with a bow, which he acknowledged distantly, he and Joyce moved away together.

"I wish you would chase Honor and bring her to reason," said Joyce childishly.

"I would much prefer to stay with you, if I may?" said he impressively. "Besides, why should I?"

"Because," said Joyce with childish impulsiveness, "Honor Bright was very fond of you."

In a flash, Dalton's eyes seemed to dilate and then contract. "What makes you think so?" he asked abruptly.

"I knew it—I felt it. She could not hide it from me."

"Did she ever say anything?" he asked with assumed indifference.

"Not in words—but when she spoke of you—oh, the light in her eyes, and the changing colour!—perhaps I should not tell you this?—but misunderstandings are wretched."

Her blue eyes apologised so prettily that he smiled with peculiar radiance.

"You are a very good friend," he said with amused indulgence.

"Who wouldn't be that to a girl like Honor!"

"And if I tell you I appreciate that, you must forgive me if I would rather not discuss Honor Bright any more. Are you very lonely now your husband has left?"

"I shall be, after today!" she pouted in self-pity.

"Then I shall call round for you tomorrow afternoon and take you for a spin?"

"I shall look forward to it. Will you teach me to drive?"

"With pleasure."

"How delightful of you!"

"The pleasure will be equally mine," he said quite charmingly for him; and after further pleasantries rather foreign to his habit, he left her and drove away.

CHAPTER XII

INFATUATION

Filled with the determination to set aside foolish jealousies and cultivate a more generous trust in human nature, the Collector returned to his administrative duties in camp which were designed to bring him personally into contact with the villagers in his jurisdiction.

His bachelor experience of social life in the East had, unfortunately, not helped to supply him with much confidence in his own sex. However, men were not all ravening wolves let loose upon society, and it was an undeniable fact that no man, however unprincipled, would dare to make love to a married woman without her encouragement, or attempt to seduce her from her lawful allegiance without her co-operation. And Joyce was incorruptible because of her love for her child.

Yet there were times when Meredith's heart yearned wistfully for his beloved wife, and for the power of second sight that he might see how things were going in his absence; and since he was denied that faculty, it was not a little comfort to him to know that Honor Bright was in intimate companionship with Joyce. He liked to think of her influence exerted to assist the development of the childlike mind; for Honor Bright was "one of the best," and would some day make some lucky fellow a splendid wife; of that there was no doubt whatever. It seemed a mystery that she was still unmarried when she had been out in India for a year or more! and Meredith wondered what men were about. It did not strike him that Honor was not to be had for the asking.

It was well, however, for the Collector's peace of mind and the work upon which he was engaged, that he did not know of the motor drives which were to provide a surprise for him one day.

"People are beginning to talk about them," Honor ventured, with reference to their frequency, shy of being misunderstood and afraid of being considered interfering; but she had not forgotten Ray Meredith's parting words spoken with wistful meaning—"Take care of my wife, she is such a kid!"

She had accepted the responsibility and it was weighing heavily upon her.

"Very impertinent of 'people,'" said Joyce in return.

"You have to live among them, and in your position they want to look up to you as a sort of 'Cæsar's wife,'" said Honor smiling. "But it is, of course, a matter that lies between you and your husband entirely. If *he* doesn't object— —"

"He knows nothing about my learning to drive, as it is to be a surprise. What concern is it of any one else?"

"We generally stand or fall by what people think of us—don't we? However much we would like to ignore the fact, it remains unquestionable. If we do things liable to misconstruction, we are likely to suffer in the eyes of the world—and you see it every day. You yourself disapproved of and condemned Mrs. Fox, whose ways none of us admire or can stand."

"Oh, Honey!" reproachfully—"would you compare me with Mrs. Fox? Why she does scandalous things!"

"God forbid that I should! but Mrs. Fox did not begin by doing scandalous things. When she grew used to doing unconventional things she became consciously scandalous. Everything happens by degrees—even deterioration."

"But you don't think there is any harm in my going for drives with Captain Dalton, Honey? He is so different. He is not the kind of man who gets women talked about, I should imagine. Why, half the time, he is glum and absent-minded, and he treats me just like a child." Joyce never resented Honor's plain-speaking.

"It is no business of mine," said Honor, "except that you are my friend and I am jealous for your honourable standing here. I know nothing of Captain Dalton, but that he is a man like most others—and you might, some day, meet with a surprise."

"What sort of surprise?" laughed Joyce sceptically.

"I don't know—but you'll remember that I warned you. Meantime, go easy with your favours. You are rather generous, you know."

Honor was thinking of Joyce's innocent demonstrativeness—inseparable from herself—which some men might not understand, and the doctor was but human after all. She had seen her toying with his watch-chain while arguing against following his advice for the good of her health; leading him by the hand to visit her baby in its crib; seizing the lapels of his coat in a moment of eager excitement. On each of these occasions Honor had been apart from them, an observer at a distance, engaged by others in conversation and desirous of appearing unconscious of the doctor's existence. Since the day she had shown silent disapproval of him on the steps of the Mission Bungalow, he had made no effort to bring about a better understanding and she was wounded to the quick, though she steeled herself to show utter indifference. Yet the sight of the doctor with Joyce in such intimate circumstances—latterly made more so by the frequent drives—had caused Honor's heart to twist with sudden anguish; for it was difficult to forget the day at his bungalow when he had fought for her life and called her the bravest girl he knew. A wordless sympathy had grown up between them since that day. His eyes had held for her a special message. Though he was "not seeking her for a wife" she felt that he had liked her more than a little, and she——?

Now they were less than strangers; and Joyce, beautiful and confiding, was innocently flattering him with her preference. Where would it end?

While Honor watched the development of Joyce's friendship with Captain Dalton, she was also aware of a change in Jack. Tommy had drawn her attention to

Mrs. Fox's efforts to enslave Jack, whose own demeanour was beginning to show that all was not right with him. A new self-consciousness was apparent in his manner towards her, and he made blundering efforts to avoid being left alone in her company. He was evidently afraid of her—afraid of himself, too—because of the evil impulses her insidious influence had aroused in him.

The fact was, Jack had arrived at a just appreciation of the truism, "Opportunity makes the thief." His respect for Mrs. Fox had expired after the episode on her moonlight verandah, and though he had made excuses for her, he was conscious they had rung hollow. Yet, in spite of his strict upbringing and the knowledge of danger, he had come to the psychological point when Opportunity was certain to make him a thief, for the memory of those kisses burned fiercely. He was as one who, by steeping himself in the vice of intoxication, begets a craving for alcohol, and he felt that his powers of resistance were on the wane. His cherished "ideal" was forgotten, and her portrait reposed face downward among envelopes and papers in his dispatch-box, while he kept out of Mrs. Meredith's way and neglected Honor Bright.

"Jack's not the same man," Tommy confided to Honor. "He eats little and talks less. That woman will bring him to grief. I'd cheerfully shoot her."

"What's the matter with Jack?" Honor asked, surprised. "What does he admire in her? I have no patience with him."

"I don't know that he admires her. It's an infatuation. She has cast a spell over him somehow, since the night he dined with her alone, and he can't resist it. She writes to him almost every day."

"And he answers her notes?"

"Of course."

"Jack is weak. I simply have no use for such weakness," said Honor contemptuously. "There is more hope for the villain who is deliberately bad than for the wobbly wretch who hasn't the strength to resist temptation. When the one repents, he is at least sincere; the other can never be depended upon to repent sincerely."

"I never heard that before," grinned Tommy. "You would rather have Jack sin deliberately with his eyes open than fail in his efforts to keep straight?"

"I have no patience for 'failures.' One could be angry with him for sinning deliberately, but hardly contemptuous. As it is, I have no opinion of Jack."

Tommy made no complaint, for it was all to his own advantage. Though he was fond of Jack he had always regarded him as a dangerous rival, who so far had been merciful in not exerting his fascinations upon the only girl in their small circle at Muktiarbad. Since he was such a fool as to prefer dangling after a married woman, ten years his senior, his blood be on his own head.

One evening, a few days later, Mrs. Fox discovered Jack Darling alone in the billiard-room knocking about the balls while waiting for someone to join him in a game. The rules of the Muktiarbad Club were lenient towards the ladies, who thus enjoyed privileges denied to them at larger stations. Mrs. Fox was therefore free to enter, and Jack was obliged to submit to his fate and comply with her request for a lesson in the science of "screws" and "potting." He had been priding himself on his wisdom and self-control in retiring from tennis and the society of the ladies, and had not reckoned on the perseverance of the one lady he wished to avoid.

They played till others arrived; Jack was oddly moved by the sight of her slender hand, exquisitely feminine and appealing, as it poised the cue or lay on the green cloth of the table. Little intimacies were inevitable as he was further called upon to instruct her in the formation of a "bridge," or the handling of a cue; and he soon forgot his desire to escape, in the involuntary thrills her contact gave him.

Eventually, she gracefully resigned in favour of a couple of members who looked their anxiety to play, and carried Jack off to escort her home.

"You are quite sure you do not mind?" she asked softly.

"Why should I mind?" he fenced awkwardly.

"Because you have behaved lately as though you did not—not—like me...."

"Have I?" he asked, flushing red in the darkness. "That isn't true."

"I thought, perhaps, it was not true. That is why I was determined to have this opportunity for a talk."

She did most of the talking while he barely listened, being conscious only of the thumping of his capitulating heart. But neither made any allusion to the tender episode on the verandah, from which Jack dated his undoing.

In a quiet lane where the shadows lay deepest, he was asked to strike a match. Convicted of lack of courtesy, Jack hurriedly produced his cigarette case and offered it to her with confused apologies.

"No thanks. Only a lighted match. I want to show you something," she said plaintively. And while he struck a light she rolled back her silk sleeve and displayed for his benefit a purple bruise on her shoulder where it curved down to the arm; an ugly, evil-looking thing staining the marble purity of the flesh.

"How did that happen?" he asked greatly shocked and very sympathetic.

"Can't you guess?"

"Good God!—is it possible? Is he such a cad as all that?" What else was Jack to think?

"Perhaps I had better say no more about it, only I thought you had better know." Only the inference was possible, and Jack stood stock-still burning with indignant fury that a woman should be subjected to such brutality at the hands of a man. The match burned down to his finger-tips and fell to the ground leaving the two in the shadows of the silent road.

"It makes me feel pretty mad—what can I do?" he asked helplessly as she drew the sleeve down.

"You can do nothing—but give me a little tenderness and love," she said with a sob, letting him take her in his arms.

"You poor little woman!"

"It is so lovely to feel that you care, Jack! Nothing matters so long as you care!" She clung to his neck inviting and returning his kisses.

Further down the lane as they walked with his arm about her, they were startlingly rung out of the way by a cyclist who had come on them unawares. It was Tommy who had neglected to light his lamp, as the night, though dark, was clear and starry and municipal regulations were lax.

"Do you think he recognised us?" Mrs. Fox asked anxiously.

"Without a doubt," Jack spoke with annoyance.

"But it's only Tommy and you are his friend. He won't give us away." She had no idea of the shame and embarrassment that Jack suffered at the thought that he had given his chum ocular proof of his folly, for Tommy had confessed that he despised Mrs. Fox, and that he had encouraged Bobby Smart to break away from her clutches. That there was truth in the gossip concerning Mrs. Fox and young Smart he could no longer doubt, but this made very little difference to him. As matters stood, he was committed and could not go back. Nor did he wish to. At least Tommy was loyal and would not give him away to the Station. Thoughts of the Station brought thoughts of Mrs. Meredith and Honor Bright whose good-fellowship he valued. Honor stood for all that was best in womanhood, and to be worthy of her companionship a man had to be as straight as a die. Joyce Meredith was "not in the same boat," though she, too, was a "bit of 'All-right.'" Her sister—? what chance had he of ever meeting her sister?—Jack laughed as he shook off a tendency to morbid regret and bade Mrs. Fox a resolute farewell at her gate. He had plenty to do preparing a judgment he had to deliver in court the following day, and begged to be excused. Another day—perhaps——

Mrs. Fox fixed the day and parted from him tenderly, full of satisfaction at the success of her clever fiction. The accident which had occasioned the bruise had been of the commonest, but it had served her gallantly.

Contrary to Jack's expectations, Tommy was not at all in the mood to rag, being silent for the greater part of dinner. However, when the genial influence of a whisky-and-soda had had time to work on his spirits, the young policeman apologised for not having carried a light on his bicycle. It was his way of introducing the subject which was haunting him with forebodings.

"That's all right," said Jack. "But as one whose job is to enforce the law, I should imagine you would be more particular."

"If that's all the law-breaking I do, I shan't come to grief, my son. It is very different in your case. 'Can a man take coals to his bosom and not be burned?'"

"What the devil are you driving at?"

"I get a tidy lot of wisdom out of old Solomon and I commend you to take up the dissertation from where I left off. You'll find a good deal to set you thinking."

"Where am I to find it?" Jack asked with determined good-humour.

"Proverbs—sixth, twenty-eighth; read from there, onward."

"Thanks. I'll see what he has to say concerning such stupendous truths."

"I commend you also to try him for advice on seeking a wife," said Tommy. "It will help you to form a judgment. Listen:

"'*Who can find a virtuous woman? for her price is far above rubies*' — —"

"Blessed old cynic!" interjected Jack, adding, he had heard that before.

"'*The heart of her husband doth safely trust in her*' —mark the word, 'trust'.... '*She will do him good, not evil all the days of her life.*' I can't remember it all, there is such a lot. He goes on to say, '*Her husband is known in the gates, when he sitteth among the elders of the land.... Strength and honour are her clothing and she shall rejoice in time to come*— —'"

"Personally, I should prefer something more decent as a garment," murmured Jack, while Tommy searched his brains.

"'*She openeth her mouth with wisdom; and in her tongue is the law of kindness. She looketh well to the ways of her household, and eateth not the bread of idleness. Her children rise up and call her blessed; her husband also, and he praiseth her. Many daughters have done virtuously, but thou excellest them all. Favour is deceitful and beauty is vain: but a woman that feareth the Lord, she shall be praised. Give her of the fruit of her hands; and let her own works praise her in the gates.*'"

"Is that all?"

"Isn't it enough?"

"And you mean to say you expect to find such a paragon of perfection in modern times?" Jack asked, pouring out some more whisky.

"Till I do, I shan't marry," said Tommy.

"Here's luck to you!" said Jack raising his glass to his lips, unconvinced. "I'm afraid you'll live to be an old bachelor."

"I'm afraid I shall, though I have found her already," murmured Tommy.

CHAPTER XIII
VANISHED

Honor Bright paid several visits to the Mission after Elsie Meek's death, hoping to be of use in cheering the bereaved mother. After the funeral most of the ladies had called to sympathise, Joyce among them, tearful and tender; but having nothing in common with Methodists who held aloof from Station society, her visit of condolence ended the intercourse, so that, but for Honor, Mrs. Meek would have been much alone. The girl would cycle down for an hour or so and chat with, or read to the grief-stricken woman while she worked garments for the converted heathen, thus affording her the priceless boon of sympathetic companionship.

During these visits it became apparent to her how much the Padre had changed. He was hardly the same man. All his dictatorial ways were gone, his self-sufficiency vanished; he was, instead, bowed down with depression, he looked older than his years, and spoke with a new and strange humility.

Very shyly, as though unaccustomed to the rôle, he was becoming the attentive husband with an anxious eye for his wife's comfort, and seeking to show her by unobtrusive services that he understood and shared her grief and was suffering the pangs of remorse. It was not easy for Mr. Meek to confess that he now realised he had been a hard husband and father, but his manner was tantamount to such a confession, and Mrs. Meek was deeply touched. The passionate love and devotion of nineteen years ago had long settled into a natural affection for the father of her child, and now when she was stricken to the earth with sorrow, the void in her heart craved to be filled, and she could feel he was striving to fill it.

"You don't know how pathetic it seems to me," she confided in Honor, "his self-conviction and efforts to atone. He must have been fond of our child, deep down, though unable to show it, not being of a demonstrative nature. I think he feels he was narrow and bigoted not to have allowed her a few innocent pleasures such as girls enjoy among young people in a Station,—and it is too late now!"

"There is nothing I can imagine so painful as unavailing remorse," said Honor.

"It makes me sorry for him and though I have found it hard to forgive him, I have uttered no word of reproach. He is so altered. Although a good man and truly religious, he was yet growing unconsciously selfish and domineering—all that has now been swept away, and he is ready for any self-sacrifice—even to allowing me to visit my family in Scotland."

"Will you go?"

Mrs. Meek's work dropped in her lap while she gave herself up to thought. "No," she said at length. "I have lost touch with my people. Though they love me dearly, and I them, I don't feel as if I could leave my husband alone now that he is so broken and sad. We share the same bereavement, and need each other now more than ever before. Besides, he hardly realises how dependent he is upon me. I have done so much for him all these years that he will be utterly stranded without me. It would be cruel."

Honor smiled at her affectionately, thinking it was very sweet—this spirit of love and forgiveness springing to life after years of habitual submission. A truly feminine quality, upon which the masculine nature has never failed to draw, and which would continue as long as women remained womanly for the salvation of men.

While at Sombari, Honor heard news of Captain Dalton's doings in the District. His fame as a surgeon had spread far and wide with various results on the ignorant and enlightened. In the case of the former, he inspired more fear than respect, and Mr. Meek could tell of mischievous rumours afloat which he had done his best to dispel so far as his influence went. One of the tales in circulation was that Captain Dalton was an agent of the Government sent to cripple the youths of the District and otherwise render them helpless in the event of a revolution.

"And when is such an event likely to happen?" the Padre had asked.

Who can tell?—Weren't there mutterings and discontent in big towns?—All who travelled and went to the cities came back with news of great things to come if all that the people demanded was not granted by the *Sarcar*.

"What are the people demanding?" Mr. Meek persisted in knowing.

That was best known to the highly educated. What did the poor agriculturist know of what was good for the country? He was like sheep led to the pasture by those in authority. But when the *Sarcar* sent among the sheep a butcher with no stomach for the suffering of the helpless ones, it was time to protest and to see to it that he was recalled or driven away. Some were for even more lawless methods of ridding the countryside of this monster who disembowelled the sick and suffering, severed limbs, and robbed people of their rights.

Mr. Meek's inquiries elicited that the doctor had performed certain surgical operations in some cases of accidental injury, which the neglect of sanitary precautions had rendered necessary. An operation for appendicitis had resulted in death through bad nursing and failure to carry out instructions. The women of a zemindar's household had fed his son on solids too soon after the removal of his appendix, which act of ignorance and disobedience had produced inflammation, agony, and death. The doctor was regarded as his murderer, and evil looks followed him whenever he passed that way.

"What butchery!" one had afterwards exclaimed at a council of five called to discuss the enormity of the doctor's conduct and his growing record of outrages upon humanity. "To extract a portion of the intestines was madness and murder, for who can exist without intestines as God made them?—and his effrontery to put the blame upon the women who in the tenderness of their hearts had fed the youth on *dhal* and rice for the restoration of his strength — *ai Khodar*! What harm was there ever in plain *dhal* and rice? It was but an excuse, and now there is Gunesh Prosad without a son to inherit his estate, and all because of this man who is sent among us to cut up human bodies while they are yet alive!"

"It is a great danger to us. Someone must teach this *Sarcari* butcher of human flesh a lesson, or where might it not end?" another had remarked in complete sympathy.

"But," put in a third cautiously, fearful of making himself unpopular by repeating the tale with which he was fit to burst, "didst hear of that legend concerning the coolie of Panipara *busti* who went forth as a beater for the hunt, the time the Collector Sahib and others took long spears and killed wild boars? He was gored, and lay on the grass disembowelled, and as one dead. Quickly on hearing of the accident came the doctor Sahib in his *hawa-ghari*, himself at the wheel, and leaping out he knelt on the grass, and in a twinkling with strange gloves, and water in a *gumla*[15], he washed the coolie's intestines and restored them where they belonged, after which with a needle, even as a *darzi* sews garments, he stitched up the wound! Those watching turned sick of stomach, but not so the doctor Sahib. Even the Collector Sahib turned his back and called for a glass of spirits. *Ai— Ma!*—how he did it was a miracle, but the man is at the hospital in the Station, recovering, and these are true words; on the head of my eldest born I swear I have repeated it just as it was told to me."

"It is a fable; believe it not. More likely he is dead and his body already cremated."

"Not so. I was told I could see him, if I willed, with mine own eyes. Many have journeyed to the Station so that they might with their own eyes behold him. The doctor Sahib may be unfeeling, even bloodthirsty, but he is devil-possessed with cunning to work magic."

"Even so, he is a danger and should be removed. Who knows what excuse he might take to use the knife on thee and me and the little ones of our households? *Tobah!* he is a wolf, not a man. And this one the *Sarcar* has sent among us to mutilate, kill, and rob us of our comforts and rights. Soon, he will take away the *jhil* from Panipara *busti* so that the people will be put to the labour of dragging water out of deep wells, and for the washing of their garments, they will have to walk many *kos* to the river!"

Mr. Meek had learned a great deal more from his converts of the sayings of the villagers and their feeling against Captain Dalton, all of which Mrs. Meek recounted to Honor in order that she might put the doctor on his guard. The latter, however, gave her no opportunity to speak to him, so she left it to Joyce to tell him of his growing unpopularity.

This Joyce did on one of their outings in the Rolls-Royce and only succeeded in bringing a smile of amusement to the doctor's lips. He had no apprehensions whatever for his safety and the subject, therefore, was speedily forgotten. Joyce

[15] Earthen receptacle.

learned how to drive, and one afternoon in December had the supreme satisfaction of motoring out to camp and back again in the doctor's car. Her pleasure in his surprise was so childlike and exuberant that Meredith had not the heart to show his disapproval of the means by which she had attained this end, and smothered his own feelings that they should not damp her spirits.

"It was very charming indeed of him to spare so much of his time to you," he said with reference to the doctor's tutelage. "But why should he take all that trouble, do you think?"

"Because he likes me, of course," she replied ingenuously. "People don't usually do things for those for whom they care nothing," she said perching on his knee and lighting his cigarette for him. Her engaging impulses of affection were most disarming to Meredith's suspicions.

"But—suppose I object to his liking you to such a remarkable extent?" he said with admirable self-control.

"But why should you? Aren't you glad?"

"Devil a bit! I am wondering whether or not I should consider it an impertinence, the way he places his leisure at your disposal."

"But you yourself say I am the Bara Memsahib of the Station. Isn't it expected of the men to show me plenty of respect and heaps of attention? You wouldn't like to see me left out in the cold?"

"So long as they remember the 'respect'——"

"Ah, now you're talking!" she said severely. "Have I ever done anything to make you doubt my right to the respect of everyone here?"

Meredith kissed away the frown, considerably lighter of heart than he had been for some time. No man looking into the sweet pure eyes could fail to respect her! A fellow would indeed be a rascal if he tried to lead such a perfect lamb astray!

So the drives continued even after the lessons were no longer necessary, Joyce often at the wheel with Captain Dalton beside her keeping strict watch over their safety and that of the car which he particularly valued, while listening idly to her prattle. The curve of her cheek and sweep of her eyelashes delighted his artistic love of beauty, so that though he had plumbed the shallow depths of her mind at the start, he was still entertained by such superficialities as artlessness and loveliness.

"When are you going to show me the ruins?" she asked once, when in full view of the tall minarets and crumbling dome of the ancient palace. "No one seems to have sufficient interest in them to show them to me."

"There is nothing much to see beyond jungle and brick-work," he said, bored at the bare idea of plodding over the ground he had already visited, which was interesting only to globe-trotters and lovers of antiquities.

"I am crazy to see some of the old enamel still to be found on the bricks if you look for it. They say it is a lost art. Are there any snakes and leopards?"

"Possibly snakes, but no leopards. They were gotten rid of long ago, I am told."

Joyce shuddered. "The thought of snakes gives me the creeps. Isn't it possible to see the place and yet avoid snakes?" she asked longingly. She looked so pretty that he relented.

"If we are careful the snakes won't trouble us. I'll take you there some day when I have a long afternoon to spare."

At this Joyce was delighted and gave him her sweetest smiles. "If it were not for you, I don't know how I should exist in Muktiarbad!" she cooed.

"Your husband would not like to hear you say that!" he remarked studying her curiously.

"He has to be away so much that I might have died of *ennui* if you hadn't taken pity on me!" she pouted.

Dalton was not ready with pretty speeches; it involved too much effort to make up insincerities, but he acknowledged that the drives had given him a great deal of pleasure. It was so difficult to rouse him to enthusiasm, and he was so complacently cynical, that Joyce took a delight in probing his silences and getting at his thoughts.

"Don't you ever really enjoy yourself?" she roguishly asked, her head on one side and arch mischief in her eyes.

"I've just said so, haven't I?"

"But you don't mean it. I wish I could understand you and all there is behind that grudging smile—what you think of people—me, for instance."

"I think if I were an artist I should like to paint a picture of you—you are so amazingly good to look at," he returned daringly.

Joyce coloured. She had asked for frankness and could not quarrel with him for having answered her bluntly. On the whole she was rather pleased, than otherwise, that he should admire her, for where was the use of being pretty if one's friends did not show that they appreciated the fact. So she beamed on him wholly unconscious of flirting and rallied him still further on his reserve.

"I don't want to be your model, but your friend. You treat me too much as a child and never give me any confidence. Today, after all these months, what do I know of you?"

"You know at least that I am very much at your service. Isn't that so?"

"You are very kind—and all that, but friends talk openly to each other. I know nothing of you, and I *do* know everything you could say would be so interesting," she sighed. "For instance, why are you never really happy?"

"I have forgotten the way," he said coolly. "Perhaps I have learned too much of life and have lost interest in it. You don't laugh when you can't see the joke, do you?"

"No."

"Nor do I. I see no joke in life worth enjoying, so I have forgotten what pleasure is."

"Can't you tell me all about it?" She pleaded.

"It's an ugly story and not for your ears. But it played the devil with me for good and all," said he grimly.

"I am so sorry," she cried sincerely shocked and grieved. "I thought you must have had a bad time to look and act as you do. Poor you!" and one small hand rested for a moment on his. It was immediately captured and held close.

"Why should you care?" he asked, his expression curiously hardening.

"Because I like you so much."

"Only *like*?" he asked with a short, unpleasant laugh.

The necessity to avoid a goat tethered by the roadside prevented her from replying; Joyce recovered her hand for the steering-wheel and they discussed the narrow escape of the goat. To Joyce it was very flattering, this unbending to her alone of all in the Station, and the growth and development of their friendship. Some day she would learn what had "played the devil" with him for good and all. On the whole he was really quite a dear.

Meredith chafed during his week-ends at the Bara Koti when it became apparent how much his wife depended on the doctor for companionship; and now that Honor was supposed to have taken a dislike to the latter and to avoid encounters with him on their doorstep, there was little help for it. The only advantage to himself to be derived from the entertainment Joyce found in the doctor's society, was her healthier condition of mind and no further insistence on a passage home for herself and the child in the spring. He had a firm faith in her virtue and goodness, and applied himself to his winter programme with feverish haste that he might be at liberty to return to her the sooner and personally take over the care of her before her innocent partiality for the Civil Surgeon became common talk. That it was innocent he would have staked his life.

Honor Bright was less sanguine, though intensely loyal. The increasing intimacy between Joyce and the doctor weighed heavily on her; and it made her rage inwardly to hear her friend discussed openly at the Club by a clique that usually looked on at the tennis. While serving her smart over-hand strokes, scraps of conversation would float to her, demoralising her play and rousing in her a fierce inclination to speak her mind.

"Where is Mrs. Meredith this evening?" a voice was heard to ask on one occasion.

"Joy-riding as usual with Captain Dalton," from Mrs. Fox venomously. "It will be interesting to watch the result when Mr. Meredith awakes to what's going on."

"What's going on?"

"The doctor is a 'dark horse.' You don't suppose he would waste so much of his valuable time if he did not hope to get some entertainment out of Mrs. Meredith? She is such a coquette." This from Mrs. Fox, maliciously.

"She's a simple little thing," said the first speaker charitably. "I shouldn't imagine there was any harm in her."

"'Still waters run deep,'" quoted Mrs. Fox.

"There is another instructive proverb I could quote," cried Honor striking savagely at a ball.

"And what is that?" from Mrs. Fox.

"About 'glass houses and stones.'"

"If that is meant for me, thanks, awfully! But so many panes have already been broken, that I am most indifferent to stones," Mrs. Fox returned languidly as she smiled on the company, who laughed in embarrassment.

"So it would appear," murmured Mrs. Ironsides to a friend.

"Hateful creature!" Honor snapped in Tommy's ear as he handed her a ball.

Jack, playing on the other side with Mr. Ironsides for his partner, had deteriorated so much of late that Tommy and Honor, who had both a genuine regard for him, were much exercised in mind.

He had lost his frank look and easy good-humour; was rarely to be seen at the Club without Mrs. Fox, whom he usually drove down in a side car attached to his motor cycle, a recent purchase,—and was no longer the same man. A constraint had arisen between him and his chum who poured out his fears to Honor in the hope of receiving advice and comfort, but he had succeeded only in alarming her.

"Can't anything be done to save him, Tommy?"

"I can't think of anything, unless Meredith gets him transferred at once."

"But who's to suggest that?"

"His wife, I should think; otherwise some day there might be an unholy row. Fox is no fool. I dare say he is biding his time. He was fond of Bobby Smart and got him out of this while there was time, but he may prefer to sacrifice Jack."

"How terrible!" Honor was sincerely afraid for Jack. He was too young to be mixed up in such a bad business, and Mrs. Fox was clever enough to play him like a fish till he was landed.

Honor walked home at dusk escorted as far as her door by Tommy. It was her intention to call on Joyce after dinner with a proposition concerning the transfer of Jack from Muktiarbad. It seemed the only thing left to do. Incidentally, she would repeat her warnings to her friend concerning herself, for which she expected no thanks. Still, it had galled her badly listening to the coarse remarks of Station people at the Club. She would speak, however disagreeable the task.

At nine o'clock when she reached the Bara Koti she discovered that Joyce was not in. Usually, she returned from her drive at dusk, but as she had not done so up to that late hour, the Collector's servants had come to the conclusion that she was dining at a neighbour's in the happy-go-lucky way that sahibs took "pot-luck" at one another's houses without reference to their domestics.

It was odd in Mrs. Meredith's case, for never before had she failed to return to her baby that she might tuck him into his little cot herself and see that all was right. The ayah was not a little perturbed, but did not voice her feelings until speaking to Honor, fearing that they were foolish and unfounded. What did the Miss-sahib think?

Honor did not know what to say. The more she thought of it the less likely did it seem that Joyce would dine out without coming home to change into dinner things and kiss her precious infant good-night. She decided to return home at once and ask what her parents thought about it.

This she did without loss of time, and Mr. and Mrs. Bright took a grave view of circumstance.

"The car has either broken down somewhere, or they have met with an accident," said Mr. Bright.

Mrs. Bright maintained a stiff reserve.

The thought of an accident caused Honor's knees to give way beneath her and she collapsed into a chair. "How shall we know? Supposing they don't return—?" The bare idea was intolerable.

"I have never liked these constant motorings in her husband's absence. Mrs. Meredith is very foolish to court gossip in the way she is doing. Presently there will be a scandal," said Mrs. Bright shortly.

"Joyce is not a flirt, Mother."

"She goes far enough to earn the reputation of one, however innocent she may be."

Honor knew it was the truth and was silent with an indefinable dread. Was Joyce altogether safe with Captain Dalton?—Should he fall in love and grow intensely attracted by her beauty and childlike charm, was he the sort to consider morality and the law? Was he strictly an honourable man? None knew him; none trusted him; not even Ray Meredith who was afraid to betray his jealousy and incur his wife's resentment; or why had he said: "Take care of my wife—she is such a kid?"

"What had best be done?" she asked anxiously.

"We had better beat up the Station and see what has happened," said Mr. Bright, rising to put his suggestion into effect. "She might be stupid enough to be dining with the doctor at his bungalow."

"Oh, never!" said Honor indignantly. "She is not so foolish as all that!" A hot flush surged over her face at the idea. Joyce dining with the doctor at his bungalow, *alone*! It was too preposterous, yet—was it? She was "such a kid," and might be foolish enough to dare any folly so long as she felt sure of herself and the purity of her own intentions.

But the pain at Honor's heart was out of all proportion to her concern at Joyce Meredith's indiscretion.

She tortured herself imagining the possible scene in Dalton's dining-room—Joyce at dinner, *tête-à-tête* with Captain Dalton!—on familiar terms with the man who rarely condescended to be agreeable to others! It was a picture inconceivably hurtful.

"You had better lose no time, Dad. If you find her—anywhere—tell her that her servants are alarmed—the ayah particularly. I shall see her in the morning," she said, resolutely shutting out the vision conjured up by imagination.

If Joyce were not dining somewhere, there must have been an accident, in which case they would have to send out search parties.

She watched her father leave in the dogcart and wondered what the upshot would be, her mind restless with forebodings.

It was fully an hour later that Mr. Bright returned home to report that Captain Dalton and Mrs. Meredith were nowhere to be found. Dalton's servants were waiting to serve him with dinner, and were growing anxious as his habits were usually automatic and punctual. He so far considered them that they were always informed of his plans. If he intended to dine out they were given liberty to spend the evening with their friends in the bazaar. As it was clear that something unusual had happened, Mr. Bright had called round on Tommy and a search was already in progress. Jack had taken the Sombari road on his motor cycle and Tommy had taken the main road in an opposite direction. It was more than possible that the car had broken down somewhere, in which case the stranded ones would probably find a bullock-cart to bring them ingloriously home.

Honor hung about on the verandah for news till midnight, and was almost speechless with alarm when both boys appeared, one after the other to report the failure of their quest. The car was nowhere to be seen.

To add to the difficulty, clouds which had gathered in the evening had discharged smart showers of rain at intervals, as is familiar to Bengal about Christmas time, and not a trace of wheel-marks could be discovered on the road.

By morning the excitement had spread all over the Station. Inquiries poured in on the Brights. The subject of Mrs. Meredith's disappearance with the doctor was discussed at every *chota hazri* table with and without sympathy, and even in the bazaar it was passed along from one to another. The Collector's memsahib had gone off with the doctor, leaving her little child to the tender mercies of an ayah! Alack! even to the homes of the mighty came shame and dishonour through a woman! And all through the European custom of giving women so much liberty! On the whole, the "black man" knew best how to protect his honour and his home!

Meanwhile, a mounted messenger had gone at great speed to inform the Collector, who arrived by midday looking dazed and ill from the shock. It was pitiful to see how helpless he had become in the face of such an appalling tragedy as the complete disappearance of his wife. Telegrams to various stations on the line had brought no information; mounted policemen had returned without having discovered a clue. The car had vanished with its occupants, though all who knew Joyce intimately, knew that she would cheerfully have given her life rather than have abandoned her child.

"One can scarcely believe that she has eloped," Mrs. Bright said to Honor. "She is so wrapped up in the child."

"Someone would have seen the car," said her husband. "It is an unaccountable thing."

Joyce eloped!—it was unthinkable.

Honor, who from anxiety, had not slept all night, mounted her bicycle and rode out into the fresh and brilliant sunlight on a forlorn hope. An idea had come to her as an inspiration which, though unlikely, was not an impossibility. In the search for the missing ones, every road in the District was being scoured without success. Since the rain had obliterated all tracks there had been nothing to guide any one in the quest, and nothing had been gleaned from villagers. No one had seen the familiar two-seater after it had passed the boundaries of the Mission, which was a circumstance as mysterious as it was unaccountable, for it must have gone somewhere.

Why not off the road? Not a soul had conceived it likely that Captain Dalton would have risked his fine machine over the bumpy side-tracks that formed short-cuts in various directions, notably one to the ruins which Joyce had often expressed a wish to see. They were not difficult of access by motor-car, although the road to them was almost covered by weeds and undergrowth. Supposing that the doctor had yielded to persuasion and taken Joyce to see the old Mogul Palace, and supposing that they had subsequently met with an accident, their plight might be truly pitiable. Very few natives found it necessary to travel by the jungle path so long disused, for the Government having constructed metalled highways in all directions, travellers had ceased to travel uncomfortably even if the old path was a short-cut between villages. Occasionally woodmen in search of timber prowled around the ancient pile and jackals gathered in packs to howl their grievances to the moon; otherwise, a stray tourist on a visit to the Station or a winter picnic party were the only visitors to the gaping halls and crumbling arches.

Just where the unused and overgrown track left the Sombari Road, Honor stepped off her bicycle and searched the ground again for a clue without success. None was to be found in the slush and puddles of the uneven way.

Nothing daunted, she led her bicycle over the ruts towards the jungle in which the palace lay buried, its dome and minarets visible through the tangled tree-tops. It was not easy going on foot, much less could it have been for a motor-car; moreover, Honor was not at all sure she liked venturing on her visit of exploration alone, but all who were capable of continuing the search were already occupied in its prosecution in different parts of the District, and there was no one she could have asked to keep her company.

It was when Honor came to shadowed glades where the undergrowth almost hid the track and obstructed her progress, that she found the first clue—snapped twigs and branches bent backward. These suggested the passage of a cumbrous body on wheels, for sodden leaves were pressed into the wet earth and creepers which had barred the way had been torn and flung on the path.

If it had been Captain Dalton's car, why had it not returned? Honor's heart grew sick with fear.

She pressed on. Presently, she came upon the car itself, beneath overhanging boughs and a dense entanglement of bamboos. It had been saturated by the rain, the hood lay back, and an empty luncheon basket lay open on the seat.

Evidently, they had left the car with the full intention of returning to it immediately, and were prevented by some unforeseen calamity. Honor quivered with alarm and misgiving. Where were they if not in the palace—killed, or injured and unable to help themselves?

Her mind flew to wild animals.

Though it had been a long accepted legend that tigers and leopards had been driven out of the neighbourhood, and had not been seen for years within a radius of twenty to thirty miles, it was still possible that a stray leopard or tiger had lately found a refuge in the neglected precincts of the ruins.

Honor was unarmed and terribly afraid. The fate that had overtaken her friends might easily be hers a few steps further. Prudence and self-preservation dictated immediate flight and a call for a search-party. At the same time, having come so far it seemed her duty to continue till she was convinced that she could do no more. There was the possibility that Captain Dalton had met with an accident and Joyce, unable to leave him, was in dire need of help. Honor felt she would cease to respect herself forever if she deserted her friends at the moment of their greatest need.

She hesitated no further, but stumbled forward over the uneven ground, desperately anxious and frightened, yet nerved to face any danger.

Another bend of the track brought the palace into view—a dark conglomerate pile of crumbling masonry which looked frowningly down upon her, its walls weather-beaten and scarred by time, and with rank vegetation sprouting from every crack. A pipal tree flourished aloft above its dome, its roots buried in the concrete and clinging to the walls; while festoons of wild convolvulus hung in profusion from the lower branches.

Moisture still dripped from the leaves, and the earth was sodden underfoot. Lofty arches yawned in the sunlight and a silence as of the grave reigned, broken only by an occasional caw from an inquisitive crow, or the intermittent chattering of apes.

Again Honor came upon signs of forcible penetration—wild creepers torn aside to make a path, and jungle hacked out of the way; no easy task. Her friends had evidently been determined not to accept defeat in their effort to reach the interior of the ruin.

It was a year since Honor had visited the spot and it seemed to her that the shape of the building had changed. One wing had partially collapsed; whether recently, or some months ago, she could not tell, but it did not look quite the same. Here and there, boulders of freshly fallen masonry strewed the path. There was no doubt that the edifice was slowly falling to pieces.

Raising her hands to her lips, she gave a loud, Australian *"coo-ee!"* and listened while its echo called back to her....

Was it an echo?

Honor held her breath to listen, and heard it again—a man's voice calling—"Hulloa!—*coo-ee!*"

CHAPTER XIV

THE INDISCRETION

Joyce had started out on her motor ride with the doctor as happy as a child on a holiday. Her baby was well and there was no cause for anxiety; in fact, all the world seemed smiling and kind. At last she was learning that a short absence from home made no difference to an infant in the care of so capable a nurse as her Madrassi ayah, trained in the way of infants by the remarkable "Barnes-Memsahib."

All things considered, there seemed no earthly reason why she should not be happy with the light-heartedness of youth helped by a kind friend to pass the time agreeably while she remained in India. In the spring — —

But she would not look ahead. Why borrow trouble? When the hot, March winds began to blow, Ray himself would recognise the necessity of sending the little one home. No father could be so selfish as to allow his own son and heir to fade away under his own eyes, and neglect the only chance of saving his little life. As to the hills! — the innumerable infantile diseases incurred in the hills owing to the dampness of the climate made life a constant terror. No! It would have to be Home in March. Passages were usually booked long beforehand but people often dropped out at the last, and a passage for a "lady and infant" could easily be found at the eleventh hour.

Meanwhile, this was December, and she was capable of enjoying herself amazingly in circumstances that were innocent and harmless.

With a friend like Captain Dalton at her service, so to speak, and Honor to love her almost as a sister would, she was very lucky and could afford to be as happy as the season would permit.

Station gossip whispered that Dalton would not have spared so much of his precious time unless he were receiving some return by way of compensation; which was a logical deduction in estimating a masculine nature not governed by religious scruples; but with this Joyce was hardly concerned, having little comprehension of all that gossips implied. She was delighted to requite so much self-sacrifice on the doctor's part with all the geniality she could command.

As a matter of fact, Captain Dalton was finding a cynical amusement in the study of this — to him — new type of feminine creature: a married woman with the mind of a child, unawakened as yet to the deeper emotions, in whom the instincts of sex were still asleep. He was quite sure that, like most pretty women, she was vain and easily led, and, if it were not himself, it would be some other fellow who would undertake her awakening, since her husband was trustingly content to leave her mental development to chance and nature.

Having passed the stage of desperate infatuation for mere physical beauty, he could play at his leisure with the idea of encompassing her ruin, as he sat beside her in his car, watching the dimples come and go. Life had done him a bad turn at the beginning of his career, and he was envious of men who had escaped suffering such as he had known. Out of sheer devilry he would like to pull Meredith's house about his ears and teach him that no woman of extraordinary physical attractions was a safe asset as a wife. Sooner or later, vanity would be her undoing and she would join the ranks of the fast and free. His experience was fairly wide and his faith, *nil*. Already Joyce Meredith coquetted delightfully. In a little while she would be doing it dangerously; by and by, audaciously, and so on, till she developed into the accomplished flirt, the sport of men in the East. He had watched the evolution till he had arrived at the theory that, with time and opportunity, the generality of women could be brought to capitulate.

This afternoon they had set out with the intention of visiting the ruins, taking with them a rug and a tea basket for a *tête-à-tête* picnic. At first Dalton had thought of leaving the car on the high road and walking the rest of the way, but on second thoughts he decided to risk the tires and springs over the bumpy ground, forcing a passage through the obstacles in the way. Remembering the nature of the jungle, he came prepared with the necessary implements for hacking a passage through, so that he was enabled to take the car much farther than he had at first thought possible. After they had partaken of refreshment under the drooping boughs of a great banyan tree, with a screen of bamboos on the west sheltering them from the afternoon sun, they proceeded on foot to the ruins, he carrying the rug in case she should need to rest.

"How fairy-like and lovely it all is!" cried Joyce clinging to his arm and picking her way among the dead leaves. The speckled sunlight dancing through the leaves, the spreading branches overhead, the graceful foliage of the tropical vegetation, the beautiful birds, made the spot peculiarly fascinating. "It gives one such a sense of isolation," she added.

"We are completely isolated," he returned. "Hardly a soul comes this way. Some months ago when I wandered down here, a native who was chopping wood said the place was haunted, for which reason the people give it a wide berth."

"Haunted!" exclaimed Joyce fearfully, as she crept closer to his side.

"The natives are terribly superstitious and easily scared. The devil is said to be in possession of the palace, and ill-luck or disaster to overtake any who enter it. Are you nervous?"

"Not if you are not. You see, I have such immense faith in you," she said with charming flattery.

"Then we'll brave the fellow together." He hacked at the creepers and tore them aside, and having cleared a path, drew her towards the gloomy walls visible through gaps in the foliage. It was a friendly little hand that nestled confidingly in his. "These wild convolvuli grow with such amazing rapidity, that in a month of rainy weather the whole path is blocked. If you were put to sleep in the ruin by a wave of the devil's wand, the creepers would make a wall and shut you in, like the princess in the fairy tale. How would you like to sleep here for a hundred years walled in by creepers as high as the tree-tops?"

"And be awakened by a splendid prince?" she laughed, entering into the spirit of his raillery.

"I can picture him tearing his way through with the instinct to kiss you, so as to learn the true meaning of Life! You don't need enchantment to turn you into the Sleeping Beauty; you are that now. It would be interesting to see what would happen were the Prince to arrive."

"He arrived when I met Ray," she said colouring richly.

"You think he did, but that was in your dreams. You are not awake yet, so your experience has yet to come." He avoided her eyes while he spoke and left her puzzled to follow his thought.

"I cannot understand you. Why should you say I am asleep?"

"Because it is written in your eyes."

"Then I am a somnambulist?" she laughed.

"Yes. A dangerous one," and they laughed together.

"Who is going to wake me?" she coquetted with a pretty drooping of her lashes.

Dalton stole a look at her pouting lips, thinking he would defer the reply to her question for a while. She put him in mind of a child consciously playing with fire, yet expecting to escape unscorched. Of course, she would have to learn her mistake. She knew perfectly that nine out of ten men would be on fire with passion for her under such intimate circumstances, and reveal the fact without loss of time; she was not quite so sound asleep as not to be aware of her own beauty and its spell, yet she dared to experiment on men and rouse their emotions. Let her, then, take the consequences!

Soon, Joyce found herself in front of the ruined palace, standing on higher ground, its dome and minarets visible for miles in a setting of dense foliage and drooping palms. It had been built in the sixteenth century for heathen worship, and subsequently converted by a Mohammedan grandee into a residence for his own accommodation and that of his harem. To Joyce it looked an irregular mass of ruined masonry, roofless in parts and overgrown with jungle. The portion which had been reserved to the women formed a separate wing which at one time had been enclosed by a high wall, but which was now reduced to mounds of fallen brick-work and shattered concrete. "The place looks almost as though it had suffered bombardment," she said, "how desolate and weird!"

"I could tell you a romance connected with that wing which savours of the *Arabian Nights*," said Dalton. "Want to hear it?"

"How do you know so much more about it than any one else?" she asked, accompanying him gingerly over the fallen masonry to gain a better view of the harem. All around them the undergrowth was dense and matted; date-palms reared themselves from thickets and mingled their drooping branches with tamarind trees, the prickly *babul*, and the wild *jamun*[16].

"I make it my business to know all about every place I live in," he returned.

"Tell me the romance," she commanded.

Dalton spread the rug on a grassy mound, and when they had seated themselves, he began his tale in true Oriental fashion, with a charm of style that captured her fancy.

"Once upon a time, when the land belonged to those who could hold it by the sword, a rich Nawab built himself a costly residence out of a heathen temple. Behold the residence!"—with a wave of his hand. "And with him dwelt his retinue and his sycophants, his child-wife, and the women who contributed to her needs and his pleasures.

"Alas, for masculine confidence! In a moment of weakness, this great prince took into his service a young warrior of Rajputana as the chief of his bodyguard—a Hindu by religion and of exclusive caste—because of his great strength and the beauty of his youth and person. This one, tradition tells, conceived a burning passion for the favourite wife of his master, having seen her face by chance, unveiled, at the bars that protected her window;—a girl of extreme loveliness, and as slender as a wand, whom custom prevented from disclosing her features to the eyes of men who were not her near relatives. She had therefore been closely guarded within the harem walls in company with other women of her lord's establishment, and left to find entertainment for herself in the priceless jewels that adorned her person.

"Every day the Rajput, by name Ramjitsu Singh, would pass and repass below the high wall that enclosed the women's quarters, hoping again to see, by favour of the gods, this beauteous vision whose wondrous charms were the talk of the bazaars; their fame having been spread by her female attendants. Small was she, they said, with eyes like a gazelle's, and lips of the redness of ripe berries. Her hands and her feet were the hands and feet of a babe, so slender were they, and soft; and the hair of her head could have robed her.

"One day, the Rajput's patience was rewarded by a sight of the beautiful face which made his senses swim as in a sea of delight. She stood again, unveiled, at the bars of her window, and gazed down at him with great sadness and yearning. Like a bird in its cage she looked upon the free world with longing, and sighed. The foolish one!—The faithless one!"

"How can you call her foolish and faithless?" Joyce interrupted indignantly.

"That is how the Indian story-teller speaks of her."

"It was only natural. Think of her youth and the conditions to which she was

---

[16] Indian blackberry.

obliged to conform!"

"Well, see what happened. Are you interested?"

"I am thrilled. Go on!"

"Thereafter, the Rajput neither ate nor slept till he had devised a plan for carrying her away; for what are laws to lovers? or bolts and bars? Neither caste nor creed can hold a man back whose soul is on fire for a woman." He paused to allow his words to take effect.

"How very romantic!" laughed Joyce, unmoved. "It is like a poem, as unreal as it is picturesque!"

"Don't you believe a man's soul can be aflame with love and desire for a woman?" he asked, picking up a stone idly and flinging it after a disturbing crow.

"Books tell one so, but how am I to know?"

"It must have been proved to you times without number!—but I said you were asleep!" he remarked with his inscrutable smile. "Know, then, that men have cheerfully risked hell for a woman's favours. They have broken every law for the transcendent bliss of lovers' kisses!—Anyhow, that's not the story.

"To proceed: Poor old Ramjitsu was ready to dare or die for his Love, as many another man has been since the world began, and will continue to be while the world lasts. Every night, when darkness covered the land, and the people within and without the palace slept, Ramjitsu Singh would climb the wall by means of a stout bamboo, and clinging to the sill, would wait for the gods to grant him the opportunity to plead his love.

"At last, one night, attracted by the silvery radiance of the moon, she came to the grating to gaze without, and hearing a quivering sigh, she turned and beheld her gallant lover. He looked like a god himself in the bright moonlight, and the words of his mouth, uttered with breathless passion, held her spellbound. With her flower-face pressed to the bars she received his caresses."

"Oh, poor little thing!" cried Joyce, her breath hurried with sympathy. "Did she love him, too?"

"She must have, in that moment, for nature at such times speaks loudly to youth. Listening to his impassioned vows, she, who was of a different religion, as apart from his as the East is from the West, was willing to place her destiny in his hands. Human nature, you will see, is stronger than caste or creed, and tradition is brought to naught by romance and passion.

"One night, when all seemingly slept, Ramjitsu, who had from time to time cautiously loosened the iron bars in their sockets, removed them altogether and received in his arms the form he coveted. Conceive that thrilling moment of ecstasy! Suddenly, however, a lightning stroke from a sword descended upon the faithless one from within, and she was slain in her lover's arms. The weight of her falling body, thus violently flung forward, unbalanced the Rajput whose foothold at the best was precarious, and together they were hurled to the paved court below, Ramjitsu breaking his neck in the fall.

"So ended the love story of the Palace—a tragedy which has remained an everlasting tribute to love, and serves as an example to the Indians of a just vengeance on the unfaithful. The spies of the Nawab had betrayed the young wife and her lover, and the husband had punished them both with death."

"Just vengeance!" repeated Joyce scornfully. "A brutal murder, I call it."

"The Mohammedans speak of it with pride."

Joyce brushed away the tears and laughed hysterically. "It is a horribly tragic tale and I wish you had not told me of it, for the memory of it will haunt me."

"Why do you mind?"

"I can't help feeling for that poor little prisoner who wanted to be loved and was killed! They had probably married her off as a little child to the Nawab whom she afterwards learned to hate."

"You wish she had escaped with the Rajput? That would have violated every law of their religion and tradition." He watched her keenly.

She looked distressed. "Why are laws so hard and fast? These poor women! Can they never choose for themselves who they will marry?"

"Never. Among Eastern races marriages are always arranged. So you don't condemn the Rajput for wanting to steal her?"

"Oh, no. How could he help it?"

"Or her for wanting to run away with him?"

"Not for *wanting* to run away. But laws have to be kept, I suppose, or no homes would be safe. Individuals have to be sacrificed to communities," she said thoughtfully. "Show me where it all happened."

He rose, and taking her by the hand, helped her to her feet, after which they passed together through a gap in the wall which led to a room on the ground floor from where a winding, brick stairway took them to the apartments above. Each step had to be carefully negotiated because of the mortar crumbling under foot, and the loosened bricks that threatened an accident. Presently, they were in a narrow corridor into which slits or loop-holes admitted the daylight. An arch at the far end from which the door had long since vanished, introduced them to a series of chambers, one leading into another. The walls were black with cobwebs and the dust of ages, while the concrete flooring was strewn with the *débris* of fallen plaster. Heavy cracks in the roof let in shafts of the fading daylight, and roots of weeds and pipal trees had penetrated and hung below. On the whole it was anything but a desirable spot in which to linger, but Joyce's desire to view the interior of the romantic chamber had to be satisfied.

"This is supposed to be the room, and that the window. You can see the holes in which the iron bars must at one time have been embedded. The story goes on to tell of great calamities befalling the fortunes of the Nawab; of battles fought in the neighbourhood between Hindus and Mohammedans, and the immediate withdrawal of the Moslems to another part of Bengal. Now let us get out. I am not at all sure the place is safe."

"Let me first take a souvenir!" she pleaded. An enamelled brick above the arch had attracted her eye. Its design and colouring were still fresh and clear despite the ages that had passed since it was fashioned. "Look at it!" she coaxed. "Isn't it wonderful? You would think it had come straight out of a jeweller's shop. How did they learn such work in those far-off days?"

"Italian workmen were known to have been imported by wealthy princes for the decoration of their temples and homes."

"Can't I have it?"

"Quite out of reach," he answered, stretching an arm upward.

"But I might try to punch it out with your knife, if you put me on your shoulder."

Dalton was sure that no effort of hers would dislodge the brick; moreover, he was doubtful of the wisdom of the experiment, considering its position in the arch; but the blue eyes lifted to his were undeniably bewitching, and the suggested method of the operation, too much of a temptation to be resisted. He would let her try till she admitted failure: the impulse to grant her the moon if she demanded it was strong at the moment, so he gave her his knife and without much effort hoisted her to his shoulder and allowed her to dig at will into the arch. Her delicate fingers would soon tire of forcing the brick from its solid bed. He, therefore, held her securely and closed his eyes not to be blinded by the fine dust that showered over them both.

"Look out!" he warned her once, when the sound of falling mortar was heavier than he had anticipated. "Don't bring the place about our ears."

"I don't want to be buried alive!" she replied. "It isn't as difficult as I imagined. See, it is already loosening."

But he could not look up out of regard for his sight. For a moment he had no actual concern with the work she was engaged upon, having allowed himself to suffer distraction. With his arms about her, his face at her waist, he was assailed with the temptation to bring matters between them to a crisis. He was done with philandering and desired to end her folly and his patience. What was easier than to draw her down to his breast that he might cover her tempting lips with kisses? Though he was not in love with Joyce after the manner of Ramjitsu, her mouth was alluringly sweet, and her possible response to his passion would reward his daring. There was the novelty, too, of acting the Prince Charming to her rôle of Sleeping Beauty; for her woman's nature was asleep and waiting only to be startled into comprehension. All the afternoon he had played with the idea till his desire for possession had mastered prudence. What right had she to imagine him a bloodless being, as passionless as a stone? He was a man, and a very human one at that. He would prove that to her without delay. What a fool he had been to have wasted so much time! He would kiss her till he infected her with his passion; which would not be difficult if she were like those of her sex who traded on a husband's trust and confidence!

The glamour of the moment intoxicated his senses: contact with her person, the perfume of her, her complete helplessness in that retired spot, assisted to turn him temporarily insane.

Just as desire was about to master reason and self-restraint, a shriek of terror from Joyce paralysed his nerves and suspended thought.

The arch, already heavily cracked and depending solely for stability upon structural pressure, being further weakened by the dislodgment of that particular brick, showed signs of collapsing.

On looking upward, Dalton saw their danger and had time only to spring backward to a far corner of the room before the arch subsided, bringing with it a portion of the roof. He stood stock still with Joyce clinging to his neck, watching the building crashing about him. The shock and vibration of the fall had brought about the collapse of precarious parts of the ruined edifice, till, roar followed roar, and the air was thick with dust.

Dalton momentarily expected the shaking floor to give way beneath their feet, or the roof to descend upon them and bury them alive. It was something to remember all his life: his impotence to help himself or his companion in the midst of the calamity, while believing himself face to face with the horror of a slow death by entombment.

After a while, when all was still and the dust began to settle, the spectacle disclosed to view beggared description.

Tons of material lay between them and the stairs up which they had come; the window was buried behind a dense mass of fallen bricks and mortar; a great hole torn in the roof showed the sky overcast with clouds. Possibly there would shortly be rain to add to their misfortune.

How was it possible to extricate themselves from their terrible predicament? Dalton cast his eyes about him towards an inner chamber, only to see that the roof there had also collapsed barricading the only other outlet.

In the midst of his anxieties he had to soothe the girl's fears. Joyce was shivering with terror and nearly speechless.

"Pull yourself together," he said shortly. "It is a devilish catastrophe, but we must face it. Just as well we are not killed!" He endeavoured to unclasp her clinging arms, but she only clung the closer.

"Oh, I am so frightened!—don't leave me!" she whimpered.

"I am not going to leave you," he said reassuringly, "but I must take a good look around." Releasing the rug from beneath a weight of *débris*, he induced her to sit down while he made a careful survey of the conditions of their prison, for that it undoubtedly was. They were as completely shut out from the outer world and as helpless as prisoners in a dungeon. Both rooms were isolated from the rest of the building; both were partially roofless and without means of exit.

Gad!—what a commotion there would be in the Station when it was discovered that they had not returned! Dalton wished with all his heart that he had left his car on the high road and not brought it into the wood. Who would think of looking for it there?

He was partly comforted by the thought of the wheel-marks left in the dust, but this source of hope was cut off when the rain began to descend later in the night.

In the meantime he had to make the best of the situation and not allow Mrs. Meredith to fret.

"You have to thank a special Providence interested in your fate that you are not buried alive," he told her cheerfully.

"And so have you," she said solemnly.

"Providence doesn't usually bother much about me; relations have long been strained. Possibly I have been preserved for your sake," he laughed.

"How can you talk in that irreverent way!" she said reproachfully.

"Sorry, if it offends you."

But Joyce fell to weeping. Was it possible that they would ever be found?— they would die of starvation—and what about her baby?

Dalton had much ado to allay all her fears. When it was discovered that they were missing, did she suppose that a stone would be left unturned to trace them? She was to cheer up and show how brave she could be.

"I am not like Honor Bright," she sobbed. "I cannot face such a horrible prospect as a night spent in this ghastly place all among snakes and creeping things!"

The mention of Honor seemed to silence the doctor completely. For some time he was moody and depressed; Joyce was allowed to weep into her hands till exhausted.

Only when it was getting dismally dark did he arouse himself from his abstraction and take up again the task of cheering her.

"Can't we dig ourselves out?" Joyce asked before the darkness descended wholly upon them.

"Without implements of any sort?" Even the knife was lost in the confusion, and in any case it would have been utterly useless.

"Do you think they are sure to find us?"

"I am confident of it—in the morning. It will be too late and dark for them to think of looking here tonight, but in the morning someone is sure to find the car and discover our whereabouts."

"How hungry we shall be!" she sighed, and Dalton laughed.

"How thirsty we shall be, is more to the point!—Poor child!" taking her hand in his and recalling how near he had been to madness. He was not too far from it even now with her hand resting confidingly in his, and the consciousness of their unique position.

"Anyhow, there is the sky and fresh air, and at least we are not quite alone. I have you!" she said with dangerous flattery.

"Yes. You have me," he returned eagerly. "And I—have—*you!*"

"What about snakes?" she asked, casting her eyes about her fearfully.

"They are more upset than we. At any rate, I don't believe we'll be troubled by snakes tonight. You will have to forget we are lost, so to speak, and talk till you are tired, and then try to sleep."

"Sleep—here?"

"On the rug."

"I couldn't. It is so uncomfortable!"

In the growing darkness, he was again mastered by the evil thoughts which had possessed him in the moments preceding the catastrophe. Their isolation produced a host of ungoverned impulses. As the evening advanced his manner changed, growing suggestive of possession; his manner became more tender.

"You will always remember tonight!—there will never be another like it in your life," he whispered, leaning towards her and stealing her hand. "You have been horribly frightened, haven't you?"

"I am more hopeful now, thinking of the morning," she returned, her soft breath on his cheek. "It is only the snakes I fear!"

Dalton drew her into his arms. "I shan't let you think of snakes, you pretty little thing! At last I have you close. You have tantalised me with your loveliness every day, till Fate has given you to me!" his lips found hers and pressed them roughly. "Wake up, sleeping Princess! see, this night is ours. Let me love you as I want to. Let me teach you how to love!"

Joyce seemed paralysed in his arms. She lay as still as death under his kisses as though mesmerised and dreaming. Emboldened by her silence Dalton continued to caress her with increasing ardour, till Joyce, coming suddenly to her senses, was seized with panic and horror.

"Who are you?" she cried in a frenzy of fear, struggling to escape. It seemed she was entrapped by some human monster in the doctor's likeness, against whom she was powerless to struggle.

"Why do you ask? You know me well—don't be foolish! Won't you let me love you?"

"Love me?—like this?—Do you forget I am married?" she gasped, still struggling to escape. "Let me go. I hate you for daring to touch me—to kiss me. I hate you! How dare you do it!" Joyce had never known such terrifying moments, even worse than when the building seemed falling about her ears. The horrors of the night were multiplying a thousandfold, now that the doctor had failed her and gone mad.

Dalton made several efforts to pacify her, thinking he had only to deal with a phase of childishness, but found her unmistakably determined to break away from him.

"Stop it, and listen to me," he said angrily. "You want it all your own way, but it is my turn now. Why did you lead me on and tempt me, if you meant to back out in the end? I could have kissed you twenty times, but refrained for reasons you would not understand. Now when those reasons are finally swept aside and I am ready to be your lover, you pretend to be surprised."

"Surprised! I am horrified! I thought so well of you—I believed you would respect me, not treat me as you might—Mrs. Fox for instance! Let me go, you coward and bully!—I have trusted you and treated you as a brother—for this?—you unspeakable cad!"

Dalton released her instantly, and she burst into tears, crying as though her heart would break. "Honor warned me, but I would not listen!" he heard her say amid her sobs.

"What did Honor warn you about?" he asked sternly.

"She said," Joyce sobbed, "to go 'easy with my favours'—that you were 'a man—like most——'"

"Did Honor say that? and why?"

"Because—she thought I was being foolish to—to become so—friendly—with you—when I am a married woman. She was right! I have been a fool!" A fresh outburst of weeping.

"Did she say that because of her contempt for me, or because you are a wife?" he pressed.

"I—don't know. All I know is that she was right and I should have listened to her warning; now I shall never, never respect myself again."

"I see no reason why you shouldn't," said Dalton, a sense of humour overcoming his wrath. "You've done nothing but tell me in polite language to go to the devil."

"You kissed me!"

"What of it? Many women in your position are kissed, and they are in no wise cast down," he laughed sardonically.

"I feel degraded—I feel unfit to kiss my own, dear little baby again!"

"You should have thought of all that when you were so anxious to charm me," he returned cruelly.

"You are a beast, and the most hateful man I know!" She made an attempt in the gloom to crawl away to some distance from him and his rug, but he ordered her to stay where she was, adding,

"I shan't trouble you again. You have nothing to fear from me."

"I don't want to share the same rug!—I wish I was a mile away!"

"The rug has done you no harm. If you prefer it, I'll shift off it. The best thing you can do is to go to sleep."

"I couldn't with this sin on my conscience."

"What sin?" he asked repressing his impatience with difficulty.

"This sin against my husband."

"You have committed none. If my kissing you was a sin, mine is the conscience to be troubled; but it was slain quite a long time ago," he added with a short laugh.

"I am not joking," she said angrily. "How do you suppose I can face my husband knowing that I have behaved so as to make another man kiss me?" What a child she seemed!

There was no doubting her distress, and Dalton exhausted every argument in his attempt to understand her attitude of mind. "What do you want me to do?" he asked finally. "If an apology is of any use, I apologise humbly for behaving as I did. I grant you, I am a perfect specimen of a cad. If it will do you any good, tell your husband all about it when you get back, and send him round to give me a horse-whipping. I promise I shall not injure a hair of his head."

"He is much more likely to shoot you."

"Even so. He is perfectly welcome to. I am not in love with my life. Only let him do it by stealth so that they don't hang him afterwards."

Joyce cried again hopelessly, till Dalton felt himself a sort of criminal.

"Please don't! I cannot tell you how sorry I am to have upset you so. I had no idea you would take it like this. There are so many women who— —"

"Like Mrs. Fox?" she interrupted scornfully.

"Perhaps. I don't know much of Mrs. Fox. She doesn't appeal to me."

"You couldn't offer me a worse insult than to think that I might be like her!"

"I am sorry. Forgive me, will you?"

"I cannot forgive myself for my blindness and folly!"

Joyce spoke as though she were shivering, and Dalton was stricken with concern. "You are cold?" he asked anxiously.

Her teeth chattered. In December the nights in Bengal are often bitter, and Joyce had left her driving cloak in the car. Dalton immediately divested himself of his coat and made her wear it. His manner having returned to the professional, she was no longer afraid of him, so obeyed meekly.

"Now the rug," said he. And she was wrapped to her ears in the rug, after which he left her to herself for the night. Both listened to the patter of the rain as it fell on the *débris* around them, and, eventually overcome with fatigue, Joyce dropped off to sleep.

CHAPTER XV

THE AFTERMATH

In the early morning, Joyce realised that she was both hungry and thirsty. Her lips were parched, her throat dry, nothing having passed them since early tea the previous afternoon, and she was at the lowest ebb of despondency and depression. Her surroundings helped to increase her misery, for the ground was a mixture of puddle and slush, and there seemed no chance of help anywhere. She seemed to have fallen into a deep crater, and but for a projection of roof that still held firm owing to a network of pipal roots, she would have been as drenched as the bricks and mortar with which she was surrounded.

To add to her alarm, she was all alone. Captain Dalton was nowhere to be seen.

Though he had behaved horribly the evening before, he had not troubled her since; the tramp of his feet as he paced up and down the circumscribed space that was left to them of the chamber, being the only evidence she had till she dropped off to sleep that she was not without company. But with the daylight he was gone, and feeling almost panic-stricken with ghostly fears and loneliness, she called aloud to him.

"Captain Dalton!"

"I'm here," his voice cheerily announced as he emerged from the inner room which had suffered an equal amount of damage. "See what the gods have sent you!" and he handed her a pipal-leaf cup, full of water to drink.

It was eagerly seized and gratefully drunk. "Where did you get it from?"

"That other room is full of branches torn from the roof when it fell in," he returned. "I discovered them by the light of a match and amused myself making cups out of the leaves by the light of a few more. They don't hold much, but I managed to set a good few to catch the rain drops as they fell, and that's better than nothing."

"Have you had any?" she asked politely.

"I was waiting for you, but I'll take a drink now." He retired and did not return till she called him again.

"I wish you would take your coat. You must be so chilled," she ventured. "The rug will do for me."

"Are you quite sure?" he asked and Joyce noticed that his hands were blue with cold. After putting on his coat he was about to retire again when she stopped him wistfully. "Please stay—I feel so frightened alone."

"I thought you preferred not to have me around," he said dropping down beside her.

For answer she wept into her arms as they rested on her knees.

"I was beastly, last night, wasn't I—poor little kid," he said in gentler tones than she had ever heard from him. "Can't you have it in your heart to forgive me?—just wipe it out as though it had never happened?"

"I can forgive you, but—I—could never wipe it out. I feel so degraded. It is like having an ugly stain on a page you had always wanted to keep clean."

Dalton studied her as something entirely new to his experience. "I have never in my life met anyone like you. It has been an eye-opener to a man like me. I didn't understand you all this time. I am just beginning to, now. Tell me frankly your idea."

"It is nothing extraordinary," she said drying her eyes. "It is only that I did not believe a gentleman could treat a decent married girl as you did me. I wanted to be like brother and sister, and I thought you understood. Anything else never entered my head as possible to self-respecting people."

"And I have spoilt all your pretty illusions!—let down my sex too, rather badly! What don't I deserve! It would relieve my feelings if you slanged me for all you are worth. Believe me, you have done no wrong. It is only that I see things crookedly, and am just what you called me, an 'unspeakable cad.' I should have respected your helplessness. Truly, I deserve to be shot."

"I *have* been very silly, I don't care what you say. But I never can remember I am grown up!" she said pathetically. "Honor told me that people would talk, but I did not believe they had any cause. Now I realise what they are thinking! and it breaks my heart. They will believe I am like Mrs. Fox. She does things that look bad, and people despise her. Now they will despise me."

"Never! they have only to look at you and hear you speak, to see what you are."

"Honor said it was not enough to be good but to avoid doing the things that make people think we are not. Now they are thinking perhaps that I flirt with you and let you kiss me!" Her face was suffused with crimson shame. Nothing was so horrible to contemplate as the fact that he had kissed her! She was stripped of self-respect forever.

Dalton might have been tempted to smile at her self-accusing attitude had it not been for her perfect sincerity. He felt overcome with contrition and longed to atone.

"You make me infinitely ashamed," he said humbly. "Perhaps if you knew what went towards making me such a brute-beast, you would feel just a little sorry for me and understand—even bring yourself to like me a little bit as you say you once did. I have never had a sister. It might have made a difference if I had." After a pause—"Some years ago there were two persons in whom I believed as—I believe—in God. One was a woman and the other, my dearest pal. He and I were like brothers. I would have trusted him with my life. I did more. I trusted him with my honour." A pause. "And he whom I trusted and loved, robbed me of all that made life dear to me, and of what I valued more than life. And the woman I loved and believed pure and true, conspired with him to betray my honour! I was their dupe. A blind confiding fool!"

"Oh!" was wrung sympathetically from Joyce.

"When I found out all I went mad, I think. I have been pretty mad—and bad—ever since; but at the time, if I could have laid hands on both I might have ended my career on the gallows. But Fate intervened. He was killed in a railway accident shortly afterwards, and a year later, she came whining to me for forgiveness."

"Did you forgive her?"

Dalton's eyes glowed with cruelty and an undying contempt. "Forgive her? Not if she had been dying! There are things impossible to forgive. She had killed my soul, destroyed my faith in human nature—which others, since, have not helped to restore!—turned me into a very devil, and without an incentive to live. Do you think I could forgive her? If I hated her then, I loathe the very memory of her now."

"Yet you tried your best to make me one of the same sort?" Joyce asked wonderingly.

"I did not believe, till you proved it to me, that women are of any other sort," he replied.

"You forget Honor Bright?"

"I never forget Honor Bright," he replied unexpectedly. "I have looked upon her as the exception that proves the rule."

"Your mother?" Joyce interposed gently.

"My father divorced her," he said harshly. "So you see I have had rather a bad education!"

"I am very sorry for you."

"You are?—that's good. Then there is hope for me."

"I am sorry that you should have such a contempt for women, owing to your unfortunate experience."

"I owe you an eternal debt of gratitude for teaching me what an egotistical jackass I have been."

"Tell me," she asked, suddenly waking up to their dust-laden condition, "am I covered with smuts and grime?"

Dalton surveyed her quizzically. "You are covered from head to foot, like a miller, with fine white dust."

"So are you!" and they laughed together for the first time since the calamity.

"Let's wash, there's a pool in the next room. Quite a respectable amount of clean water is collected about the floor."

He showed her the pool and left her to make her toilet while he explored their prison for some possibility of escape. Putting his hands to his mouth he sent forth stentorian cries for help with no result. Without a pick-axe to work with, he saw no chance of cutting a way through the tons of material that lay around them.

It was midday, when Joyce was feeling weak with hunger, and Dalton fighting a strong tendency to pessimism, that he heard Honor's "*Coo-ee!*" and replied.

"Thank God!—at last here's someone to the rescue!" he exclaimed, and Joyce burst into tears.

When Honor was able to locate the spot from which the answering voice proceeded, she contrived with difficulty to get near enough to the opening to hear what had happened. It was good to know, however terrible had been the experience of the pair, that both were unhurt, and that Joyce was bearing up wonderfully.

"I shall run back and get help at once, cheer up!" she called out.

"We don't, either of us, feel cheerful, I can assure you. It has been ghastly here all night," the doctor shouted back.

"But it is great to have found you! I am so thankful," and she sped to her bicycle and travelled at top speed to the Mission. Mr. Meek could provide the labour at a moment's notice for the work of digging out the imprisoned couple, and to him she went direct.

Immediately the Settlement hummed with activities; coolies swarmed to the spot with pickaxes and spades, crowbars and ropes, and as news flies from village to village with almost the rapidity of "wireless," hundreds of natives gathered at the scene to view operations, the women with infants astride one hip, and naked children swarming around. They camped on the ground chewing *pan* and parched rice, and chattered incessantly of the mysterious workings of Providence, the folly of humanity, and the decrees of Fate.

The bare-footed, semi-nude rescuers, climbed over the face of the ruins with complete disregard of life and limb, and with wary tread and light touch, began the work of removing the *débris*.

In due course, the rescue was effected, and Joyce was assisted to climb out of the wrecked chamber to safety. Honor half-supported her to the car which Captain Dalton drove in silence to the Bara Koti. His eyes avoided Honor's and in manner he was quiet and constrained.

"So you never got the souvenir after all!" she said to Joyce when she had heard a disjointed account of the catastrophe.

"I should have hated to look at it again, if I had," was the hysterical reply. "I shan't want to pass this road again, or get a glimpse of that terrible place as long as I live. I hate India more than ever, and Ray must send me home at once. Otherwise, I shall live in dread of some other calamity befalling either Baby or me. Oh, Honor, persuade him to let me go!"

By the time she was put to bed she was suffering from nervous prostration. Meredith, who had returned from his fruitless search, looked like a man walking in his sleep. His wife had clung to his neck in passionate relief, but she had avoided his lips as she had never done before, and a sword seemed to have entered his heart.

"Oh, I am so glad to be back!" she kept repeating, with her babe pressed to her bosom.

"Memsahib habbing one great fright!" commiserated the ayah.

Silent and stunned, Meredith hovered about the room. He had uttered no word of reproach to his wife for her imprudence,—she had suffered enough, mentally and physically; but resentment was fierce within him towards the doctor. The impulse to walk round and horse-whip him for having had the impudence to lead his foolish, but adored girl-wife into such a scrape, was well-nigh unconquerable, and he refrained only for fear that scandalous tongues would give the unhappy event a sinister character.

"Kiss me, Sweet," he once whispered, leaning over her in passionate anxiety. He wanted to look deep into her eyes; not to see them fall away from his with a shrinking expression foreign to them.

Joyce offered her cheek.

"Your lips," he commanded.

But Joyce fell to weeping broken-heartedly. Meredith kissed her cheek with a pain at his heart, and turned away.

"Won't you tell me everything?" he asked another time, studying her intently. Normally, he imagined she would have babbled childishly of all her experiences, and have been insatiable in her demands for petting. Why did she seem crushed and silent as to details? Honor had said the shock would account for her shaken and hysterical state; but it did not explain her strange aloofness.

"You know it all," Joyce returned listlessly, the tears springing to her eyes at his first question as to the experience she had undergone.

"I know the barest outline—and that from Honor Bright. You wanted a particular stone for a souvenir, and in digging it out, the arch collapsed, which brought down a large bit of the roof and a lot more besides. What happened after that? How did you manage to spend the night? It must have been horrible!"

"Some day I may be able to talk about it, but not now," she cried with quivering lips. "It is cruel to question me now."

Meredith leaned back in despair. "I hope Dalton was properly careful of you?" he asked, devoured with jealousy.

"He gave me his coat and his rug, and made cups out of pipal leaves to catch the raindrops as they fell. We were so thirsty," she said monotonously.

"Rather a brainy idea!"

"Please don't recall all that to me. I don't want to think of it!" she cried; and that was all Meredith could learn of the events of that night.

The following day it was discovered that the doctor was suffering from a feverish chill and was confined to bed. By nightfall, it was reported by Jack who had been to visit him, that he was in a high fever, and that the Railway doctor had been called in by the Civil Hospital Assistant for a consultation.

The next day it was known that Captain Dalton was seriously ill with pneumonia; a *locum* arrived from headquarters, nurses were telegraphed for, and for some days his life hung in the balance.

Joyce, who still kept her bed with shaken nerves, incapable of interesting herself in her usual pursuits, was startled out of her lethargy at the news. "If he dies, it will be my fault," she cried. "Oh, Honor! I was so cold that he gave me his coat as well as the rug, and did without them himself till morning. He must have taken a chill, for he looked so bad in the dawn."

"He did what any other decent man would have done in his place."

"It was rather surprising of him, considering how fiercely we quarrelled!" and feeling the need of confession, she poured out the whole story of her shame into her friend's ears. "Even now I grow hot with humiliation when I think of it! I cannot understand why he did it, for it was not as if he had fallen in love! Only because he thought I was a—a—flirt, like others he had known."

Honor's face was very white as she listened, silent and stricken.

"I just had to tell you, dear, or the load of it on my mind would have killed me. I feel as if I were guilty of a crime against Ray; and, poor darling, he does not understand what is wrong!"

"Why don't you tell him and get it over? He loves you enough to make the telling easy. And if you love him enough, why, it can only end happily," said Honor with an effort.

"There would be a tragedy!—I dare not. Ray would kill him for having dared to insult me like that! You have no idea of what I have been through! Captain Dalton said I was asleep and needed awakening! I have awakened in right earnest and know that I have been a wicked fool. How I long to be loved and forgiven! Oh, Honor! when Ray looks at me so anxiously and lovingly, I just want to be allowed to cry my heart out in his arms and confess everything; but I simply cannot, with this dread of consequences. Nor can I make up to him with this wretched thing on my conscience! Why didn't I listen to you!"

"There is not much use in crying over spilt milk, is there? The best thing you can do is to bury it and be everything to your husband that he wishes. You must try to atone. If you love him——"

"I do! There is no other man in the world so much to me. I did not realise how much I cared till Captain Dalton made me, by his outrageous behaviour! I am not fit for Ray's love after knowing how I have lowered myself!"

"You will not mend matters by creating a misunderstanding between yourself and your husband. What is he to think if you continue to shrink from his caresses?"

"He will think I don't care at all, and that is so untrue!"

"Can't you see that, with your own hand, you are building up a barrier between you which will be difficult to pull down at will?"

"When I am able to tell him all about it, he will understand. At present I feel shamed and degraded. I feel myself a cheat! I, whom he believes a good and virtuous wife, have actually been kissed by a man who thought I was the sort to permit an intrigue! Don't you see, that if I behaved as though nothing wrong had happened, I would be putting myself on a par with Judas?"

Having wrought herself up to the point of hysteria, she was not to be reasoned with.

"How I wish I had never set foot in that dreadful place! It seems, after all, that the devil is really in possession of it, and that disaster overtakes people who enter there."

"Disaster invariably overtakes people who give the devil his chance," said Honor unable to resist a smile.

"I dare say you are right. I have been very foolish, for I had no idea of the sort of man I was growing so intimate with. But he was truly sorry, and tried afterwards in a hundred ways to show how he regretted his behaviour. Indeed, I think, on the whole, he received quite a good moral lesson for thinking most women are without any conscience," and Joyce proceeded to relate the sequel of her story, which involved that of the doctor's past.

"It is a most painful history," said Honor gravely.

"And he has never known home-life; his mother was a wicked woman, and was divorced!"

"How pitiful!"

"It quite accounts,—doesn't it?—for his badness?"

"I don't think he is at all bad," Honor said unexpectedly. "He's been badly hit and wants to hit back; that's about what it is. To him women are all alike"—

"Not you!—he said you were, to his mind, the 'exception that proves the rule.'" Joyce interrupted.

Honor coloured as she continued,—"And he has very little respect for the sex. He requires to meet with some good, wholesome examples to set him right, poor fellow!"

"He thinks the world of you, Honey!"

"Does he?" with an embarrassed laugh. "Then he takes a queer way of showing it."

"That was your fault. You turned him down over Elsie Meek's case, and he was too proud to plead for himself. But I have watched him, Honey, and there isn't a thing you say or do he misses, when you and he are in the same room."

"Your imagination!" Honor said uncomfortably. "You forget he has just been trying to make love to you!"

"True. But he has never been *in love* with me. It was sheer devilment. Even I could tell that. Love is such a different thing. Ray loves me. There is no mistaking it, for it is in his eyes all the time, and proved in a thousand ways."

"Did Captain Dalton say much more about that girl who jilted him?" Honor asked with embarrassment. Joyce had failed to grasp the full significance of Dalton's unhappy experience, and Honor had accordingly derived a wrong impression.

"Only that he loathes her now. That she killed his soul!—which is absurd, seeing that the soul is immortal."

"It can therefore be resurrected."

How, and in which way, Honor had not the slightest idea, but her heart instead of recoiling from the sinner after all she had heard, warmed with sympathy towards him. She could not help a feeling of pity and tolerance for the unfortunate victim of deception who through disillusionment and wounded pride, had gone astray.

When Honor returned home, it was to hear that her mother had gone over to the doctor's bungalow to nurse the patient till professional nurses should arrive; and had left word that her daughter should follow her.

"We have to do our 'duty to our neighbour' no matter how much we may disapprove of him and as no one in the Station is capable of tending the sick with patience and intelligence, I must do it with your help."

So Honor superintended the making of beef-tea for the sick-room, fetched and carried, ran messages, and made herself generally useful, much to Tommy's disgust. It was hateful to him that a man so generally disliked as the Civil Surgeon, should be tenderly cared for by the women he had systematically slighted.

"I don't see it at all," he grumbled to Honor when he caught her on the road on her way home for dinner. "Surely his servants could do what is necessary till the nurses arrive?"

"The least little neglect might cost him his life, Tommy."

"It wouldn't be your fault. For weeks the fellow has not gone near your people."

"Would you have us punish him for that by letting him die of neglect?"

"It is no business of mine, of course."

Honor quite agreed with him, but softened her reproof with a demand for his help. "At any rate, it is everyone's duty to lend a helping hand in times of trouble. We want a message sent to the doctor-*babu* at the government dispensary, and it is a mercy I have met you." She gave him a list of the things required by the local Railway doctor who was in charge of the case, and Tommy cycled away, obliged to content himself with the joy of serving her whenever and wherever possible.

That evening, while Honor was left on guard at Dalton's bedside to see that he made no attempt in his delirium to rise, she experienced a sudden sinking of the heart in the thought that he might die.

He was very ill.... Pneumonia was one of the most deadly diseases. As yet there was no means of knowing how it would go with him. With gnawing anxiety she watched his flushed face and closed eyes and the rapid rise and fall of his chest. How strong and well-built he was! and yet he lay as weak and helpless as a child.

The thought that he might die was intolerable. It gave her a sense of wild protest, a desire to fight with all power of her mind and will against such a dire possibility. He must not die till he had recovered his faith in human nature, his belief in womanhood. If there were any truth in the New Philosophy he would not die if her determination could sustain him, and help him over the crisis.

"Honey...?" the sick man muttered. His eyes had unclosed and were looking full at her.

"Yes?" she replied, trembling from head to foot with startled surprise at hearing him speak her name.

"Have they let you come at last?" he asked in weak tones.

"They sent for me to help," she returned gently.

"Was it because I wanted you so much? My soul has been crying out for you. There is only one face I see in my dreams, and it is yours. You will not leave me?" he asked breathlessly.

"I will stay as long as they let me," she said kneeling at the bedside that she might not miss a syllable that fell from his lips.

"How did you know that I loved you all the time?"

"I did not know." Surely it was wrong for him to speak when he was so ill? yet she longed to hear more. Every word thrilled her through and through.

"Ever since that day—you remember?—when you came to me for help in your danger and suspense; when I saw into that brave, staunch heart of yours, and, for the first time, knew a true woman!" His face was alight with emotion. It was transformed.

"Oh, hush!—you must not talk."

"Yes. I am horribly ill," he panted. "It is ghastly being tucked up like this, unable to get up. But it is worth while if you will stay with me." A pause while he frowned, chasing a thought. "What was I saying? My mind is so confused."

"It does not matter, I understand."

He caught her hand and pressed it to his burning lips, then laid the cool palm against his rough, unshaven cheek.

"If I have longed for anything it is for this—to hold your hand—so—to feel that you'd care just a little bit whether I lived or died—nobody else does on this wide earth!"

"I care a very great deal," she said brokenly. "So much, that I beg of you not to talk. It must hurt."

"Every breath is pain. If I give a shout you must not mind. It is a relief sometimes. Pleurisy is devilish. They told you, I suppose, I have that as well? If I don't pull through— —"

"Stop! You shall not say that. You *will* get well. I know it. I am sure of it," she said. "Try to rest and sleep."

"I shall try, if you say you love me."

"I *love* you," Honor said with fervour. It did not matter to her that he might presently be rambling and forget all about her and his fevered dreams of her. It was the truth that she loved him, and she spoke from her heart.

He did not seem to hear her, for, already his thoughts wandered. "I keep thinking and dreaming the wildest things and get horribly mixed," he said frowning and puzzled. "Was I buried for days and nights in the ruins—with someone? then how is it I am here?"

"You were buried for one night with Mrs. Meredith, and you were both rescued in the morning."

His eyes contracted suddenly. "A pretty little creature—dear little thing!— brainless, but beautiful. One could be almost fond of her if she did not bore one to tears!" He turned painfully on his side and Honor placed a pillow under his shoulders. "Ah, that's easier!—thanks, nurse," he said mechanically. "Tears?... What about tears? Ah, Mrs. Meredith's tears. She cried almost as much as the rain, poor kid! and we were nearly washed out—like 'Alice,'" and he laughed huskily, forgetful that he was again in possession of Honor's hand which he held in a vice. "I am a damned fool to have tried it on with her. Beastly low-down trick," he muttered almost inaudibly. "'You unspeakable cad!' she said, and, by God! I deserved it. I should have known that she was not the sort to play that rotten game. Ah, well! it is only another item on the debit side of the ledger!" His eyes closed and he drifted into unconsciousness. Honor's hand slipped from his hold and she rose to her knees, choked with grief and longing. Oh, for the right to nurse him tenderly! "Oh, God! give him to me!" she cried in frenzied prayer.

Dalton did not recognise her again after that, and the next morning Mrs. Bright handed over the case to the nurses from Calcutta.

CHAPTER XVI
CORNERED

When Joyce made her final plea to be sent home to her people without waiting for the spring, it met with little opposition. Meredith had come to the point of almost welcoming a break in the impossible deadlock at which his domestic life had arrived. His beloved one's nerves had broken down from one cause and another, and she was drifting into the habits of a confirmed invalid. If he did not let her go, he would, perhaps, have to stand aside and watch her increasing intimacy with the doctor whom he could not challenge without creating a disgusting scandal; which would make life in Bengal intolerable for himself as well as for her. So he agreed to her departure with the child in the hope that "absence would make her heart grow fonder," and that she would come back to him, restored, when the cold season returned and made life in India not only tolerable, but pleasant.

Hurried arrangements were put through, a passage secured, and Joyce roused herself to bid her friends a formal farewell.

At the Brights', only Honor was at home, her mother having driven to the bazaar for muslin to make new curtains. Christmas was approaching and a general "spring cleaning" was in full swing in order that everything should look fresh for the season.

"It is the greatest day in the year, and even the natives expect us to honour it. Our festival, you know," Honor explained.

"It always looks so odd to have to celebrate Christmas with a warm sun shining and all the trees in full leaf!" said Joyce. "That is why it never feels Christmas to me. I miss the home aspect,—frost and snow, and landscapes bleak and bare."

"The advantage lies with us. We can calculate on the weather with confidence, and it is so much more comfortable to feel warm. And then everything looks so bright!"

"I am glad you like it since you have to stay. I hate India more than ever."

Honor looked earnestly at her, and wonderingly. "Isn't it rather a wrench to you to leave your husband?" Joyce had grown so apathetic and cold.

For answer her friend broke down completely, and wept as though her heart would break. "We seem to be drifting apart. Oh, Honey, I love him so!"

"Then why go?"

"I must. I want to think things over and recover by myself. I am trying to forget all about that night in the ruins, and hoping for time to put things to rights. Perhaps I shall return quite soon. Perhaps, if the doctor is transferred, I shall find courage to write and tell Ray all about *it*. I am all nerves, sometimes I believe I am ill, for I can't sleep well and have all sorts of horrid dreams about cholera, and snakes, and Baby dying of convulsions! So, you see, a change is what I most need; and I am so homesick for Mother and Kitty! I cry at a word. I start at every sound, and if Baby should fall ill, it would be the last straw."

"But what is to happen when you are away, if, while you are here you feel you are drifting apart?"

"When I am away, he will forget my silly ways and remember only that I am his wife and how much he loves me. He *does* love me, nothing can alter that; but lately I have held aloof from him for reasons I have explained to you, and he is hurt. You may not understand how desperately mean I feel, and how unfit to kiss him and receive his kisses after what has happened. For the life of me I could not keep it up without telling him all. And how could I, when Captain Dalton is convalescent and my husband will have to meet him when he is able to get about again? Already he is talking of going round to chat with him. You see, he does not know!"

Honor was deeply perplexed. "Of course, you must do as you please, but in your place, I would tell him everything, and as he knows how dearly you love him, and only him, he will, I am certain, give up all desire for revenge. At a push, he might ask for a transfer."

Joyce shuddered. "I'd rather leave things to time. Later on, I can tell him all about it, and, perhaps, by then, Captain Dalton will have been transferred. Don't you love me, Honey?"

"Of course I love you."

Joyce flung her arms round Honor's neck and kissed her warmly. "You were looking so cold and disapproving! Take care of Ray for me, will you? and write often to me about him. I shall miss him terribly," and she sobbed unrestrainedly.

When Meredith saw her safely to Bombay, preparatory to her embarkation, he allowed himself to show something of the grief he felt at having to give up for an indefinite time what he most valued on earth. In the seclusion of their room at the hotel, he held her close in his arms and devoured her flower-like face with eyes of hungry passion.

"So, not content with holding yourself aloof from me, you are leaving me to shift for myself, the best way I can!" he said grimly.

Joyce's lips quivered piteously and she hid her face in his shirt-front.

"Has it never occurred to you," he said, "that a man parted too long from his wife, might get used to doing without her altogether?"

Two arms clung closer in protest. "But never you!" she replied with confidence.

"Even I," he said cruelly. He wanted to hurt her since she had walked over him, metaphorically, with hobnailed boots. "India is a land of many temptations."

"But you love me!"

"God knows I do. But I am only a very ordinary human man whose wife prefers to live away from him in a distant land."

"Ray, you are saying that only to be cruel!"

"Because I am beginning to think you have no very real love for me."

"I love you, and no one else!"

"I have seen very little evidence of love, as I understand it. A great many things count with you above me. The child comes first! God knows that I have idolised you. Perhaps this is my punishment! but I worshipped you, and today you are deliberately straining the cord that binds us together. The strands will presently be so weak that they will snap altogether. Then all the splicing afterwards will never restore it to its original strength. It will be a patched-up thing—its perfection gone. Remember, a big breach between husband and wife may be mended—but never again is there restored what has been lost!" He lifted her chin and kissed her cold lips roughly. "When do you mean to return? Can't you suggest an idea of the time?"

"Whenever you can get leave to fetch me," she answered with sobbing breath.

"I swear to God I will not do so!" he broke out. "You may stay as long as you choose. I shall then understand how much I count with you. I refuse to drag back an unwilling wife."

"Oh, Ray! Don't talk like that! Won't you believe that I love you?"

"I would sell my soul to believe it ... to bank all my faith on it!"

"It is true!"

"Prove it now."

"How can I?"

"Let me cancel the passage, and come back with me."

Her face fell. "I could not do that after all the arrangements have been made. Mother will be so disappointed—besides, people will think me mad!"

Meredith released her and turned away, a fury of jealousy at his heart. "Ever since that night at the ruins you have become a changed being. I tried not to think so, but, by God! you have forced me to. One might almost imagine you are running away from Captain Dalton. Is there anything between you?" he asked coming back to face her, white and shaken.

Joyce burst into tears. "I don't understand what you are accusing me of!" she sobbed, panic-stricken.

"Are you in love with that man?"

This was something tangible and Joyce was roused to an outburst of honest indignation. "No!—no! A thousand times, no! How dare you think so! How dare you imply I am lying? I have said I love you, but I shall hate you if you hurt me so!"

Meredith's face lightened as he swung about the room. "It all comes back to the same thing in the end. It is good-bye, maybe, for years!"

Early the next morning, he saw his wife on board with the child and ayah, and then returned to his duties at Muktiarbad, a lonely and heavy-hearted man.

Captain Dalton recovered, was granted sick leave by the Government, and disappeared from the District for a sea trip to Ceylon.

Tommy mentioned the fact to Honor having just learned it from him on the platform of the railway station where he was awaiting the Calcutta express, surrounded with baggage and with servants in attendance. He was looking like a ghost and was in the vilest of tempers; not even having the grace to shake hands on saying good-bye!

Honor turned aside that the boy might not see the disappointment in her face. Her heart was wrung with pain. Not once had Captain Dalton made an effort to see her.

Her father had smoked a cigar with the invalid one evening when he was allowed to sit up on a lounge in his own sitting-room, and had been asked to convey thanks and gratitude to Mrs. Bright for her many kindnesses to the patient in his illness; but there had been no reference to "Miss Bright"; nor did he give any sign that he remembered what had passed between them at his bedside, the one and only time that he had seemed to recognise her and had spoken unforgettable words.

It was cruel; it was humiliating!

Honor had been trying by degrees to teach herself to believe that he had spoken under the influence of delirium. Perhaps he had been thinking of someone else outside her knowledge? But she could not forget how sanely he had recalled the time he had treated her for snake-bite. His words were burned into her brain as with fire—"When you came to me for help in your danger and suspense; when I saw into that brave, staunch heart of yours, and, for the first time, knew a true woman!"

There was no delirium in that!

What did it all mean? If he really loved her, why did he not want her as she wanted him? Why did he treat her with such indifference and wound her to the heart?

There was no answer to her questioning. Captain Dalton was, as always, unaccountable, and Honor lifted her head proudly, and determined to think no more of him. She gave herself up to the arrangements for a happy Christmas, and, for the next week, was the busiest person at Muktiarbad.

Tommy, claiming assistance from his chum, Jack, was ready to draw up a programme for a gala week. There would have to be polo, tennis, and golf tournaments if the residents entered into the spirit of enjoyment and were sporting enough to fill the Station with guests.

"Who do you suppose will care to come to a dead-and-alive hole like this?"

Jack remarked, throwing cold water, to begin with, on his friend's enthusiasms. "It will be a waste of energy especially when they are having a race meeting at Hazrigunge!"

"Even this dead-and-alive hole might be made entertaining if we put our shoulders to the wheel."

"There are not enough of us. You might count the doctor out—he's away. Meredith is no good. His wife's left him for the present and he lives in the jungles with a gun. With half-a-dozen men, one girl, and a host of Mrs. Grundies, you are brave if you think you can manage to engineer a good time. Take my advice, old son, and leave people to spend their time as they please. After all, Christmas is a time for the kiddies; not old stagers like you and me."

Jack's spirits were conspicuously below par, and there had been signs and symptoms of boredom, reminiscent of Bobby Smart whenever he had been seen in company with Mrs. Fox.

"Can't you work up some little interest?" Tommy asked impatiently. "It's beastly selfish of you, to say the least of it."

"I might spend Christmas in town."

"I might have known that. I heard something last night about Mrs. Fox having an invitation to spend Christmas with friends in Calcutta," was the pointed rejoinder.

"Pity you did not think of it before."

"Chuck it, Jack!" said Tommy earnestly, putting a hand affectionately on his friend's shoulder.

"I wish to God I could," was the gloomy reply. "It's so easy to get into trouble, but so devilishly difficult to get out of it again, decently."

"I'd do it indecently, if it comes to that! You think it's 'playing the game' to keep on with an affair of that sort? It's a damned low-down sort of game, anyhow, with no rules to keep; so chuck it before worse happens."

Jack lighted a cigarette deliberately and made no reply. His good-looking, young face was looking lean and thoughtful; he had suddenly changed from boyish youth to *blasé* middle age; the elasticity of his nature was gone; his laugh was rarely heard, and he seemed to keep out of the way of his friends. Even Tommy had ceased to share his confidence. There was a rumour that the Collector had spoken to him like a father and was seriously thinking of having him transferred—a suggestion which had been made by his wife, prompted by Honor. But transfers were not effected in a twinkling, and Jack still remained at Mrs. Fox's beck and call, took her out in his side car, and was often missing of an evening when it was expected of him to turn up at a special gathering of his friends.

In desperation Tommy confided to Honor that Christmas was going to be as dull as Good Friday, as there would be nothing doing. And Honor not to be beaten, collected subscriptions, sent out invitations, and threw herself heartily into the task of organizing a good time.

In the end, Christmas week at Muktiarbad was a season of mild amusement and effortless good-fellowship. A few guests arrived to assist in making merry, and there was no discordant note to jar the harmony of the gatherings.

Jack arrived at the crisis of his life, on Christmas Eve, in Calcutta, when he felt that the invisible bonds threatening to enslave him were suddenly tightened, rendering his escape well-nigh impossible.

He had taken a box at the theatre, from which he and Mrs. Fox watched the "Bandmann Troupe" in their latest success.

"What a mercy we are not staying at the same hotel, Jack," said Mrs. Fox. "It did feel rotten at first, but as it turns out, it will be all for the best, old thing. I have extraordinary news for you."

"You have?—out with it!" he said absently. She had so often surprises on him which generally ended in some new suggestion of intrigue, that he was both unmoved and incurious.

"First tell me how fond you are of me. You haven't said much about it since we came to town."

"We haven't been so very much alone, have we?"

"No, worse luck! but there is no reason why you should not make up for it whenever we are together. You must have heaps of quite charming things to say? In fact, you do love me tremendously, Jack, don't you?" she coaxed.

"I thought I had proved it sufficiently," he said colouring with annoyance while he tried to look amiable.

"You are a darling—like your silly old name which I adore! What a topping world this is! You don't know how much you have altered everything for me. I feel such a kid, and everyone tells me I might be in my teens!" she said with a pitiable attempt to be kittenish.

Jack turned away, sickened by her vain folly, and frowned involuntarily. What an outrageous ass he had been! However, some day he would break away from his chains; only, he must do it decently. Let her down gently, so to speak, as she was so damned dependent on his passion, which had long since died a natural death.

Mrs. Fox snuggled her hand into his. "Say something nice, my Beauty Boy," she wheedled.

Jack squirmed inwardly; nevertheless, to oblige her he admired her gown and called up the ghost of the smile which had once been his special charm.

"How lovely it would be if you and I were husband and wife, Jack?—sitting here, together, in the eyes of all the world?"

"Lovely," echoed Jack, dutifully.

"You would never fail me, dearest, would you? Say, supposing I were, by some miracle, free?"

Knowing that she was securely bound, Jack felt safe in assuring her that he would never dream of failing her. It was his belief that this, and other vows he had unthinkingly made, were impossible of fulfilment in their circumstances.

"What a boy it is!—always so shy of letting himself go. Look at me. I want to see if your eyes are speaking the truth. There is something of importance I have to tell you relating to our two selves and the future."

Jack obeyed, curious and not a little anxious because of the half-suppressed note of excitement she could not keep out of her voice. The shaded lights of the theatre were not too dim to show the fine lines at the corners of her mouth and the obvious effort to supply by art what nature had failed to perpetuate. But the egotism of a woman grown used to her power to charm, dies hard.

Jack's eyes fell nervously before the questioning in hers.

"Tell me, don't you believe we could be very happy together?"

"Why should you doubt me?" he said evasively.

"I don't doubt you, but I want the joy of hearing you say so. To me it is so wonderful,—what is about to happen,—that I am afraid I shall wake up and find it is all a dream!" she said fatuously, gazing with adoration at Jack's fine physique and boyish, handsome face. "You have often feared possibilities, and said you would stand by me if anything went wrong between Barry and myself."

Jack remembered having often said much that had made him hotly uncomfortable to recall afterwards.

"Didn't you, Jack, dear?"

"Of course," he said desperately. "What else do you suppose, unless I am a howling cad?"

"I know you are not, that is why I simply adore you. You are so true, so sincere! My beau ideal of manhood!—--"

"Well, it is like this. Barry has come to the conclusion that it isn't fair to either of us to keep dragging at our chains when we have long ceased to care for each other, so he wrote, yesterday, to tell me that he would put no obstacle in my way if I wished to divorce him. There is someone he is keen on and whom he will marry in due course. I can do the same. He has heard about you—just rumour—but as a woman is always the one to suffer most in a suit for divorce he has most generously suggested that the initiative should come from me. Rather decent of him, what?"

"Tremendously decent," said Jack his heart becoming like lead in his breast. For a moment the lights of the theatre swam; he felt deadly sick and cold, and failed to take in the sense of what she continued to say. In the midst of his mental upheaval the lights mercifully went down and the curtain up, so that much of his emotion passed unnoticed.

"Why Jack!—think of it, we shall be able to marry after it is all finished!—only a few months to wait!"

"Yes," said he with dry lips.

"Try to look as if you are glad!" she teased. "You know you are crazy with delight. It is what we were longing for. Be a little responsive, old dear," she said, giving his hand a squeeze.

Jack returned the pressure, feeling like a trapped creature with no hope of escape. Marriage with Mrs. Barrington Fox had never at any time entered into his calculations. He was too young, to begin with, and certainly did not wish to be tied down to the woman who had played upon his untried passions.

Waves of self-disgust and dread seemed to overwhelm him.

He sat on for the next few minutes seeing nothing, hearing nothing, saying nothing, while he anathematised himself mentally as every kind of a fool, Barrington Fox as a contemptible blackguard, and the woman beside him as something unspeakable. He could not deny his own culpability; but he had felt all along that a nature like his was as wax in such unscrupulous and experienced hands.

He had been weak—yes, damnably weak! that was about the sum and total of it. And he would have to spend the rest of his life in paying for it!

What would the mater say? He thought of her first; the proud and handsome dame who had placed all her hopes on her eldest son—who thought no one good enough to be his wife.

His pater?—and the girls?

He had never associated them in his thoughts with Mrs. Fox, nor dreamed of their meeting even as acquaintances. The contrast was too glaring.

His career?

Well!—the Government did not approve discreditable marriages; but, on the other hand, it did not actively interfere with a Service man's private affairs. A good officer might make his way in spite of an unfortunate marriage. There were worse instances in the "Indian Civil" than his. But he was certain, at any rate, he would be socially done for!

Gradually he had come to realise that all the stories concerning Mrs. Fox must have been true, and that she had been tolerated by society purely on account of her husband—and he was now proved no better than she!

Be that as it may, he saw no way out of his dilemma save by dishonouring his written and spoken word. One was as good as the other and he felt himself hopelessly snared. The lady would have to become his wife, and he would spend the rest of his life dominated by her personality, fettered by her jealous suspicions, and suffering in a thousand other ways, as men suffer, who rashly marry women several years older than themselves.

Mrs. Fox laughed merrily at the comic situation in the performance to give Jack time to recover himself, but her eyes gleamed anxiously.

She was sufficiently woman of the world and quick-witted enough to comprehend the shock to Jack and his consequent stupefaction. But he was young enough for his nature to be played upon, and she was determined not to lose her advantage. She banked all her hopes on his sense of honour, and continued to thank her stars that her luck was "set fair."

CHAPTER XVII
BREAKING BOUNDS

Honor lived in dread of Captain Dalton's return to the Station.

Did he remember anything of what had passed between them in the hour which she had spent at his bedside? Or had he completely forgotten the episode and her confession? She would have been glad to think he had forgotten, for she had brought herself to believe that he had been labouring under the influence of delusions. If it were true that he loved her, his manner would have been very different in the days preceding his illness. True, she had been aloof; but men in love are not usually balked by such trifles as had stood in his way.

No. He had been dreaming.

His fever-stricken brain had been wandering among unrealities, and her face had filled the imagination of the moment. Facts and fancies had intermingled, till they had misled him in his delirium into believing that it was she he loved.

The truth was, she argued to herself, that he loved nobody. It was certain that a woman by her treachery and double dealing had killed his better nature, or drugged it; and his capacity for love and trust had gone. If it were not so, he would have loved Joyce who was beautiful and winning, and have respected her because of her ingenuous innocence. It was a thousand pities that such a strong character had been tricked and perverted!

And now that there was no one to monopolise his leisure moments, it was to be hoped that he would, on his return, confine himself to his music and the treatise he was at work upon. It would be a relief, Honor felt, if he would only continue to keep out of her way; otherwise, life would be intolerable. It was the acme of humiliation to have discovered herself in love with a man who had no need of her whatever! and the sooner she could find something to do outside the District, either in a hospital or in connection with some charitable organisation, the better it would be for her peace of mind and self-respect.

However, when she broached the subject of work away from home, her parents would hear nothing of it.

"Our only child, and not to live with us!" Mrs. Bright exclaimed, horrified. "What is the use of having a daughter if we are to let her leave us—except to be married?"

"I shall never marry. I have no vocation in that line, so should lead some sort of useful life."

"And isn't your life useful? What should I do alone when your father is in camp? If either of us was ill, whom do you think we would look to, but you? Surely, Honey, you are not bored with your own home?"

"Never, Mother dear! I am too happy with you and Dad. But most girls do something now-a-days. It is only that I feel it such a waste of energy to stay at home doing nothing but please myself."

"You have your duty to us, and your 'duty to your neighbour'."

"Which latter consists of meeting him collectively at the Club, helping to amuse him with tennis and golf, and listening to a lot of scandal!"

"My dear! since when have you turned cynical? You are, I am sure, a great comfort to Mrs. Meek; and the families of our servants simply worship you."

"For converting my cast-off garments to their use in winter. My old navy skirt has certainly made an excellent pair of pyjamas for Kareem's young hopeful, and the sweeper's youngster looks like nothing on earth in bloomers and my old golf jersey!"

"The *saice*, too, is delighted with those jackets you turned out from my old red flannel petticoat. The twins are as snug in them as a pair of kittens," laughed Mrs. Bright.

"I want to hear no more of that rot about your wanting work while I am above ground," said Mr. Bright, looking up from his newspaper and regarding his daughter severely. "It will be time enough to let you go when some fellow comes along and wants to carry you off; but to let you go and tinker at other people's jobs is not at all to my liking when you have a home and duties to perform with regard to it."

And that was the end of all argument. Not having a combative nature, nor a taste for debate, Honor adjourned to the store cupboard and gave Kareem the stores for the day.

"Please be obdurate in the matter of the *ghi*[17], Honey," was her mother's parting injunction. "He would swim in it if you allowed him. Two *chattaks* for curry are ample. The dear rascal is not above saving the surplus, if he gets it, and selling it back to me."

"Memsahib's orders" admitted of no palava, and Kareem who was faithful unto death, but not above commercial dishonesty, submitted to the mandate with the air of a martyr. "Whatever I am told, that will I do; but if the food is not to the sahib's liking, I have nothing to say." Having expressed his views on the matter of his restrictions he withdrew with his tray full of stores, a bearded, black-browed ruffian in appearance, clad in a jacket and loin-cloth, but of a character capable of the highest self-sacrifice and devotion.

It was still early enough after her morning's duties were over, for a tramp along the Panipara Jhil for snipe, the sport Honor most enjoyed and at which she was gradually becoming proficient. She would be all alone, that bright January

---

[17] Butter converted into oil by boiling.

day, as Tommy, her faithful and devoted lover, was prevented by his duties from waiting on her.

Jack, too, was at work down at the Courts,—not that he was likely to offer his escort in these days of his unhappy bondage to Mrs. Fox; but Honor's thoughts strayed persistently to him with anxious concern. He had returned from Calcutta after Christmas looking jaded and depressed. Tommy had been unable to make anything of him till, one day, his attention was caught by a paragraph in the *Statesman* concerning an application for a dissolution of marriage from her husband, on the usual grounds, by Mrs. Barrington Fox.

"Good God! a walkover for her!" he exclaimed in consternation. Being full of concern for Jack, he forthwith proceeded with the news to Miss Bright, and they lamented together in bitterness over the young man's impending ruin. "She has played her cards like a sharper, and I have no doubt that that old idiot, Jack, is done for," Tommy observed.

"But why should he marry her?" Honor protested. "Two wrongs don't make a right."

"He feels, I suppose, in honour bound to marry her."

"In honour bound to punish himself by rewarding her dishonesty?"

"He shared it."

"Hers was the greater sin. She tempted him. Think of her age and his, her experience of life and his!—I don't see it!"

"Men have a special code of honour, it seems."

"Tommy, it is a case of kidnapping. Jack's only a foolish, weak boy, deserving of punishment, but it isn't fair that the punishment should be life-long!"

"He is pretty sick of himself, I can vouch for that."

Jack's undoing was a source of depression to Honor Bright, and the question of how to save him was with her continually.

It was a cold day with a pleasant warmth in the sunshine as Honor swung along the roads on foot, her gun under her arm, and a bag of cartridges slung from her shoulder. She was dressed in a Norfolk jacket and short skirt of tweed, with top boots as a protection from snakes, and her free and graceful carriage was a beautiful thing to see. So thought the doctor as he watched her from behind a pillar in his bungalow verandah.

He had returned by the last train the previous night a few days before he was expected, and, as yet, no one besides his servants and the *locum* knew of it.

When Honor had passed he began making hasty preparations to go out. His shot gun was taken down from a rack, examined, cleaned, and oiled afresh; cartridges were dropped into his pocket; thick boots suitable to muddy places were pulled on, accompanied by much impatience and a few swear words.

Would he have the motor? Yes—no! The motor could be taken by a mechanic to a certain point by the Panipara Jhil and left there for his convenience.

In the meantime, Honor tramped through the fields taking all the short cuts she knew, and was soon on the fringe of the grass in complete enjoyment of the wildness of the scene and its solitude. The slanting rays of the morning sun filtering through the trees, cast checkered lights upon the lilies and weeds that floated on the water. Little islands dotted the surface, covered with rushes and date palms, the wild plum, and the *babul*—all growing thickly together. The air was full of the odour of decaying vegetation and the noise of jungle fowl, teal, and duck. The latter could be seen fluttering their pinions among the lotus flowers, and bobbing about on the surface of the water, thoroughly at home in their native element; occasionally a flock would rise and settle again not far from the same spot, vigilant with the instinct of approaching danger. In the far distance, Panipara village could be seen, its dark, thatched roofs seeming to fringe the *jhil* at its farther verge.

Honor filled the breach of her light gun with a couple of No. 8 cartridges, and warily skirted the brink. In places the pools were so shallow that a man might have waded knee deep from island to island; but the soft mud was treacherous, and flat-bottomed canoes were generally hired at Panipara by sportsmen who went duck-shooting. As Honor was after snipe, she kept to the banks and picked her way fearlessly along the tangled paths, her high boots a protection from thorns and snakes.

Birds sang lustily in the trees; the throaty trill of the tufted bulbul sounding inexpressibly sweet,—the thyial, too, like a glorified canary, made music for her by the way.

For nearly an hour Honor wandered over the marshy ground of both banks, often imagining she heard footsteps and rustlings among the long grass that screened the view. The sounds ceased when she paused to listen, so she concluded that her imagination had played her false. At length, just as she was beginning to despair of success, a couple of snipe rose like a flash from almost under her feet, and were gone before she could raise her gun to her shoulder. Immediately she was startled by the sound of a shot fired somewhere in her neighbourhood! She had no idea that any one else was out shooting that morning. She looked around. Beyond a thin veil of smoke hanging over the water, there was nothing to be seen.

Who could it be, but a native *shikari*?—for there were a few in the District licensed to carry firearms, who supplied the residents of the Station with birds for their tables. Satisfied with her theory, she pressed on a little farther and was rewarded by another chance at a snipe. As the bird headed for a clump of bushes, she fired, and simultaneously with her shot there came an involuntary cry—a sharp exclamation of pain, and for a second she was rooted to the spot, forgetting everything but the fear that someone at hand had been hit.

Dropping her gun in the grass, she ran forward in dismay, brushed aside the screen of weeds and jungle, and came face to face with Captain Dalton leaning against the trunk of a tree, holding his wrist.

"Oh!—have I hurt you?" she cried in an intensity of alarm rather than of surprise at finding him there, when she believed him at least some hundreds of miles away.

Dalton never looked at her, nor replied, but releasing his wrist, allowed the blood to drip to the ground from a trivial wound. A stray shot from the many in the cartridge had scratched the skin upon a vein, and the occasion was serving him well.

But out of all proportion to the injury was his pallor and the emotion that swept his face and held him quivering and tongue-tied.

"What can I do?" Honor cried in her distress. The sight of blood was enough to rend her tender heart; and to know that it had been shed by an act of hers, shook her to the foundations of her being.

Dalton produced a handkerchief in silence and passing it to her, allowed her to bandage the wound as well as she could. He was concerned only with watching the beautiful, sunburnt fingers that moved tremblingly to aid him, or the sympathetic face that bent over the task.

When the bandage was completed, their eyes met, and the same moment Honor was in his arms, clasped close to his breast while he murmured his adoration.

"I love you!—my God! how I love you! and I want you so! Oh, my precious little girl!—my Honey—my love!"

Honor asked no questions, but welcomed, with a sob of joy, the gift of love that flooded her heart to overflowing. She clung to his neck with loving abandonment and yielded her lips to his generously. With her great nature, she could do nothing by halves, so gave of her love with no grudging hand.

"Since when have you loved me, my Sweet?" he asked in tones that were music to her ears.

"From the moment you kissed my hand and called me 'brave'!"

"And yet you plunged that dagger in my heart when you said in my hearing—'I have no interest in Captain Dalton'?"

Honor recalled her conversation with Joyce and blushed. "It was not true!" she confessed.

"I deserved it—and more!" he said humbly with suffering in his eyes.

"And when did *you* begin to—care?" she asked shyly.

"From the moment I looked into your eyes at my bungalow, and saw heroism, truth, and purity."

It was sweet hearing, though she was convinced that he exaggerated her qualities. "Why then did you hide it so long?"

"I was fighting the biggest fight of my life."

"And have you won?"

"Won?" he laughed harshly. "No. I have lost, but it's worth it," kissing her defiantly. "Can you guess how much I love you? When I was ill I used to dream of you. I even thought you came to me and said you loved me!"

"I did. I was beside you, but you were delirious with fever, and I was sure afterwards that what you said meant nothing."

"You were there? I often wondered about it, but dared not ask for fear of dis-illusionment. The dream was so dear!"

"And when you recovered, you never tried to see me!"

"I was fighting my big fight which I have lost," he returned recklessly.

"So I tried to teach myself to forget."

"And you couldn't?"

"Oh, no. It was too late!" she sighed happily.

"Blessed fidelity! and now you confess that you love me. Say it!"

"I love you!" A few minutes passed in silence while he demonstrated his transports of delight in true lover fashion.

"When you were angry with me over Elsie Meek's case, I went mad and did a succession of hideous things. How can you love such a monster?"

Honor drew his face closer and laid her cheek to his.

"I hated everybody—I even tried to hate you, but it was impossible. I resented the happiness of other men. I tried my best to break up a man's home after partaking of his hospitality. Do you care to kiss me now?"

Honor kissed him tenderly. "I watched it all with such suffering!"

"You did? God forgive me! Did you know that it is not to my credit that Mrs. Meredith is an honest woman today?"

"I know all about it."

"She told you? I might have known it! Women like Joyce Meredith talk. But she is a good little woman. As for me!—I am unfit to kiss your boot. Even now, I am the greatest blackguard unhung,—the meanest coward, for I cannot bring my-self to renounce my heart's desire!" He held her from him and looked into her face with haggard eyes. "Send me away! Say you will have nothing to do with me!—I shall then trouble you no more."

With a happy laugh Honor flung herself on his breast. "Send you away?—now?" The thing was clearly impossible. And why should she? However wickedly he had behaved in the past it mattered nothing to her, for the present was hers and all the future. What a glorious prospect!

"You haven't the foggiest idea what a scoundrel I am!"

"Then I must have a special leaning towards scoundrels!" she replied, her face hidden on his shoulder.

"God knows the biggest thing in my life is my love for you," he said brokenly. "My dream-girl! If I lose you, I lose everything. You will not fail me, Honey?" he asked solemnly. "If all the world should wish to part us, you will still hold to me?"

"I could not change. Whatever happens, I shall always love you, even if all the world were against you."

He was not satisfied. For many minutes he held her to his heart, covering her face with passionate, lingering kisses.

"And all this while we are forgetting that your wrist is hurt!" she exclaimed.

"Damn my wrist! Look at me. Your eyes cannot lie!"

Honor lifted her eyes, clear and sweet to his, full of the love and loyalty she felt, and saw an unutterable sadness in the depths of his soul. He should have been rejoicing, yet he was like a man burdened with a great remorse.

"Say, 'Brian, I am yours till death.'"

Honor repeated the words gravely.

He continued: "'I swear that, when you are ready to take me away, I will go with you, and none shall hold me back.' Say that."

Honor said it faithfully. "I don't care if we have the quietest of weddings," she added, "so long as it is in a church."

After a pregnant pause, he said tentatively, "Mr. Meek, I dare say, could tie the knot."

"When may I tell Mother?"

"Will she keep it to herself?"

"She will tell Father, of course."

"Can't we have our happiness all to ourselves for a little while?"

Honor thought she could understand his deep sensitiveness of criticism and questions—he was so unlike all the other men she knew—and consented. Moreover, she loved him and wanted to please him. There was no wrong in keeping secret what concerned themselves so closely, till he was ready to make it public. Her own dear mother, from whom she had kept nothing in her life, would be the first to understand and appreciate her motive, as she was the most sympathetic woman in the world, and wanted nothing so much as her child's happiness.

"I will do exactly as you wish, dear," she said, glad to offer an early proof of her great affection.

Dalton kissed her rapturously, in unceasing wonderment at her condescension in loving one so utterly unworthy. He seemed unable to grasp the truth, and kept asking her repeatedly for assurances.

The heat of the sun's rays now penetrating their shadowed retreat and striking down upon her bared head, awakened Honor to a sense of time and the realisation that it was midday.

"When shall I hold you in my arms again?" he asked before finally releasing her.

"The question is, where?—if it is to be kept a secret between us, only?" she asked wistfully, compunction already pulling at her conscience. Secrecy savoured of intrigue, and all things underhand were abominable to her.

"I am so glad my bungalow is so near to yours—only the two gardens and a hedge between! I might almost signal to you to meet me somewhere?" he said hesitatingly as though expecting a rebuke.

"No, Brian. I'll have nothing to do with signalling," she said definitely. "We'll meet every day at the Club if you like, and leave the rest to chance."

"I could not build my hopes on chance. It would drive me crazy, as I am not a patient man. Can't I see you alone—say in the lane—after dinner?"

"No." She shook her head decidedly. "I couldn't do things by stealth! I cannot deceive—it's no use expecting it of me!"

"I knew that; and it's that which I worship in you! But I am an exacting and selfish brute. Well!—I'll not complain, Sweetheart!" He released her, still with the gloom of a profound sadness in his eyes, and, together, they walked back to find his car.

CHAPTER XVIII

SECRET JOYS

Honor seemed to walk on air all day. The whole world had changed for her in a twinkling, and her heart sang for very joy at being alive. God had answered her appeal and had given her the love of this lonely man whose soul was sick and wanted tender nursing back to health. Henceforward it would be her privilege to restore to him his lost ideals and revive his faith in God and human nature. Her belief in the power of truth and love being securely established, she had no fears for a future spent with Brian Dalton, for all his failures and misdeeds.

Her only regret was, having to keep her happiness to herself for the present, when she longed to share it with her mother: and to atone for her enforced reserve, she tried to be more than ever attentive and considerate to her while she looked forward to the time, not far distant, when she would obtain her forgiveness and blessing.

Captain Dalton's professional duties kept him engaged till dusk, when, much to the surprise of the members, he reappeared at the Club. He was impatient to meet Honor again and to exact from her lips renewed assurances of her unchanged feelings and good faith, for he was restless and unable to accept the astounding truth, being suspicious of his good fortune and distrustful of circumstances.

On the whole, the meeting was unsatisfactory on account of the lack of opportunity for a *tête-à-tête*. Constant interruptions owing to Honor's popularity, had the effect of driving him into his accustomed aloofness of manner tinged with aggressiveness towards offending persons. Tommy's persistent claims on Honor's comradeship were particularly aggravating, and not to be borne.

"I shall wring his neck if he butts in again," Dalton muttered viciously.

"We have known each other since we were children," Honor put in as a softener.

"I can't stick it here for another minute," he said with a suppressed curse. "Let's get out of this!"

To Honor, it was joy to be with him even in the midst of a company of others. Her satisfaction lay in the knowledge that she was beloved and his whispered endearments gave her bliss. His voice at her ear was the sweetest music she had ever heard when it said, "Honey!" or "Sweetheart!" and asked her to repeat that she loved him. "You know I do," she once answered. Thereupon their eyes met for a brief moment and her senses swooned under the intensity of his gaze. In that fraction of time he had, by suggestion, kissed her with such passion and longing—as at the *jhil*—that her breath fluttered in a sob, her eyes were blinded. He was teaching her to want him even as he wanted her till she was thrilled at the strength of their love. It was glorious that they were both young, with so many years of their lives before them in which to grow nearer to each other. "And they twain shall be one flesh," seemed the most blessed psychological miracle that her virgin mind could conceive.

"Where shall we go?" she answered indulging his demand to take her away from the Club.

"We can go for a spin in my car."

"It is so dark!"

"Do you mind?" His voice sounded hurt, and Honor, who was sensitive to its inflection, immediately yielded. She feared venomous tongues, but, the most deadly of them all being absent—Mrs. Fox having taken up her abode in Calcutta while her case was pending—she was reassured.

"Mother dear, I am going for a little run in Captain Dalton's car, if you don't mind," she called softly to Mrs. Bright who was busy organising a bridge party in the Ladies' Room.

Mrs. Bright looked surprised. Doubtful thoughts flashed through her mind,—fear of gossip, reluctance to stand in the way of innocent pleasure, and wonder that the doctor should have shown a sudden inclination towards sociability. Seeing a critical expression lurking in Mrs. Ironsides' eye her dignity was immediately in arms.

"Certainly, darling, but don't be late. Mind you wrap up properly," she returned cordially. Mrs. Ironsides would have to appreciate the fact that Honor had her mother's fullest trust and confidence. However, throughout the ensuing rubber she could not avoid mentally speculating on the possibility of the most eligible bachelor in the District beginning to consider her child from a matrimonial point of view.

Miss Bright passed out into the darkness with Captain Dalton, her eyes shining with a new beauty, and Tommy watched her, filled with dismay. What was the meaning of it? Honor with the doctor, of all men! The doctor paying Honor marked attentions, and she accepting them with sweet graciousness! He forgot to pull at his cigar which went out while he stared into the night with eyes that saw only the look in the girl's eyes as she walked beside Dalton towards his car.

The motor drive was repeated occasionally, and it became an ordinary event for Honor to shoot duck on the Panipara Jhil in his company. "It is better than tramping the *jhil* alone," Mrs. Bright said, when the subject was mentioned in her presence. "I have always felt anxious while she has been absent on her snipe-shooting expeditions alone, but am so much easier in mind now that the doctor has taken charge of her. He is such an unerring shot, I am told; and she is learning to be so careful under his guidance."

It was the least of the lessons Honor learned from the doctor. He taught her the delights of a perfect companionship founded on mutual love; a man's reverence for the woman he respects: a complete knowledge of her own heart; its power of devotion, its great depths, and stores of feeling.

Sometimes Ray Meredith joined them in his fleeting visits to the Station—a lonely and pathetic being, in need of companionship, and grateful for friendly attentions. His wife wrote regularly, he said, and she and the child were well. Otherwise, he spoke little of his absent family. Sometimes Tommy would meet them on the *jhil* and share their picnic luncheon. Jack was never accorded an invitation. On these occasions, the lovers would play at being ordinary friends but with poor success. Honor would avoid meeting the doctor's eyes, while the doctor's eyes were unable to stray long from contemplation of her engaging face which had never looked so lovable and full of charm.

With a quickened intuition, Tommy realised that his own sun had set, and he went about his business, a very subdued being; one who had lost all interest in his occupations and who was finding very little in life worth living for.

When Honor was alone with Dalton, they would discuss the future, and plan their Elysium together. He was engaged in making arrangements for taking up a practice in Melbourne, where a colleague, formerly his senior, had retired and was eager for his young brains in partnership. When everything was settled, her parents were to be told, after which they would be quietly married at the Mission, and leave for Australia. "You will not mind such a hole-and-corner sort of wedding?" he asked anxiously.

"What does it matter, so long as we are married?" she replied. "I have always hated a big, ostentatious wedding."

"I should loathe it!" he said strongly. "And what about Australia?"

"Anywhere with you—even if it is to the South Pole!"

Dalton kissed her to express his delight in her thoroughness. "How glad I shall be when I have you all to myself!—I shall spend every day of my life in proving to you how much I value your love, and you shall give this poor devil a chance to take up his life again. Honey!—sometimes I am sleepless with fears. It seems to me too good to be true. I am overcome with dread lest I should never carry it through! Something will be sure to happen to stop it. If so, I am done for! It will be the end of me!" He looked as if haunted with forebodings of evil.

Honor enfolded him in her embrace. Her tender arms clung about his neck and she kissed him tenderly in her desire to bring him comfort. "Why should anything happen to interfere? God knows how much we care, and He will be merciful." She fancied he alluded to sudden death.

"Ah! yes. Your God to whom you pray for safety every night of your life, may see fit to save you from such as I. I'm not good enough to take you, Honey; that's straight."

"You shall not say that," she protested laying her soft palm across his mouth. "Who is good in this world? Not I, by any means! So we are a pair in need of protection, and are both determined to begin a new life together in gratitude for the

Divine Countenance."

Dalton suppressed a sound that was almost a sob while he defiantly blinked away a tear. "Sweet little Puritan!—" He covered her hand with kisses. "But it will be a terrible day for me when that martinet of a conscience sits in judgment on my sins. It makes me wish with all my heart that I may be dead before then! I'd risk damnation to——"

"Oh, hush!——"

"To have you mine, anyway. Does that shock you? It's the truth," and Honor was pained and greatly puzzled.

But he was not often in such a strange frame of mind. There were times when he was a different man, almost boyish in his merriment, and full of a determined optimism. He would build castles in the air for them both to live in, and make her laugh just for the sake of admiring her beautiful teeth.

It was early in March when Honor, having lost much of her reserve, discussed Jack's affair with Dalton and deplored his inevitable ruin. "Tommy says he'll be done for in every way if he marries her, but he will do so in spite of everything."

"More fool he."

"He's been very weak and very wicked," sighed Honor; "but *she* began it. We watched it start, and Jack walk, as it were, blindfold into a trap. It seems terrible that she should escape and he receive all the punishment!"

"Generally, it is the other way about!"

"Jack's punishment will be life-long. He will never be a happy man. Already, he is almost ill for thinking of it. His people are so proud and would never receive Mrs. Fox. Can't anything be done? You don't think he is obliged to marry her?"

"Not Mrs. Fox. Circumstances alter cases. She had her eyes wide open and played her cards for this. It would serve a woman like that jolly well right if young Darling gave her the slip. Tell Tommy to prevail on him to see me. What he wants is a medical certificate and leave home for six months. I'm very much mistaken if that doesn't change the complexion of things considerably."

"But he has no real illness!"

"I dare say I'll find him really ill when I overhaul him. He looks on the verge of a break-down. I have never seen a lad go off as he has done the past few months."

"That is because, at heart, Jack is not really a bad fellow. It is just that he is deplorably weak; and remorse for having yielded to temptation, is tormenting his soul. In proper hands he would shape quite well."

Dalton was as good as his word, for, when Jack visited him for a medical opinion on his run-down health, he was ready with the certificate which was to obtain six months' leave for him in Europe.

And while the young man waited on tenterhooks for sanction to leave India, and the routine of station-life continued as usual, the doctor awoke to the fact of his own increasing unpopularity with the natives of Panipara. Joyce Meredith had once tried to warn him, at which he had been considerably amused. After that, the arrival on the scene of a surveyor and the taking in hand of preliminary measures, showed that the Government were seriously considering the drainage scheme; hence personal hostilities against the author of it became active, and the gravity of his position was forced upon him.

The villagers scowled whenever he passed and repassed in his journeys about the District, and offered him open insolence in lonely places; while, on one occasion, a large mob had gathered to waylay the car, but had melted away at sight of Honor beside him. They had recognised the daughter of the senior police official, and were afraid,—or had caught sight of shot guns in the car; whereupon, discretion had prevailed.

Recognising symptoms as dangerous, Dalton refrained from taking Honor motoring with him, and had given up their joint expeditions to the *jhil*, at which Mrs. Bright was well pleased. Captain Dalton had, apparently, not proposed to Honor, and it was high time that he ceased making her conspicuous by his attentions. She had expected something to come of them but, so far, the only result was gossip and chaff on the part of ladies when they met at the Club, which was excessively annoying.

Didn't Honor see that matters were going a bit too far? Was it prudent for a young girl to get herself talked about—especially with a young man who had already caused plenty of gossip in the Station? Honor allowed that she had, perhaps, been a little unwise not to have considered the opinion of the neighbours, but her dear mother need not make herself anxious, as she and Captain Dalton understood each other perfectly.

That being the case, Mrs. Bright was consoled; for what is an "understanding" between a man and a maid, if not an unofficial engagement? Like most mothers, Mrs. Bright was anxious, at heart, to see her daughter happily settled in life; and the doctor, though not a wealthy man or popular, was, at least, a rising one in his profession, and considered a good match.

Honor, however, paid little attention to gossip and chaff, her mind being filled with anxiety and growing alarm for her lover's safety. She had quickly divined the increasing antagonism of the Panipara villagers towards him; and knowing his recklessness lived in continual dread.

"I shall not know a moment's peace while this sort of thing goes on," she fretted. "Can't you get a transfer till we are married?"

"And leave my little love?" It was unthinkable.

"It would make no difference in our feelings for each other."

"I couldn't do it, apart from the fact that it would look like running away. You little know what it means to me to see you every day."

Latterly he had spent most of his evenings at the Blights', who took compassion on his loneliness and were complaisant of his obvious attachment to Honor. Mrs. Bright, in her tactful way, gave him many opportunities of having Honor to himself in the drawing-room while she betook herself to her husband's own particular sanctum to indulge in confidential chat. "It is plain to see that he worships our Honey, and it is best they should meet here, since meet they must, in her own home," she would explain. "I dare say we shall be hearing something one of these days."

"He improves on acquaintance, and certainly has a devilish fine voice. I could listen to him all night," said her husband, nevertheless, obeying the hint and remaining a voluntary exile in his study.

Considering that his opportunities for snatching whatever of happiness he could out of his life in the present lay in Muktiarbad, it was not likely that Dalton was inclined to seek a transfer and thus run away from bodily danger;—not even when a parcel containing a bomb was placed on his writing-table, which, owing to some technical defect, failed to go off when it was opened. The incident gave Tommy and his subordinates some work to do, trying to trace the culprit who had placed it there, but the matter was treated with unconcern by the doctor himself.

CHAPTER XIX
THE DELUGE

One day, at the close of April, when the thermometer was unusually high, Ray Meredith fell a victim to a stroke of the sun, and had to be carried in from camp like a dead man. His friends were thrown into consternation, telegrams were flashed to headquarters, and even the bazaar discussed his danger with bated breath. Captain Dalton, always at his best in critical moments, rose all at once to great heights in the estimation of the District. It was told of him how he was not only physician but nurse to the Collector, and no woman could have been more deft or capable in the sick-room than he was. But no one knew that a sense of obligation to his conscience as well as to the sick man was driving him hard, so that, for the time being, all personal considerations were swept aside,—even his cherished plans which were nearing completion,—in order that he might save a useful life to which he owed some reparation.

Mrs. Bright was filled with admiration, and Honor with adoration. Both held themselves in readiness to be of use as necessity might demand, and were full of concern for Joyce so far away. Yet no cable was sent to tell her of her husband's state.

"From a rational point of view, it would be folly," said Mrs. Bright. "If he should die, we can send a cable to prepare her, and follow it up with another soon afterwards. Should he recover, we will have given her a nasty fright for nothing. By the time mail day comes round, we shall have something definite to say, and a letter will do quite well." To this Honor was obliged to agree, but it seemed terrible to her loving heart that a wife should be in ignorance of her husband's peril, and thus be deprived of importuning the Almighty with prayers for his recovery. So much of good in life depended on prayer, that she felt it necessary to pray on behalf of Joyce for the life of the husband so precious to her. According to her convictions, God works through the agency of his creatures, and as no stone was being left unturned by the doctor whose whole heart was in his profession, Ray Meredith stood a good chance if God were merciful to the reckless man who had scorned the deadly rays of an Indian sun.

"I am so thankful he has you to take care of him," she once said during a private interlude, when Dalton held her in his arms under the great trees of the avenue and kissed her good-night. "Poor, poor Joyce! She would break her heart if she were to lose him—and she away! She would never forgive herself for going."

"If, in spite of all our efforts, he should not recover, you may take it that he is fated to die of this stroke. One can't kick against Fate."

"There is no such thing as Fate! If you do your best, God helping, he will recover, I am sure of it. I am praying so hard for his wife's sake. If we keep in touch with God and do our best unremittingly, it is all that is wanted of us."

"If any one's prayers ever reach heaven, I am sure yours do!... Do you ever pray for me?"

"Always!"

"What for, specially?"

Honor hesitated for a moment, then murmured, "That we may never be parted in life, and that I may succeed in making you happy."

Dalton kissed her reverently. "Any more than that? Do you never say, 'Make him a good boy'? I need that more than anything. It is what mothers teach their kiddies to say, but it's forgotten when they grow up."

"I'll say that, too, if you wish it."

"Say it every night of your life; and also that my sins may be forgiven me. They are many!"

The evening the nurse arrived from Calcutta to take charge of the case, Meredith was improving in spite of the insupportable heat. *Punkhas* waved unceasingly in the bungalows, and quantities of ice were consumed. People moved about without energy, mopping their faces and yearning for the relief of a nor'wester, while a "brain-fever" bird cried its melancholy cadences with aggravating monotony, from a tree in the Collector's garden, where every leaf and twig had a thick coating of dust. A grey pall in the north-west tantalised with its suggestion of a possible thunderstorm, which, if it burst, would instantly cool the overcharged atmosphere; and anxious eyes glanced at it with longing.

Honor drove to the railway station in the Daimler to fetch the expected nurse, and was in time to meet the express as it steamed in with its long train of coaches, in which every window gaped, revealing in the third-class compartments the spectacle of semi-nude humanity packed like sheep in pens, perspiring, and anxious for the moment of release.

When the crowd on the platform had thinned, she saw a lady in a nurse's cloak and bonnet, waiting by her trunks, the belabelled condition of which advertised the fact that the owner was a much travelled person.

She was strikingly handsome in a bold and arresting way, with dark eyes capable of expressing much, and full, red lips parted upon slightly prominent teeth. She looked as if she could be extremely fascinating, but there was something about her that did not inspire Honor with confidence,—though she freely admired her grace and aplomb,—and she thought she looked more like an actress than a nurse. Surely the stage would have better suited one of her type! She wondered.

"I have been sent to fetch you. My name is Honor Bright."

"Oh, how d'you do! How kind you are! You see, I have 'some' luggage," was the reply.

"It will all fit on the car," and signing to a couple of coolie porters, Honor gave them directions and led the way through the booking office to the entrance porch. After they had taken their seats and the car had started, the nurse learned all about the case, in which she showed only a passing interest. "A married man, did you say?" she asked carelessly.

Honor had not said so, but answered in the affirmative.

"Wife at home?"

"In England; yes."

"And what's your doctor like? I always like to know for one has so much to do with the doctor, and it's just as well to understand something about him before-hand," she said, with ill-concealed eagerness.

"I should not describe Captain Dalton better than to say he is very direct and never wastes words," said Honor, smiling at her first impressions of Brian Dalton. Her secret knowledge of him thrilled her happily.

"And what of his looks? Is he as handsome as" —she bit her lips, stumbled in her sentence, and concluded, "as his pictures? I have seen his portrait in a photo group of surgeons at the Presidency General Hospital, in Calcutta."

"I have never thought about his being handsome," said Honor. "He has a strong face, and an expressive one—on occasions."

"I am told he is a hard man. How does he impress you?"

"I dare say he could be as hard as flint; but I have not experienced that side of his nature."

"It's a funny little place, this," said the nurse who had not troubled to give Honor her name. "I rather fancy it. I suppose you manage to have quite good times since everyone must know everyone else quite intimately. Like a large family!"

"I am quite fond of it, for I have many good friends."

"I could imagine putting up with it for a change; but to live here year in and year out, so far away from town and the bustle of life, would bore me stiff. How-ever, *chacun à son goût!*"

At the house, the nurse was shown her room and left to unpack and arrange her things, and change into nursing attire. Tea was served to her in the morn-ing-room though it was nearing the dinner hour, and Honor remained to enter-tain her till the doctor returned from another case; Mrs. Bright having temporary charge of the patient.

Soon afterwards, Captain Dalton arrived and Honor saw him step briskly into the room. She retired to a distant corner, herself, leaving him to confer with the nurse and acquaint her with the nature of the case, utterly unprepared for the scene that followed.

For a moment, she was paralysed at the sight of the doctor's ghastly pallor and startled eyes as they lighted upon the stranger's face.

"You?" he breathed through stiffened lips.

"Yes, Brian. I was given the chance as Nurse Grey was ill. I had to see you again!" her voice was fiercely agitated. "Won't you hear me?"

"Good God! Don't you understand that you are nothing to me?—less than nothing!" His eyes blazed.

"Yet you never divorced me! That gave me hope. Have you no forgiveness? No pity?"

A stony silence.

"Oh, you are hard!—*hard*! It is not fair to punish any one forever for one mistake——"

"Mistake, do you call it?"

"Sin, if you will have it. Are *you* sinless? After all, we are but human, and we forgive as we hope to be forgiven." She made a movement as if to fall at his feet, and Honor rushed blindly from the room. Her one instinct was to get away somewhere and hide—hide from the knowledge so ruthlessly thrust upon her. It was too horrible to contemplate. She shuddered from head to foot, and shivered as with ague. Out into the open she ran, among the dust-laden crotons and azaleas, and the florid shrubberies of the Indian garden, now bathed in soft moonlight. Scarcely heeding her footsteps, she stumbled to a bench beneath a laburnum. If it harboured reptiles, she was indifferent. Let her be bitten and die! She was crushed and bowed to the earth with a burden of grief too great to endure,—too hopeless to think upon.

What was it that he had offered her? Had he meant to insult her?

Never! He loved her too well. He would have killed himself rather than have treated her lightly.

What was it then?

Her mind refused to act. It acknowledged only one thought, and that was, severance—immediate, final—from the being she loved most on earth. That was inevitable.

Brian Dalton was married. He had been married all the time. Joyce had misunderstood; or he had lied to her.

No. She would not allow to herself that he had lied. His was not a petty nature given to lying, or to the faults of the weak and timid. He was a daring and defiant sinner, "risking damnation," as he had once said, for the desire of his heart. She could now understand his bitterness, his recurring moods of sadness and almost of remorse; for he was plotting all the while against the honour of the girl he respected as well as loved.

Consecutive thought was impossible; she was bewildered and numbed by the suddenness of the blow. Through it all she moaned as though in physical pain, "Brian!—oh, Brian!" Not for a minute did she doubt that he loved her. He had given abundant evidence of his sincerity; but unable to get her by fair means, he had determined to try foul. He had fought the fight of his life, and had failed.

"Yes—I had to see you again," the nurse had said. And then,—"You never divorced me!"

The words, "never divorced me," kept repeating in her brain. The nurse had spoken, forgetful of Honor's presence or imagining that she had left the room. He, too, had seemingly forgotten her presence or failed to notice that she was still in the room.

She was handsome, this woman who had been—*was*—his wife! Honor recalled the flashing eyes, the sensuous mouth, and quailed. Having once loved her, might he not be won to love her again? She was his. He had no right to think of another.

No other had any right to think of him!

Honor writhed in misery.

"Are you sinless?" his wife had asked him.

From his own showing, he was a most deliberate sinner, ready to sacrifice an innocent soul for his own gratification. Only a miracle had stopped him.

Words he had spoken returned to her mind—

"Your God to whom you pray every night of your life will see fit to save you from such as I!"

The pathos of his dread, the wistful appeal in his voice, had touched her deeply. She could hear it still, and her heart went out to him in sympathy. Her poor, unhappy darling! But,—had God really interfered to save her from the pit he was digging for her feet?

If he were free, she would have no wish to be saved from him, sinner though he were. She would take him gladly, and, God helping, slay the demon in him forever.

But he was not free. The task was not for her.

The Church would not marry them if it were known that he was not free.

It did not enter into her consciousness that she could go to him in spite of God or the law. Defiance of laws, human and divine, was impossible to Honor who had been reared to respect both from her cradle.

Therefore, all was at an end; and yet, she had no anger in her heart towards Brian Dalton; only love and pity, and grief for the parting which was inevitable—a blasting, desolating grief.

Presently, footsteps sounded on the gravel. Someone was wandering in the garden in search of her. It was a man's tread. It was Dalton's; she recognised the impatience, the determination in it, inseparable from the man. Yet she made no sign. She dared not, though she wanted him with all her heart. Sobs threatened to strangle her and were fiercely suppressed. What right had she to his love now that she knew all? What use had she for his explanations and apologies? She was choked, dry-eyed, frightened.

She was afraid of herself, for, at the first sound of his footsteps, the beating of her heart had deafened her. She wanted him as much as he wanted her, and she trembled, feeling powerless to deny her love its human expression. It was compelling. What could be the end of it?

She bowed her face upon her quivering arms whispering, "God help me!—God help me," yet straining her ears to catch every sound without. And she made no resistance when Dalton at last found her, and, seating himself at her side, drew her tenderly to his breast.

It was long before either spoke. Honor felt it was for the last time. He feared it might be for the last time.

"You know?" he asked in a voice hoarse and strange.

"Yes," she whispered trembling as she clung to him.

"Yet you do not spurn me?"

"How could I, when I love you so!"

"Such a scoundrel as Brian Dalton?"

"I only know how much I love you!"

An inarticulate sound resembling a stifled sob came from him. After a while——

"What are you going to do with me, Sweet?"

What answer could she give him but one? "What I must!" Yet she clung all the closer.

"Though you love me?"

"I shall love you till I die. But we have to—we must—part!"

His arms about her were like bands of iron. He was scarcely aware of the force with which he crushed her to him.

"It cannot be done," he said almost to himself.

"Why did you not divorce her?" Honor asked resentfully.

"To punish her. Ah!—my God!—Punishments come home to roost. Some day I will tell you the whole sordid story. There is no time now—I have to go back to Meredith."

"We must say good-bye here," she returned with a desperate attempt to be calm.

"Never 'good-bye'!" Yet he had no hope. Honor's conscience had decided—the conscience he had once feared would sit in judgment on his sin against herself; and yet it had uttered no word of reproach.

For a full minute he held her away from himself, trying by the light of the moon to see the look in her eyes. He wanted to plead with her to fly with him to another land where none should know their history; but his words died in his throat as he gazed upon her white and stricken face. "Honey, be merciful to me in your thoughts!" he cried, instead, kissing her forehead, her eyes, and denying himself her lips.

"Just let me go right away. Give me courage—help me!"

"And what of me?"

"I leave you the gift of my heart. I can never take it back."

"Do you forgive me?"

"Love always forgives."

"God bless you! I think I must have been insane. I would have earned your hatred in time. How shall I face life without you?"

Honor gave him her lips sadly. "In our different ways—we shall face it. Just at first it will be very hard, but not impossible if we have courage to do what is right. To stay on here after this, is more than I can bear; so I must go away—just for a bit, to learn how to be brave. When I come back—if you are still here, we might both bear it better."

"My poor Honey! What a beast I have been! As for me—you will find me here right enough. I shall not go to Australia *now!*—but I shall never bear it better."

They parted a little later in heavy sorrow. Honor left him bowed and broken on the garden bench, and stumbled home unseeingly.

Afterwards, she learned in one of Dalton's letters—for he would not be denied that medium of communion with her—the full story of his past humiliation.

He had married a nurse at Guy's when he had been a medical student, and she had left him six months later for his best friend. She had been proved as faithless as she was handsome, with a baleful influence over men. Not long afterwards, the man she had led astray was killed in a railway accident, and since then, she had, on various occasions, tried, without success, to persuade Dalton to take her back. Apparently, she had not resigned hope with the years, for she had followed him to India, believing that time was her greatest ally, since it dims the memory of wrongs.

When he had discovered her presence in Calcutta, and learned that she had joined a nursing home in a fashionable quarter, he had applied for a transfer to quiet Muktiarbad, giving as his reason, his need of rest from his too strenuous labours in the capital. His desire was to gain time and to keep out of the way of any possibility of coming into professional contact with his wife.

At Muktiarbad he was able to forget his troubles, and, to his relief, seemed to have been forgotten by the Government and left to enjoy his peace undisturbed. However, through her connection with a nurses' association, his wife had accidentally learned of Nurse Grey's summons to Muktiarbad and had cleverly contrived to work things so as to go herself, instead.

"If I had only done the right thing in the beginning, and severed the tie, legally, things might have been very different today," was the burden of his cry. Instead, in the recklessness of despair, he had cut the ground from under his own feet, and by his desire for revenge, destroyed any possibility of future happiness for himself. Passion for the woman was dead. Her beauty revolted him; her character he loathed and despised. "It is amazing to me," he wrote in deep contrition and humility, "that such an egotistical, conscienceless blackguard as I, should have been given the inestimable boon of your wonderful love!—to be allowed to retain in my keeping such a pure and faithful heart! It is my most treasured possession. My feeling for Honor Bright is my religion. To the memory of her, Brian Dalton, one-time scoundrel, kneels in worship."

When Mrs. Bright returned home from Meredith's bedside and found Honor nerveless and prostrated with white cheeks and dark rings round her eyes, she was convinced that it was high time her daughter was sent to the hills.

"I told you so in March when the weather grew unbearable; and now, you, too, have got a touch of the sun!" But Honor's cheek was cool and symptoms of sun or heat stroke were lacking. "How do you feel?" the anxious lady questioned. Being in ignorance of the nurse's identity and having no clue to Honor's state, she was worried and at a loss.

"I am only feeling rather exhausted, Mother darling," said Honor wearily. Since she had not taken her mother into her confidence while she was happy, she felt she had no right to burden her with her sorrow.

"Shall I ask Captain Dalton to come and see you?"

"Not on any account!" Honor hastened to say.

"I know it is rather embarrassing when a doctor is an intimate friend—and an unmarried man! Still, considering—" Mrs. Bright was thinking of the "understanding" and wondering when it was going to become something definite. However, Honor was not the girl to hector or question on matters that concerned herself alone. The question of her indisposition was more pressing than any. "Have you a headache?" she asked anxiously.

Honor could truthfully say that her head ached. "When I have slept, it will, I dare say, wear off."

"I hope so, for I should not like to think that you are going to be ill."

"I am not ill; but, perhaps, dear, if you can spare me, I had better get away tomorrow before the heat becomes worse. May is always such an appalling month in the plains."

"I shall speak to your father immediately about it," Mrs. Bright said, relieved to find something she could do to avert a break-down of her daughter's usually excellent health. "The Mackenzies at Mussoorie will be delighted to have you for a month or two as a paying guest. We have only to wire. And if they have no room, they can secure one for you near by."

"That will be all right," said Honor listlessly. "I'll start tomorrow night, if possible."

"It shall be possible. Such a sudden collapse!" commented Mrs. Bright. "I do hope you will feel more fit in the morning."

"I'll be quite fit, never fear," said Honor. "Tonight I am only a bit 'off colour,' as Tommy says," and she tried to smile.

"I'll send a message down to the *dhobi* to get your wash ready by noon tomorrow. At these times one realises how infinitely more convenient is a *dhobi* than an English Laundry Company," and Mrs. Bright bustled away that she might lose no time in letting the washerman know what was expected of him. Though the laundry had been taken away that very morning, she had not the slightest doubt that the task would be completed to perfection before noon, for she knew the laundryman of India to be as remarkable in his line as the Indian cook is in his.

The following evening, Honor left Muktiarbad station, with the faithful Tommy to see her off in the train; and her mother was there to give her a last hug and sundry forgotten injunctions at the eleventh hour. "Mind you telegraph on your arrival—and don't forget to wear a woollen vest next to your skin. It is so necessary to ward off colds. Give Alice Mackenzie my love and say that I shall try to come up in the rains. Good-bye, darling, and take care of yourself! If you want more money, don't fail to let me know. Have you got your umbrella? Thank goodness! I thought it was forgotten. Write soon; I hope you'll pick up and look better when I see you next."

The train moved off and Mrs. Bright remarked to Tommy that she was quite alarmed to see such a sudden change in her beloved child. Really, she should have insisted upon her going away, the latest, a month ago.

"What is the matter? I, too, have been aghast at the change. Honey looks positively ill," said Tommy.

"Nothing is the matter but the heat, it seems. I wonder why Captain Dalton never came to see her off. I told him, when I was at the Bara Koti this morning, that she was leaving by the 7:20. And they are such good friends. I feel quite hurt."

"He is out somewhere in the District this evening. I saw him take the main road in his car a little while ago, and travelling at break-neck speed," said Tommy.

"Someone else taken ill somewhere, I suppose."

"Very likely."

"Still, I think he might have made a point of saying 'good-bye.'"

Tommy wondered, but said nothing. He had long made up his mind, as had others in the Station, that Captain Dalton and Honor Bright were engaged. He had also heard of lovers' quarrels and was ready, by the look on Honor's face, to believe that a very serious misunderstanding had taken place. Her abstraction, her ghastly pallor and haunted eyes had given him positive suffering and a feeling of blind sympathy, which had only found vent in loading the compartment with newspapers and magazines snatched from Wheeler's bookstall.

To Honor's surprise, Captain Dalton appeared at a wayside station, and leant his arms on the open window. The sight of him, his set face and brooding eyes, made her heart stand still, while a sudden faintness seized her. Behind him the

Station hawkers were shouting their wares, native travellers were bustling to and fro, and the air was alive with sound, so that in the midst of all that confusion they were absolutely alone.

"I am glad you have no one in with you," he said quietly. "I so wanted a few words with you."

"How is Mr. Meredith?" Honor asked, trying to speak naturally.

He took both her hands and held them close, deaf to the question. Meredith was out of danger and the nurse had become interested in her charge. What were they and all else to the lovers so parted!

"Have you nothing to say to me?"

"I have said all that there is to say," she replied tremulously.

"I am going to write to you, and you must write to me. Do you understand that this is imperative?"

"Is it?" she asked with beating heart. Oh, that they might at least hug to themselves that innocent joy!

"If I do not write to you or hear from you, I shall be doing something desperate. I cannot be responsible for myself. It will be the only thing to keep me sane. You cannot dream how I am being punished. Don't add to my punishment if you have any pity." His anguished eyes and quivering lips were convincing. "You will have no fault to find with my letters," he added while she hesitated.

Honor promised.

A bell clanged noisily and the engine whistled.

"Oh, Honey!—how can you leave me like this?" he whispered holding her eyes with his.

Honor moved impulsively towards him and their lips met in a passionate and lingering kiss. The strength to resist his unspoken appeal was melted by that silent demand. After all, they were parting!

"Good-bye," she said, the tears falling.

He stepped back as the train began to move, his gaze riveted on her face, and jaws set with stern self-repression.

CHAPTER XX
THE "IDEAL"

While Raymond Meredith convalesced at Darjeeling in the care of Nurse Dalton—the identity of whose name with that of the doctor being generally understood at Muktiarbad to be a mere freak of coincidence—his family in Surrey waxed strong and healthy in the glorious summer weather. Baby Douglas, who lived out of doors, had cheeks like a damask rose, while his mother gained gracious curves which added to her already radiant beauty. Even her pretty little sister who had recently put up her hair, was eclipsed. But only in point of looks.

Kitty was not one to be overlooked in any company, by any means. What she lacked in regularity of feature, she made up for in charm of expression, a delightful speaking voice, and a ready tongue. Bright eyes given to laughter, the gleam of white teeth, curving red lips mobile and piquant, a dimpled cheek, laughter creases at the corners of the full-lidded, soft eyes, that had a roguish trick of quizzing—eyes that had borrowed their hue from the summer sky, with lashes like her sister's, and an indefinable little nose, made up a whole which was positively unfair to the rest of her sex, judging from the fact that every other girl was superfluous when Kitty was on the scene. And she was not blind to her own success, yet she was merciful out of the tenderness of her naturally good heart that never inflicted suffering wantonly; and if it happened that, owing to her irresistible fascination, she was the means of causing pain, to her credit be it said, that she was clever at healing the wounds she unwittingly inflicted, which saved unhappy consequences to unfortunate victims, and bound them to her as friends for life.

"I am so afraid of your becoming a flirt," Joyce once said reproachfully, after one of these instances was explained and apologised for. "You should think twice before you let yourself become too friendly. It will prevent any foolish mistakes in the end. Of course I speak from bitter experience."

Kitty, who was aware of that experience, sighed repentently. "Why didn't Providence make me a boy? I love them all so much."

"You would then, with your thoughtlessness, have broken some poor girl's heart. Half a dozen, perhaps."

"It is very difficult to know what to do," said Kitty with the roguish twinkle reasserting itself in her eyes.

"You have to nip all silly sentimentality in the bud. The real thing is never silly," said Joyce out of her superior wisdom.

"That's the difficulty. I never notice the bud till it is a full-blown passion-flower! I think I should become a nun."

Joyce hugged her by way of appreciation, unable to resist the dimple which fascinated even a sister.

There is nothing so winning as an imperishable sense of humour. Vivaciousness, and an infectious gaiety which radiates like the sun and dispels the shadows of depression in a moment—these were Kitty's chief assets. She had danced through childhood like a sunbeam. She had been the merriest of flappers and was now a sorceress to beguile with her arts in innocent and unconscious charm. Kitty's laughter, accompanied by that irresistible dimple, was the most captivating thing. Tender smiles greeted the sight of her from aged lips, and masculine youth felt drawn as by a magnet.

So it came to pass, that Jack Darling who was spending six months medical leave in England, fell a victim to Kitty's charm shortly before Mrs. Fox's decree nisi against her husband became absolute.

It was at the Victoria Underground station, near the booking-office, that they met. Believing that the wide hat and muslin gown could belong to none other than Mrs. Meredith who he knew was "at home," he pushed through the crowd and presented himself.

"Such a pleasure, Mrs. Meredith!" It is always such a pleasure to meet friends in London with whom one has been intimate in a distant land. Especially is it true of friends from India.

But two remarkably beautiful eyes turned full upon him in blank amazement and a hint of a twinkle in their cerulean depths. They said plainly, "You've made a mistake, bold Sir, but how delightful that you should know my sister!"

Before she could speak, Jack was apologising profusely, hat in hand, and blushing to the roots of his shining, well-brushed hair.

Restored to health after a yachting cruise off the coast of Scotland, Jack was a splendid specimen of manhood to look upon, though still inwardly depressed with the sense of the Inevitable awaiting him in the East. ("Such a lamb!" was Kitty's description, which was her highest praise.)

"I am so sorry—I—I do beg your pardon, but I would have sworn—in fact any one would be ready to swear——"

"That I am my sister?" she laughed, showing the engaging string of pearls and the irrepressible dimple. "Thank you so much. I always appreciate a compliment when it is sincere, for I am a great admirer of Mrs. Meredith."

"Then—then you are Miss Wynthrop—*Kitty*?" he said, blushing still more furiously. "I beg your pardon," he added apologising for his boldness in using her Christian name. "We used to talk so much about you at Muktiarbad. But you are even more—at least I was thinking of your photograph," he concluded lamely.

He had thought it a charming photograph of a girl, and now the original in natural colouring, youth, and perfect health had thrown his mind into chaos. Fragments of forgotten verses he had composed to his "Ideal," before the baneful influence of Mrs. Fox had drugged his senses and threatened the ruin of his career, now returned to haunt his memory and justify their extravagance.

At last she was before him in the flesh, not secretly reposing on a piece of pasteboard at the bottom of a dispatch-box left behind in India!

"Yes, I am Kitty," she answered with animation. "But you? I am sure I know you? My sister has a photograph of a Station group—ah, you are 'Jack'! I can't remember the other name."

"Darling!" he prompted eagerly with a suspicion of fervour. To hear her pronounce his name was to listen to the most adorable music.

"Of course! Fancy my forgetting! And your chum in the police is Tommy Deare? How perfectly priceless! I know you both intimately. You live in a little three-roomed bungalow near the Courts, all among weeds and snakes, and never go to church unless you are caught and taken!"

"You've got it exactly!" he returned delighted. Was there ever such a girl before? *Why is a dimple in the left cheek like—nothing on earth?* he wondered ecstatically. *Because it is so absolutely divine!* he concluded, mentally, to his own intense satisfaction at the inspiration.

"Now what a pity I am not my sister!" she said mischievously. "What a great deal you must have in common."

"I shall call on your sister if I may. At present—I am quite content," he returned wishing his appointment at a fashionable club in Mayfair at Jericho. For a dime he would let it slide and follow her to the ends of London.

"I am sure my sister will be delighted," said Kitty cordially. Then followed an exchange of addresses, Jack's being the name of a well-known club. "Mother always welcomes Joyce's friends from India. They come for a week-end and usually stay a week. The name India is a passport to our house."

"Of course I led up to it," the minx said to Joyce on describing the meeting. "I couldn't dream of letting him vanish and be lost to us, when he is the most delightful boy I have ever met."

"A very naughty boy, I am afraid, though I have a soft corner for him," said Mrs. Meredith, who considered the recital of Jack's misdeeds unfit for Kitty's ears.

"It is the naughty ones that are generally so nice," Kitty said with a sigh. "They are so human and attractive."

"Because they are naughty?" Joyce was shocked to hear such radical sentiments from little Kitty.

"It always strikes me that if they are capable of great naughtiness, they are equally capable of much good. It is the force that I admire. It only wants proper direction." (Which remark proved that Kitty's mind was capable of sympathetic understanding.)

Jack and Kitty enjoyed their chance meeting so much that they missed their respective trains repeatedly. Hers on the "West bound" platform, and his on the "East," might have rumbled in and out of the station beneath them, *ad infinitum*, had not Kitty recollected that she was due to have tea with an aunt at Richmond, who was impervious to diplomacy and dimples and with whom no excuses concerning Fate and an Affinity at the Victoria Underground, would avail, if the kettle were over-boiled and the tea delayed. So Kitty reluctantly bade him adieu.

"You are surely not going all that long way alone?" asked Jack, whose young sisters travelled the length and breadth of London unescorted.

"Do you think it unsafe?" asked the minx, seeing through his idea and encouraging the development of possibilities.

"One hears so much about girls mysteriously disappearing from London, you know," he murmured. "I couldn't bear to hear of such a thing happening to you, so I'll come as far as Richmond station, if I may?"

"That will be charming of you! Are you sure it will not be taking you much out of your way?"

"Not at all," Jack returned with gallantry, breaking his engagement without compunction. Thereupon, he bought their tickets, and sitting beside her on the crimson velvet seats of a Richmond "Non-stop," plunged recklessly into love at first sight. The moral obligation oppressing his mind was swept away for the time being. How was it possible for it to be otherwise, when he had come into the presence of his "Ideal" in the flesh?

And Kitty, complete mistress of the situation, did not let him guess by word or look that she had been equally impressed. It was thrilling to think that this godlike person had a photograph of herself tucked away somewhere among his goods and chattels. Naughty Joyce had confessed the fact to her long ago, and she was beginning to feel that she now had him in the hollow of her hand. She had no hesitation in improving the acquaintance begun in such an unorthodox fashion; a friend of her sister's was, naturally, a friend of hers. Such being the case, she could afford to expand genially and to fan the flame her portrait had kindled, experiencing for the first time in her life an answering glow.

Jack returned to London, deep in day-dreams and oblivious of his surroundings. Kitty's face and Kitty's voice were with him all the way; and he groaned in spirit at the thought of his madness and folly in the past.

It was inconceivable that he could have been such a fool; that he should have allowed himself to forget the high standards of life he had cherished, for a low intrigue! The idea of being tied for life to Mrs. Fox had been distasteful all along; but now it was intolerable! After the vision of Kitty Wynthrop, it was impossible, any longer, to contemplate marriage with a woman of Mrs. Fox's type! Whatever she might think of him, he would not do it. He would infinitely rather put an end to his life!

Of course, he was dishonourable. That went without saying. He had failed ignominiously from the outset to behave as an upright and honourable man. Self-analysis laid his pride in the dust and made him writhe in self-condemnation.

If Kitty only knew, she would despise him as he deserved! She was so pure, so perfectly wonderful! What a wife she would make! and so on, and so forth. Jack endured agonies of remorse for a week, during which time he was lost to the world; and then, with a temperamental rebound he called at Wynthrop Manor with the humble determination of laying himself at Kitty's feet that she might walk over him as she willed. Big, ingenuous men, like Jack Darling, are happiest when doormats to the women they love.

Joyce Meredith was delighted to see him. His presence in England argued that he had shaken himself free of the toils of that scheming flirt, Mrs. Fox, and she was ready to help him to recover his forgotten ideals. She had never really believed Jack as guilty as he was reputed to be, and, like nine out of ten women, put all the blame on the woman. Anyhow, she was sure that gossip and scandal had exaggerated everything, which was the most charitable way to look at the affair. As a Christian woman, it was her duty to think kindly of the erring, and sit in judgment on no one. She, therefore, welcomed Jack with great amiability and earned his everlasting gratitude by putting no obstacles in the way of his courtship of Kitty.

About this time, she received a letter from Honor telling her of Meredith being down with sunstroke, and was rudely awakened to the fact that she had been taking too much for granted where India and her husband's health were concerned.

Though Honor wrote that he was out of danger and slowly recovering, — that a nurse was expected that very day, — the little wife was beside herself with anxiety and alarm, and wanted to take the first steamer sailing for Bombay that she might be with him, to leave him no more.

"I should never have come away!" she cried inconsolably.

"I could never understand how you brought yourself to do so," said Kitty ruthlessly.

"I have been a selfish wretch, thinking only of myself, and of my anxieties for Baby!"

"Well, you've got Baby, any way."

"But if I should lose Ray, what is Baby to me!"

Kitty, who had not the heart to add to her beloved sister's agony, did her best to comfort her. "He was out of danger when Miss Bright wrote—let me see—that was about three weeks ago, or nearly, and, as you have had no cable since, it follows that he is all right by now."

"But I ought to go straight to him!"

"And they might be sending him straight home to you!"

It was not at all an unlikely possibility, so Joyce cabled to her husband to inquire his plans.

The answer came from Darjeeling that, in view of the great heat in the Red Sea at that season of the year, he was recuperating in the hills.

She was then persuaded by relatives and friends to possess her soul in patience and adhere to her original plan of returning to India in the autumn,—the best time for arriving in the East. By then she would be able to decide whether to take her baby out to India, or leave him behind in the care of the grandparents and a capable nurse.

A slight indisposition to the infant owing to the disturbances of teething, decided her to remain, and to pour out her heart to her husband in a letter telling him of her longing to be with him during his convalescence.

Somehow the written words did not adequately convey her depth of feeling, and Joyce was dissatisfied, especially with the passage which referred to the baby's indisposition:

"If Baby were not teething and in uncertain health, I would leave immediately for India,—but I am advised to hold on till the autumn when I can better decide whether I should leave him behind, or not. I am, of course, comforted to know that you are getting better, and, perhaps, it will be as well on account of the heat in the Red Sea and of the unhealthiness of the rains if I do exercise a little patience and wait. However, dearest, cable if you are not quite well by the time this reaches you, and I shall take my passage at once."

"It sounds rather as if I am placing the baby before him," she said to Kitty.

"And haven't you done so all along?"

Joyce looked perplexed. "If I have, it is only because it seemed to me the wee darling needed me more than Ray did."

"I wonder!" said Kitty out of a new perception of life and the needs of love. "After all, there are many to look after Baby if you must leave him in England. If I were in your place, and if there was nobody to take charge of him, I'd keep him out there, somehow. There must be good places in the hills, you have such a choice of stations,—and even babies have to take their chance, same as their daddies! It must be terribly lonely for a man when his wife, whom he adores as Ray adores you, leaves him and comes away home for the sake of the child! Personally, I couldn't do it."

Kitty's candid views carried conviction and aroused reflection. Gradually Joyce became aware of a great longing to be again with her splendid husband and feel anew his love and devotion.

As no answering cable arrived from Darjeeling requesting her presence in India, and as the weekly letters mentioned that he was convalescing satisfactorily, Joyce was beginning to nurse a creeping fear that her husband had, perhaps, learned to do very well without her. But pride sealed her lips and her letters to him contained no reference to any such thought. His, to her, since his illness, had become erratic and brief. He would begin by expressing a great distaste for the pen, allude to a feeling of incurable lassitude, curse an elusive memory, and, after giving her news of little consequence to themselves, would conclude in the manner that had become a formula of late:—"Your affectionate husband, Ray."

However, Joyce was determined not to borrow trouble. When they came together again it would surely be all right. Sunstroke was a paralysing illness and recovery from its effects was slow, she was assured; so, for a while, she must expect his mind to feel lethargic. With the restoration of perfect health his old tenderness would return, for true love could never die!

To Jack, the summer months were paradise, for the beautiful environs of Wynthrop Manor gave him many opportunities for uninterrupted companionship with Kitty. They walked, fished, golfed, and played tennis together. He was in love in the wild tempestuous way of youth, and ready, if need be, to die for the object of his adoration.

But Kitty was not too easy to win. The more attracted she felt, the more elusive she became. She would surround herself constantly with girl friends, that Jack might have no doubts concerning his choice; clever girls, and pretty girls were invited there for tennis and tea during Jack's lengthy visit to the Manor, till he was nearly distracted with impatience. Yet he hesitated to speak from an overwhelming sense of his utter unworthiness.

Could he dare to ask her to be his wife, and allow her to believe him all that a young girl's fancy might paint him? Would she consent to marry him if she were aware of the peculiar situation in which he stood with regard to Mrs. Fox whose letters still arrived at his chambers, and to whom he still wrote, only to keep her from following him to England?

She had threatened to do so at all costs, if he neglected to keep in touch with her, and the fear of bringing about such an undesirable climax had obliged him to temporise.

Early in August, when the Great War broke out, and all England was in the turmoil of mobilisation, and the manhood of the nation was flocking to join the Colours, Jack complied with the demands of his conscience and called at the India Office for permission to resign his service that he might join the Army. But the Secretary of State flatly refused his application and he was told, instead, to hold himself in readiness for an immediate recall to his duties in the East. No civil officer of the Indian Government was eligible for a commission in His Majesty's Forces except with the sanction of that Government alone. Thereupon, Jack, deeply depressed in spirit at his impending exile, joined Joyce and Kitty at Eastbourne whither they had gone for a change.

For the time being, civil life and economic conditions were disorganised. All England was in a turmoil of preparation for the Titanic struggle on the fields of France. People were becoming alive to the fact that even a democracy has its obligations to the State which guarantees it freedom; for freedom can only depend upon victory over autocracy and militarism. Private property was commandeered for the needs of the Army; public buildings became hospitals; motor cars and horses were requisitioned and carried off. Self-sacrifice became the order of the day. For weeks, no dependence could be placed upon railway time-tables, and all personal and individual concerns were forgotten in the overwhelming needs of the hour. A peace-loving people, averse to war, aware of all the horrors it entailed, yet rose to the supreme occasion, mindful of the great traditions of their forefathers, and stood ready for any sacrifice in the cause of honour, freedom, and the Right.

When Jack was asked to describe the state of London, he felt that it wanted more than words to paint its state in those historic days. The people having spent their feelings in a great outburst of loyalty and patriotism, were beginning dimly to realise the gigantic task to which the nation was pledged,—a nation, which, but for its Navy, was totally unprepared for war, and yet ready to withstand a formidable European Power that had secretly and thoroughly organised and planned for over forty years to strike a blow for world-domination. Right was in conflict with Might, and the end no man could then see; yet London was confident; but London was also very grave.

About this time, Joyce, to her great dismay, received a cable from her husband forbidding her to travel on the high seas till security thereon, for passengers, was assured. She had not realised till she received the message, how much she had been depending for happiness on the prospect of their reunion in the autumn. If the war was to stand in the way of her return to India, it might then be years before she should see her husband again—which would be unthinkable!

In the presence of Kitty's romance she was learning to comprehend the extent of her own loss,—her deplorable lack of appreciation in the past;—and she recognised that she had only herself to blame. Ray had loved her greatly; how greatly, she was only now beginning to understand, and her very soul hungered for that love with a nostalgia that was making her ill. If, by her folly, she had sacrificed that devotion—if he had ceased to love her altogether, and had met another more responsive and appreciative than she had been, she would not want to live; for even her beloved babe would no longer suffice to fill her life.

Memory recalled for her torment, certain words of his at parting. He had been wounded at her determination to leave him so soon after their marriage, and being ignorant of the true cause of her nervous break-down, he had expressed little sympathy, and had accused her of failure of affection for him. "Remember, a big breach between husband and wife may be mended, but never again is there restored what has been lost!" he had said. Also: "You are straining the cord that binds us together; the strands will presently be so weak that they will snap altogether. Then all the splicing afterwards will never restore it to its original strength. It will be a patched-up thing; its perfection gone!"

Had she done this terrible thing by her own shortsightedness and folly?

Little did he guess at the time of their parting that she was suffering tortures of self-contempt and nervous dread of his scorn, were he to know all that was on her mind!

And now, after this lapse of months, she was longing to make full confession and atonement. With her in his arms and their love fully restored, he would surely forgive her her foolishness and the silence which he had mistaken for lack of affection.

But, the war!

She would not be able to go to him now, and he would continue to believe that she had failed him! Her affectionate letters had not convinced him, for actions speak louder than words. Gradually an icy atmosphere of indifference had breathed forth at her from his letters, and she had been filled with secret uneasiness and fears. He was indeed learning to do without her.

Possibly the cord that had bound them together had snapped!

Upon this, came a letter one day, from Honor Bright.

Honor had been spending the hot months at Mussoorie in the Himalayas, which the Brights had always preferred to Darjeeling; and, after the monsoons had broken, her mother had joined her there till the middle of July, when they had returned together to Muktiarbad. For months Joyce and Honor had corresponded, fitfully, so that it was no surprise to the former when the Indian mail brought her a letter in her friend's hand-writing, the contents of which were acutely disturbing. Joyce read and re-read the letter, filled with alarm and foreboding.

What was Honor hinting at? and had she any grounds for hinting at all?

Honor was evidently perturbed about something in connection with Ray, or why this strange appeal to his wife to let nothing come in the way of her returning to her place beside her husband, no matter what the difficulties? "'It is not good,' we are told, 'for a man to live alone,' and please remember that there is no such thing as infallibility in human nature. Sometimes temptations are so strong that one needs to be superhuman to withstand them. Why expect too much of Life?" stared up at Joyce from the page.

"I would not write as I am doing, believe me, dear Joyce," the letter concluded, "if I were not so fond of you both that I feel your married happiness a personal concern. It is the biggest thing in the world; don't therefore, I implore you, gamble with it. If you will only look ahead and think a bit of the future without the love of your husband,—the grey years deprived of his tender devotion,—you will realise how lonely will be your life! Dearest, hold on to the blessed gift while it is yours and do not let it pass out of your possession. I have watched it happen before! 'That what we have we prize not to the worth whiles we enjoy it, but being lack'd and lost, why, then we rack the value, then we find the virtue that possession did not show us whiles it was ours.' This is so true also of love which, so often, is not appreciated while it is ours! And love can starve and die for want of sustenance, which is propinquity and a proper response. You see, I have kept my eyes open and am a silent student of human nature! I have come across a few devils in society; but in my experience, 'The female of the species is more deadly than the male,' and I believe the Lord's prayer is directed chiefly against her. She goes out of her way to dig pitfalls for the unwary and the best have been known to succumb. That is why a wife's place should be beside her husband throughout life, as the whole fabric of their happiness depends upon their unity. Separations make for misunderstandings and division; so, whatever happens, come out. Men and babies want looking after, and to my mind, Man is the greater baby of the two, for he wants more than a nurse to care for his bodily wants. He needs a wife with a combination of virtues, the chief among them being *tolerance*. My mother's life has demonstrated this to me with beautiful clearness, hence my understanding.

"You might be anxious at having to travel alone at such a time, but in your place I would take any risk to be with my husband, if I loved him deeply. That is the crux of the matter. Later on, conditions may become still more difficult. Cable when you are leaving, and *don't hesitate.*"

The appeal was very sincere, and thrilled Joyce with apprehensions. To be urged to travel at the risk of capture by German raiders at large on the high seas, that she might rejoin her husband without loss of time, argued that something was seriously wrong. Honor was her true friend and would not counsel such a step without reference to that husband, unless something was decidedly wrong. Whom was she to obey? Her husband, who had cabled to her to stay where she was? or Honor, who was urging her to go out at once?

While Joyce pondered over her dilemma, the fate of two people dear to her was being decided elsewhere.

CHAPTER XXI

THE REAL THING

Jack had come to the conclusion that it was impossible to part from Kitty Wynthrop with his love unconfessed. It was unthinkable that he should go out to India, loving Kitty as he did, and marry—Mrs. Fox! Bah! he consigned the latter, remorselessly, to perdition.

Whatever befell, he would speak to Kitty that very night—dear little girl!—he had wasted too much time already over his confounded doubts and fears, and had little enough time to spare. If she favoured him—why, he would be the luckiest, as well as the happiest of men! Some day, when he was absolutely sure of her and her love, he would confess his misconduct in the past, lest she should hear of it from others—she might; there was no knowing, with all those meddlesome cats about!—and perhaps he would obtain her forgiveness, after which he would be faithful unto her as long as they both should live. How fellows could—damn!

Jack was shaving at the time and had gashed his chin in his agitation.

He was confident, while he soothed the spot with an antiseptic, that such a darling little girl as she, would never hold up against him anything he had done in pre-Kitty days. It would be unjust and unreasonable. Why, hang it all! who was there that was human who hadn't some little—or big—scrape to his discredit in his bachelor days? Unfortunately, fellows were not gifted with second sight to know how they would feel when they came to be properly in love with the only girl in the world for them! The sickening sense of self-disgust— —

Another accident with the razor, and Jack paid more attention for a time to the matter in hand.

When he was putting the finishing touches to his tie, his fingers betrayed by their unsteadiness, his agitated frame of mind.

The worst of it was the blessed uncertainty of the whole affair. A fellow could never be sure of a girl like Kitty, or at any time take her feelings for granted. The least little bit of a liberty, and—hands off! Yet she was adorable and, often, sweetly encouraging. Certain little concessions had been treasured in mind and dreamed of at night, such as a dainty wrist held out to him for glove-buttons to be fastened; his blundering fingers allowed to assist her with her theatre wrap; their shoulders touching at a picture palace—a fact of which she had been unconscious, but which had thrilled him to the foundations of his being. They were hopeful signs; but the indifference with which she could drop him for a whole day, so as to keep some idiotic engagement with giggling flappers, was enough to send any lover crazy!

Jack hurried downstairs in time to hang about the hotel passage, waiting for Kitty to arrive by the lift with her sister so that he could accompany them to the dining-hall.

On this occasion Kitty was alone, Joyce having confessed to a headache, and they dined at their little table *tête-à-tête*.

"I can't think what is troubling her," the little sister remarked, "for she is fearfully worried, I know."

"Something, perhaps, in that letter you took to her a little while ago?" suggested Jack.

"It was from a friend of hers at Muktiarbad."

"Honor Bright?"

"Yes—a strange idea to name a girl 'Honor'!"

"Her surname must have suggested it."

"Perhaps I should call it a happy idea. But supposing her character did not bear out the selection?"

"In her case, I should say it suits her admirably. She's a topping good sort."

"Is she pretty?"

"My chum used to think so, but not I. She's good to look at, anyway, and there's something straight and clean about her that does a fellow good. She has fine eyes and nice teeth which go far towards beauty."

"I wonder what she could have written about, to upset my sister so completely?"

They wondered together, and grew more confidential over their mutual interest in the subject. Jack enjoyed every minute of the meal, trying to imagine he was dining with his wife,—an idea full of charm.

After dinner was over and Kitty had satisfied herself that Joyce was no worse, they strolled in the hotel gardens, at the corner of which was a summer-house. Jack who was trembling from head to foot with impatience and longing, drew her suddenly within where the shadows were darkening, and blurted out his tale of consuming passion. "Can't you see it without the need of words? I am mad for love of you! If you don't want me, in mercy say so, and I shall go out there and drown myself."

He would have said a great deal more, only there was no need, for Kitty confessed that she wanted him more than anything on earth, and was only waiting for the initiative to come from him.

Her frank response enraptured Jack, and he caught her to his breast inarticulate with joy, while she, free of artificial coyness, surrendered herself to his embrace and gave him her sweet lips again and again.

Jack felt that he would have liked to have kicked himself all round Eastbourne for imagining that he had ever before known what it was to love! This was the real thing, and the bliss of it was unspeakable.

"And why didn't you give me the least bit of inkling that you had a soft corner in your heart for a blighter like me?" he asked when it was possible to indulge in connected conversation.

"Why did you take so long to know your own mind?"

"My mind was made up the instant I found out that you were not Mrs. Meredith the afternoon I met you in front of the booking-office at Victoria. You surely have not forgotten our very first meeting? I could tell you in detail what you wore!"

Of course she had not, though she feigned to seem retrospective.

"I believe you were wearing a shot brown tie," she ventured, perfectly aware that she was correct.

"You remember that?" (An interlude of ecstasy.) "I went all the way to Richmond just to be able to look at you for a bit longer. I have been in love with you for quite a year!"

Doubt being cast upon his veracity, he explained his possession of her photograph, which fact she had long been aware of.

"I used to write poems about your eyes and your lips which I thought the most alluring in the world. Did I dream I should ever see and kiss them in reality?"

Silence again for a further interval of rapture.

"Now you will know how I have been feeling about going out to India! How is it possible for me to leave you behind? Can't we be married in a week?"

"We could," said Kitty, "but you forget there are others who will have something to say to that."

"Your parents?"

"Undoubtedly. One daughter in India is enough for Mother. I am not at all sure she will consent." It was very mischievous of her to distress him for the sake of delighting in the proofs of his abject slavery to herself, but Kitty was nothing if not human, and realising the completeness of her own surrender, was pleased to get back a little of her own.

His woe-begone look was almost melodramatic. "If they refuse their consent, what will you do?"

"I suppose I shall have to obey. I'm not of age, you know," said Kitty knowing full well that she was bound to have her own way, her parents having long ago resigned themselves to her strength of character and determination.

"Then I'll desert and enlist under another name that I might be killed by a German bullet," he said gloomily.

"But you mightn't be killed. You might just be smashed up instead, invalided out without a limb, or, worse still, be made unrecognisable!"

Horrible prospect! Jack's military ardour cooled visibly. "Anyhow, it would be their fault."

"And I should chase after you and beg of you to marry me, all the same,—limbless and unrecognisable as you may be!"

"You would? You said just now you would have to obey."

"Of course I would obey, but only for a time. Do you think I shall ever give you up, even if the skies were to fall?"

That finished it. Jack was in heaven again, and the time passed with amazing rapidity.

Meanwhile, Joyce had been to see Baby Douglas asleep in his crib and was weighing the pros and cons of her problem with agonised uncertainty. He was now as healthy as any normal infant of his age, and was in the care of an experienced and trustworthy nurse. At Wynthrop Manor he would be in the lap of luxury, wanting for nothing, and his grandparents would be sure to bring him up in the way he should go, till she and Ray came home together on his next furlough ... (after the War!—whenever that might be!). But all her baby's pretty ways and unfolding intelligence would be for others to enjoy! She, his devoted mother, would be thousands of miles away!

The thought brought forth a flood of tears, and expressions of sympathy from the nurse. "If it makes you feel so badly, I wouldn't go if I were you."

"It breaks my heart!"

"There now, don't take on so. Give up the idea. You will feel easier in mind to leave him when he is a bit older."

"It will be just as bad—perhaps worse!" cried Joyce, thinking of the possibility of a loveless reunion with Ray, if she stayed away too long! In that case she would have no compensation for her act of self-sacrifice.

"Then take him with you, I have no objection to the voyage, or serving in India which I have often wished to see."

"Oh, no. Baby is best here, for his own sake. In India I have all sorts of anxieties. I would have to go alone."

"But there are many ladies who stay in Europe for the sake of their children, leaving their husbands in India. In my last place, my mistress, whose husband was a Forest officer living in lonely places among the blacks, spent most of her time with her people in England as she could not abide the natives, and the climate upset her nerves. Only, occasionally, she visited him in the East, and sometimes he came home."

"What a life!" sighed Joyce. "I know it is done, but it isn't right"—she was thinking of Honor's letter. "Both go different ways, and what love and happiness is there for them?"

"But that is always so when ladies have husbands in India!"

"It need not be so. It makes me wonder why men marry when they know the risk they run of broken domestic ties, and the burdens they have to bear! It isn't worth while, if a man is to become only the means of providing money for the comforts of his family, and keeping very little, or none for himself—poor dear!"

Decidedly, Joyce Meredith's views had undergone a change.

The questions pressing on her mind were—Where was she most needed? and where, most, lay her heart's desire?

In her case, duty and desire were no longer in conflict. Clearly, her place was beside her husband as long as she was capable of enduring the climate, and her heart was sick with longing for him.

"I shall be going out almost immediately—as soon as it can possibly be arranged," she said coming to a sudden decision. "Pack the trunks early in the morning, and we shall return home in the afternoon to fix this up. It will be a great comfort to me, nurse, to know that you will stay with Baby."

"I'll stay as long as you want me, ma'am, and you need have no fears," said the woman who was sincerely attached to her charge, and who was aware that her devotion received ample recognition.

On her way to her own room, Joyce met two embarrassed and happy people waiting to waylay her with their news.

"Take us into your room for a little while, do, there's a darling, we've so much to tell you!"

Joyce was hustled into her own room by her little sister with Jack's big form looming in the rear, and the wonderful tale was told and her congratulations solicited.

"Of course I saw it coming," said Joyce kissing them both. "You were like ostriches with your heads in the sand ——"

"In the clouds, rather. I have been seeing a little bit of heaven, Mrs. Meredith," said Jack.

"Now please come back to earth, and tell me your plans, for I have decided to join my husband as soon as it is possible to get a passage."

"You?—with Baby?" from Kitty.

"No. Baby must stay behind."

"Then that was what gave you a headache? You ought to be ashamed of yourself to have a headache at the prospect of going back to Ray!" Kitty teased.

"Say, 'at the prospect of leaving Baby.'"

"Can't you take him?" said Jack. "There are crowds of youngsters of his age getting rosy and fat in the hills all the summer."

"I shouldn't feel safe about him. He'll be best with Grannie."

"Bravo!" cried Kitty. "Jack's got to go very soon, so we can all three go together." Jack's face showed intense appreciation.

"You don't mean to say you are thinking of marrying at once?"

"Why not?" from him.

"Of course not," said Kitty ruthlessly. "But as it is not good for you to travel alone in these exciting times, you *must* take me with you—engaged to Jack—and to be married when we have time to look around. Has anyone any objections?"

"You darling!" gasped Jack.

"Well, let's see what Mother has to say about it," said Joyce. "Meantime I shall pack a few things before getting to bed."

"Then you won't be so heartless as to turn us out. Come Jack, and let us talk it over"; and Jack, nothing loath, drew her on his knee in the one big chair by the window, and for some little time Joyce had ceased to exist for them. Neither seemed to mind the fact of her presence; it was sympathetic and that was quite enough, so they felt at liberty to continue to enjoy their mutual delight in the knowledge that they had become engaged.

Joyce suffered a pang of jealous longing for her own dear lover-husband, when she saw the look on Jack's face while he held Kitty to his breast and kissed her yielding lips. And Kitty, with her arms wound about her boy's neck and her face uplifted to his!—It was her hour, and Joyce knew that her own was yet to come. She had indeed been the Sleeping Beauty who had slept too long under the kisses of her Prince. She had never really understood her own heart, or realised love till now. Could there ever be a moment more wonderful on this old earth, than that in which two lips met in mutual passion?—two souls fused in divine ecstasy?

"Blessed darlings!" she murmured to herself, turning aside not to intrude on their sacred joy yet conscious of the fervour of the clinging kisses, the incoherent whispers, the bounding hearts! It was all as God had meant it to be when he created Man and gave him Woman for his mate.

"My place is indeed with my husband," she muttered to herself.

CHAPTER XXII

A DESPERATE RESORT

In the early days of the Great War, a voyage to India had no terrors for the travelled. Before the Hun had proved himself a savage in warfare, indifferent to all international laws and the dictates of humanity, the only anxieties and drawbacks suffered on the way, were those in relation to the risk of encountering mines, or the delays caused by the changing of routes. The nerves of the public had not been harrowed by tales of atrocities on the high seas, and the nation confidingly believed that the glorious traditions of naval warfare were respected even by Germany. It had yet to learn what manner of people the Allies were fighting. The difficulties and dangers of a sea voyage only added to the thrill of expectancy, and the contingency of meeting with German raiders on the way, was like having a bit of Marryat's novels in real life; fear was an unknown quantity.

As Kitty anticipated, she met with little opposition from her parents in the matter of her engagement, or of her voyage to India under her sister's chaperonage, with the prospect of a wedding at the end of it. Since she had always managed things her own way, there was little use wasting time in argument. Jack was a very fine fellow indeed, and Kitty might do worse than marry him. At all events, he was the man of her own choice.

Accordingly, a trousseau was acquired regardless of cost, and, the moment Jack's orders arrived recalling him to duty — which was towards the end of August — trunks were packed, passages were booked, and the party crossed to France, *en route* to Marseilles.

Jack's feelings can be better imagined than described. In his wildest dreams he had not hoped for such luck as a speedy marriage with Kitty, and he was rendered, for a time, incapable of coherent thought. They boarded the mail boat at Marseilles and settled down as an engaged couple to enjoy the days at sea to the extent of their capacity.

Beyond an occasional cruiser in the distance, or a destroyer there was nothing throughout the voyage to remind them of the war; and, from the point of view of belligerency, it was both uneventful and calm.

As recognised lovers, Kitty and Jack had the choice of sheltered nooks and were left to themselves, undisturbed, except by camera fiends who snapped them at embarrassing moments and made themselves generally obnoxious.

Being absorbed in his happiness, Jack had given no thought to Mrs. Fox who was awaiting him in Calcutta, till, one day, in the Arabian Sea, the imminent prospect of their meeting filled him with uneasiness and obliged him to consider his position seriously. As far as he knew, she was expecting to fall into his arms on his reappearance in India. She knew nothing of his new-found happiness and was very likely wondering at his reason for having missed so many mails. She would not follow him to England since she was aware that all leave was cancelled.

So awkward was the situation, that Jack was greatly disturbed and sought the advice of a ship-board acquaintance who happened to be a young man of wide experience in the affairs of the heart.

"I should tell my *fiancée*, in your place," said he. "Put it to her straight. The great thing is to get your story in before the other has a chance to cut the ground from under your feet. That is, if she is the sort to do it."

"She's the sort right enough," said Jack miserably. "She would do it to spite me for breaking my word to her; but—damn it!—I'd rather be shot than become her husband, now that I am crazy after the sweetest girl in the world, and she is ready to marry me!"

"Then have it over. It is better than someone telling her at a tea-party,—'Didn't he ever confess himself to you?—naughty boy'! and so on. Or the disappointed one butting in with—'Hands off! He is promised to me!' which is more than likely."

So Jack decided to make his confession, prostrate at her feet, metaphorically.

While the lovers were living in a world of their own, Joyce was learning many things, chiefly courage and patience. Her fellow-passengers courted her society; she was considered the loveliest of women; and all combined to spoil her with flattery and attentions. However, she was too much absorbed in her own thoughts, her manner was too cold and aloof to lend encouragement to flatterers who vied with each other in serving her and disputed among themselves for her favours. She took no real interest in what was going on, to realise the half of it; and her indifference rendered her the more alluring. But Joyce had had a life-long lesson at Muktiarbad, and not being by nature, a flirt, the result was that the childish coquetries of the past were abandoned for a dignity and reserve that would have satisfied the most jealous of husbands.

She had not cabled to India. A desire to read her fate in her husband's eyes had fixed her determination to take him by surprise. She would then know at the first glance whether she were welcome or had ceased to reign supreme in his heart.

Honor had advised her to cable. But this was entirely her own affair and she would go through with it. She had a right to expect her husband's love and loyalty; and this being the case, there could be no objection to her taking him unawares. Joy does not kill; and if she did not bring him happiness, it were as well for her not to be deceived. Such was her logic, which she kept to herself, being too proud to share her doubts with Kitty.

One day, as she lay in a deck chair, apparently dozing with her book open on her lap, she overheard two women gossiping together behind the angle of the saloon. They were talking of friends in Darjeeling, and their voices had lulled her into a state of semi-consciousness, till the name "Meredith" made her alive to the fact that her husband was under discussion.

"Not the planter, Tom Meredith, but the I. C. S. man."

"Any relation of the pretty creature with us?"

"I am sure I can't say. He is married, I am told, with a wife at home. 'When the cat's away, the mice *will* play,' you know! She is a widow, or passes for one, and neither cares a snap of the finger for the talk about them. All Darjeeling is scandalised, and that's saying a good deal! My friend writes that the woman nursed him while he was ill from sunstroke in some outlandish station in Bengal, and they became fearfully intimate. These nurses know a thing or two and can make themselves indispensable if they like. Men generally find them irresistible. However, it is rather rough on his wife at home, when you come to think of it."

"What has the nurse to do with him, now that he has recovered?"

"Ah, that's the point! She stays at the same hotel nominally looking after a delicate baby whose parents are in the plains; but the kid gets precious little of her attention. It is left to the ayah's tender mercies while the nurse goes about with Mr. Meredith. They are never seen apart, and she spends most of her time in his rooms. It puts me in mind of that divorce case you may remember two years ago at Simla, when"—and the conversation was diverted into other channels.

Meanwhile, Joyce was hot and cold with conflicting emotions. Without question, it was her husband they had been discussing, for he was in the Indian Civil Service, and had been sent to Darjeeling to convalesce after the sunstroke, which had seized him in the District of Muktiarbad, the "outlandish station" referred to.

By the light of this conversation Honor's letter was explained. She, too, had heard of the doings at Darjeeling, and in her anxiety had written that letter imploring her friend to return.

Well—she was returning, but to what?

Her husband was apparently content to be without her—which would account for the cable message he had sent her on the outbreak of war, forbidding her to travel.

Joyce rose from her deck chair with a face as white as the foam on the crested waves, and stumbled to her cabin. "It is nothing," she explained to fellow-passengers who offered assistance thinking she was likely to collapse, "only a stupid attack of dizziness—I thought I was a better sailor, that's all," and she tried to smile.

Kitty was sent to her in hot haste to see what she could do, and was told the same thing. "I'll be all right after a bit."

"Are you sure?"

"Perfectly," was the assured answer, for Joyce was already determined not to go down under the blow, but to fight to a finish. Ray—her husband—false to her? The shame of it—the humiliation, would be unbearable, if what she had heard were true! It was possible that gossip had exaggerated the state of things between him and that woman who had nursed him. Scandalmongers never did give any one the benefit of a doubt. For instance, scandal might have been busy with her own name and that of Captain Dalton, but she was innocent in act and thought. She would not judge hastily; but she would allow no woman to dare to come between herself and her husband. He was her own man. God had given him to her, and she was glad she had taken the journey at all costs to put matters right and send the depraved creature—who was trying to take her place—about her own business. But if Ray had been false to her—she knew he could not lie to her—she would....

Joyce seemed to arrive against a blank wall in her mind as she faced such an unthinkable problem as Ray's unfaithfulness.

Later in the evening when she returned to the deck having gained the mastery over her nerves, it was to find that an unhappy breach had come to pass between Kitty and Jack.

Dancing was in full swing on the hurricane deck, a band was discoursing dreamy melodies, and Jack with his back to the sea was leaning against the taffrail and glowering at the ship's doctor who was dancing with Kitty.

As the evening lengthened, it was evident that the latter was bent upon inflicting all manner of snubs and punishments on her distracted lover by the taffrail, which in a certain measure, recoiled upon herself. Finally, when "lights-out" obliged dancing to come abruptly to an end, Kitty retired to her cabin without so much as a good-night to Jack who looked as if he had come to the end of all things.

"What is wrong?" Joyce asked her before turning into her berth. "Can I help?"

"We've had a disagreement. That is all," said Kitty curtly, looking white and angry. "You have heard of lovers' quarrels, I suppose?"

"There is no need to snap my head off," said Joyce. "I am only sorry to see it happen. Life is too short for misunderstandings."

"I quite agree with you. But this is not a misunderstanding. I have been deliberately deceived."

"How do you mean?"

"What's the use of discussing it?"

"There is no use if you are determined not to be helped."

"What can you do? What can any one do? This is a matter which is only between us. I am sorry I did not know all about it before, or I would not have become engaged."

A light dawned on Joyce's mind. "Oh—I see. Jack's been telling you about his foolishness in the past!"

"You call it foolishness?"

"Wasn't it the height of folly to have been silly about a married woman? and one who isn't worth a thought?"

"It was something worse than folly when it came to his being *engaged to marry* her all this time—even when he proposed to me! How dared he do it? How had he the nerve to ask me to be his wife when he knew she was waiting to marry him on his return to India, having won her decree?"

"I heard she had divorced her husband—the designing wretch! She is a perfectly horrid woman. Poor Jack! I don't wonder at his meaning to throw her over after knowing you!"

"But to be engaged to two women at the same time!—it is wicked and humiliating! Why didn't you tell me of her?"

"It is something to know that you have saved him from making the mistake of his life!"—ignoring the question.

This was an inspiration on the part of Joyce, and Kitty was rendered dumb. Joyce immediately pursued her advantage.

"To have been compelled to marry Mrs. Fox into whose snare he had fallen, would have been a dreadful thing for poor Jack, who, at the most, is only an overgrown schoolboy without much experience of the world. I did not tell you of it as I thought it was over and done with."

"As a man of honour, he is bound to keep his word to her and marry her as he said he would,"—obstinately.

"I would rather see him dead. There is no honour about Mrs. Fox or her methods. She deliberately set out to work this thing, and her punishment is in your hands. Jack loves you. You have no right to force him into marriage with a woman who will ruin his life for him."

"I think he has behaved abominably."

"If you are looking for perfection in the man you intend to marry, you had better make up your mind to live an old maid. Good-night!" and having delivered her parting shot, Joyce turned away, feeling no longer the same childish creature of a few months ago. She had awakened in right earnest.

Needless to say, Jack spent the night in his clothes on deck. Sleep was impossible; and, in the hope that she would relent and creep on deck to find him and retract the hard things she had said, he haunted the companion till the stars paled and the day began to break.

But Kitty, though very loving, had a temper that was not easily calmed. Jack had behaved abominably right through, and should not get things all his own way, she decided, and while relenting inwardly, she maintained towards him an attitude of cold disapproval. She had given him back the ring—which at that moment was burning a hole in his waistcoat pocket—and had had nothing more to say to him, though, when he was not conscious of the fact, her eyes often dwelt upon him with wistful yearning. He might deserve punishment, but there was no doubt about it, that he was the only man in the world for her! She loved everything about him, from his curly blond head to the soles of his manly feet. He was by far the best-looking boy on the ship, and the most simple-minded! Besides, what was unforgettable, he was a prince of lovers! Was she going to allow Mrs. Fox to take him?— —

Kitty flushed in hot indignation at the thought, but it was right and proper that he should suffer for his weakness and folly. Of course, she would have to forgive him or be miserable for the rest of her life, but—not yet.

The punishment might have continued for days, if Jack's own precipitancy had not brought about almost a tragedy.

In the morning he gravitated to his friend again, and in a burst of confidence, related the outcome of his having adopted the course that had been advised. His friend, wise in the ways of women, listened with his tongue in his cheek. Not being in love, himself, he could afford to see the humourous side of Jack's trouble. This time he suggested a ruse.

"Excite her pity, my dear fellow. Do something to rouse her heart. It is only suffering from shock and will come to the scratch when it is stirred by pity. The best thing to do is to get seriously ill. Too much grief—mental strain—has brought on a heart attack. Lie down to it and kick up a devil of a fuss. I'll tip the doctor a wink and we'll do it in style. What do you say to that? When she hears you are on the verge of heart failure, all through her, she'll fall on your neck and wipe out the past."

"Go to blazes!—I'm not going to do any play-acting and drag the whole ship into the secret, only to lose any possible chance I might have had if ever it leaked out."

"Then we'll have to think of something else."

"I think I'll just drop overboard, and end everything," said Jack melodramatically. "That will show her how I have felt over her treatment of me!"

"But you'll not be there to enjoy it. Happy thought. Can you swim?"

"Like a fish."

"Good! You can go overboard if she remains relentless, and the thought that she has driven you to commit suicide, will bring her to you weeping and repentant the minute you are restored to consciousness."

"What the devil do you mean?"

"Why just an accident, done on purpose. To all it will appear an accident. To *her*,—attempted suicide. To you and me, simply bluff. I'll be the first to see you go, and a life-buoy will go after you in a trice. Only let's know when you contemplate bringing it off, so that I can be stationed near one. There'll be no time lost. 'Man overboard!' and the engines will be stopped, reversed, a boat lowered, and there you are! You'll be fished out apparently drowned—or nearly—and with hot water bottles and brandy you'll be well enough to see Miss Kitty in your cabin in half an hour."

"What price, sharks?" asked Jack, to whom the adventure strongly appealed,— as an adventure, if nothing else. He could imagine the commotion on the ship, and

Kitty, white with anxiety and self-reproach, hanging over the rails as she watched his chances of recovery from the briny deep.

"Fellows have been known to fall overboard in the Arabian Sea, and one never hears of sharks. You'll have to risk it. Take a sailor's knife; then, if you are attacked you can put up a fight till you are picked up."

All day Kitty avoided Jack and surrounded herself with the callow youth of the vessel. She appeared in high spirits, played deck quoits, and did not give him a minute's chance to get a word with her, till the idea in his mind, of attempted suicide, took root and developed after serious and profound thinking. Something would have to be done. He could not exist another day apart from Kitty, severed from her heart, and condemned to wear his out in agonies of despair and remorse.

The following morning, after breakfast, Kitty's attitude being unchanged, Jack hung upon the taffrail, and, surveying the clear, emerald-green waves as they heaved past the sides of the ship, telegraphed with his eyes to his resourceful friend.

The sea was choppy and glittered like jewels in the sunlight. Sea-gulls skimmed the surface and circled in the wake of the steamer, which was travelling fast, the speed of the engines causing a gentle vibration of the decks, while the ratlins trembled in the breeze.

It would require some nerve to plunge into the waves, fully clothed; but he was in light, deck shoes which could be kicked off; and his coat could easily be sacrificed in the water. It was an old suit!

Sharks?—

They had seen none since entering these waters. Besides, he was ready to take his chance, or to fight, if it came to the push.

Above all, his act must be made to appear an accident. Kitty, alone, should think as she pleased, being in a position to supply a possible motive; and, doubtless, her feelings would be heart-rending.

Jack nerved himself to bring this just punishment upon her obduracy and took up his position on the taffrail with his back to the sea.

His first act was to note whether Kitty, who was promenading the deck with a subaltern—called to active service—had any idea of his peril. She had always discouraged his sitting on the taffrail, saying that it "got on her nerves."

Kitty glanced towards him, and with an air of indifference continued promenading.

Jack's already sore heart was lacerated. Could there be any sharks about?

His friend and ally was to be seen idly lounging in the neighbourhood of a life-buoy suspended against the rails, further aft.

Just as he was about to let go, someone lounging up, remarked on his unhealthy pallor. "Feeling the motion of the vessel?" he asked Jack, who did not know what it was to feel sea-sick.

"Not in the least," said Jack wishing him to the devil.

"It must be the smell of kippers. Frankly, I can't stand them. The stink hangs about all morning, till one feels one is breathing as well as eating kippers."

"They have an unholy smell," Jack agreed, wondering when the fellow would move on, or whether his inopportune presence was to be taken as a warning not to put his mad intention into effect. He was superstitious enough to believe in omens.

"I rather like *bumlas*, do you?" was the next remark.

"I don't know—oh, yes, I think they are topping."

"Sort of jelly-substance, and when fried crisp, the last word!"

"Oh, damn!" said Jack aching for him to go.

"What's that?" the man asked, protruding an ear forward. "The wind makes a devil of a noise in these ropes——"

Someone called him off for quoits, and Jack started to tune up his nerves again for the plunge.

Children ran between him and the line of chairs he faced. He could see Joyce Meredith listening idly while the ship's doctor talked to her. At that moment the subaltern took Kitty's hand in his to examine a ring she was wearing,—an heirloom, with a story,—and this gave the final stimulus to Jack's sporting resolve. He was seen suddenly to lose his balance, throw out his arms, and disappear over the side.

On the instant there was wild confusion. Chairs were flung back, children shrieked, women fell fainting on the deck. Someone had shouted, "Man overboard!" which was taken up vociferously in every key by, at least, a hundred throats, and in less than a minute the engines were silent, the vessel moving only with its headway. Then, with a blast of steam, they were reversed. Meanwhile, the after part of the hurricane deck, and the poop of the second saloon, were packed with eager souls scanning the surface of the water in the hope of catching sight of their unfortunate fellow-passenger.

Again the vessel stopped, and a boat was lowered.

"Wonderful presence of mind," the doctor said to Joyce as she, too, anxiously strained her eyes to look for the reappearance of Jack's form in the water, which had been seen, and then lost sight of. "Did you hear how a fellow kept his head when he saw young Darling go over, sending a life-buoy the same moment after him? Splendid, I call that!"

Joyce was deeply impressed. "He has probably saved Jack's life! Good man! does any one know where my sister is?"

Kitty was nowhere to be seen. Joyce presently found her in the saloon crouching on a sofa with her hands over her ears.

"He is drowned, I know he is drowned, and I shall never see him any more! I have killed him just as surely as if I sent him over with my own hands!—oh, let me die!" She was beside herself, and her suffering would not only have more than healed Jack's injured feelings, but have made him sue for pardon.

Joyce took her in her arms and they clung together, fearful of what they should presently hear. The shrieks of the women and children were mingled with the voices of the men shouting instructions from the deck to the officer in the boat. Nothing definite could be gleaned from the excited ejaculations of the onlookers.

"What made me do it! — why did I let myself behave so!" Kitty cried shivering from the force of her emotions. "I shall never be able to ask his forgiveness for my hardness, and yet in my heart I was melted towards him and longing to tell him so, — only waiting till the evening when we could be more alone. Oh, I am terribly punished for daring to punish my poor Jack!"

"We are not to give up hope, dearest, but are to will with might and main that he be saved. It all helps. Honor Bright says it is scientifically possible to impose will-power on the forces of nature. It is a way God works for us and with us."

"It is useless to tell me all that when I cannot even think!" wailed Kitty.

"But there is a great deal in heaven and earth that is not 'dreamt of in our philosophy,'" Joyce repeated.

"Oh, my poor Jack! — Go, Joyce, and ask what is happening, now! I cannot bear this stillness." For a sudden hush seemed to have fallen on the company on deck.

At that moment, a distant cheer came from over the water. It was taken up by those watching from the ship and loud "Hurrahs!" sounded again and again.

"Oh, thank God! — he must be safe!" cried Joyce.

Kitty seemed to crumple up as she burst into a passion of tears.

Neither she nor Joyce had any idea that the rescue of Jack Darling was a touch and go. He had gone overboard confident of being able to keep afloat till he was picked up, and willing to accept his fate if it worked out otherwise. Having, in his despair, become temporarily insane, he was hardly accountable for his actions till his immersion in the waves brought him rudely to his senses. After coming to the surface, he looked about for the steamer, and was astounded to see it already so far away that it seemed to him impossible for a boat's crew to descry him in that heaving expanse of ocean. To add to his dismay, the vessel seemed to steam on as though determined to leave him to his fate.

The prospect was horrible!

In a flash, he saw himself swimming till exhausted and a prey to sharks. Life became all at once very dear. Whether with, or without Kitty, it would be better to live, than to die this slow and lonely death! He had been nothing but a damned idiot to have allowed himself to be dragged into such a dangerous piece of melodrama, and all for nothing! With a little patience and perseverance he might have gained his end without all this miserable fuss! No abuse was strong enough for his folly.

At that moment he espied the life-buoy, which he was fearing he would never find, and eagerly scrambled into it. Ah, that was better! Though he could swim like a fish, there was no doubt about it that he was grateful for support in the restless waters. Sometimes he was on the top of a wave where he was able to see the far distant ship; then, with a smart buffeting, he would find himself at the bottom of a trough with, what looked like green mountains of water threatening to engulf him.

It was an immense relief to his mind when it became apparent that the vessel was steaming back on her course, and the sight of the boat being lowered gave him new life and confidence.

But before it could reach him, symptoms of cramp in one leg had set in—possibly, because of late he had entirely neglected his exercises. The first twinge scared him mightily. If it should increase, he would be doubled up in the water and, in spite of the buoy, go down like a stone. The prospect racked him with suspense. The cramp again seized him with demoniacal violence and a red-hot band seemed to tighten round about his limb....

Was it cramp, or the jaws of a shark?

Petrifying thought!

If ever he had been punished in his life for folly, he was being punished now!

He glanced wildly over his shoulder, then at the advancing boat. He tried to call aloud, but his voice was choked with spray. The pain intensified. It seemed to rise into his thigh and the leg felt wrenched from its socket. Surely this was the end? A shark— —?

Jack remembered no more. He had fainted with the pain of severe cramp combined with the shock of terror. He had never been wanting in courage, but physical agony, and the notion of falling a prey to sharks before he had time to show fight, had caused him to swoon.

And it was at that moment that the boat reached him, and eager hands snatched him into safety.

Before the boat reached the ship he had recovered, and after a stiff dose of brandy, was able to take an interest in his rescue.

"I could have sworn a shark had got me," he explained. "The pain was so excruciating."

"In the water, cramp is the very devil!" said the third officer.

It was a shamed and chastened young man who disappeared into his cabin, amid hearty congratulations, to change into dry garments. In the face of so much honest relief and thankfulness, he felt a very worm for his deceit and trickery. It had been a mean game—a dirty trick he had played everybody, and Kitty in particular; which might easily have cost him his life. Truly, he had come to the conclusion that he was not fit to aspire to any nice girl. Kitty was properly fastidious, and she was not to be blamed for having recoiled from his unsavoury story, though it had been the barest outline of his misdemeanours that he had given her. All the same, it was hardly a yarn for the ears of even modern eighteen!

She being his promised wife, he had felt it due to her to reveal his past—(lest others should do so!)—and he had no right to rebel against her verdict, however blasting to his life and happiness—and so on, and so forth.

In downright self-disgust he kept his cabin, pleading the effects of cramp and exhaustion, and emerged only when it was dark, to drop into a deck chair behind a windlass, and brood upon his sins, staring out upon the moonlit sea.

Here Kitty came to him with healing, and here we take our leave of them for the present, feeling perfectly sure that Jack was not likely to damage his chances of reconciliation by any further confessions,—not even concerning his latest and maddest adventure. Confession may be good for the soul, but Jack had learned that there are circumstances when it is better to be silent.

CHAPTER XXIII
TEMPORISINGS

While Jack counted the days to the arrival of the ship at Bombay, and Joyce lived in anticipation of the reunion with her husband; while Honor watched for the coming of Joyce and an end to an impossible situation in Darjeeling; while Dalton played at friendship with the girl he adored, since to desire more was like asking for the moon; and while Tommy was breaking his heart with disappointment, and tormenting the Government of Bengal for permission to join the Indian Army reserve, instead of continuing to serve that Government by safe-guarding his District, it seemed almost inconceivable that thousands of miles away, the destinies of nations were in the melting pot, and the map of Europe in process of re-making.

Immense armies were in training; miracles of organisation were taking place within the British Empire. Always the greatest Naval Power, she was rapidly becoming, also, a great Military Power.

The grand old army of "Contemptibles" was covering itself with imperishable glory; Indian and Colonial troops were mobilising for the assistance of the Motherland. In all parts of the world the clarion cry was sounded—"To arms!"

The War was the absorbing topic in all the cities of the world.

But at little Muktiarbad and similar rural districts, the placid monotony of daily life was barely stirred.

There was "a war on," of course, they said in the bazaars. India was involved—that, also, was a matter of course. The fighting sons of India could not be left out of such a fateful occasion as a war which called for loyalty and support. But it was an impersonal matter to native Muktiarbad. Doubtless, one of these wise dispensations of the Almighty, that helped to thin out the too rapidly increasing population of the world! It had no bearing on the lives and fortunes of the cultivator and the shop-keeper, save, that, in the case of the latter, it enabled him to put up his prices. But since the sun rose and set exactly as usual, and the flowers bloomed, and the seasons remained unchanged, and the daily life of the District continued undisturbed, where was the need to worry?

True, there was occasionally talk in the bazaar of battles lost and won; but talk was the life of the bazaar. Whatever happened, or did not happen, the bazaar always knew about it and spread rumours that none heeded, for rumours are always unreliable. What did they amount to, anyway? Nothing came of them, so far as the countryside was concerned.

Now and again, it was said, that So-and-So, generally a stout Pathan, who had seen active service on the frontier, had packed his bundle and was off on his own initiative to offer his strong right arm for the cause of the *Sarcar* who was his father and his mother. His ancestors had fought and bled—or died; won medals and gained pensions; he, too, would gain medals and a pension, or lose his life if God so willed it. *"Kismet ke bat!"*[18] Where was he going? God knew! Some day, if it was so willed, he would return to tell.

Like as not, he would never return. When youth went a-travelling, the attractions of the great world seldom released him from their thrall.

At the court-house, the Magistrate and Collector, officiating for Meredith who was still on leave at Darjeeling, tried cases and settled disputes, while the court-yard in front was covered with squatting humanity, chewing *pân* and awaiting their individual turns to be called up before the *Hakim* to tell—anything but the truth!

At the Club, the sahibs and memsahibs played tennis and bridge and enjoyed their cold drinks as usual, just as though there were no sanguinary battles raging afar, such as the world had never known in all its history.

Once, during the month of August, a strange *babu* had appeared in the bazaar, and, perching himself upon a cask, had talked sedition for about an hour to apathetic ears. Muktiarbad, being mainly Mohammedan, did not like gentlemen of the Brahmin persuasion; so he had departed much disheartened. Shortly after, another agitator—a Mohammedan this time—had endeavoured to incite the peace-loving population to revolt by preaching religious antagonism towards Christians.

But Muktiarbad was not to be roused. "Live and let live" was the prevailing sentiment among its people. Besides, what was the use of rebelling, since it would be futile against such a mighty race as the British, who were also good rulers, taking no advantage to themselves from their might, and giving each man according to his due? The needs of the village folk were mainly personal, and so long as these were supplied, what cared they if the rulers of the land were Christians. They never interfered with the Moslem religion; why should Moslems interfere with theirs? And so this man also departed discouraged.

At Panipara, interest centred chiefly on the fact that the Government had decided that the *jhil* should be drained. The Great War was a secondary matter. Wells were already in process of construction and, at the end of the rains, before the water of the wide morass could be poisoned with germs, usually bred in the drought of winter and spring, the drainage was to be taken in hand and the health of the District safeguarded forever. All this interference and annoyance had sprung from the doctor Sahib, who was thereby the most unpopular sahib that had ever been put in charge of the sanitation of a District. He was cursed by the ignorant in the Muktiarbad bazaar and at Panipara village itself, but so far his person had been respected, as it was known by some occult means that he secretly carried firearms wherever he went.

[18] With Fate lay the decision.

In July, Honor had returned with her mother from Mussoorie in the Himalayas, physically and mentally stronger for her prolonged absence.

Captain Dalton and she had corresponded as friends, all expressions of personal feeling being rigorously excluded from the closely written pages. Both had bravely "played the game," the faithfulness and regularity of the letters, alone testifying to their unchanged devotion.

When they met again, Honor having braced herself to the ordeal, had sustained it courageously, no one guessing how much it had cost her to smile and shake hands with the doctor as naturally as she had done, the moment before, with Tommy; for the meeting had taken place, unexpectedly, at the Club.

Captain Dalton retired to his bungalow shortly afterwards, and the tension had lifted. He had gone, Honor knew, instinctively, because he could not bear to stand by, listening indifferently to the general conversation when his heart was filled with longing to speak to her alone. She had experienced the same inward impatience, but had learned a greater self-control.

By and by, their meetings became frequent; but the self-imposed restraint, mutually practised, had a wearing effect on the nerves of both.

And all the while, gossip in connection with Ray Meredith filtered through from various sources, and caused no little comment among his friends.

At last a letter to Mrs. Bright from Mrs. Ironsides, who was spending a month at the Sanitorium, placed it beyond doubt that Ray Meredith was very securely in the toils of his former nurse who was in the same hotel, in charge of a child suffering from jaundice.

"She has been in Darjeeling, with one pretext and another, I am told, ever since Mr. Meredith recovered," the lady wrote, "and people are beginning to look askance at her for the flagrant manner in which she flaunts her ascendancy over him. It is a thousand pities his wife is not with him, for he is at the woman's heels morning, noon, and night. Rumour says their rooms adjoin! I should feel inclined to blame him soundly were it not for the fact that he looks very delicate since his illness, and that people recovering from sunstroke are not altogether themselves. Possibly he is merely drifting for want of someone sufficiently interested in him to save him! Whatever it is, this Mrs. Dalton must be an abandoned creature, for she is indifferent to the fact that she is creating a disgusting scandal. When you think of how devoted that man was to his pretty little wife, you feel inclined, to believe anything of men! But, as I say, he cannot be himself. Let us hope it is only due to the sunstroke, and that his wife will come out soon and look after him."

Honor took this news to heart and wrote the appeal to Joyce of which the reader is already aware: she also gradually brought her mind to the point of speaking frankly to Captain Dalton on the subject.

Since her return from the hills, two weeks before, she had not met him alone, so that when she asked him, in a little note to see her at the Club next morning on a matter of some anxiety, he was naturally full of wonderment as he drove to keep the appointment.

The marker, alone, was in possession of the Club and in his office, when Dalton arrived, so that the meeting was undisturbed.

"You are surprised that I should have sent for you?" Honor said, as she stepped off her bicycle, having greeted him with a friendly nod. Had she given him her hand he would have noticed that it was trembling.

"Pleased, as well as surprised," said he, feasting his soul on the wholesome, girlish face with its frank, trustworthy eyes. "Has anything happened?" He was longing to hear that her request was prompted only by her great desire to have speech with him alone; but even as the thought crossed his mind, he knew that Honor would never have made an assignation with him for any personal reason. Not with those truthful eyes!

"A great deal seems to be happening," she said as they walked into the building side by side, and found themselves seats in the verandah. Dalton had hoped she would have led him to one of the public rooms where, at least, they would have been safe from the curious eyes of passing natives; but that she did not, was consistent with her character, for she was as open as the day.

Seated beside him, she told him of Mrs. Ironside's letter and of her own, unhappy fears for Joyce, and her future relations with her husband.

"She should not have gone home so soon after her marriage," said Dalton. "I guessed how it would be when the nurse took on the job, for Meredith is a very charming fellow, and she is a woman without a conscience."

"Brian, we must stop it!" It had been "Brian" and "Honey" in the letters.

"Not even an angel from heaven could, if Meredith is infatuated. I tell you, she is a clever fiend."

"It rests with you!" said Honor appealingly.

"With me?" surprised.

"Joyce and her husband love each other. I will not believe that he has ceased to care. Doesn't sunstroke somewhat dull memory?"

"For a time, yes,—possibly. Sometimes altogether. Meredith, however, is all right, or will be when he regains his normal vigour."

"I take it that he is not his normal self, and that when he is, he will be ashamed of the part he is now playing. Joyce's happiness is at stake. She is a simple little thing and very fond of him. Their happiness must be saved—even at a sacrifice."

"Well?"

"Oh, Brian!—you will have to take your wife back!"

Dalton stared dumbly at her. That Honor should ask him to take back the woman who had wrecked his life and whom he despised as the commonest prostitute in the land!——

"*You* ask me that?" he breathed.

Honor bent her head. She could not but realise that the step she proposed was a terrible outrage.

"Why, Honey!" His voice was choked. "Have you any idea of what you are asking me to do?"

"It will be a great sacrifice—which—which I shall—share—" words failed her and she looked away with a pathetic trembling of her lip.

"*You* would wish it?" in wounded tones.

"I would hate the thought of it!—yet, something must be done. She might find it more profitable to return to you and leave Mr. Meredith in peace."

A painful silence.

"Honey, if she lived with me I should surely murder her! Do you know how I detest the woman? Do you imagine I could take her back as a wife? I would rather be shot."

Honor buried her face in her hands. In her heart of hearts she was singing a pæan of thanksgiving that he was still hers—only hers, though divided from her by an impassable gulf!

"You could bear to see me reconciled to her?"

No answer.

"Honey," he cried desperately. "I would do anything in the world for you!"

"But you cannot sacrifice yourself for a good woman's happiness?" she questioned, hardly knowing what she said.

"Why should I for Mrs. Meredith?"

"Because you once owed her a debt—she was very good to you after——"

"My God!—yes!"

"This will kill her. She will hear—there are so many who will be ready to give her chapter and verse of the scandal against her husband. But if this—nurse—were with you, it would, perhaps, all blow over."

"Is it really your wish that I should do this thing? Remember, she is hateful to me—and she can never, in any sense, be my wife again!"

"I am—glad!" she could not help exclaiming. "Then the sacrifice will not be so terrible, after all!"

"Perhaps not," he answered, his eyes full on hers with a passion of longing. "Will you let me think it over?"

"Decide quickly!" she begged him.

"There is nothing I would not do for you," he repeated.

Honor rose with her gracious smile of gratitude and trust, and they parted without touching hands. When she returned home, the reaction from the strain of their meeting prostrated her for hours. Her parents feared that the climate of Muktiarbad was, at last, telling on her healthy constitution as it had told on Ray Meredith's.

"Perhaps we shall have to send you home!" her mother sighed anxiously.

"Not a bit of it!" Honor asserted. "The cold weather will put me to rights very soon."

"Perhaps you have something on your mind, darling?"

"I have. I am worrying badly for Joyce Meredith."

"Joyce will get nothing more than she deserves. Why should you suffer? It is nobody's business to meddle between husband and wife."

"Somebody is already meddling, so it may need counter-meddling to put it right."

"I shouldn't bother my head. We have enough to do without trying to act Providence in the case of fools."

"We are not trying to act Providence, but Providence needs to use us. It seems we are just so many pawns in the great Game."

"It has often puzzled me what Captain Dalton has been after," said Mrs. Bright, eyeing her daughter rather narrowly. Fear had preyed considerably on her mind, that the doctor had been playing fast and loose with her child, to her sorrow. "You and he have been fast friends. Once you told me there was an 'understanding'; but nothing seems to have come of it, though you have corresponded very regularly."

"I showed you some of his letters, darling," Honor temporised, faithful to her intention of bearing her own burdens alone, if possible.

"Nice, manly letters they were, and most interesting of his work and things in general. But I am none the wiser."

"What did you understand of our friendship?"

"That there was an 'understanding,'" her mother repeated.

"I do dislike that word in the sense you are applying it!" said Honor with a forced laugh. "We are not going to get married, anyway, for Captain Dalton is a married man."

"Honey!" Mrs. Bright was dumbfounded. "Since when have you known this?"

"For quite a long time; since early summer, in fact. You have met his wife— Mrs. Dalton, the nurse. Everyone here fancied her name was a coincidence. She worked to come here that she might see her husband and get him to take her back." Having said so much, Honor went on to explain further the cause of the breach between husband and wife and the irrevocable nature of it. "I am telling you this, dear, as you have a right to know the truth, being my mother. It is, however, a personal confidence, which no one else need share," Honor concluded.

"Why did you not mention it to me before?" Mrs. Bright asked while a light dawned on her mind.

"Because I have been very sorry for him, and, somehow, I felt I ought to respect his confidence. But it will, inevitably, be known in time, and then you will be able to say you were not uninformed."

"Honor, are you in love with Captain Dalton?" Mrs. Bright asked pointedly.

Honor winced. "Yes, Mother. And he loves me."

Mrs. Bright looked faint. "*You*, my child, in love with a married man!" This was, indeed, a blow! It accounted, fully, for Honor's discouragement of eligible suitors in Mussoorie, which had greatly vexed her mother at the time. "This is dreadful!"

"Not at all, except for the fact that it is naturally a grief to me, — to us both; for, as you see, we can never marry."

Mrs. Bright was entirely astray. When other girls were convicted of being in love with married men, it had always sounded so immoral! But no one could think of Honor as such. She was plainly an upright and honourable girl.

"Yet you encouraged his writing, and answered his letters! You meet, to all appearances, as if nothing is wrong. What am I to make of it?"

"That we are very much to be pitied. Writing and meeting openly are all that are left to us."

"He should have gone away—severed his connection with Muktiarbad. Not have stayed to fan the flame!"

"Life is too short for needless sacrifices, Mother darling. Having made the greatest, we refuse to suffer more than we need. Sometimes, if you are starving for food, a bare crust will keep you alive. We are subsisting on bare crusts and are grateful."

"I consider Captain Dalton has not behaved at all well. He knew his position and went out of his way to make you care!"

"Ah, no!—it just happened!" said Honor, her eyes suddenly flooded with tears.

Mrs. Bright looked at her daughter's white and sorrowful face, and away again. She could not bear to see the suffering there. All the traditions of her life caused her to stand aghast at the idea of dalliance with a sin so subtle and alluring as this. It should be the root-and-branch method. Nothing else would suffice to save her child! Yet her own eyes overflowed in sympathy.

"Oh, my poor little Honey!" She held out her arms and Honor took refuge in them to weep unrestrainedly. "We are trying to be so good!" she cried.

After kissing her daughter tenderly, Mrs. Bright said: "You cannot temporise with forbidden fruit, Honey. Eve did, you know. You are but human, therefore fallible, however good you are trying to be. The time will come when the heart, torn with longing, becomes too weak to resist. Specious arguments are insidious and irresistible, and you will go down. *Let him that thinketh he standeth take heed lest he fall!* That is why we pray, *Lead us not into temptation, but deliver us from evil.* Our Lord understood human nature better than we ever shall, that is why there is only one thing to do, and that is, to fly from temptation. We pray to be 'delivered,' but praying alone doesn't suffice if we are to be honest with ourselves and God. There is nothing that will save us, but *doing right.*"

"We are doing nothing wrong!" Honor pleaded.

"The wrong lies in the lack of moral courage to deal drastically with the wound. If poison remains, it is bound to fester. Captain Dalton should go away."

"We were obliged to let ourselves down gently. It has been so miserable!" Down went Honor's head on her mother's shoulder, and the tears fell fast.

Tears also fell on her dark head. Mrs. Bright's heart was wrung with pity. She had said enough for the present, so now devoted herself to soothing her beloved child's sorrow with her never-failing sympathy. Honor was a good girl, and to be trusted entirely to look her trouble squarely in the face and conquer it; and the mother's heart was lifted in prayer that she might be enabled to aid and strengthen her child.

It was very shortly after this that war broke out, and there was so much to think of and talk about in the Station, that private affairs were temporarily set aside. The newspapers were read eagerly in detail; correspondence with dear ones over the seas was quickened with new interest; and everyone, even in such a little place as Muktiarbad, found plenty to do to help in the common cause. War-work parties were organised, at which the ladies engaged in knitting woollen comforts for the troops, and in making up parcels to be dispatched to the front and to prisoners in Germany; and every member had some bit of war news to discuss with the others at the Club as they rested from their games under the waving *punkha*.

"It will drive me silly," Tommy had said from the first, "if I have to loaf about in a place like this when all my pals and school contemporaries have volunteered, or are in the thick of it, doing their bit."

"You are doing your bit, just as any one who is killing Germans," said Mrs. Ironsides who had returned from Darjeeling. "What is to become of us all, if all medically fit civil officers are sent to fight? Why, we should be murdered in our beds, if it were not for the Police!"

Tommy thought he would cheerfully risk Mrs. Ironsides being murdered in her bed, if the Government would only allow him to serve "for the duration"; and he continued to send in applications for leave to join up, with a persistency worthy of the Great Cause, in the hopes that constant dripping would wear away the stony indifference with which they were treated.

One evening, towards the end of September, Captain Dalton sought Honor at the Club. He had news for her, the gravity of which shadowed his deep-set eyes and heightened the grim setting of his jaw.

In a room full of people engrossed in one another, he gravitated to her, as usual, but surprised her by asking her to grant him a few words in private. "Come out with me to the tennis courts," he commanded with a definiteness she felt powerless to slight.

It was dark on the tennis courts with only a young moon shining; nevertheless, Honor accompanied him forth, realising the fatefulness of the coming interview. When they had reached the shadow of the Duranta hedge that separated the courts from the building, and were seated on a bench, he told her in a few words that he had decided to comply with her wishes in the matter of his wife. It had taken him two months to bring himself to the point of making the sacrifice, but at last it was made.

"Of course I am doing it to please you. You have set your heart on helping Joyce Meredith, and as this is the only way, it shall be done though it takes a mighty effort in the doing. I am writing to tell her that she may return to my protection openly, as my wife; but, needless to say, my wife only in name. If it will give her a chance to right herself in the eyes of the world and help her to live as an honest woman, she is welcome to make the fullest use of my offer. It certainly might keep her from tampering further with Meredith's loyalty to his wife. But I question whether it is not too late!"

"It is never too late!" said Honor, feeling numb and paralysed.

"That will be up to Mrs. Meredith. She is an unsophisticated little thing, and, I dare say, Meredith will keep his mouth shut."

It was plain to judge that he was again full of envy of other men's chances of happiness, for his tones reminded Honor of the man he was when they first met. It was too dark to see his face.

"If she accepts your offer will she come here?" Honor asked shrinkingly.

"She will have to if she comes at once. But I expect soon to be put on active service. My application to serve with the Army is receiving consideration, and it is possible I shall have to go to France or Egypt as there may be trouble with Turkey. In that case she will choose her residence. Another medical officer will occupy my bungalow."

So it had come at last!

Honor had been fearing that the war would, in its relentlessness, claim him also. It was said in the papers that there was a scandalous shortage of surgeons for a war of such magnitude.

Suddenly she was seized with shivering. "You will go and we shall never meet again!" fell from her lips independent of her will.

Dalton took her with determination in his arms and kissed her passionately on the lips. "My own love!" he moaned over her. "My precious one!"

This was what her mother had meant when she had spoken of her becoming, in time, too weak to resist. For the moment her will was as weak as water; she could only cling to him and yield to their mutual craving for demonstrations of love. It was wrong, of course,—but, even so, it was heaven so long as they could banish memory and think only of the joy of enfolding arms, the meeting of loving lips!

"I shall be going away and we might never meet again!" he echoed her words in passionate despair. "Pity me a little, when we meet, and let us be happy! Promise!"

"I dare not promise," she cried, quivering with emotion in his arms. "I love you, but help me to do right!"

For some time neither spoke while Dalton seemed struggling with the might of his desire. They rested on the iron bench wrapped in each other's arms, speechless for many moments till the peacefulness and silence of the night brought them sanity and calm. Then, kissing her once more with the tenderness of renunciation, he put her aside and rose to his feet.

"I wonder you care for such a worthless hound as myself!" he said at length. "I have no self-control. Go in, darling, I am going home to scourge myself for attempting to lead you against the dictates of your conscience. Forgive me, Honey, I was mad!"

Honor left him, shaken in every nerve, her self-confidence shattered. "Let him that thinketh he standeth, take heed lest he fall!" But it rejoiced her that Brian Dalton had fought his battle with himself alone, and had conquered. How much his appreciation of her high sense of honour had contributed to his victory, she would never know.

CHAPTER XXIV

SUSPENSE

The next morning Honor received a telegram from Joyce to meet her at the Grand Hotel in Calcutta without delay, and she was only too glad for a respite of even a few days from the pain of schooling herself to avoid the man she loved. Her parents having no objection, she caught the express at midday, and was in Calcutta the same night, her mind lightened of one of its burdens. At least the little wife had acted upon advice and was going to her husband without waste of time, after which all would surely be well for them both.

Joyce was prepared for her coming, and they talked to a late hour, she, betraying her trouble by her anxious questioning, which Honor skilfully parried.

"You must not put too much faith in gossip," said Honor after learning of the conversation which had been overheard on the ship. "Have you wired?"

Joyce confessed her intention to take her husband by surprise. "Only, now that it has come to the point, I am as nervous as I can be."

"You had better wire. It will bring your husband down half-way to meet you and give him some happy hours of anticipation."

"You are not sincere when you say that," said Joyce unexpectedly, "or why did you tell me to stop at nothing to come out?"

Joyce was no longer the same, ingenuous little girl Honor had parted from at Muktiarbad eight months ago. Her manner had acquired assurance, her carriage a becoming dignity, and there was about her an air of thoughtfulness and reserve, new to her.

"I said it was not good for man to live alone, nor is it."

"And you knew there was someone trying to supplant me in his affections?"

"I knew he was exposed to the influence of a woman without a conscience." Honor then told her precisely who Nurse Dalton was, and how her flagrant pursuit of Ray Meredith had aroused the anxious concern of his friends. Not another word would she add as fuel to the fire of Joyce's jealous imagination.

"Well, I shall be able to find out all about this for myself when I am there!" sighed Joyce when she had heard the woman's history.

Honor prayed inwardly that Mrs. Dalton would have received Captain Dalton's offer before then, and have lost no time in arranging to come away. She could not prevail on Joyce to telegraph to her husband of her arrival in India, or that he was to expect her in Darjeeling as soon as the railway service could take her there. As it was no part of a friend's duty to interfere in the affairs of husband and wife, she desisted from further persuasion, content to leave the issue to a Higher Power.

They passed on to other topics, and Honor was intensely pleased to learn from Joyce of Jack's happy fate as Kitty's accepted lover; and, further, that the two were married by special licence soon after landing at Bombay.

"They are so happy! Last night they left for the new station to which he is appointed, as mentioned in the *Gazette* yesterday. During the few hours they were in town they tried to keep out of the way of Mrs. Fox — perhaps you know Jack had allowed her to believe he would marry her?"

Honor believed she had heard the rumour.

"However, as ill-luck would have it, he and Kitty ran into her, so to speak, in the foyer of this hotel! I was there, and, believe me, I was never so uncomfortable in my life! Kitty was looking charming, and so smart. Happiness agrees with her, for I have never seen her look better in my life. We were waiting for a taxi, when who should come in but Mrs. Fox with some friends! Mistaking Kitty for me, — people say we are very much alike, — she held out her hand and said in her affected way — you remember? — 'Oh, how d'you do, Mrs. Meredith. I had no idea you had come out again!' Then, seeing her mistake, she apologised, for I was following Kitty to the door.

"'It's my sister,' said I, feeling dreadfully embarrassed at having to make the introduction. 'Mrs. Darling, Mrs. Fox,' I said, and just at that moment Jack came in and straight up to us, with no eyes for any one but his wife. 'Come, dear, I have managed to get a taxi for the luggage,' and then his eyes fell on Mrs. Fox. Really, poor Jack! he turned quite pale. But Kitty who knew all about that affair and had forgiven it, smiled graciously at Mrs. Fox who was paralysed with shock, and said — 'I am so sorry we haven't a moment. My husband and I are tied to time and have to catch a train. Good-bye,' — with a bow, — 'so pleased to have met you!'

"Jack also bowed, speechless, as he hurried after Kitty. We all three fairly ran, though we had plenty of time for their train; but if looks could have killed, I am sure Jack would have died on the spot."

To Honor's credit be it known that she suffered a twinge of pity for Mrs. Fox; a passing twinge, such as one might feel for people when they come to grief by their own act.

"I wonder what Mrs. Fox will do, now," Honor remarked after expressing her hearty congratulations for the happy pair. Jack did not deserve such happiness, but if every sinner had his deserts, there would be too many miserable people in the world today.

"Mrs. Gupp who shares my table at meals, knows Mrs. Fox pretty well and has very little to say in her favour. She was maliciously amused over the affair, and is of opinion that Mrs. Fox will have to go home at once. The story is already common property."

Honor thought Joyce lovelier than ever with her air of dignified reserve. She had grown self-reliant and there was a tinge of hauteur in her manner which seemed to add to her stature and give a regal carriage to her beautiful head.

"So you are travelling all alone to Darjeeling?" Honor asked wistfully, wondering what was going to be the upshot of that journey.

"It is nothing at all. I have hardly the patience to wait for trains. There is so much at stake. If I could only be sure that Ray loves me as he used to do, I would be crazy for joy! I should never leave him again—not for anything in the world!" and she hid her face in Honor's neck while the tears flowed.

"Not even if you come across snakes and are obliged to put up with mosquitoes and the heat?" quizzed Honor.

"I'll face anything but the loss of my husband's love. What a fool I have been! a blind, childish fool! Why, that affair with Captain Dalton which I exaggerated and worried over, might have been made all right in good time. I ought to have listened to you, and set myself to make Ray so happy that he would have had nothing to forgive! After all, it wasn't as if I was wilfully to blame?"

"I told you that before you went home."

"And it came to me only when I began to fear that I was losing his love! That was a contingency I never believed possible. He was always so mad about me, spoiling me in every way and treating me as a little queen! Oh, Honor what a mess I have made of things!"

"Don't do anything in the heat of passion, dear," Honor advised thoughtfully. "Remember he has had sunstroke. A man is hardly himself for months after such an illness—sometimes for years. It affects people differently. Some are irritable, some have clouded memories; for the brain is the seat of the trouble."

"Are you trying to prepare me to find Ray insane?" Joyce asked with frightened eyes.

"Not at all. He is as sane as you or I, but his impulses are not so much under control, and his judgment is likely to err since that shock to his brain."

"Then he is not to be held accountable for anything he has done of late?" indignantly.

"You might take all I have said into consideration if you are required to forgive anything he has been weak or foolish enough to have done since his illness."

Joyce laughed bitterly. "I wonder what you would feel inclined to do in my place?"

"Do you really wish to know?"

"I do," said Joyce as a challenge, while drying her eyes.

"The chief thing to be considered, is the future. That must be saved at all costs. A mistake in the present, committed in haste, might affect your future life; and not only yours, but your baby's as well. You are about to deal with baby's daddy as well as your husband, and the whole of your world is looking on. You might take a prejudiced view of things that have occurred. You might, in your anger and humiliation, feel unforgiving towards him, and so, break up your home. I question whether anything ought to weigh against your love for your husband, if in your heart you love him and he loves you."

"Loving me, could he be disloyal?"

Honor hesitated. "It is possible he has been suffering from a clouded mind. Things have not been correctly focussed, as it were. And while in that condition, if he was tempted to drift into actual wrong-doing, I should imagine that self-loathing and remorse would afterwards be a worse punishment for him than you could possibly conceive of. This is presuming he has done anything to be ashamed of. In that case, I could not be harsh. Love always forgives—even to 'seventy times seven.'"

"Honey, you are an idealist! I wonder how many women could exercise so much forbearance! Think of the anger, the humiliation, the resentment! It is an outrage to one's faith and trust!"

"If you had remained within reach of him so that when he was ill you could have gone to him at once, there would have been nothing to forgive. But for a frivolous reason you put the seas between you and threw his love back into his face. You are also very much to blame," said Honor boldly.

Joyce covered her face with her hands and wept silently.

Honor saw her into her train at Sealdah Station the following day, and after an afternoon spent in shopping for her mother, returned to Muktiarbad.

Joyce spent an uncomfortable night in the train on account of the muggy heat which was barely rendered tolerable by electric fans in the compartment, and was glad when the time came to transfer herself and her baggage into the toy railway of the Himalayas, which rattled briskly up the slopes by tortuous tracks into higher altitudes and cooler climes.

A party of ladies known to each other occupied the same compartment and chattered of all they did in Darjeeling last year, and all they meant to do. Joyce paid little heed while silently watching the changing views as the train wound its way along the mountain sides. The infinite grandeur of Nature on which humanity had set its stamp, thrilled her with wonderment and delight. All personal troubles were forgotten for a while as the glorious scenery unfolded to her vision.

Surely her eyes must have been holden when she saw it a year ago!

Heavy mists sweeping the mountain sides frequently obliterated a picture of purple distances and rugged heights. Anon, there was a blaze of sunlight revealing wooded spurs with zinc-roofed cottages and grey villages nestling on their slopes. Green valleys lay at the foot of frowning precipices, and round many a bend and curve were glimpses of tea gardens with the bushes laid out in serried rows; and cumbrous, zinc-roofed tea factories looking strangely incongruous in their wild and glorious setting.

With a rush of sound, a waterfall would be seen, as a curve was rounded, tumbling over rocks and rushing under a bridge on its way to join some mighty river in the plains. The plains were often visible, stretching like a grey sea to the horizon, their surface marked by the silver tracery of streams. Now and then, Joyce could catch a glimpse of the Everlasting Snows, with Kinchin-junga, Nursing, and Pundeem, a mighty group glittering in the sunlight in stately magnificence, their peaks inaccessible to man. Beside the road, a stout parapet of boulders covered by ferns and lichen, stood, in places, between the passengers and certain death, a thousand feet below; while up the steep banks rose forests of *sal* and fir, climbing towards the sky.

Wherever there were homesteads perched among the rocks, children of the mountains would run forth like sure-footed goats to view the passing train, their round and ruddy cheeks besmeared with dirt and chapped with cold; their flat faces, high cheek bones, and slanting eyes, revealing their Lepcha strain.

And all the while the temperature continued to fall; and the atmosphere grew moist and cold and exhilarating in its freshness.

A block in the line occasioned by a local landslip—a frequent occurrence on the hill-railway—detained the train till the afternoon, at Kurseong, where the passengers left their carriages for luncheon at the hotel.

At Sonada, further on, two ladies entered the compartment and audibly discussed certain doings at Darjeeling where they appeared to be residing. When Joyce heard her husband's name, she set herself to listen, determined not to miss a word.

"I suppose she will be there," said one. "Wherever Mr. Meredith goes he manages to get an invitation for her,—and people don't much like it, but there's his position, you know!"

"I know. They are seldom seen apart. A handsome woman in her way, but utterly regardless! Her dress, for instance, at the Shrubbery Ball was indeed up to date—just a band under the armpits for a bodice. I never saw any one off the stage so disgustingly naked!"

"He looks to me rather 'fed up.' And the way she takes charge of him in public requires nerve! he simply falls into line just as if he can't help himself. Got into the habit, so to speak!"

"What are you going to wear tonight?" and the conversation drifted to the Planters' Ball at the Club. The Governor and his wife were expected to be present with their suite, and the house-party from the Shrubbery.

"It is a wonder to me," said the first speaker, "that Mrs. Dalton is received at Government House." Joyce again held her breath.

"Oh, but her position makes that all right. Her husband is an I.M.S. man, a rising surgeon, somewhere in the plains. They don't get on, but that's nobody's business; and in Darjeeling one has to shut one's eyes. If you begin to point the finger of scorn, you'll be kept fairly busy" (with a mischievous laugh). "And after all, if her husband doesn't mind, it's nobody's business. All the same, she's been cut by a good few, and if he doesn't look out, he'll end in the divorce court—or she will!"

They laughed as at a great joke, and, others listening, smiled in sympathy, while Joyce turned her burning face away.

It seemed that there was no getting away from the story of her husband's shame. But for her having left him, this would never have been!

When the train drew up at the platform of the station in Darjeeling, she pulled herself together and stepped bravely out of her compartment, head erect, and manner perfectly composed. The need to have herself well in hand, gave her strength of mind for the occasion, so that none of her old friends—were she to come unexpectedly upon any—should think her crushed and miserable; a poor, humiliated wife! No! the world should see a laughing face.

As the roads of the Station were very familiar to her, she climbed the path leading to the Cosmopolitan Hotel, at which her husband was staying. It rose by easy stages to a higher level and passed by red-brick villas built on the English plan, with pent roofs and homely chimney-pots. In parts the road was clear, in others, heavily shaded by tall firs, through the branches of which could be seen the Snowy Range bathed in the soft afterglow of a lurid sunset. Preceding her was a Lepcha boy from Sikkim, carrying her trunk mountaineer fashion on his back, strapped to his forehead; and it was a mystery how he lifted himself as well as his burden up the short cuts, without pausing to draw breath.

CHAPTER XXV
THE MEETING

While Joyce climbed the road preceded by her Lepcha coolie, a scene of dramatic possibilities was taking place in a room of the hotel to which she was bound.

It was Mr. Meredith's sitting-room, comfortably furnished; a fire was burning cheerfully in the grate, and the actors were himself and Mrs. Dalton, who had called upon him in a crisis of her affairs.

She was eager and excited, bold, and yet somewhat baffled.

He was nervous and uncomfortable, while fidgeting with a letter in his fingers.

"He has made a rather sporting offer, don't you think?" she asked with biting sarcasm, her eyes studying his face.

"What are you going to do?"

"Surely!—that's for you to say."

"Me?" (irritably).

"Of course. You know that he and I parted long ago over incompatibility of temper, and that his offer is made only to save his precious honour. He has heard rumours! There is no love in it; instead, it is carefully ruled out. I may return to his protection whenever I like; but as his wife *only in name.*"

"It will be better than this knock-about sort of life you have led, with an allowance wholly inadequate to your needs" (conciliatingly).

"But is there nothing else in life for a young woman of my years and temperament? What about you and me?" (tenderly).

Meredith reddened as he said resolutely, "That page will have to be turned down for good, in the fullest sense of the word."

It was a page of which he was heartily ashamed. The shame was inevitable, the affair having been, from the first, a comedy of degrees in which his heart had never been involved; begun while he was a helpless invalid dependent upon this woman for nursing and companionship. That she had started the flirtation, and had taken advantage of his loneliness and temporary weakness to bring him almost to the verge of a deep dishonour, were memories he would have given much to forget. Mrs. Dalton was a type of woman he had always held in contempt; but he had failed to identify her as such, till his normal health had reasserted itself. Latterly he had allowed himself to drift with the tide while looking for a means of escape from his intolerable position.

"Do you mean that?" she asked with whitening lips.

"I think it is the only thing to do," he replied.

"If you say that for my sake, then I might just as well be frank. You know I love you, Ray Meredith, and I believe you love me, only you have never quite let yourself go, for some hidden reason—possibly your career? It can't be consideration for that bloodless and callous creature, your wife? I refuse to believe that you have any feeling for a woman who has placed her child before her husband and is content to live apart from him when she knows that men are but human after all! Your career is safe. A man's private life is his own affair. If we throw in our lot together, we can after the divorce marry and live happily ever after, as the good little story books tell us in the nursery." She laughed tenderly. "My husband will gladly have done with me, for I can tell who it is he wants. I paid a stolen visit to his bungalow at Muktiarbad and snapshots of her live all about him in his den. Can I tolerate the position I shall occupy in his house, knowing all the while it has been flung at me like a bone to a dog? If he could marry her tomorrow he would; only she isn't the sort, I am told, who would take him unless I am dead! Now, this is frankness indeed!"

Meredith was silent.

"Can't you speak?"

"I have spoken."

"And is that all?" she cried passionately, creeping nearer, her dark eyes compelling his surrender. "Don't you know that all Darjeeling is talking of us? That, for your sake, people are treating me abominably while they smile kindly on you? I am only a woman, therefore may be crushed. My God!—and you would turn me down, like a 'page' for 'good'!"

"Perhaps I should not put it like that," he said nervously as he trifled with Captain Dalton's letter to his wife, and allowed it to fall to the floor. His cigarette case suggested comfort and was drawn forth as a diversion.

"Put it as you like, it is rather a knock-out blow for me!"

"Say, rather, that it is a mercy things have not gone too far, and that you can accept your husband's 'sporting' offer with a clear—a clear"—*conscience* was scarcely a suitable word. He was certain she had smothered it long ago.

"Oh, damn my husband! I want nothing to do with him since knowing you! Ray, old dear, have you ceased to love me?—I don't believe it!" She flung her arms about his neck and laid her cheek to his. In her tones was beguilement, in her eyes the lure of an evil thing. Her back was turned to the door so that she did not see that it had opened suddenly to admit someone. Both had been too preoccupied to hear the gentle knock.

Meredith looked up and saw his wife enter,—his little Joyce, whom he imagined was in England. For a moment he was petrified—the next instant he shook himself free of Mrs. Dalton's embrace, and stood apart, convicted and ashamed.

Joyce stood stock still as if paralysed, and could only murmur conventionally, "I am sorry," purely a mechanical expression of apology such as she would have made to a stranger. "No one answered my knock, so I came in."

The very air was electrical. Meredith could only utter his wife's name in blank amazement. What could he say under such damning circumstances? Mrs. Dalton laughed hysterically.

Collecting her scattered wits, Joyce explained, reaching a hand out to a cabinet for support: "I came out with the mails. There was a hint of *this*, only I dared not let myself believe it. It seemed impossible from my knowledge of you. But it appears I was wrong," her lip curled. Turning to Mrs. Dalton she said coldly, "Perhaps you will be good enough to leave us together?"

Standing there erect in her pride and beauty, dressed exquisitely, yet simply, she was a revelation to the woman who had sought to rob her and was now brazen enough to carry off the situation with effrontery.

"It was pretty smart of you to act the spy, stealing on us without warning! However, we are not afraid. Do your worst!"

"I am waiting for you to leave the room," said Joyce with immovable calm. Her queenlike dignity was something new to her husband, and it commanded Mrs. Dalton's unwilling respect and obedience.

Meredith walked swiftly to the door and held it open for the lady to pass out, his features rigid, his eyes bent on the carpet at his feet, nor did he raise them when she brushed past him and lightly touched his hand as it held the door-knob.

"Why didn't you cable? — or wire from Calcutta?" he asked through white lips.

Joyce looked in scornful silence at him and then said with a perceptible shrug, "I am glad I did neither."

"Things look pretty bad against me, I admit," he said bitterly. "Is it any use for me to ask you not to judge me too hastily? The situation you surprised was not of my creating."

Joyce laughed suddenly, a strained and mirthless laugh as she mentally recalled the words, "The woman gave me, and I did eat."

"Judge you hastily? Such a situation requires no explanation. It is plainly a confession of guilt, or it could not have been."

"By that do you mean you will take action?"

"Action? — do you mean, divorce you?"

"Yes."

"Perhaps you would like to marry Mrs. Dalton if her husband gives her up!" she said bitterly, hardly recognising the tones of her own voice.

"Good God! — never!" he shuddered involuntarily.

"I do not understand you."

"You would not believe me if I told you."

"I am beginning to understand more of men than I did when we parted. It seems, you could make love to this lady without being in love with her? You even humiliated me in the eyes of the world, merely for the sake of a vulgar intrigue?"

She astonished Meredith with every word she spoke. His little Joyce had suddenly become a woman, a thousand times more wonderful than he had ever known her.

"I am innocent of anything but an ordinary flirtation, of which I am heartily ashamed, believe it or not," he returned pacing the floor restlessly, his face pallid, his eyes miserable. "What are you going to do?" coming to a stop before her. It was as well that he should know the worst she contemplated.

"I don't know ... but I cannot advertise my shame to the world!" she said icily as she turned to leave the room.

"Where are you going?"

"There is my trunk. I shall need to engage a room."

"Sit down by the fire, and I will see to everything for you."

Joyce sank nervelessly into a chair and saw him leave the room, only to re-enter shortly afterwards with the news that the hotel, being full, she would have to occupy his own bedroom while he made shift with the dressing-room attached.

Joyce scarcely heeded him. So long as he was not to share her room, nothing mattered. "And what about the Planters' Ball tonight?" she asked to his profound surprise. "Are you going?"

"I was, but not now. How can you ask?" What on earth was she after?

"Why not? I would rather you kept your engagement—and—took me."

Meredith stared, wide-eyed. "You?" For the moment he thought her mind deranged. How could she contemplate taking part in a frivolous social function in the midst of their tragedy? Their lives were sundered; their happiness blasted; and she was thinking of the Planters' Ball!

Joyce was thinking of the women who were expecting to enjoy the spectacle of Ray Meredith's flirtation with Mrs. Dalton; and no doubt there were a great many others also prepared to amuse themselves at his expense, and her eyes hardened. A jealous determination to punish the woman who had spoiled the happy relations between husband and wife, possessed her, so that the idea of slighting her publicly at this grand ball was a temptation. That her husband would slight Mrs. Dalton, she had no doubt. There was no mistaking the look in his eyes. Honor Bright had said that, were he guilty of wrong-doing, self-loathing and remorse would punish him more heavily than she could conceive of! He was already ashamed, and would yet repent in the dust at his wife's feet. When that came to pass, she might see fit to relent—not now. Now her whole soul was in revolt. Her heart felt like stone in her breast. What would another woman have done in her place? She had no experience. Honor had advised her against precipitancy. She would act with infinite deliberation, surpassing anything Honor would have counselled. Honor had talked of love! For the moment she had lost her faith in love, and knew no feeling so strong as revenge. She would go to the ball, and Ray should have no eyes for any other woman but his wife. It had been so in the past, and it would be so again, or she would hate to live. People had always said that she was pretty, and she had been glad for his sake. She was more than glad now; for it put the strongest weapon for punishment into her hand.

Meanwhile, her husband was amazed that she should think of the ball, and, doubtless, feared she was mad!

"I am not insane, if that is what is on your mind. But I have to think of the future," she said coldly. The future was another point that Honor said, would have to be considered. "We shall go to this dance together to keep up appearances. For the same reason, we shall, if you have no objection, dance a great deal together. For Baby's sake the world must think that we are rejoiced to come together again after so many months apart, and it might help to make people forget the ugly things they have been saying. Do you mind?"

"Not at all. You shall do as you please, in this, as in everything else."

"I have no doubt Mrs. Dalton will find someone in the hotel to escort her?"

"She can take care of herself."

"Very well then," looking at her watch, "perhaps I had better dress, for it is rather near the dinner hour."

"And is that all you have to say to me?" he asked with quivering lips.

"What would you have me say?"

"Anything would be better than this coldness—this avoidance of all that is most vital to us both. Even if you raved and stormed, I could stand it better, for I might have a chance to explain. Things are not as bad as you think."

"They are bad enough for me!" she returned calmly, her lovely profile and the lowered sweep of her eyelashes, her straight carriage and the gentle curve of her bosom, outlined against the dark hangings of the window.

"Will you listen to me for a bit?"

"I would rather not."

"Then you condemn me outright?"

"You have condemned yourself."

"You cannot have forgotten my love for you?" he cried desperately.

She turned and lifted grave, blue eyes to his face in mute condemnation.

"You do not understand—I have been ill—I don't seem to have been myself for a long time, I—I—it seemed to me that you did not care a farthing what became of me. You left it to me to cable if I wanted you when you should have known that I was yearning for nothing so much as a sight of your face. It was pointed out to me that any woman with a spark of true love for her own man, would have let nothing stand in the way of her joining him the moment she heard of his illness. Did you?" He laughed harshly. "No! It was the old story, 'Baby,' and always, 'Baby!'

God!—you never cared."

"I cared so much, that I never wanted to amuse myself with another man though I had plenty of opportunities." Yet, his passionate denunciation had gone home.

"Joyce, am I to have no chance?"

With a gesture of disgust, she dismissed the subject peremptorily, and passed out of the sitting-room, trembling with emotion from head to foot.

In the adjoining apartment, which was his bedroom, she struggled with the straps of her fibre trunk till they were taken out of her hands and the leathers unbuckled, by her husband who had followed her in. Joyce watched him with a pain at her heart as he bent over his task. A lump came into her throat too big to swallow. She felt choked with a rising hysteria which only a great effort of will controlled. He looked so handsome, so like the lover-husband she had known, that it was all she could do not to fling herself into his arms and say "Let us forget everything and remember only our love!" Her natural place was in his arms now that she had come out all that distance to be with him; instead, they had not even exchanged the most formal of greetings! He had been false to her—a crime no woman feels disposed to forgive.

"I had to come in here as this is the only way to my dressing-room," Meredith explained as he rose to his feet.

Joyce thanked him coldly and watched him pass through the heavy curtains which separated the two rooms and was the only apology for a door. When he was gone, she writhed in anguish. Oh, if she could have crushed her pride and called out to him to come back!

It was not so easy, however, and she hardened her heart for the task that lay before her.

While dressing, her trembling fingers almost refusing their work, she wondered how Mrs. Dalton would behave when they met again? If she would have the audacity to speak to Ray? A woman of her sort would be equal to any impertinence. Why had she not returned to her husband, who, Honor had said, was willing to take her back? At all events, Joyce was infinitely glad she was on the spot to curtail the woman's opportunities for further mischief. It was worth the risk of the journey.

When she slipped on her evening gown, a rich, black *crêpe de chine*, she was seized with consternation when she remembered that it fastened at the back. Under no circumstance would it meet without assistance. A maid, or an ayah?—Both were equally impossible to procure at a moment's notice.

She made several futile efforts, then looked about her in dismay! What was to be done? Flushed, and in despair, she cast a glance at the curtains behind which lay her only hope. Her husband had often officiated with the hooks and eyes, and was otherwise expert as a maid. The only alternative was to forego the ball and her great reprisal; and this was unthinkable now that all her hopes were centred on revenge. Had Joyce belonged to a lower order of society, she would probably have gratified her wrath by making a scene and scratching out the woman's eyes, or tearing out her hair in handfuls. As it was, the picture of Mrs. Dalton seated as a wall-flower, openly despised and neglected by the man she had tried to seduce from his allegiance, appealed powerfully to her imagination.

Timidly she called, "Can you help me, please?"

There was no answer.

"Ray!" her voice was still more diffident, but her call met with immediate response. Ray who had not yet begun to change for dinner, was with her in an instant.

"I cannot dress without help. Will you please?" she asked frigidly.

Meredith took infinite pains, his face, as reflected in the mirror, looking haggard and pale. He had never seen his wife in black, which was an excellent foil to her fair beauty, and the sight of her rendered him tongue-tied. He had nothing to say even when she dismissed him with a "Thanks, I'll manage very well, now."

When Joyce entered the winter-garden,—the principal lounge of the hotel, with glazed roof and walls, its interior full of flowering orchids, palms, and tropical plants of varied beauty, she saw Mrs. Dalton already there, resplendent in crimson satin and jewellery, cultivating the acquaintance of new-comers to Darjeeling who had arrived by the train that day. It was a daring gown for colour and cut, and Joyce was put in mind of the description she had overheard in the train, of the lady's ball-room attire. Mrs. Dalton evidently set a high value on the generous curves of her handsome shoulders, for she displayed them with liberality.

Ray entering soon afterwards, performed a few introductions with a self-control that was remarkable, considering his shaken nerves, after which they passed into the glare of the dining-hall to the table at which he had always dined in company with men.

Joyce excelled him in her power to sustain the rôle she had marked out for them both. Her manner was winning and delightful, and, but for Meredith's inner knowledge, it might have misled his hopes disastrously.

"Yes," she once said with subtle meaning as she smiled at an ardent admirer who had been captivated at first sight, "I would not cable or wire, for I wanted to give my dear husband the surprise of his life. You can imagine his feelings! It is a mercy that joy seldom kills, or he might have died on the spot. And I am so glad I came, though I had to leave my wee baby with his grannie. But things might have become too difficult later, owing to the war; and I could not be parted from Ray indefinitely; could I, dear?" to her husband.

Ray smiled unsteadily.

"India is such a delightful country. Nothing will induce me to leave it in a hurry again. Do you know Muktiarbad? No? It's a little paradise though officials will call it a Penal Settlement!"

"Lucky dog, your husband!" said an admirer fatuously. "And so plucky of you to go to the ball tonight, after your long and fatiguing journey. I hope I may have a dance?"

"Certainly. You surely did not think I would deprive my husband of this pleasure when he is, I am sure, one of the best dancers in Darjeeling? I should never have been forgiven by his friends!"

"May I have the first 'Boston'?"

"That is for my husband to decide," she said archly with the familiar play of the eyelashes and dimple peeping in and out of her cheek. "He has first choice of the dances on my programme."

"We'll see about the programme when we are there," said Meredith quietly. His position was more than he could support.

"I mean to enjoy myself thoroughly tonight!" sighed Joyce.

Meredith stole a glance at his wife and noted the feverish light of excitement in her eyes, under which blue shadows of fatigue lay, and the nervous movement of her fingers as they crumbled her bread into morsels. He could see that she, too, was suffering from nerves.

"Damn the ball!" he cursed inwardly. He had no interest in it; no wish to be there.

"Are you sure you are not too tired?" he asked her, longing for a loophole for escape.

"Not in the least," she replied, over-doing her part by touching his hand lightly with her fingers. It was a graceful mark of confidence and affection which won the indulgence of all the men at that table; but to Meredith it was deliberate cruelty. Her touch was an electric shock, and his heart stood still for a moment while the room swam before his eyes. He made no reply, but having finished dinner, rose abruptly, without waiting for the initiative to come from her. Across the room was the woman who had often hung upon his breast with her cheap caresses and offers of love which he had been too weak to spurn altogether. Already the sight of her flaunting charms nauseated him.

A 'rickshaw carried Joyce to the Club while her husband accompanied her on foot. When he tried to engage her in conversation, he had to learn that her bright speeches were only for others. When they were alone, she was dumb. It was clear that he had sinned in her eyes past all hope of forgiveness.

At the ball, Meredith went through his part as in a dream. He smiled to order, made many introductions, and danced with his wife, and no other. Obedient to her example, he made idle conversation while they danced together, though his heart was on fire with longing; and when he was not dancing with her, he could but watch her from the doorways, remembering the existence of friends only when they accosted him; appearing hopelessly absent and inconsequent the while.

It seemed to him that his life was broken and ended.

"You're a dark horse, you blighter," he was chaffed. "Keeping it up your sleeve all this time that your wife was on her way out!"

"Introduce me, old son," said the *aide-de-camp* to the Governor. "Mrs. Meredith dances divinely."

"Let me congratulate you, Meredith," said the Governor, in his friendliest manner. "Your wife is the most charming little woman I have met for some time. I have quite lost my heart to her!" He patted Ray's shoulder to impress the fact on "this foolish fellow" who had scarcely "played the game" in his lovely little lady's absence. "It was a damned shame!"

Joyce was unquestionably the "belle of the ball"; there were no two opinions about that. Few remembered that she had been at Darjeeling the previous season, since she had kept to her hotel as a semi-invalid with a very young child; so that she had the additional advantage of being fresh. India loves new sensations and is grateful to those who supply them, gratis.

Men surrounded her and paid her marked attentions, fought with each other, good-naturedly, for portions of dances, and served her as a princess at the suppers. Yet, in spite of her bewildering success, she never forgot the object that had taken her there, and was more than repaid. Her manner to her husband was faultless, and it kept him regardful of her slightest wish. Her mission was to charm all, her husband in particular, so that Mrs. Dalton's humiliation should be complete; and before midnight, victory was achieved. Mrs. Dalton ordered her 'rickshaw at the stroke of twelve, and retired from the ball, her almost empty programme in pieces on the floor. She had been overlooked by men, cut by women, and obliged to look on, with a raging heart, at Mrs. Meredith's triumph. Ray Meredith, with the rudeness of utter contempt, had left her absolutely alone. The cruelty of his behaviour had been insupportable. When, on one occasion, she had seized the chance of a word with him, he was deaf to her exhortations, and she was shaken off with a contemptuous disregard for her feelings.

When she left the building, it was to suffer the tortures of a woman scorned. She was learning to swallow that bitterest of all pills, the knowledge that she was utterly despised by the man for whom she had been willing to lower her womanhood in the dust.

She had come to the realisation of the fact that the woman who lowers herself in the eyes of men, will inevitably find herself shamed and scorned.

When she arrived at the hotel, she brooded far into the night over her bedroom fire, reviewing bitterly her moral decline from the day of her first great mistake. Feeling unable to face the people who had known her in the Station, she departed the next morning for Muktiarbad, leaving her infantile charge and its ayah to the tender mercies of the Sanitarium.

CHAPTER XXVI

THE FAIR

The *méla*[19] week was a great event at Muktiarbad, for the Europeans as well as the natives of the District, as it gave the officials a holiday, brought people together, and encouraged healthy competition in arts, crafts, and various industries of the country. Prizes were offered for the best exhibits, and local shopkeepers took advantage of the opportunity to advance their own interests by placing on the market, articles of use and ornament from all parts of India. Eager crowds, garbed in all the hues of the rainbow created a kaleidoscope of colour as they jostled one another among the booths, bent on bargaining or on sight-seeing. Merry-go-rounds, puppet shows, monkey-dances, juggling, and cocoanut shies, entertained adults as well as children, while the noise and confusion of tongues was Bedlam.

The fair was usually held at the crossroads where a large irregular patch of green afforded ample space for the pens, stalls, booths, and side-shows that contributed towards the joys of the occasion; and to it came people from miles around, and even from distant parts of the District.

Just when this annual *fête* was at its height, Mrs. Dalton arrived at Muktiarbad to take up her abode under her husband's roof, thus providing enough of a sensation among his neighbours to last beyond the regulation nine days for wonderment.

That the Civil Surgeon should prove a married man was not so outrageous as his having neglected to admit, while she was among them, that Nurse Dalton was his wife, instead of misleading them tacitly into thinking that the name was a coincidence. It was unpardonable! And now, to add insult to injury, after she had made herself conspicuous in Darjeeling by flirting openly with her late patient, the Station of Muktiarbad was expected to forget and forgive, and take the black sheep to its bosom. Unheard of audacity!

How far Ray Meredith was to blame for the gossip concerning himself and the lady, was immaterial, since his wife was reported happy and content,—besides, he was a man, and women are notoriously hard upon women; as was proved when the ladies of the Station were ready to throw stones at the erring one the instant it was known that the doctor took every chance to keep out of his wife's way, and was seldom found at home. Why the two had come together again when there was no love lost between them, was a mystery to all and a challenge to their sense of propriety.

[19] Fair.

When Mrs. Dalton, as in duty bound, called on everybody, she was received without cordiality by her sex, who met immediately afterwards to consult what response to her overtures was demanded by common civility. Some proposed the snub direct, by ignoring her altogether; others were for dropping cards into her "Not-at-home box" at the gate when it was ascertained that it was up; while Mrs. Bright decided to return her call and let civilities end there.

Tommy listened with indifference to the female cackle at the Club till Honor's name was introduced, and then he could no longer hold his peace. "What about Honor Bright?" someone had asked meaningly.

"What about her?" said Tommy, his eyes following the girl's lithe movements on the tennis court.

"It was popularly supposed that she was engaged to Captain Dalton, and yet she knew all along that he was a married man!"

"Has any one in this company got anything to say that is detrimental to Miss Bright?" he asked with eyes flashing.

Thus challenged, the speaker collapsed into silence.

"Honor is one of the very best," said Mrs. Ironsides vehemently. "Let there be no mistake about that!" This was the last word on the subject, and Tommy retired victoriously, cursing feminine tongues that would never mind their own business. His relief when he discovered that Captain Dalton was no longer in competition with himself for Honor's hand, was great, till he realised, later that his own chances were *nil*.

The Government of Bengal having at last yielded to his importunities to be allowed to join the Indian Army Reserve, he was waiting, like Dalton, for orders, brimful of martial ardour while he packed and sorted his kit. Jack's belongings were to be sent on to him; while his own, salvaged from the wreck of patriotic-dinner parties at which his bachelor friends had drunk to the confusion of the enemy till they were themselves confused, were to be sold to his successor and to friends in the District. Mr. Ironsides had bespoken his gun, a local Rajah his ponies; and his dogs were to be distributed among friends. There remained personal treasures, chief among them being a gold napkin ring,—a christening present twenty-two years ago,—which was to be given to Honor as a keepsake. Should he fall in battle, it would serve to remind her tenderly of his unfaltering love. Thoughts of wooing and marriage were out of place and of secondary importance beside the needs of the Great War, into which he was going heart and soul.

Poor old Jack! Tommy could pity him despite the fact that he was married to the girl of his heart. How it was possible for any fellow to "sit tight in his job" while all his pals were in the thick of the fight, was inconceivable. But Jack put the blame on the Government and settled down to enjoy his Elysium. It was clear that Mrs. Darling was going to have it all her own way in the future to Jack's supreme delight. According to her, "There was a place for every man, and every man should be kept in it." It was, further, a husband's duty to "obey his wife." As for the war!—he must remember that "They also serve who stand and wait,"—or, as she put it—"administer justice in the land in which it has pleased the Almighty to place them." The "Almighty," in this case, being the Government of India.

These sentiments quoted in a humorous letter from the young magistrate, brought forth an appreciative reply and a wedding present which made a gap in Tommy's small savings, for he was infinitely relieved at his friend's escape from the clutches of a certain lady. It was a satisfaction to know that at last Jack would be in agreement with Solomon on the subject of a wife.

Honor Bright first met Mrs. Dalton at the *mêla*, not having been at home when that lady had called. She was making a tour of the exhibits with friends from Hazrigunge when she was joined by the Meeks who were charitably piloting the lonely new-comer about the grounds. Mr. Meek, glad of an amiable listener, was discoursing on the merits of his live-stock which had won prizes, and was pointing them out in their pens. Husband and wife, in their isolation at the Mission, heard little or nothing of Station gossip, and to them Mrs. Dalton appeared very superior to her unfriendly husband whom they had never liked. Small wonder that his wife had been unable to agree with such a domineering nature!

Honor thought her greatly altered and believed she could divine the cause. Since happiness has its source from within, it was not surprising that Mrs. Dalton had failed to find it in the life she had led. Her eyes had a wistful appeal; her manner was deprecating. The old confidence and daring were gone, never to return. Something had happened to bring disillusionment, and the lesson had sunk deeper.

"I saw so little of you when I was last here," she said to Honor after shaking hands. "You went directly to the hills, you remember? I do hope we shall be friends?"

"You are very kind," said Honor with embarrassment, as she had no inclination for friendship with Brian Dalton's wife.

"We have so many tastes in common, I believe, and might do things together. In a quiet station like this, it is the only way to kill time."

"I am very busy now-a-days," said Honor whose time was always too well occupied to admit of practising such an accomplishment. "There are ambulance classes at the Railway Institute; the work-society for knitting comforts for the soldiers and sailors; the bazaar at Hazrigunge for the Belgian Relief Fund, and other duties, so that I have quite a lot to do."

"I wish that I, too, might help!"

"The secretary would be glad, I am sure. She is Mrs. Ironsides. I should advise you to apply to her." With a smile and bow, Honor passed on, followed by Mrs. Dalton's gloomy gaze.

"Honor Bright is a very dear friend of mine," said Mrs. Meek, kindly. "Don't you think she is a very refreshing specimen of girlhood? My husband thinks she is very good-looking, but I say she is good to look at. A distinction without a difference, you will say? but not so; the difference lies in expression, which makes the matter of features immaterial. Honor has such a frank and truthful face, and a nature of the very kindest."

"I am just wondering why it is she is not married?"

"She will marry the right man when he comes along. So far I have not seen one good enough."

"It is rather wonderful how everyone loves her! Most people have enemies and detractors, but Miss Bright seems a universal favourite."

"It is not really surprising. She is universally respected and beloved. Even the natives look up to her."

"'Respected!'" echoed Mrs. Dalton to herself bitterly. The lack of self-respect had always been the rock on which her life had been shipwrecked. She had failed to mark it on her chart, and was now a derelict. A jealous pang went through her and she remarked with a tinge of spite, "In fact, Miss Bright is so good that, like the Pharisee of old, she thanks God she is not as other women are!"

"You do her injustice. I know no one more charitable," said Mrs. Meek warmly.

"I apologise," said Mrs. Dalton with a sudden revulsion of feeling. "Believe me, I have reason to know that, for she tried to do me a good turn, I don't know why,—considering the circumstances,—but I must find an opportunity for thanking her." Yet Mrs. Meek saw only discontent and unhappiness in her companion's face, and wondered.

Meanwhile, Honor passed beyond their range of vision and was making household purchases for her mother: *jharunsé*[20] made at Cawnpur, lace at the Mission, a pair of garden shears, and trifles that appealed to her as useful for the Hazrigunge bazaar.

While selecting a rush basket for flowers at a stall for the sale of wicker-work made by low-caste Hindus at Panipara, she overheard a conversation in the vernacular between one of the workers and an outsider of evil appearance. Their words were often unintelligible being drowned in the noises prevailing around her, but the drift of their talk held Honor rigid and attentive, with every faculty alert, and fear at her heart. Feeling secure in the midst of so much distraction, they spoke unreservedly.

"These reeds of Panipara are unsurpassed," said the outsider viciously. "Where will you get others for your trade, now that the *jhil*, is being drained? Look you, it is the work of Dalton Sahib, this butcher of human flesh!"

"Alack! my trade is ruined. I shall have to move on and seek a living elsewhere, or die of want!"

"Thus you are turned from the village of your forefathers where you have worked,—and they before you,—at basket-plaiting and mat-making. What does he deserve for his wanton act?"

"May he die, and jackals eat his flesh!"

---

[20] Dish-cloths.

"That is a just saying, my brother! Even I have suffered—" for a few minutes Honor heard nothing but the loud laughter of some Bengali students who were passing. "My only child it was," the voice proceeded agitatedly; "he was rendered unconscious, and while lying helpless on a table at the hospital, and I his father crying in the yard below, this ruthless one cut open his bowels and removed a part of the intestines! Can anyone live without that which is necessary to life. In agony my son died, calling aloud to his mother and father,—and we, powerless to save him! *Ai Khodar!* Listening my liver dried up and my heart hardened as a stone, while I took vows on his dead body to find a way to punish this murderer. No matter how long I have to wait, I shall—" again his words were lost.

"But brother, this is idle talk! will you risk——?"

"Care must be taken to find one suited to the job; he must have experience and courage, and"—he glanced suspiciously at Honor and dropped his voice, fearing that she might be one of those Memsahibs, who understood Bengali. So many did not.

"There is one man at Panipara—of daring inconceivable. Three months he served in gaol for—he fears neither the law nor——"

"Ss-s-h! I will see him. Tell me where—?" Their heads drew closer as their voices were lowered to continue their plotting.

Honor could hear no more. She had drawn too near and their suspicions were aroused, so that whatever else they had to say was lost in mumbling.

Her heart hammered and her pulses throbbed with fear. What were these men thinking of doing in their revenge? Was the doctor's life in actual danger?

Her friends, at another stall where brasses and wood-carving were displayed, were signalling for her to join them. She looked around for help, but not a policeman was in sight. Even then, she could have done nothing, for the evil-looking Indian had slipped away and was lost in the crowds. She had no positive evidence to offer that would satisfy the law. The basket-weaver, looking innocent and bland, sat on his haunches shouting out to the public to inspect his goods.

Honor, therefore, controlled her excitement, and decided to warn Captain Dalton again on his return to the Station, and consult her father on the subject. With an anxious heart, she joined her friends who were looking on at a monkey dance.

"*Bibi Johorun,*" the female monkey, dressed in skirt and shawl, and cap on her head adorned with a red feather, hopped to the measure of the little drum the man rattled rhythmically with a turn of his wrist; while her husband, the male, in coat and brass buttons, sat on a toy stool awaiting his turn to be called up for the War. Presently the pair would embrace in farewell, he would shoulder his mimic gun to the delight of the spectators, and proceed to march to battle to the time of the drum. Honor knew the routine perfectly. Meanwhile his expression of sleepy indifference under the rakish khaki cap as he blinked and chewed the nuts offered by the public, was human in its comprehension. When the crowd grew pressing, Honor left with her party, hearing for some distance the man's monotonous singsong voice urging Johorun to dance for her reward, failing which there would be a certainty of chastisement.

> *"Natcho-jee, Johorun, natcho-jee!*
> *Paisa milé ga.*
> *Paisa, na courie, thuphur milé, ga!"*

That evening, at the Club, Mrs. Dalton drew Honor apart from the rest of the company and they paced the grass together while it grew dusk. She was evidently much agitated, and after making some clumsy attempts to lead up to the subject, she suddenly broke out with the question.

"Tell me why you told my husband to take me back?"

As Honor was not ready with her reply, she continued,

"He told me in his specially cruel fashion, that I owed the concession to you, for I had charged him with being in love with you."

Honor drew back shocked at her bad taste. "That is hardly the thing for you, his wife, to tell me!"

"I don't say it from any evil motive!—oh, I wish you to believe that I am past all that—I have no longer any use for malice, and hatred—even jealousy! I only want to understand you. I am a woman, too; if I cared about a man who loved me as he loves you, I should want to kill the woman who stood in my way! There is something eternally primitive about love in its relation to the sexes!"

"There is love—and *love*. Perhaps you don't know—apart from everything— that Joyce Meredith is my dear friend? She has a right to be happy in her married life."

"I see. So you sacrificed yourself and ordered him to come to the rescue! He would do anything in the world for you."

"He and I can never be anything to each other," said Honor firmly.

"I am beginning to feel truly sorry for my husband. Perhaps you don't believe it? But, since he despises me so absolutely, it seems a shame that he should be tied to me for life! He should have given me my liberty long ago. You know why we parted?"

"Yes, I know."

"He might then have married you——"

"Please do not speak to me in this way or I must refuse to walk with you," said Honor indignantly.

"Oh, no, don't!—please don't go before you hear what I have to say!" Mrs. Dalton cried earnestly. "I have no tact, and always say the wrong thing. The fact is, I am a most miserable woman, feeling every day the consequences of my first mistake. If you knew what a bankrupt I am in love and all that goes towards making life worth living, you would have the heart to feel a little pity for me!"

"I do pity you," said Honor, relenting.

"If he would only forgive me! But he is so hard. He spurns my every effort to humble myself. He has no faith in me. I killed it! But if he would only give me a chance, I would be a better woman, I swear it! A kind word and look—oh, what wouldn't I do to atone! Miss Bright, you can help me!"

"I?"

"Yes. You! Natures like yours are great." Mrs. Dalton's voice broke with a sob and she wrung her hands in genuine emotion. "You may not credit me with sincerity, but I am not wholly bad. Brian is my husband—whenever I look at him I realise all that I have lost forever—unless, a miracle happens and he forgives me! If he could do that, I would be his slave. I would be at his feet! What a life is mine! The emptiness of it!—the futility of it! Who cares for women like myself? Women at a loose end who have spoilt their lives, and are trying to patch up some kind of forbidden happiness for themselves? It is just a form of gambling; wild excitement while it lasts. But it never lasts long! Think what I feel tonight! Here am I, a married woman among so many—with a fine husband,—he is that!—hard and cold, yet such a *man*!—and I might have been so happy. I might have had children!" Mrs. Dalton broke down into violent sobbing and Honor guided her to a bench that she might weep unrestrainedly and so find relief.

It was a strange position for herself, who a moment ago was filled with repulsion, to find that she could fold the unhappy woman in her arms and attempt to console her with words.

"I quite understand. Believe me, I *do* understand. It has been like losing the substance for the shadow."

"Just that. Oh, why couldn't I have looked ahead and seen this day! But I was mad and blind. Women must be insane when they commit these irrevocable acts! It is only men who can retrieve such mistakes—women, *never*!"

"It is unfair to us," said Honor for her sex.

"It is damned unfair!" said Mrs. Dalton fiercely. "Why can't he forgive me and let me have another chance? God forgives; why not man?"

"Perhaps he might—some day."

"Do you say that? Oh, Miss Bright!—now I know why everyone loves you." She seized Honor's hand and kissed it passionately. "Will you plead for me? This is what I want of you. Will you do it? He would listen to you if he listened to no one else in the world. I am truly heart-broken, and done with folly and conscious wrong-doing. Jesus Christ said, 'Thy sins are forgiven thee, go and sin no more.'"

"I will do my best for you," said Honor quietly.

"God bless you—oh, God bless you and reward you! Brian is away for a few days. I will let you know when he returns, and you can come to the bungalow. Will you promise?"

"I promise," said Honor bravely. "But he is giving his services to the war. He will be leaving shortly for the front?"

"I know it. And I shall follow him wherever he goes, like a dog, just to be near and serve him. It is the least I can do. They want nurses at the front."

They talked for a while longer and when they parted at the gate of the Club, it was understood that Honor would accept an invitation to tea at the Daltons' bungalow as soon as the doctor was back.

CHAPTER XXVII

A DIFFICULT TASK

The sun had long set and a grey dusk had fallen when Dalton, weary and despondent, returned to the Station after a dull round of inspection during which he had occupied comfortless *dâk* bungalows. Lights were appearing in many windows and were to be seen streaming from the reception rooms of the Club, where guests for the gala week were being entertained. As he passed, he could hear the click of the billiard balls and the sound of merry laughter. Somewhere in those lighted rooms was Honor Bright, perhaps, shedding the sunshine of her presence on her friends! His eyes strained wistfully to catch a glimpse of the beloved form, but in vain, for the Duranta hedge effectually obscured the view.

Three days had passed since he had fled incontinently from the impossible conditions of his home, only to find himself compelled, when no further excuses for his absence were to be found, to return to it bitterly disgusted with life and feverishly impatient to escape altogether from an intolerable presence. One hope alone remained to him, and that was, that the Government would accept his offer for service at the front.

Although in his relations towards his wife he was almost a stranger, he had paid her the compliment of letting her know the date and hour of his return; not from any impulse towards friendliness, but from an instinctive pride of race, which made it impossible for him to slight a white woman in the eyes of the natives. However far apart their lives were sundered, his servants, at least, would have to respect her as the Memsahib and the mistress of his house; any other position for her—a British lady in India—was unthinkable.

And Mrs. Dalton was under no delusion respecting his object. The formal note had no special meaning for her.

There was a light in the drawing-room, Dalton noticed, as he drove up to the steps; and as he descended from his car, a servant, salaaming, informed him that the Memsahib was entertaining a lady visitor. Receiving no encouragement to become communicative, he said no more, but hurriedly assisted other domestics to minister to his master's comforts. The Sahib had no interest in the Memsahib's doings, it was plain to all; and it was greatly to be deplored that he should have saddled himself with her presence in his bungalow where he had so long enjoyed freedom and solitude.

In his private apartments, all was ready for Dalton's reception; refreshments were produced like magic; the lowered lights raised; and he was able to rest and recover at his leisure from the fatigues of the day. Seated at his desk in his comfortable study, he smoked and read the letters that had accumulated in his absence while his mind subconsciously dwelt on thoughts of Honor.

Where was she? What was she doing? How was she enduring their miserable separation? Was it preying upon her as on him?

Would he ever have the chance to hold her in his arms again and read the truth in her dear eyes? Or must he go to his grave with this ache of unfulfilled longing forever denied to him?

The thought was insupportable. Every fibre of his being craved for her with a desire so intense and compelling, that he was incapable of concentrating his mind on any subject.

While brooding in the deepest melancholy, a sound at his verandah door arrested his attention. It was distinctly the *frou-frou* of a woman's skirts. Could it be possible that his wife was seeking to force an interview with him?

There came a light knock on the shutters of the open door which was screened with a cretonne curtain.

"Come in," he said impatiently, resenting the disturbance, and the curtain was raised to admit the diffident intruder.

It was Honor, looking very white, yet as always, brave and sweet.

"Honey!" he started to his feet deeply moved. The harshness vanished from his face which was now alight with wonderment and love. Dressed in a muslin frock and straw hat, she looked simple and fresh, and yet carried the air and distinction which had always marked her in any company. But though she smiled into his eyes there was something in her expression that forbade him to hope for any crumbs of comfort from her visit.

"Good evening," she said trying to speak in ordinary tones while the wild beating of her heart made her momentarily faint. "I came, as I wanted so much to tell you something."

He gave her his seat and leaned against the table looking down at her. "I think I know why you have come. Not on your own account,—that would be impossible to you,—but it is on some dear, quixotic errand for another. You have come straight from—Mrs. Dalton." He could not bring himself to say, "my wife."

Honor bent her head, looking distressed. Her mission was becoming more difficult than she had anticipated.

"Honey," he said reproachfully, "don't you think I have done enough?"

"There is a little more you could do," she returned, lifting pleading eyes to his face.

"For her? Do you think she deserves the half of the consideration she has received? Other women who have sinned against the law and every code of honour have been regarded as outcasts from society. Honest women bar their doors to such as she. I cannot bear to see you with her!—a girl like you cannot understand—I cannot explain"—he broke off with a gesture of impatience and helplessness.

"I understand quite well," said Honor lifting her head courageously. "I feel that life is terribly unjust. There are men who are even worse than she, and yet their sins are covered, and society allows them to marry pure, honest girls! Is that right or just?"

It was Dalton's turn to lower his gaze.

Honor continued speaking. She did not allow her maidenly reserve to stand in the way of her frank denouncement of the injustice of human and social laws. Very quietly and logically she stated the case while Dalton with arms folded on his breast, listened, ashamed for himself and his sex. Before she had finished, he came and knelt beside her chair, and, gripping the arms of it with shaking hands, humbled himself to the dust.

"We are all a cursed lot of Pharisees!" he cried. "Don't turn away from me with disgust! Pity me and love me still though I am unfit to kiss the hem of your skirt." Nevertheless, he bent and pressed his lips to the border of her gown.

"Ah, don't!" she cried, the tears flooding her eyes. "You and I cannot think of love any more! It must be friendship or nothing. Today I have realised as I never did before, that there are higher duties for some of us, to which we must give the first place, even at the sacrifice of love."

"Honey, you don't know what you are saying!" he cried passionately. "Dearest, you cannot forbid me to love you! It is an unalterable fact. I cannot change it, even at your bidding."

"I know—it is quite true of love, for it is a sacred thing and belongs to the heart. But it can be locked away—put out of sight—*buried*," she returned, her voice breaking. "The higher duty is—the *saving of a soul*. Dare we withhold our forgiveness from a repentant sinner? Your wife is truly a very miserable woman. She is on her knees to you. Can you afford to refuse her?—or will you rather say, 'Go and sin no more'? Which of us is without sin? If you repulse her now, it might lead to her ruin, body and soul?"

"You are asking more of me than I can do. I can never again look upon her as a wife. Feeling as I do, it would be a violation of the best instincts of my nature."

"I am not asking that of you."

"What, then, is it I must do? for you know that I would give all I possess to please you."

Honor's tears fell fast, unheeded. "*Only be kind to her*. Let her feel that she has something to live for. At present she has nothing."

"I tell you, she is false. She has played upon your sympathies and led you to believe in her."

"I believe in her only because it is impossible to doubt her wretchedness, or her repentance."

"She lied to you!"

"She told me the truth concerning herself. She did not spare herself. Hers is, indeed, a 'broken and a contrite heart' which even God does not despise," said Honor reverently.

"You wish me to be kind to her?—Tell me how, when we live under the same roof and I can never regard her as my wife?"

His eyes gazed upon the girl's face with wistful yearning. She was his soul's mate,—she of the pure eyes and tender mouth! He could be kind to *her* all the days of his life. He could love and cherish *her*, in sickness and in health. Would to God she could belong to him!

But she was talking of his duty to another whom he despised!

Honor pleaded long with all her gentle tact, that he would try to practice tolerance and kindness. The future would take care of itself.

"Kindness from you is all she craves, and a chance to prove her sincerity."

"In what way can I be kind?" he repeated.

"By being thoughtful of her needs, considerate, and forbearing. Speak gently, and do not grudge her your smiles when there is need to show appreciation."

"And if I bring myself to do all these things, do you believe she will be content? Oh, Honey!—what a burden you are laying on my shoulders! Do you know that I find it difficult to be even decently polite to her? That is why I keep out of her way. And what is my reward to be?"

"If we do our duty day by day, it is enough. We should not look for reward, yet, I am confident we shall receive it, never fear! It works out right in the end."

"When I am dead?"—bitterly. "There is only one thing I want. Given that, I would ask nothing more of life!"

He rose and stood aside to set her free, for Honor indicated that her visit was at an end.

"Good-bye, and God bless you, Brian," she said with trembling lips, giving him both her hands.

Dalton made no reply, but stooping, kissed them tenderly; for the moment he was incapable of speech. Then going to the door he held the curtain aside to allow her to pass out.

Honor found her way home, shaken with emotion. She had won her point, but Mrs. Dalton would have to discover for herself the result of the interview which she had contrived to bring about; and if it helped her to begin afresh, the pain it had cost would not have been in vain.

So deeply engrossed had she been in the purpose of her visit, that she had forgotten to repeat to Captain Dalton the conversation she had overheard at the *méla*. Her father had scoffed at it, and Tommy had treated it with indifference, explaining that all pioneers of progress in India had to put up with opposition, threats, and bluff. The natives of Bengal were too cowardly to risk their necks—didn't she remember her Macaulay? After all, there was really nothing tangible to worry about.

Nevertheless, the matter so preyed upon her mind, that she wrote a note after dinner to Mrs. Dalton, telling her all about it, and asking her to persuade her husband to be always on his guard against sudden surprises, as she believed men were plotting against his life. It would give the poor woman an opportunity to begin friendly relations with her husband, and possibly help to bring about a better understanding between them.

The note was entrusted to an orderly, who dropped it in the pocket of his tunic and postponed the delivery of it to a more convenient season, his friends from the bazaar having gathered at the door of his *basha*[21], behind the bungalow, for a smoke, and to gossip about their exploits at the *méla*.

It was not till they had gone, that he was recalled to a sense of duty with regard to the note, and the hour was then late. However, it was as much as his place was worth for him to leave the delivery of it till the morning; so, making his way across to the Civil Surgeon's bungalow, he aroused Mrs. Dalton's ayah, who, in her turn, roused her mistress, and handed her the communication from Honor.

Thus does Fate control the destinies of individuals; for, had the orderly done his duty earlier, there might have been a very different ending to this story.

Meanwhile, a letter by the last post from Joyce in Darjeeling, engaged Honor till close upon midnight. It had given her much to think about, and called for a reply of congratulations, as it was written at a time of intense joy and thanksgiving over the restoration of happy relations with her husband:

Joyce had written at great length, beginning her letter with a description of her journey and the miserable thoughts that had occupied her all the way. After giving a brief outline of the circumstances connected with her arrival at her husband's rooms, she continued:

"You can imagine the shock it was to find her there and so very much at home! I could have killed her! But I did nothing melodramatic, believe me. I was too stunned. Instead, I boiled with the desire for a reprisal. Since I could not fight her like a savage, being, of course, a highly civilised person, I fought her with the only weapons at my command. I went to the Planters' Ball, tired though I was, and made an amazing hit. Did you ever imagine that I was an actress, born? If you had seen me dance and smile while my heart was breaking, you would have had to revise all previous impressions of little Me.

"Ray looked completely dazed at first, and could hardly believe his eyes. I obliged him to keep up appearances, so that we danced a great deal together, and he had my sweetest smiles, though he knew all the while that my heart was turned to stone. I was an angel to him before others, but alone with him I was adamant. And Mrs. Dalton had the lesson of her life. I saw to it that Ray dropped her entirely, and as people are like sheep, there was no one brave enough to have anything to do with her. Her humiliation was complete. Before half the night was over, she left, looking mad with everybody. Even those who had been in the habit

---

[21] Dwelling.

of speaking to her, gave her a wide berth, so you can imagine how comforted I felt!—though I am inclined, now, to be a weeny bit sorry for her. It must have been an appalling experience, and only a woman can appreciate what it must have felt like. However, it will do her good to realise how much it is all worth in the end! It seems like becoming all of a sudden bankrupt of friends and love, and of all that makes life so dear and good. I am surprised that Captain Dalton has cared to take her back, but I suppose it is to save her from worse. If that is so, he can't be so bad after all!

"I am rather ashamed of the part I played at the ball, for I took a wicked pleasure in Ray's misery. He looked so white and ill all the time, and whenever we danced I could see how he was just aching to kiss me as he used to do. His eyes gave him away all the time! But he never dared, even when we sat out in sheltered nooks, for I was a cruel devil, and 'rubbed it in' every time I got the chance. But, darling, consider how sore I felt—and how angry!

"So I flirted mildly all the evening just to show that two could play the same game! Of course, in cold blood, I simply hated myself for behaving so despicably. I did not know I had it in me, but one never knows oneself till things happen to rouse one thoroughly. In the end I had a splitting headache and felt on the verge of hysteria. It was all I could do not to break down while Ray was unhooking my frock at the back. It was the only ball-gown in my trunk, the other not having arrived—the sort of thing that leaves one at the mercy of some charitable person. That was Ray! Though we were quarrelling desperately, he hooked and unhooked me without a word of protest, and oh, the misery of his dear, handsome face in the mirror! I could have hugged it to my breast and cried upon the squiggly little curls that never lie flat. Oh, I do love him so! But I was too proud to relent so soon, and tried to keep up my rage, which all the while was cooling fast.

"When Ray left me, after the little business of the hooks and eyes, he retired to his dressing-room, where I supposed he had caused a bed to be made up for himself on the floor. The hotel was so packed, there was no help for it. Well, how was it possible for me to sleep when I thought of his lying on the draughty floor, and myself in possession of his comfortable bed? I tossed and turned and wondered about him, seeing all the while his unhappy face in the mirror. I remembered about your saying how a man punishes himself by remorse far more than others can punish him, and I knew that my poor boy was suffering terribly. That made me think of tragedies with razors and things, till I could not lie down another minute, but had to get out of bed to peep and see that he was safe. Very softly I tip-toed to the curtain which hangs between the rooms, and put my eyes to the edge.

"Do you know, Honey darling, the poor fellow had no bed at all! His servant had not been given any order, and my dear, precious husband was sitting in the cold, before a dead fire, looking the picture of desolation and grief. It made me cry like anything to see his head bowed upon his arms, his whole attitude so dejected! and by the heaving of his shoulders, I knew he was crying. Think of it!—crying because of what he had done! and for my cruelty and unforgivingness! It is dreadful to see a strong man all broken up and humiliated for the sake of his wife. Oh, Honey! I could bear it no longer, and fairly ran to him.

"Of course you can imagine the rest. It is too sacred to relate, and I thrill all over at the memory of it. How we clung together—mingling our tears! Oh, what a blessed thing is love!

"There is no more to tell, except that we are enjoying a second honeymoon, far more wonderful than the first. And you may be quite, quite sure that I shall never leave my beloved husband again, unless I am forced. He and I shall go home every three years to Baby who is well cared for by his grannie. Of course I miss him dreadfully!—but then, there's Ray!—a big baby in his way, and one can't cut one's self in two, can one? so, all things considered, I feel I must just hold on out here for his sake till we can go home together. It is wonderful how different India now seems to me! I verily believe I hated it before, because I was blind or asleep. Love makes Paradise of any place!

"I have told Ray all about that time in the ruins, and we both agree that I was a little silly to let my dread of his view of it keep me silent. My folly nearly spoiled both our lives. I should have trusted my husband more. Anyhow, I am wiser now."

Honor sat long over this very human document, moved to laughter and tears. So Joyce had pardoned her sinner and had come into her reward! Another sinner, far more culpable would also find happiness through forgiveness, and her husband come into his reward, some day! It was Life, with its eternal give and take, and its exchange which was seldom just. Yet, in proportion to the kindness and generosity with which Brian Dalton treated his contrite wife, would be her gratitude and devotion; and time would bring healing and forgetfulness of wrongs.

But some there were who gave always, expecting nothing in return, and they, too, won happiness with the years—virtue being its own reward!

For the first time Honor was conscious of a great bitterness of spirit as she sought oblivion in sleep.

She had just turned down the wick of her bedroom lamp—for it was customary in those parts to sleep with a light burning low all night in a bedchamber because of the lurking danger from snakes—when she heard a sudden sound in the distance that rooted her to the spot. The next instant her mother who had been awakened by it, called out from the adjoining room:

"Honor, are you awake?"

"Yes. Did you hear that, Mother?"

"I was just wondering what it was. It sounded like a pistol shot."

"I thought so, too. Listen!—there are voices."

Mr. Bright, who was also disturbed, suggested in sleepy tones that his wife and daughter should go to sleep and leave other people to mind their own business. It was not part of his duty to look for trouble. It came fast enough to him in the ordinary channels. If any one had been killed, they would hear of it in due course.

"How cold-blooded!" said Mrs. Bright.

"We have quite enough of crime by day, my dear, without looking for it with a lantern at night."

But the distant voices increased in agitation, and grew confused.

Drawing the window curtain aside, Honor looked out into the night and saw unmistakable signs of alarm at Dalton's bungalow. Lights hurried to and fro and conflicting orders were shouted by one servant to another. In fact, it was very evident that something had gone seriously wrong.

"I wonder what could have happened?" said Mrs. Bright looking over her daughter's shoulder. "See, there is someone coming to tell us about it."

A single light was moving swiftly towards the hedge that divided the two gardens. Honor felt her heart paralysing as she watched the progress of the lantern; a hand seemed tightening upon her throat and her limbs grew palsied with fear. What was it they were coming so quickly to say?

An evil, dark face had risen before her imagination, and she heard again the voice speaking to the basket-maker at the *méla*, vowing to take the life of the surgeon who had been the cause of his only son's death. "Oh, God!—oh, God!" burst from her lips.

"Honey! Honey! What is it you fear?" Mrs. Bright cried, gripping her by the shoulders.

But Honor broke away from her mother and, with shaking fingers, flung on her out-door clothes.

"Surely you are not going out?"

"Can't you understand, Mother?" she cried in strained, unnatural tones. "They have killed him! I know they have killed him!"

"Sahib! Sahib!" called voices loudly on the verandah.

The coolies pulling at the *punkha* joined in a chorus of "Sahib, Sahib!"

"We are sent to call the *Bara Sahib*. Haste and wake him. A great calamity hath befallen."

"A murder has been committed, wake the Sahib!"

"Good God!" exclaimed Mr. Bright springing from his bed. "What are they saying? A murder? Where?"

"At Captain Dalton's bungalow. The doctor has been murdered!—how terrible! Honor always said people were plotting against his life," said Mrs. Bright, horror-stricken.

"Good God!" said Mr. Bright again as he pulled on his boots. "Tell them I will be with them in a minute. Send someone to call Tommy Deare, quickly."

In the meantime, Honor was speeding across the grass on her way to the scene of the tragedy.

CHAPTER XXVIII
THE ATONEMENT

When Honor's letter of warning was received by Mrs. Dalton, she was greatly disturbed in mind at the apparent gravity of its purport.

On being awakened, she had carried the letter to the table, raised the light, and read all that Honor had to say, after which she felt undecided how to act. The lateness of the hour made it certain that her husband was sound asleep after his fatiguing day, and to rouse him for the purpose of passing on a caution which he had previously disregarded, would be, she thought, both inconsiderate and tactless. Besides, no good could be gained by disturbing him, as no action could possibly be taken at the moment, even presuming that he were disposed to move in the matter. It seemed, therefore, wisest to allow the letter to stand over till the morning. Attempts had been made on his life, but Mrs. Dalton had understood that the enmity and ill feeling in the District had practically died down. Yet, here it was shown to be smouldering dangerously and an imminent menace to her husband, sleeping or waking.

Though she was not passionately fond of him, and was unlikely ever to be, — having grown weary of strenuous emotions and the disappointments of life, — she valued the legal tie that bound them together as her sheet anchor in a life of vicissitudes. The unwonted ease she enjoyed in Dalton's home made it a haven of rest after her many storms. Under the shelter of his protection, she looked forward to regaining, at least, her good name and standing, if not the place she had rightly forfeited in his esteem. She had a glimmer of hope that the future held some promise through Honor's intervention on her behalf.

Honor had done an inconceivable thing. In Mrs. Dalton's view it was incomprehensible. Her reverence for the Divine Law had caused her to renounce the man she loved, and to plead with him for the woman who had lost all moral claim to his regard or consideration. She was wonderful! and Mrs. Dalton was filled with admiration and respect.

At dinner that evening she had gleaned the first-fruits of Honor's sacrifice, for he had been less taciturn, and had even responded to his wife's efforts to engage him in ordinary conversation. Instead of sitting in silence throughout the meal, or exchanging banal remarks about the food or the weather, they had discussed the war and all that India was going to do to prove her loyalty to the Crown. He had spoken of the advance in science and surgery, bound to result from the lessons of the war; and had told her of his wishes and intentions regarding herself should he be suddenly called upon to start for Europe. The generosity and consideration shown in his arrangement for her, had touched her deeply, and she had been only too willing to express her concurrence. It was the first time she had known the sensation of a genuine and impersonal interest in an intellectual man's conversation; and she was happier than she had been for many a day. She lay down again, but sleep would not come to her eyes, and her thoughts were busy with the subject of Honor's letter. She reasoned with herself to no purpose, for the stillness of the night bred new fears and intensified the lurking danger.

What should she do? waken her husband?—or wait till the morning?

Would it not be best to watch over him silently while he slept? It might move him to gratitude when he should learn of the sacrifice of her night's rest!

The weather was warm and muggy in spite of the *punkha* waving in the room, pulled by the uncertain hand of a coolie half-asleep in the verandah. There was another waving in like manner, she knew, in her husband's room at the extreme end of the bungalow; and in both apartments were windows thrown wide open to the night air—as was customary in the plains—with short curtains of lawn to screen the interior from public view. Outside, the shrill chirping of crickets vibrated in the air, and the occasional croak of a bull-frog from a pond in the garden, could be heard. Otherwise, the silence of the night was oppressive and ominous.

Open windows not far from the ground offered an easy opportunity for entrance into the house of evil characters bent on mischief, and even the drowsy *punkha* coolie in the verandah would be none the wiser.

The thought was disquieting and banished sleep from her eyes.

Impelled almost against her inclinations by an inward force too urgent to resist, Mrs. Dalton slipped on her kimona, and with her feet in slippers, went forth to satisfy herself, personally, that all was well with her husband. He did not desire her interest; he had no wish that she should sacrifice her rest, nevertheless, a sense of undefined apprehension made it impossible for her return to her bed and sleep.

On her way to his bedchamber through the rooms that intervened, she could hear the squeak of the ungreased *punkha* wheel as the rope passed to and fro over it. It was proof positive that he was asleep, or he could not have tolerated the noise for a moment. Suddenly, however, it ceased, and Mrs. Dalton, comprehending the reason of its stoppage, smiled to herself, appreciating the frailty of the *punkha wallah*.

Arriving on the spot with the intention of stirring up the slumbering coolie, she was surprised to find that he had deserted his post after the manner of new hands unaccustomed to the task. This one, she remembered, had been engaged that very day. The rope hung idly against the wall under the wheel, and Mrs. Dalton was in momentary expectation of a curse from within as the mosquitoes settled on the sleeper.

The culprit being nowhere in sight, she applied her eye to the edge of the curtain and looked towards the bed. Her husband lay, as she expected, fast asleep, tired out thoroughly, and unconscious of externals. Suddenly, as she peered at him, she became aware of a dark form moving between her vision and the sleeper.

Paralysed with fear and incapable of uttering a sound, she saw the figure of an Indian clothed only in a narrow loin-cloth, creeping stealthily towards the bed.

Who was he? and what was he trying to do?

Mrs. Dalton was rooted to the spot and dumb with terror.

Something gleamed in his hand—a steel blade had caught the reflection of the lowered flame of a lamp hanging on the wall. The man's purpose was plain, for thieves do not usually carry knives. He was there to commit murder. Oh, God!

What was she to do?—She was powerless to move. Fear made her a coward, a helpless, nerveless creature. Like one in a horrible dream, her tongue refused to utter a warning, or her constricted throat to produce a sound.

And there was not a moment to lose as the figure was stealthily nearing the sleeper. Thoughts flashed through her brain with lightning rapidity. If the man were not stopped, somehow, and at any cost, in another moment she would see Honor's fears justified and Brian killed while asleep in his bed. How was it possible for her to witness such a deed and not raise a finger to save him?

But she was defenceless!

The man raised his right arm, and the sight of the knife fully exposed, gave the impetus needed to galvanise Mrs. Dalton's nerves into sudden and fierce activity. Without a thought for her own danger, she sprang into the room and flung herself upon the Indian, clasping him round the waist and holding him back as in a vice.

"Brian!" she shrieked in strangled tones, finding her voice at last. "Brian! Help! Murder!"

A fierce struggle ensued. The native tried to free himself in vain; her arms tightened about him as he flung himself from side to side, and did not loose their hold even when he struck at her with his knife over his shoulder, once, twice, thrice, burying the blade deep every time.

Only one idea obsessed Mrs. Dalton, and that was to hold on till the assassin could be secured. He should not escape to remain a menace to her husband's life!

Her cries aroused Dalton from his profound sleep. He had long been in the habit of placing a loaded revolver under his pillow at night for self-protection from possible attempts on his life, and instantly realising the situation, leaped out of bed, and fired point blank at the Indian's head as the knife descended once more on his poor doomed wife.

As the man dropped dead, Mrs. Dalton fell into her husband's arms, an unforgettable sight.

Dalton carried her to his bed and laid her in it, a dying woman, while the terror-stricken servants crowded into the room. He gave them his orders and they sped in various directions—one to inform the police, another to rouse Mr. Bright. Someone took the car for the assistant surgeon, while others brought in more lamps and fetched and carried all that was necessary for the work of First Aid.

With her life ebbing fast, Mrs. Dalton made a pitiful attempt to explain the reason of her presence on her husband's side of the house, afraid that he would misunderstand her motive; and he was filled with sorrow and self-reproach. "I came to see that you were safe—I only wanted to watch over you, for I had been warned that you were in danger. Miss Bright wrote—her letter is on my table, read it."

"I understand," he said with the utmost gentleness, "and I cannot find words to tell you how I honour your wonderful courage and sacrifice."

"It was the only thing to do. I could not call out—I had no voice! I was so dreadfully afraid!"

"Afraid for me!—and not for yourself!"

"I had no time to think of that."

"It was heroism! You did a thing which, in battle, would have won you the Victoria Cross!"

"Thank God I was able!" she panted.

"I do not deserve it. Will you forgive me?" he asked brokenly.

"It is I who have to ask that!"

"The past is all wiped out today, so far as I am concerned. God bless you!"

"Ah, thank you for that!—May God forgive me for the mistakes and the folly—the wrong-doing! It is too late now to retrieve them! Ah, those words, 'too late'!—on how many graves?... the words, 'too late'!... Yet—Honor would say it is never too late while there is breath in which to call on—the name of the Lord."

"God is very merciful to all sinners who repent," said Dalton. "I, too, am a sinner. I have been a Pharisee and hypocrite all my life; may I, too, be forgiven!"

"Perhaps this will be taken into the account—my atonement," she sighed feebly.

"You have done what few women in your place would have had the courage to do. I shall remember it all the days of my life with gratitude and remorse."

For a while they were silent as he did all he could to ease her suffering.

"This is death!" she whispered, searching for his face with glazing eyes. "Tell Honor—I wish her the happiness she deserves.... You will love her as you could never have loved me. It is for the best...!"

Dalton stooped low and kissed her on the forehead and as he straightened himself he saw that she was dead.

When Honor arrived in the verandah and heard the story of the tragedy, her heart bounded with a very human relief at the thought that a most precious life had been spared. For a moment she had room for no other thought in her mind. "Thank God, Brian is safe!" she cried to her soul.

Afterwards she could afford to dwell on the miracle of Mrs. Dalton's sacrifice. Who would have thought her capable of such an act of heroism? Truly, one never knows how much of good there is in human nature, howsoever perverted! Poor

Mrs. Dalton! She had, indeed, atoned. She had given her all—her very life for the man she had wronged, and whose pride she had lowered in the dust. It was a magnificent act, the memory of which would wipe out every wrong she had done, and silence every tongue that spoke ill of her.

"Is she still living?" Honor asked one of the servants, fearfully.

"She died but a moment ago," said the *bearer*, "for the Sahib has retired into another room and all is silent."

Elsewhere, too, all was still. In the presence of death, voices were hushed, as the servants hung about waiting for the coming of those who had been called.

"It is a terrible sight," Honor heard one say to another; "the body of that *punkha* coolie lying just where he fell. Some *domes*[22] must be fetched to remove him."

"The Sahib says, let no one lay a hand on him till the police arrive; such is the custom when an inquiry has to beheld."

Seeing that her presence was unnecessary, Honor passed out into the darkness and ran swiftly home.

It was discovered later, at the inquest, that the discharge of a *punkha* coolie had given Dalton's watchful enemies the opportunity they had been seeking to carry out their plan of revenge; and that the man who had been engaged to fill the vacant post was a marked character, living in the village of Panipara, who was well known to the police. Doubtless he had been heavily bribed for the perpetration of the intended crime which had so strangely miscarried. The instigators pointed to their own complicity by disappearing from the District, and the vain search for them occupied Mr. Bright and his staff for many months. As well might one look for a needle in a stack of hay, as expect to find fugitive criminals among the numerous villages of Bengal.

Captain Dalton left for Europe soon after his wife's funeral, his services having been placed at the disposal of the War Office, and Honor treasured in her memory his brief words spoken in farewell as he held her hands in his. "We have both a great deal to do while the War lasts. Will you follow me, and let us work together?" In the moment of parting, it was not possible to keep out of his eyes all his lips could not say, and Honor promised.

---

[22] Low-caste Hindus.

EPILOGUE: ALL'S WELL

It was something more than four years later, when the Armistice was signed amid world-wide rejoicings of the Allied Nations, that a young soldier, bronzed and upright, rang the bell of a beautiful flat in Brighton, over-looking the sea. Above his breast pocket, on the left, were two ribbons, the D.S.O. and the M.C., the sight of which had won him glances of approval and soft looks of admiration, all the way along. Those bits of ribbon told wordlessly of self-sacrifice and devotion to duty; valour and endurance;—they suggested to the subconscious mind, danger, bodily discomfort, and endurance to the limit of human suffering, so that this brisk little freckled officer of very ordinary looks, was marked for all time, by those who knew, as one of the many special heroes of the most terrible war the world has ever known.

He was shown into the drawing-room, and, in a moment, a gracious lady swept in with welcome in her eyes and both hands extended.

"Oh, Tommy!—how good it is to see you safe!"

"And to see you looking so fit, Honey—dear old girl!"

"I was beginning to feel quite anxious, as you had not written for a month!"

"There was so much doing. Besides, I was reserving it all for our meeting."

They had much to talk about; he, of his vicissitudes in Mesopotamia, and she, of her husband and his work in the war-hospital in Brighton to which he was attached. Last of all, Tommy asked to see his god-son to whom he had yet to be introduced.

"He is such a perfect darling!" said Honor beaming upon her visitor happily; "the very image of Brian." Pressing a bell, she gave her orders which were promptly obeyed by a nurse who entered with the baby, a lusty boy with grey-green eyes, and lips firmly locked in a cupid's bow.

"Hullo!" said Tommy, "shake hands with 'Uncle'!"

"Say, 'How do'?" said Honor, kissing the velvet cheek.

"'Ow do!" said Baby staring at the pretty coloured ribbons on the khaki tunic.

"This is the age at which I like them best," said Tommy admiringly. "He's 'some' kid! Do you remember trying to interest me in the Meredith infant when it was a glorified dummy in long clothes?"

"Yes, and you wasted your energies trying to fix its attention when it did not know you from a mango tree!" They laughed heartily at the recollection.

"Where are the Merediths, by the way?"

"They are stationed at Darjeeling, which suits the baby very well—perhaps you don't know that there is another baby?"

"I believe Jack wrote something of the sort, some little time back."

"A baby girl this time, and getting on splendidly."

"Where is the first?—still with the grandparents?"

"Yes. I saw him not long ago—such a beautiful boy and so independent! The old people are so proud of him. Do you know that Jack and Kitty are at home?"

"No! When did they come? I did not know that women were allowed passages?"

"They managed to 'wangle' it, somehow. Jack had malaria and was ordered home by the doctors. It was a most exciting voyage, from all accounts, for their boat was chased by a submarine in the Bay of Biscay and escaped two torpedoes by a miracle."

"Horrible!"

"Kitty says she would not have missed the experience for anything; but Jack declares the anxiety has taken ten years off his life."

"Dear old Jack! Where are they? I shall look them up."

"Staying with his people. They are in love with Kitty and can't make enough of her."

"And what are your plans now that the war is over?"

"Brian expects to return to India, in which case, we go with him."

"You'll take the baby?"

"Most assuredly! Master Tommy is not going to be left behind by his Mummy—not on any account!"

"But the climate? I thought it does not agree with babies?"

"It agrees quite well; at least for the first few years. I am not so sure about it later on, but, 'sufficient unto the day is the evil thereof.' We'll begin to think about sending him home when he turns seven. You see, we have the hills, and life is too short for unnecessary partings."

"I am with you there! How are Mr. and Mrs. Bright?"

"As usual, thank you. Father retires after the New Year, and they will live in Edinburgh. And what of your plans, Tommy?"

"I dare say I shall be back in the Police again, before long."

"And have you not found any one yet as a life-partner, to make India worth while?" she asked kindly.

Tommy smiled. "I am in no hurry, being difficult to please. I shall have to find the lady whose price, according to old Solomon, is 'far above rubies,' or remain in single blessedness all my days."

"You'll find her right enough if you *know where* to look, and *how!*" said Honor laughing. "Her natural element is the country home."

THE END.

Lector House believes that a society develops through a two-fold approach of continuous learning and adaptation, which is derived from the study of classic literary works spread across the historic timeline of literature records. Therefore, we aim at reviving, repairing and redeveloping all those inaccessible or damaged but historically as well as culturally important literature across subjects so that the future generations may have an opportunity to study and learn from past works to embark upon a journey of creating a better future.

This book is a result of an effort made by Lector House towards making a contribution to the preservation and repair of original ancient works which might hold historical significance to the approach of continuous learning across subjects.

HAPPY READING & LEARNING!

LECTOR HOUSE LLP
E-MAIL: lectorpublishing@gmail.com